MANNINGS OF MORMONVILLE

JEFF CALL

Jeff Call

ISBN: 172962027X
ISBN-13: 978-1729620373

DEDICATION

To my family: CherRon, Ryan, Brayden,
Landon, Austin, Carson and Janson

Reviews of *Mormonville*, Book I

"As you read this book, you will have an unsurpassed amusing, emotional and spiritual experience. You will see yourself or your fellow members and leaders on every page. You will smile and laugh as you are reminded that we are indeed a peculiar people. Suddenly and often a pure and plain incident of gospel living will send a surge of joy into the most tender part of your heart. Through an inside and outside examination of the church and the gospel, you will desire to cheer for the Saints, and to give thanks to the Lord for this treasured way of life." — *George Durrant, author and teacher*

"Widely hailed by readers as one of the most powerful and through-provoking LDS novels ever published. Luke Manning's personal journey will deeply affect your own life." — *Cedar Fort Publishing.*

AUTHOR'S INTRODUCTION & ACKNOWLEDGMENTS

When *Mormonville* was published in 2002, I figured that was the end of the story about Luke Manning.

However, over the ensuing months, many readers told me they wanted to know more about the fate of Luke and other characters. So I set out to explore what happened next.

In 2004, *Return to Mormonville: Worlds Apart* was published, and, once again, I thought the story was over. But as the years passed, something kept telling me there was still more to write.

It took a long time but finally, in 2018, the third installment of what's become the *Mormonville* series was birthed with *Mannings of Mormonville* — 16 years after the debut of the first book, and 14 years after the sequel. That's an eternity between books in a series, I know. But I'm hoping that those who have read the first two books will enjoy catching up on the latest with Luke and Hayley Manning and their growing family.

I believe that this third book in the series can be enjoyed and understood without having to read the first two. However, if you read *Mannings of Mormonville* first, I hope you will go back and read the first two books as prequels.

Mannings of Mormonville is my first self-published book, so in some ways, this feels a lot like being published for the first time. I express gratitude to Ken Meyers and Chad Daybell for their keen copyediting skills, constructive criticism, and valuable feedback. Ken also helped design the cover, and I'm indebted to him for his efforts to make that possible, since my graphic design skills are nonexistent.

I also thank my family members for putting up with my somewhat glorified hobby of writing LDS fiction. They are a constant source of inspiration.

CHAPTER 1

LUKE MANNING'S INTESTINAL TRACT felt tighter than a trampoline spring and his stomach was turning triple salchows.

He didn't know exactly why he felt like he was about to leap out of an airplane without a parachute, but he had a general idea. He had experienced this feeling before, and something told him his life was about to change — again.

Clad in a light blue dress shirt, a fluorescent orange tie, and khaki pants, Luke, sitting in a red upholstered chair, stretched out his tall, athletic frame. He fidgeted, then drummed his fingers on the table next to him in the foyer outside the stake president's office of the Helaman Utah North Stake, as Tabernacle Choir music emanated reverently from a CD player.

Next to him, his wife, Hayley, 31-and-a-half weeks pregnant and expecting the Manning family's seventh child, tried to find a comfortable position in her chair. Fanning herself with the recent July edition of the *Ensign*, Hayley was wilting in the scorching summer heat.

"Luke, calm down. You're making me nervous," she whispered. "Not to mention the other people here."

Hayley placed the magazine on the table and rested her moisturized hands on her protruding belly.

"You're acting like we're going into surgery," she said. "This is not the emergency room."

"This might be *worse* than surgery," Luke said.

Then he remembered the woman he was talking to had already survived three C-sections.

Hayley smiled the smile that launched a thousand trips to the grocery store. For her, Luke would do just about anything. With Hayley as his wife, Luke felt like he had won the lottery — in one of the few states in the country without legalized gambling.

The Mannings had been summoned for an appointment with the stake president, which typically warranted worry, but that anxiousness was somewhat tempered by the fact that the President of the Helaman Utah North Stake happened to be Ben Kimball, Luke's best friend.

The two of them had grown close, like brothers, in the years since Luke first arrived in the small town of Helaman, Utah, in Utah County. Ben liked to say he had a front-row seat as he witnessed Luke's conversion to The Church of Jesus Christ of Latter-day Saints.

Since his baptism, Luke's life had moved at blurring speed. One day he woke up to find himself married with six children — and counting. His brood was comprised of a 15-year-old daughter, three sons, a set of twin girls, and a baby girl warming up in a cramped bullpen.

Luke found himself mired in his mid-40s, with something resembling a life preserver starting to form around his midsection. He had bills to pay and an endless list of household projects to do.

In many respects, Luke had turned into the person that, years earlier, he had ridiculed and denigrated when he arrived in Utah, incognito, as an undercover reporter. Heck, he had written a whole book on everything that was wrong with the Church and its peculiar culture. Fortunately for him, it was never published.

What Luke had lost with an unpublished book, he gained in the form of a beautiful, smart, generous, and patient wife.

There was a time when Luke thought writing a book on the Mormons was the toughest job in the history of journalism. But he eventually learned that being a successful husband and father, while maintaining his sanity, was by far a greater challenge.

The Mannings had celebrated a wedding anniversary a couple of months earlier. It wasn't the celebration that Luke had been hoping for — he wanted to take Hayley to Hawaii for a week of sun, luaus, and relaxation on a beach. But that plan was postponed indefinitely. It was bad timing for taking such a vacation — with Hayley expecting and all the other kids to care for. Plus, it would have been expensive and the Mannings weren't exactly in a financial position to purchase airfare, let alone lodging, food, and entertainment.

Where had the time gone? Luke's life was unrecognizable from the one he had when he arrived in Helaman as a swinging bachelor and fiercely independent journalist from New York City.

Luke gazed at the painting on the wall in the foyer of Jesus Christ kneeling in the Garden of Gethsemane, and he gripped the armrests of the chair tighter.

Then he noticed Hayley vigorously rubbing her right temple.

"Another headache?"

"It's nothing worse than usual," she said. "Maybe it's just sympathy pains."

"I'm pretty sure this meeting is for you, not me," Luke said, patting her knee.

"Then why are *you* so nervous?" Hayley asked.

Just then the stake president's door swung open, and a couple, huddled together, shedding tears, emerged.

Luke and Hayley shot nervous glances at each other.

President Benjamin Kimball strode from his office into the waiting area, wearing a crisp white shirt, a navy blue suit, and his benevolent smile.

Luke gulped, took a deep breath, and stood up. Hayley maneuvered out of her chair with Luke's assistance.

"Luke and Hayley, thanks for coming," Ben said.

"Hi, Ben," Luke said, shaking Ben's hand. "I mean, President Kimball."

"It's always good to see you," Ben said, adjusting his black-rimmed glasses as he ushered them into his office. "Come in and have a seat."

"Is this about my subscription to *The Friend* expiring?" Luke joked, pulling out his wallet. "I can't believe I allowed that to lapse. Do you take credit cards?"

Ben laughed like he usually did at Luke's attempts at humor. Hayley rolled her eyes.

"Trust me, it's nothing like that," Ben said, settling into the chair behind his desk.

"If this is about that comment I made about polygamy in gospel doctrine last week," Luke added, "I'm really sorry."

"What was that?" Ben asked, fiddling with the Windsor knot in his plaid tie.

"Never mind," Hayley said.

"How are you two, anyway?" Ben asked. "I wish we still lived in your ward."

"We're only two blocks away from each other," Hayley said. "At least we're in the stake boundaries."

"For now," Luke interjected.

"What do you mean, *for now*?" Ben asked.

"Didn't you notice the 'for sale' sign in our yard?" Luke quipped.

"When did this happen?" Ben said.

"Right after your executive secretary called to set up this appointment," Luke joked.

"Well, I'm very grateful that you're still around," said Ben, who was also the manager of Kimball's Market, the town's most popular grocery store — and the town's only grocery store.

"OK, what's this all about?" Luke blurted out. "I'm dying over here. I haven't eaten in two days because of this meeting. Forty-eight hour fasts put me in a bad mood. Put us out of our misery."

A wan smile graced Ben's lips.

"The reason I've asked you both to come in tonight is because I have a calling to extend to you, Luke."

"That's what I was afraid of," Luke said. "Please, don't call me to be a stake basketball official again. The last game I reffed we had to bail six members of the stake out of jail. And one of them was me."

Ben ignored Luke's flippancy.

"I want you to know I've prayed hard about this. I've fasted about this. I fought the Lord on this. I didn't want to call you to this position. But the Lord did. Luke, you're the man He wants to serve as the new elders quorum president of your ward."

In that instant, Hayley nearly collapsed. For a moment, she thought her water broke. Luke felt like he was plummeting to his demise, in slow motion, in a runaway elevator. He sat in silence for a moment before letting out an awkward laugh.

"You're kidding, right, Ben? I mean, President Kimball."

"I've been wrestling with this for weeks," Ben said. "But you are the one the Lord wants to serve in this position at this time. I'm not exactly sure why. I tried to talk myself out of it. I know better than most about the stress you're under and the challenges you're facing. But if there's one thing I've learned, it's not to argue with the Lord. He's in charge. I just do what He wants me to do. I try to stay out of His way."

Hayley grabbed a tissue from off of Ben's desk while Luke squirmed in his seat.

"I was under the impression that if I grew facial hair, this wouldn't happen," Luke said, stroking his salt-and-pepper goatee.

"Oh, by the way," Ben said, "you'll need to shave that off."

Luke's head dropped dramatically before it bobbed up again.

"We've got six kids, with one coming any minute," Luke pleaded, pointing at Hayley's stomach, while trying hard to be respectful of Ben's calling. In Luke's estimation, Ben was a quintessential member of the Church who should have been translated long ago.

"Yes, I know," Ben said. "And I can assure you the Lord knows, too."

"You're really scraping the bottom of the barrel on this one," Luke said. "I'm way busy with the kids and my freelance career. What if I can't attend a meeting for one reason or another?"

"That's why you have counselors," Ben said.

"Luke," Hayley said, "since you've joined the Church, you've never turned down a calling."

"Yeah, well there's a first time for everything. *Elders Quorum President?* I just learned how to consecrate oil last month. There are so many others who are more qualified, who know more than me. I'm sorry, but I don't think I can do this."

"Believe me, I know how you're feeling," Ben said. "That's how I felt when I was called as a missionary. Then elders quorum president. Then bishop. Then stake president. But what you have to understand is, it's the Lord that's calling you to this position. Not me."

"Don't try to absolve yourself from blame," Luke said.

"It feels overwhelming, I know," Ben said. "But if you put your trust in the Lord, He will help you."

Luke stared at the floor, and ran his hands through his hairline, which was starting to recede.

"Surely there are many others in our ward who can do it better than I could," Luke said. "How about Brother Bosworth? I know for a fact that he goes to the temple every Tuesday and Thursday — because he told me — and I've seen his family group sheets on his iPad. He's related to Benjamin Franklin *and* Brigham Young. That guy is organized. He served a mission to Outer Mongolia. I'm convinced he has memorized all of the Doctrine and Covenants. I didn't serve a mission. I didn't join the Church until I was in my late 20s. There are Primary-aged kids — namely my own — who know more about the Church than I do."

"Luke, you may not feel qualified right now, but you will," Ben said. "I can assure you, whom the Lord calls, the Lord qualifies."

Then Ben pointed to the painting of the Savior behind his desk. "This is His Church. There's a reason He's calling you to this position."

Hayley stared at the ceiling, as if summoning divine assistance from ministering angels.

"Hayley," Ben said, "what are you thinking about?"

"Are you absolutely sure about this, President?" she asked.

"Right now, I've never been more sure about a calling I've extended in the five years that I've been stake president. And Luke certainly wouldn't be called to this calling without having a wife like you by his side."

Luke arose and started pacing around the office, thinking aloud.

"This would mean a lot of meetings, wouldn't it?" Luke said.

"Yes," Ben said.

"You know how I feel about meetings. I am hopelessly allergic to them. I break out in hives during stake conference."

"Yeah, I know. But this calling isn't about meetings. It's about ministering to those in need."

"Remember when Jim Parsons was elders quorum president? Remember how he seriously injured his back after helping the Reynolds move their piano?"

"Yeah, I remember. He was in traction for three months."

"This would mean teaching lessons, wouldn't it?" Luke said, continuing his stream of consciousness.

"Yes," Ben said. "And it would mean being on the front lines of helping people with their lives. It would mean learning how to minister to others the way the Lord would do it. I know you're worthy to fulfill this calling. Whether you realize it or not, you're a great example and your unique perspective — being a convert with an amazing conversion story — will bless others' lives."

Ben paused. Luke kept pacing.

"I'll be honest with you. This is going to be tough, Luke. This calling is going to stretch you like salt water taffy," Ben continued. "You'll talk to couples going through marital troubles. You may get phone calls in the middle of the night. You might spend a lot of time in the hospital visiting the sick and afflicted, giving blessings. Yes, you might develop chronic back problems from helping people move in and out. But I promise you, Luke, that you'll receive greater blessings than you can imagine. You'll bless your family in ways you can't imagine. You'll draw closer to the Savior, and love people like He does. I'll admit, I don't know specifically *why* the Lord would want you to serve in this position at this time. All I know is, He does."

Ben always seemed to know exactly what to say.

Luke remembered what the Lord had already done for him. A rush of memories flooded his mind. The Lord had rescued him, both physically and spiritually, on several occasions, in miraculous ways. He thought about his wife and children. Wasn't what the Lord was asking him to give miniscule in comparison to what he had already received?

"Luke, are you willing to accept this calling, and magnify it to the best of your ability?" Ben asked.

Luke stopped pacing, though he noticed his hands were sweaty and shaking.

"Are you sure I can do this?"

"Yes," Ben said, "but maybe I'm not the One you should be asking."

Luke thought about that. Ben had a good point.

"Will you excuse me for a minute?" Luke asked.

"Sure," Ben said.

"I'll be back soon," Luke promised as he strode out the door.

If there were one thing that Luke had a strong testimony of, it was prayer. And this was an occasion when he needed some heavenly confirmation. He trudged down the hallway and past the cultural hall, where he heard the sound of basketballs pounding on the hardwood floor. He needed a place to be alone. He remembered a bathroom at the end of the hall, near the back exit, that was usually empty. He went into the large stall that led to the baptismal font where he had baptized his children. Luke locked the door, and then dropped to his knees.

As he prayed silently and earnestly, he was reminded of the time when he asked God if the Book of Mormon were true and if Joseph Smith were a prophet. It reminded him of the time when he offered plaintive pleadings while he was being held captive by fanatical, bloodthirsty terrorists in a remote part of Africa.

When Luke finished, after asking for assurance that this was God's will, he remained on his knees for a moment. Then it came — an undeniable, familiar peace and serenity that filled his soul. It was as if a legion of angels was lifting him off the ground, turning him around, and kicking him back in the direction of the stake president's office.

As Luke returned, Hayley looked at him with concern.

"Well, did you get your answer?" Ben asked.

"Yes," he said.

"Will you accept this calling, Luke?"

Luke exhaled and nodded. "Yes."

"Great!" Ben said. "Hayley, do you support Luke in this calling?"

"Of course," she said, wiping tears from her eyes.

"Hayley, this calling will require Luke to be gone from home for long periods at a time because of meetings and other activities," Ben said. "I apologize in advance."

"Is there a support group for wives of elders quorum presidents?" Hayley asked, half-joking.

"Yes," Ben said. "I think it's called Relief Society."

Hayley smiled.

"Hayley, I know you will support your husband in this calling," Ben said. "He will come back to you a better man, a better husband and father. And I promise that the Lord will more than compensate you for the time Luke spends in His service."

Ben then looked squarely into Luke's eyes.

"Your number one priority will always be with your wife, then your children. Hayley comes before everything else, OK?"

"OK," Luke said, placing his hand on Hayley's.

"We'd like to take care of your sustaining and setting apart next Sunday. That means I need the names of your counselors by tomorrow morning."

"Tomorrow?"

"Yes. And remember to shave your facial hair before Sunday."

"Seriously?" Luke asked.

"Seriously," Ben said, grinning.

Ben made his way around the desk and embraced Luke.

"Welcome aboard, Luke," Ben said. "I mean, President Manning."

CHAPTER 2

THE FOLLOWING MORNING, after a fitful night's sleep, Luke stood in front of the mirror and reluctantly shaved off his goatee, flecks of gray hair swirling around the sink and down the drain.

Clean-shaven, he saw himself in a different way — or at least tried to.

President Manning.

President?

All night long, that word haunted him.

President was one title he never thought he would hold, not in any capacity whatsoever — not in politics, not in the Rotary Club, not in the Church — never in his wildest dreams. Or his worst nightmares.

No, Luke didn't see this coming. Some of his previous, low-profile callings — including ward bulletin editor, Cub Scout Pack Night Coordinator, assistant Sunday School secretary, Physical Facilities Representative — were designed, he believed, to keep him behind the scenes where he could do the least amount of damage. Some of those, Luke thought, sounded like made-up callings.

Ironically, for years, Luke had teased Hayley that she would eventually be called as the Relief Society President or Primary President or Young Women's President. Luke always promised he'd be her "third counselor." Luke knew that Hayley, as a returned missionary, and diligent student of the gospel and Church history, and because of her inherently charitable nature, was infinitely qualified to be an auxiliary president.

Luke never pictured himself as an auxiliary president or even a member of an auxiliary presidency.

Hayley had been the Primary chorister for years and she loved that calling. She enjoyed being with the children and singing her favorite Primary song, "I Am A Child of God" with them. She always had the family sing it every Monday for family home evening. The kids would complain when they sang, "I Am a Child of God" each week but Hayley insisted.

"It teaches the plan of salvation in a simple way so that anyone can understand," Hayley would say. "And you can't help but feel the Spirit when you sing it."

To Luke, the word "president" connoted power as well as mistrust. Since joining the Church, he learned to be a little more trusting of people, but he was innately distrustful. As a journalist, he distrusted people. Having been abandoned by his dad, and later by his mom, and as a kid growing up in foster homes, it was hard for him to trust anyone, especially those in power. It was embedded in his soul.

Yes, this would take some getting used to — people addressing him as "President." He knew it would make him feel uncomfortable, especially since he didn't feel worthy of that title. All the elders quorum presidents he had met in his relatively short time in the Church were amazing men. Almost every member of the quorum was an Eagle Scout, a returned missionary, and a BYU graduate.

Luke was none of those things.

So how could *he* be called as president? How could he lead *them?*

A year or so after his baptism, Luke received his patriarchal blessing. He understood that a patriarch wasn't the Church's version of a fortuneteller, but Luke was a little disappointed that he wasn't promised that he would become a world-famous journalist. On the other hand, the part about having children who would bless his life came true. But there certainly was no hint in his patriarchal blessing that he would be any type of leader in the Church. And he had been just fine with that. He was content with sitting anonymously in the back of the congregation. That's where he felt comfortable.

Luke had always found it interesting that in any given ward, the

Lord could find the right people to fill all the callings, even Scoutmaster. But Luke's new calling didn't make much sense to him.

Either consciously or subconsciously, Luke always measured himself against five-generation members of the Church, and he knew he could never live up to them, or to the impossibly high expectations. Everyone in the ward, it seemed, had astonishing stories about their pioneer ancestors. Every 24th of July, people in the ward would share jaw-dropping tales, worthy of a motion picture produced by Cecil B. DeMille, about their pioneer forebears.

Some well-meaning ward members would tell Luke, "As a convert, *you're* the pioneer of your family!"

They were trying to be nice, but to Luke, it seemed to be a little patronizing, like a backhanded compliment, like being called a "sweet spirit."

Luke knew next-to-nothing about his family history, and he wasn't sure he wanted to know anything about it. He did know that his father, Damon Lane Manning was a drunk, a dead-beat dad, and a convicted felon. For Luke, thinking about his family history was depressing and torturous, not uplifting and inspiring.

One time Luke was trying to encourage two of his sons, Brian and Benjamin, to stop fighting and apologize to each other.

"Heavenly Father won't forgive you if you don't forgive others," Luke told them. And those words burned his ears as soon as they escaped his lips. He knew he was a hypocrite. After all these years, he had never forgiven his dad. And he figured there was no way he ever could in this life because his dad had died many years earlier.

Luke's trepidation about being the new elders quorum president aside, maybe, he thought, the calling provided a measure of validation. A sign that maybe President Ben Kimball, and the Lord, could trust him. Maybe he had finally *arrived* in the Church.

When Bishop Tompkins learned that Luke had accepted the calling — and he was skeptical that he would — he called him on the phone the following day.

"Congratulations," Bishop Tompkins said.

"That doesn't sound like the right word. I think the word you're looking for is 'condolences.'"

"I'm looking forward to working with you," Bishop Tompkins said, paying no heed to Luke's sarcasm. "You'll be serving side-by-side with me. Be prepared to provide counsel to brethren with marital difficulties, lead soul-stirring discussions, and become an expert in moving couches and pianos up and down stairs."

"Helping guys with their marriages? I thought that was your responsibility."

"Well, it is. But you'll be helping me. And you'll be heavily involved in helping those in our ward who are out of work or underemployed find better employment."

Luke wanted to remind the bishop that he was one of those underemployed ward members, but he didn't.

"In my calling, my main focus is on the youth," the bishop said. "I want you to be in charge of the adults. Maybe you can resolve problems before they ever get to me."

Luke's stomach twisted violently.

"Being in the Lord's service is exhausting at times," Bishop Tompkins added, "but it's always rewarding."

When the phone call was over, Luke didn't feel any better. He felt as if a sumo wrestler had been strapped to his back.

Luke didn't think he was capable of handling these new responsibilities. The timing of this calling was interesting, he thought, if not vexing. Lately he had been feeling like he was going through the motions when it came to living the gospel amid the chaos of life. Luke realized he had become complacent and casual about reading scriptures, praying, and attending the temple.

Nothing like a new calling to jolt him out of the stultifying doldrums and force him to rise from the dust.

Luke had written down in his journal something Ben had taught at a stake priesthood meeting several years earlier. In light of his new assignment, he looked it up.

"Conversion to the gospel is continuous. We don't just arrive at a destination and presume we're done," Ben said. "We must endure to the end. Our testimonies grow, or shrivel, based on how much we nourish or neglect them and based on our ever-changing circumstances. I've known plenty of people who were 'converted,' only to fall away later. That's why we need to feed our testimonies daily."

Meanwhile, Luke couldn't shake the gnawing fear that he wasn't worthy. He barely felt worthy to call himself a member of the Church, let alone a leader of a quorum of elders. He knew that through baptism he had been forgiven of past mistakes and sins. But what about his former disposition to do evil from his days when he lived in New York

City? Luke knew all about the demons that plagued his father and he knew the devil had a detailed scouting report on him and would exploit his vulnerabilities whenever he could.

Before he moved to Utah, Luke liked to work hard and play hard. He was sinning in ways he didn't even know were sinful — until he came to Utah. He had no idea that God didn't even want him to drink a cup of coffee. But that was the least of his offenses. What if those bad tendencies returned?

The Book of Mormon story about the Anti-Nephi-Lehies that converted to the gospel of Jesus Christ was one of Luke's favorites. Those people put aside their weapons of war, and buried them deep in the ground so they would never fight against God, or anyone else, anymore. Luke had symbolically buried his own weapons in his own life, but he knew his weaknesses.

Luke battled those feelings of guilt about past sins, but Ben once told him that those feelings were, in a way, a blessing because they would serve as a warning system — from the Holy Ghost — and would help him avoid making the same mistakes again.

"I wish I could be baptized all over again," Luke once told Ben, who replied, "You can. We have that opportunity every week when we partake of the sacrament."

Luke was always grateful and humbled that Hayley could love him unconditionally and forgive him for his past mistakes. She explained to him that she wasn't perfect, either — though their sins may have been different. All that mattered to Hayley was that the Lord had forgiven him, just as He had forgiven her. To her, it was about where Luke was going, not where he had been.

The most important thing in Luke's life was his family, and he didn't want to do anything to jeopardize losing his wife and children. One of the most powerful principles that attracted him to the Church was marriage without an expiration date, and the idea of eternal families.

Luke had grown up as a ward of the state of New York, never dreaming he'd end up as part of a ward in Utah. His upbringing explained why he was so motivated to be a dependable father, and to be there for his children — just like he had learned that Heavenly Father was there for him. Luke knew that God had offered him a second chance, over and over and over and over and over again. Luke didn't want to let Him, or his family, down.

Jeff Call

After Luke and Hayley got married, they made their home in Helaman, a place where the town's movie theater was closed on Sundays and never showed R-rated films. Luke liked the people of Helaman because they were, generally speaking, genuine, kind, and and compassionate. And he loved the wide-open spaces, in sharp contrast to New York City. It was well documented that Helaman, and the surrounding metropolitan area of Utah County, was one of the most religious places in the entire country, with ubiquitous meetinghouses. To say that Helaman was "predominantly" Mormon would be the equivalent of saying the Vatican was "predominantly" Catholic.

But at times, Luke felt like a foreigner in his own ward. The culture was so different from what he had been accustomed to in New York City. The gospel he embraced wholeheartedly, but some of the views, traditions, and cultural idiosyncrasies of Utah County Mormondom puzzled him, and frustrated him, at times.

That's why Luke adamantly refused to put vinyl stick figures representing his family members — like he saw plastered on almost every other sport-utility vehicle in Utah County — on the back window of his Suburban.

When Luke first arrived in Utah County, he presumed everyone he met was a member of the Church. And he had about a 90 percent chance of being right, it seemed. If there were any doubt, all he had to do was offer the person in question a cup of coffee. Their answer told him everything he needed to know about their religious and political persuasions.

Luke had arrived in Utah not knowing a single Mormon. Years later, all of his friends and acquaintances, it seemed, were Latter-day Saints. He didn't know any alcoholics in his circle of friends in Utah, but he knew quite a few with a crippling addiction to Diet Coke.

Sometimes, he felt like he needed to escape the provincial bubble of Utah County. He wanted to get away and take his family with him. Luke was secure in the knowledge that his family was eternally sealed. At times, though, he lamented that his family, living in Utah, was hermetically sealed.

Luke wanted his children to know how it felt to be a minority — in terms of race, religion or both. He knew that atmosphere could not be replicated in Utah County. Luke didn't want his children to avoid people who didn't talk, think, and act like they did. He wanted to inculcate a feeling in his children that they could be confident in their beliefs, and yet be able to carry on a civil conversation with anyone — including Democrats — without being condescending or offended.

And some of the Mormon traditions nearly drove him to drinking again (the closest he came since joining the Church was non-alcoholic sparkling apple cider on New Year's Eve). For example, he relished the experience of giving a name and a blessing to his children. What he didn't enjoy was all the pomp and circumstance that existed on the periphery of such monumental, memorable ordinances. In preparation for all the friends and family that would be coming over to the house after those occasions, he and Hayley spent an exorbitant amount of time cleaning the house, sprucing up the yard, setting up chairs, and buying and preparing food — leaving them exhausted for the Big Day. The whole purpose for the get-togethers seemed to be lost in the act of entertaining and feeding extended family and other guests, as if the reason why they were gathering was an afterthought.

The night before his son Benjamin's baby blessing, Luke cleaned the windows, mowed the lawn, and vacuumed the house. He accidentally dropped a 12-pound frozen ham on his toe and he limped up to the front of the chapel the next day for the blessing.

"You think baby blessings are tough," Ben said when Luke told him his plight, "missionary farewells are baby blessings on performance-enhancing drugs."

Ben would know. He had a son serving a mission in Asunción, Paraguay. A photo of Elder Kimball, surrounded by smiling, diminutive Paraguayans in a tin-and-wood hut and a brick-and-clay oven, sat on Ben's desk in the stake president's office.

What made those special days meaningful to Luke was performing the actual ordinance, and the way it made him feel. To him, the rest didn't really matter, though it seemed to matter greatly to everyone else.

Another thing that attracted him to the Church was the way most members lived their lives without pretense, with a deep commitment to serve and love one another. Luke had also experienced the joy and contentment that resulted from mingling with members of the Church, and ministering to others in simple ways.

Many of those lessons about service and selflessness he learned at home, trying to care for his wife and children, and he had the dishpan hands and bloodshot eyes to prove it. No, life at home rarely was a Norman Rockwell painting.

Being a father and a husband was kind of like sprinting blindfolded through a minefield, Luke decided.

Maybe he was experiencing a mid-life crisis fraught with turmoil, but Luke didn't seem to be living up to his lofty expectations for himself. He felt like he didn't excel at anything. He was merely average in any one of his many responsibilities — as a provider, a father, a husband, and a member of the Church. He wasn't excellent. He wanted to excel, but it was as if time constraints prevented that from happening. He knew that Hayley deserved someone who was excellent. Luke secretly feared that she wished she were married to someone who was.

Luke wondered if there were a way he could clone himself, or figure out a way for his body to function without sleep. If he didn't have to sleep, he was certain he would have time to accomplish all of his duties and achieve all of his goals. He wasn't sleeping much anyway.

In the middle of the night, days after he was called to be elders quorum president, Luke arose from bed, staggered into his office in the darkness, stepped on Jacob's Stegosaurus toy, avoided a curse word with a groan, then knelt next to his chair and asked Father in Heaven to either take away his trials or to take him away. Far away.

CHAPTER 3

YEARS EARLIER, NOT LONG AFTER returning from Africa, where he had been held captive by terrorists for months — before the birth of his eldest daughter, Esther — Luke had fielded numerous lucrative offers from publishers for the rights to his book about his terrifying experience.

A bidding war ensued, and he signed with Harper-Collins, a major publisher based in New York City.

The contract included a six-figure advance, and with most of that money, Luke and Hayley built a tasteful, comfortable, split-level home next to Hayley's parents' house on a lot that previously, for generations, had been farmland. The Mannings paid cash for the house, thanks to that advance.

While the home certainly wasn't ostentatious, the Mannings figured it was large enough to accommodate the large family they were anticipating. Hayley, who was shrewd with money, set aside a savings account for a rainy day. Having no mortgage payments was a blessing.

The home included five bedrooms, a spacious kitchen, a spacious living room, three bathrooms, a finished basement, a playroom for the kids, a craft room for Hayley, and an office for Luke.

While the house was being built, Luke and Hayley lived with Hayley's parents. He poured his soul into his book, which he titled

Grace Under African Skies — My capture by Sudanese terrorists, and the miraculous escape.

Luke wrote in between baby feedings. He wrote at the Helaman City Library. He wrote at the Helaman City Park. He wrote at the dinner table. He wrote while Hayley slept. It seemed he wrote while *he* slept.

It took him eight months of constant work to complete the manuscript — a poignant narrative spooled together from detailed descriptions of his harrowing ordeal — and he was proud of the final product. Months after that, the book debuted, and he went on a whirlwind book tour around the country.

For Luke, it felt good to finally publish a book, especially after the book project that brought him to Utah in the first place never materialized.

Grace Under African Skies rocketed to the Top 10 on the *New York Times' Bestsellers* list. Luke made appearances on *Good Morning America* and the *Today Show*, among many other television and radio programs. He traveled from coast-to-coast attending book signings, and doing interviews. Hollywood studios were lining up to acquire the movie rights.

One studio was prepared to offer a significant amount of money for the rights to the book but when Luke asked the executives about their vision for the movie, they said they would remove all references to Luke's reliance on his faith or God, while focusing on the terrorism and violence and the Special Forces' daring attempt to rescue him.

Luke didn't feel good about that, no matter how much money the studio was offering. To him, God and the story were inseparable. There was no story without Him. As part of the contract he had negotiated with his publisher, Luke had the power to decline the offer, figuring others would be coming in. Instead, the offers dwindled. A faith-based movie studio showed some interest in the book but ultimately opted not to pursue the project because there was "too much Mormonism" in the story.

Book sales were brisk at first but over the years, the royalties dried up.

For a while, Luke was a celebrity of sorts, especially in his home ward and stake. Ben Kimball had arranged for Luke to do a couple of firesides to share his conversion and experiences, and he traveled around the state of Utah telling his story to standing-room-only crowds stretching to the nethermost parts of cultural halls.

But as the years passed, his celebrity status faded away. His book became a muted memory. One day after sacrament meeting, a ward member, Brother Hansen, approached Luke.

"Didn't you used to be an author?"

"Um, yeah," Luke said, though in his mind, he still considered himself an author. He didn't know whether or not he should be offended. He didn't know if the ward member was implying that he was washed up as a writer.

"Well, I saw your book and bought it the other day," Brother Hansen said.

"Oh, really? Where?" Luke asked.

"Deseret Industries. It was a bargain! I paid $1.75!"

Brother Hansen meant well, but that's not exactly what an author wants to hear.

When the book was published, times were good. He was married to a gorgeous, saintly woman. He had a baby daughter, Esther. And he was secure in his faith and his purpose in life.

Then life inexorably marched on.

The Manning's' other children came in relatively rapid succession — Brian Khalid (13), Benjamin Woodard (11), Jacob Lucas (8), and twins Ashley Jane and Lindsay Anne (4).

Hayley brought into the marriage a sizeable sum of money. Her dream was to be a stay-at-home mom, with a house full of kids. She had worked as a registered nurse before marriage, and she discovered that, while caring for the children, her medical background came in handy on a regular basis. She considered herself a practicing nurse —it was just that she drew no paycheck for her work at home.

Meanwhile, Luke embarked on a freelance career in journalism, with little pressure or stress because they were living comfortably. In reality, fatherhood became Luke's full-time job, with plenty of overtime hours.

Luke decided he would work as a freelance journalist because he liked the flexibility. Best of all, he didn't have a boss to report to — except for Hayley.

But finding opportunities for freelance income were intermittent and sporadic, and Luke spent almost all of his time with his family, which he enjoyed. As the kids got older, life got busier and more expensive.

Every time Luke tried to go into his office at home to get some work done, the kids would interrupt, asking for a drink, or he'd have to referee an argument. Or Esther would start playing the violin. Or Hayley would ask Luke to go to the store or run an errand. As a result, he struggled to get much accomplished in terms of earning a steady income.

The Manning's' bills were manageable at first. But that was changing. With little money coming in, over time, the Mannings had to start dipping into their reservoir of savings.

Years flew by like months, months flew by like weeks, weeks flew by like days, as if Luke were flipping through the pages of a book. The family calendar looked like something out of a multi-variable calculus assignment.

For a guy who had never changed a diaper or ironed a shirt or made pancakes before he got married, Luke considered himself almost fully domesticated. He honed his skills over the years as a diaper-changer, sandwich-maker, and toilet-scrubber, among other things. He had never felt so exhausted.

Hayley was pushed to her limits as well. She had always looked forward to settling down, getting married in the temple, and raising a righteous posterity. But being a stay-at-home mom didn't always feel like she thought it would, or should. She constantly felt worn down. She felt like she was always telling Luke what to do. She didn't want to be a nag, but she realized that if she didn't point out what needed to be done, it wouldn't get done, and the house would be a federal disaster area.

Besides that, when Hayley looked in the mirror, she saw a woman who was emotionally and physically spent, a woman who felt her beauty and youth melting away — even though to Luke, she looked more beautiful than ever.

When Luke looked in the mirror, he saw a man he barely recognized. He remembered an article he wrote when he worked in New York where he described a politician he had covered as "paunchy." He noticed that description was starting to fit him — and he was horrified.

Before she became pregnant for the final time, Hayley informed Luke that she was 25 pounds heavier than she was on her wedding day.

Luke replied that he gained the same amount of weight since they got married.

"But at least you have a good excuse," Luke said. "You've had multiple pregnancies, including a set of twins."

That didn't make Hayley feel any better.

"I think you look amazing," Luke added.

She didn't feel amazing. Small wrinkles were forming around her eyes. And when she found her first gray hair, she felt like crying.

Hayley could have provided a substantial salary working as a registered nurse. But at the time she quit, she and Luke had decided it was more important for their family to have two parents at home than two incomes.

At that moment, however, they had zero incomes.

Hayley said if something didn't change soon, she would have to go back to work at the hospital and Luke would stay home with the kids.

Luke didn't want that to happen for approximately one billion reasons. He knew how much Hayley wanted to be at home, and he would feel like a failure in his responsibility to provide for his family. He didn't want Hayley to have to worry about money.

That's why Luke couldn't wait for the day that his book hit the big screen. He dreamed of walking down the red carpet for the world premiere in Hollywood, and having Brad Pitt play him in the lead role. He was sure it would be a blockbuster film, and the money would start rolling in again. But he wanted it to be on his terms. To not acknowledge God's role in his rescue, he thought, would not only be showing a lack of gratitude, but it also would be a lie.

As the years passed, that dream of a movie seemed to drift further away and out of his grasp. Not only did movie studios lose interest, but his agent did, too.

So Luke focused his efforts on doing small freelance projects. He dabbled in some newspaper and magazine stories that brought in a decent income, but nothing consistent.

The Mannings found their bank account shrinking while their bills multiplied. Brian needed braces. The Suburban needed new tires. Esther needed a new wardrobe. The boys were constantly foraging for food and could seemingly eat a year's supply of sustenance in a matter of hours. One afternoon, Luke once caught Jacob shoving handfuls of potato pearls into his mouth.

The twin girls had been successfully potty trained, but the baby on the way would ensure more years of diapers.

In his younger days, Luke figured he would become rich enough to hire a maid and a chauffeur, only to discover, much to his dismay, that he *was* a maid and a chauffeur.

There was a time, back in New York, when Luke thought he would never have kids. They weren't in his life plans. He didn't believe in marriage and he had no desire to be a father.

But that was all before he arrived in Mormonville.

Luke and Hayley seemed beset by one crisis after another. They were becoming experts in crisis management. Or crisis mismanagement.

A few days before Luke was set apart as elders quorum president, Hayley accompanied him to the mall, where they picked out and purchased a navy blue suit, a couple of new ties, a pair of shiny black shoes and three white shirts. Hayley had found a store holding a big sale. It set the Mannings back financially a bit, but Luke had to look the part of the elders quorum president, right?

Even with a new ensemble, and freshly clean-shaven, Luke may have looked the part, but he certainly didn't feel the part.

CHAPTER 4

WHEN LUKE WAS SUSTAINED as elders quorum president, it was a surreal event for him — and for almost everyone else in the ward.

President Ben Kimball presented his name for a sustaining vote in front of the quorum, and Luke stood to the sound of audible gasps.

Brother Bosworth was incredulous and wondered aloud if a mistake had been made or if a practical joke had been perpetrated. The rest of the quorum was supportive and happy for Luke. Everyone was genuinely surprised but no one more so than Luke himself.

Ben, as stake president, placed his hands on Luke's head to set him apart. Luke felt the weight of the hands of the entire stake presidency on his head, not to mention the weight of the calling.

He felt good about his choice of counselors and secretary, and he told them after he was set apart that he would rely on them heavily as he tried to figure out what he was supposed to be doing. Luke's mood brightened considerably when President Kimball handed him a key to the Church. He now had the keys to the Melchizedek Priesthood in his ward, and the key to the building.

Ready or not, he was Luke Manning, elders quorum president.

Almost every day, Luke would throw on a pair of shorts, high-tops, and his favorite New York Mets T-shirt and head to the church gym to play basketball in the cultural hall — by himself. And Hayley was fine with that. She knew he needed a break.

It was Luke's escape, his hardwood-floor nirvana. It became his guilty pleasure. Having a key to the church was Luke's favorite perk of the calling. It was during those morning basketball sessions that Luke could really be alone and think. And he had a lot to think about.

Luke would shoot basket after basket after basket, his mind working overdrive. An hour passed quickly. But it was therapeutic. He felt better equipped to deal with the challenges facing at him as a father, husband and elders quorum president. Plus, it was a great way for Luke to get exercise so he could lose those 25 extra pounds he had packed on since getting married.

Before they wed in the Salt Lake Temple, Luke and Hayley never really discussed how many children they wanted. On one hand, they would have felt extremely blessed to have one child. But Luke knew Hayley wanted a big family. Besides, Luke was an only child, so the idea of a lot of kids seemed appealing to him — especially when he discovered he instantly loved his beautiful daughter Esther. But, he wondered, did he have enough love in his heart for more than one? Could he love each child equally? He wondered how Heavenly Father could love each of his billions of children. The way Luke saw it, "billions and billions served" was a tagline that predated McDonald's.

At the same time, Luke marveled at Hayley's willingness to subject herself to the pain and discomfort she incurred with each pregnancy and risk her life to bring children into the world. Hayley was the bravest, most giving person he knew. The only thing that could come close to rivaling the Lord's love for His children, Luke decided, was a mother's love for her children. And he saw that on a daily basis in the way Hayley interacted with, cared for, and nurtured their kids.

Luke rarely saw what it meant to be a real father while he was growing up. But he watched his friend, Ben, very closely.

About 10 years into their marriage, when Luke and Hayley found out they were expecting twins — they already had four kids at that point — it took them a while to get over the initial shock.

Those two babies turned out to be identical twin girls, Ashley and Lindsay. Each baby weighed less than six pounds at birth, small enough to fit in one of Luke's hands. Luke thought it was a miracle that they were born at all. They were so small and fragile. All he wanted to do was protect them. He determined not let them date until they were in their 30s, if at all.

The girls were on baby formula, so Luke and Hayley would give the twins their bottles. When it came to early-morning feedings, Hayley liked to play classical music because she had learned that it would be good for the babies' mental and emotional development and she had done it for the other kids. The problem was, that music would put Luke to sleep. Luke wanted to play Jimmy Buffett or Bruce Springsteen songs, but Hayley nixed that idea.

Hayley took countless pictures of the girls sleeping in their crib together. Every night, she would place them apart but soon they would be next to each other, snuggling, holding hands or touching each other in some way, as if they were back in the womb. The good news for Luke and Hayley was, as they grew older, they could entertain themselves for hours.

And they did.

Ashley and Hayley were indeed identical twins in every sense. Luke always mixed them up. Sometimes, he realized he couldn't even correctly identify his own flesh and blood. To help him, he'd put a red ribbon in Lindsay's hair and a blue one in Ashley's. He wrote their names on the bottom of their shoes.

While the twins were small at birth, their lungs were fully developed from the beginning, something Luke and Hayley noticed every time they were hungry or needed a diaper change. Unfortunately, Ashley and Lindsay were born without a mute button.

When the twins were infants, Luke would carry them into church in their car seats, one in each arm. People would smile when they saw him coming into the chapel, and Luke joked that it was his "Sunday workout." And when the twins were two, and each would scream and squirm during sacrament meeting, Luke would carry both girls out to the foyer at once — one in each arm. They were his church hall pass.

When the twins were two-and-a-half, Ashley became severely ill with a high fever, stomach pains and vomiting. Doctors hospitalized Ashley and the Mannings left Lindsay, and the rest of the kids, with Hayley's parents. Luke and Hayley remained in the hospital for days watching over their daughter as doctors tried to figure out the cause of the illness. They performed tests. They treated her with antibiotics but nothing seemed to work. Ashley lay motionless in bed, barely able to move, hooked up to tubes and monitors. The doctors were stumped.

Ward members, as well as friends and family, held a special fast for Ashley. Luke and Ben gave her a blessing.

Meanwhile, Lindsay begged and begged to go to the hospital.

While staying with Hayley's parents, she would wake up in the middle of the night asking to see Ashley.

Hayley finally had her mom bring Lindsay to the hospital room. Lindsay ran to Ashley's bed and started climbing the rail. Luke tried to grab her, but Hayley told him to put her in the bed with her sister.

"But what about all this expensive, sensitive medical equipment?" Luke asked. "We don't need a bill for broken stuff on top of what we're paying. The nurse won't be happy with us."

"I'm a nurse, too," Hayley said. "More importantly, I'm their Mom. This is the first time they've ever been apart. They need to be together."

Once on the bed, Lindsay curled up next to a sleeping Ashley, placing her arm over her chest and holding her hand. Lindsay just lay there, staring at Ashley. Soon, a smile came over Ashley's face. Within an hour, Ashley's vital signs improved and her fever went away.

At first, the doctors and nurses discouraged having Lindsay and Ashley together, but when they saw the results, they relented. And they were astonished.

Ashley and Lindsay slept the entire night together in the bed and Ashley continued to improve.

Luke and Hayley were awakened early the next morning to the sound of both of the girls giggling. By noon, Ashley was released from the hospital with no signs of illness.

"It's like a miracle," the doctor said. "I've never seen anything like it."

"Love is more powerful than medicine," Hayley whispered to Luke.

After the twins were born, Luke believed they would not have any more children. Twins seemed to be a fitting double exclamation point to their procreation efforts.

But Hayley felt strongly that one more spirit was waiting to join their family. She was right. Four years later, she became pregnant. She just didn't know how difficult that pregnancy would be.

A couple of weeks after Luke received his new calling as elders quorum president, Hayley, just weeks away from her due date, was holding on to Luke's arm as they walked into the church. Without warning, Hayley felt light-headed, lost her footing, and nearly toppled to the ground. Luke caught her in time, but she didn't feel well throughout sacrament meeting.

"Luke," she said after the closing prayer, "you need to take me home."

Ordinarily, Luke would have jumped at the chance at skipping out on the final two hours of the block of meetings but he was supposed to conduct elders quorum meeting. He had spent much of the week preparing a couple of great icebreakers to open with.

Of course, Luke put Hayley first, so he made other arrangements and asked one of his counselors, Brother Garcia, to conduct in his place.

Luke helped Hayley into the house and it was clear she was in a lot of pain. She was a tough farm girl, she had been through five previous pregnancies, and she wasn't prone to complaining. So Luke knew this was serious. They went to the emergency room and an on-call doctor performed an ultrasound.

The doctor looked grim when he delivered the news.

"Mrs. Manning, I'm putting you on mandatory bed rest. That means you stay flat in bed at all times, except to go to the bathroom and shower and your doctor visits. If you don't stay on bed rest, you could lose this baby."

Hayley had been proud that she had gone almost full term with the twins without going on bed rest.

"I'm not saying this to scare you," the doctor said. "It's a reality. Mr. Manning, this means you are going to need to take care of the house while she's down and take care of her. You'll need to take time off work."

"No problem," Luke said.

"Mrs. Manning — no vacuuming, cleaning or doing dishes. Your husband will have to manage all that. Do you have any other children?"

"Six," Luke and Hayley chorused.

The doctor's voice said, "OK." His face said, *Heaven help you.*

Luke knew he'd need heaven's help.

Hayley wasn't one for lounging in bed all day, even when she was deathly ill or on vacation. Once they went to a hotel and while Luke was in the shower, Hayley made the bed, tidied up the bathroom sink, and cleaned the toilet.

"There are hotel maids that can do that," Luke pointed out.

"I just can't look at an unmade bed," Hayley said. "It drives me crazy."

So the notion that Hayley would actually stay in bed for weeks seemed ridiculous to Luke. But he knew that Hayley would do it to save their baby daughter.

Luke picked up on a few things over the years from Hayley about the nursing profession. He became an expert on the Heimlich maneuver, and he had to use it a couple of times, like when Jacob choked on a corn dog when he was three.

Two weeks into Hayley's bed rest, Luke was more fatigued and frazzled than ever. He'd clean the bathroom and 10 minutes later, it was dirty again. Five minutes after clearing the sink of dishes, he'd walk into the kitchen and see two filthy plates and five cups in the sink. He tried to fill the irreplaceable void Hayley left and realized he could never match her abilities.

Fortunately, Hayley's mom, who lived next door, would come over and help on a regular basis. But she was getting older and she couldn't do as much as she used to around the house.

Luke thought about Hayley, who dealt with cleaning up messes on a daily basis without saying a word about it. How was she able to maintain an orderly house, and keep the kids in line, without losing her mind?

At nights, the whole family would sit on Luke and Hayley's bed to read scriptures and hold family prayer.

Every day for weeks, there would be a knock on the door with members of the ward Relief Society standing on the porch holding casseroles, Jell-O and brownies, or some variation of that meal. Every time he heard that doorbell ring, he would salivate like Pavlov's dog, and sigh with relief.

CHAPTER 5

THE NEW SCHOOL YEAR started, and Luke was relieved to have the four oldest kids — Esther, Brian, Benjamin and Jacob — gone most of the day, thinking he'd have more time for his writing projects.

Since Hayley was bedridden, she asked Luke to take a picture of the kids on their first day of school. It took him 10 minutes to get them all to smile at the same time.

When Luke took Esther to her first day of high school, he felt old. George Burns old. Methuselah old.

The 1980s — when Luke went to high school — seemed like such a long, long time ago, a time his kids believed were a period immediately following the Stone Age. When Luke would turn on some of his '80s tunes while he did the dishes, he was surprised that Esther actually recognized some of those songs.

"How do you know this music?" he'd ask her.

"They play this sometimes at church dances, when they play the 'oldies.'"

Oldies? He remembered when he was really young that his mom would sometimes spin Buddy Holly tunes on the record player. To him, that qualified as the "oldies." Back then, he considered anything by the Beach Boys or the Beatles as "oldies."

It never occurred to him that stuff he listened to in high school on his boom box, that adults always told him to turn down, would be considered "old" music.

"These song aren't 'oldies,'" Luke would tell Esther. "They're 'classic.'"

"No, dad, this isn't *classical* music. That's Beethoven, Chopin, and Bach."

When he'd think about the fact he was born in the 1960s, it did sound like eons ago. It *was* last century, after all.

In high school, Luke used a computer with floppy disks, listened to music on tapes, and when he watched television and wanted to change one of the four channels, he stood up, walked to the TV, and turned a knob by hand. If he wanted to communicate with his friends, he used a rotary phone.

Just before her fifteenth birthday, Esther had insisted she needed a smartphone, as if her entire future depended upon it.

"Everyone has a smartphone," she said. "It's the way we talk to each other. Without one, I'll be a social outcast."

"Except you don't talk, you text, right?" Hayley said.

"Same thing," Esther said.

"What I don't get," Luke said, "is why do you text someone who is in the same room, sitting right next to you?"

Esther looked at Luke as if he had the IQ of a ferret.

An '80s version of a text message was a note he'd write in class, fold into the shape of a football, and flick it with his finger to one of his classmates.

"Your generation will never get texting," Esther said. "It's how we communicate."

"I never had a cell phone when I was in high school," Luke said, "and I survived."

"There probably weren't any phones at all when you were in high school," Esther said. "Didn't you use telegrams back then?"

Luke couldn't tell if she was joking or not.

"Actually, we communicated through smoke signals," he said.

"It's all I really want for my birthday," Esther said. "Without a smartphone, my life might as well be over."

After deliberating, Luke and Hayley decided to give Esther her own smartphone, with ground rules that Esther begrudgingly agreed to, such as relinquishing her phone at any time for her parents to look at.

Every night, she would have to leave it in her parents' bedroom by 10 p.m.

Luke and Hayley figured it would be good to give Esther a phone in case she found herself in danger, and to communicate with her friends. Plus, they realized Esther needed to be technologically savvy because this was the type of world she was growing up in. She quickly learned to have in-depth conversations with friends that her parents couldn't understand by using esoteric acronyms and Emojis.

"She's fluent in Emoji," Luke told Hayley. "I don't see any benefit to it, unless she's called to serve an Emoji-speaking mission."

How could my little girl be a sophomore at Helaman High School? Luke wondered as he passed an army of teenage kids making their way to school. How did Esther transform from a sweet little girl that always wanted to sit on his lap and read books with him into an emotional, opinionated teenager that seemed to avoid him? She preferred texting with friends and going to movies with them to spending time with him. When she was young, she loved watching a basketball game on TV with him or going to get a milkshake together. Now? She spent much of her time locked in the bathroom or staring blankly into her phone.

Luke wished he could go back in time, or at least make time slow down. It was all going too fast. He remembered thinking that he'd be so happy when all of his kids were out of diapers, only to discover that the diaper stage was a breeze compared to the teenager stage.

Esther was a good but headstrong girl — like her mother. Soon after turning 15, Esther broached the subject of boys and dating with her parents. Esther understood the family rule that no dating was allowed until the age of 16. Dating was a subject that scared Luke to death. Esther was a younger version of her mother, and Luke remembered what he was like when he was those boys' age. He noticed the way boys looked at her. It was enough to make him want to buy a rifle, and he didn't even like guns.

"Can I go with my friends to Eric Cutler's house Saturday night?" Esther asked.

"What?" Luke asked.

"I know we're not supposed to date until we're 16," she said, "but this isn't a date. It's hanging out. And hanging out is not dating."

"Who's going to be there?" Hayley probed.

"Me, Bethany, Katie, Eric, John and Jordan," Esther said.

"So, three boys and three girls?" Hayley said.

"I wasn't counting, but yeah. So?"

"What are you going to be doing?"

"Just talking or playing games. Maybe we'll watch a movie."

"That sounds like a date to me," Hayley said. "Not until you're 16."

Esther stormed out of the kitchen. "You're ruining my social life!" she shouted and didn't speak to her parents for a week.

But Esther was also in touch with her natural nurturing traits that endeared her to her younger siblings. Jacob and the twins, especially, adored her. And she was a big help around the house.

Being musically inclined, Hayley started Esther out young with violin lessons — at age four — and she had an unmistakable talent for it. It wasn't like Brian and Benjamin with piano lessons. They had to either be bribed or threatened to get them in the same room with the piano, let alone play it. Their love was basketball, and they were dribbling and shooting whenever they could. With them, the piano didn't take.

Esther liked the piano, but she loved the violin.

Luke wanted to put in earplugs as she would play discordant notes in her early days of learning the instrument. Her violin numbers sounded like cats and mice fighting inside an oil drum. But Hayley patiently helped her every day, and gradually the cacophony disappeared and Esther played real, distinguishable music. She had perfect pitch and could play almost anything she heard.

After several years, she played at school concerts and in sacrament meetings. The bishop liked having her play when there was a missionary farewell. She had the congregation in tears with her rendition of "God Be With You 'Til We Meet Again."

Luke, and others, could feel the emotion behind the music. It indeed was gift.

But as much as he enjoyed her talent, almost every time he wrote out a substantial check to the violin teacher, Sister Halford, he resented it. That was a lot of money.

Hayley insisted it was worth every penny.

"It's a wise investment," she'd tell Luke, "you'll see. It's already paying off."

One day when Luke picked up Esther from violin lessons, Sister Halford ran out to the car to talk to Luke.

"Esther is so talented," she said. "She has a bright future."

To Luke, it was just a line Sister Halford was using to encourage Esther to keep taking violin lessons and squeeze more money out of him. All he could think of was all the money he had paid Sister Halford that year. She also told him that she would have to push back a couple of lessons because she and her husband were leaving for a Mexican Riviera cruise soon.

With my money, Luke thought.

Luke felt the same way about paying Esther's orthodontist, who bought himself a new motorboat not long after Esther got braces.

"I paid for that," Luke would say every time they drove past the orthodontist's house, with the boat gleaming in the driveway.

Luke didn't think Esther needed braces. He never had braces, and he turned out just fine. Besides, what was the point of his daughter looking even better than she already did? There were already enough boys sniffing around the house. But he knew it was no use arguing with the orthodontist, or his wife, about it.

Esther became so accomplished on the violin that Hayley thought that maybe she could get a college scholarship. But Luke didn't even like thinking about being old enough to have a daughter in *college*.

And he certainly didn't want to think about her dating in college, praying she didn't go out with anybody like the college version of himself.

Esther had a not-so-secret crush on singer David Archuleta, a famous member of the Church. She had downloaded all of his music and hung a poster of him, as a missionary, on her wall. One day Luke overheard Esther saying to one of her friends, "Do you think David Archuleta would ask me to prom when I turn 16?"

Luke decided he'd approve of that, if it ever happened. Luke had watched David Archuleta and how he represented the Church on *American Idol*. He was a kid Luke could trust with his daughter. He didn't feel that way about most other young men.

When it came to his daughter, any boy over the age of 15 was a menace to society, as far as Luke was concerned.

"Dad," Esther said as they pulled into the Helaman High parking lot, "could you drop me off at the other side of the school?"

"Why? I thought your first class was here by the main doors."

"Dad, please take me down there," she said, slumping in the passenger's seat. "You're so oblivious."

"Sorry," Luke said, "I hadn't noticed."

39

Then it hit him. She was embarrassed to be seen in the same car with him. It was a painful revelation. He kept driving past the main doors.

"Have a great day," Luke said as Esther exited the car. She gave him a partial smile, thanked him for the ride, and quickly shut the door. He watched her backtrack to the front of the school, where she caught up with her friends. She seemed sullen sitting there in the car. He saw that once she was with her friends, she was smiling and laughing like she was out on parole.

Then Luke remembered that when he was a teenager, he had treated his foster parents the same way. Even worse.

This is payback, Luke thought, *with compound interest.*

Luke was bracing for the time when his other kids would become teenagers. He shuddered at the thought.

Brian was happiest with a ball of some shape in his hands, and he was the most athletic of the Manning boys. He was tall for his age and was always chosen for Little League All-Star teams. In his first ward basketball game as a deacon, Brian dribbled circles around his opponents and scored 26 points, including four 3-pointers.

He watched ESPN constantly and his favorite show was *SportsCenter*. His life goals included going on a mission, playing college football and college basketball at BYU, then splitting his time between the NBA and the NFL and then, like Bo Jackson, becoming a Major League Baseball player as a hobby.

Benjamin loved sports, too, but he had an intellectual, studious side. He was clever, a deep thinker and had a curious mind. From the time he was a toddler he was drawn to books. He'd always read books way above his grade level. Luke would get up in the morning and find him rummaging through his bookshelves in his office looking for reading material. One summer, he read the entire *The Work and the Glory* series.

And, like Luke, Benjamin loved to write.

Sometimes Benjamin would use words that made it appear that he had swallowed a thesaurus. When it came to speaking, he was too smart for his own good. With so many multi-syllabic words floating around in his head, he'd frequently get confused and mix up words. Some adults, noticing his precociousness, would talk to him as if he were a grad student.

Once, Benjamin's teacher told him, trying to pay him a

compliment, "You're a voracious reader."

"Oh sorry," he replied, "I'll try to do better."

Benjamin gave a talk in Primary that he wrote himself, and quoted the Book of Mormon: "Behold, David and Solomon truly had many wives and *porcupines*, which thing was abominable before me, saith the Lord."

There were some muffled laughs from the teachers in opening exercises, but nobody wanted to correct him because it was easier to let it go than explain the meaning of "concubines" to Primary kids.

Luke told Hayley that Benjamin was the family's resident malapropism expert.

Jacob loved spending all of his time outside, exploring, as if he were in his own little world. He could spend hours digging holes in the backyard, searching for fascinating rocks and bugs. His teachers, and school counselors, told Luke and Hayley that Jacob had a learning disability, and attention deficit hyperactivity disorder.

When he was six, Jacob decided to run away from home after getting into a fight with Benjamin. He put Graham crackers, a flashlight, and a Spiderman toy into his pillowcase, slung it over his shoulder, and disappeared into the night.

"Let him go," Luke told Hayley. "He'll be back in 10 minutes when he realizes how cold it is out there."

After 15 minutes went by, Hayley ordered Luke to go find Jacob. Luke drove around for a while before finding him at the school playground, hunkered down for the night.

"You need to come home," Luke said.

"Do I have to?"

"Yes. Mom says so."

"Where have you been?" Hayley asked Jacob when he and Luke returned home. "We've been worried sick."

"I ran away from home," Jacob said. "But I would have come home for breakfast, Mom."

Growing up, Luke had been so excited for certain milestones to cap segments of his life. Like getting a driver's license or graduating from high school. Never would he have to go through that, or worry about those things, again.

But he was wrong.

Luke learned that parents re-live everything through their children. The first day of kindergarten, the first playground fight, the first day of high school, the first time driving a car, the first date, the first kiss.

Luke wasn't sure if he would be able to go through childhood again and again and again vicariously through his kids. His overarching goal as a dad was to make sure their childhood experiences would be better than his were.

CHAPTER 6

AS HAYLEY CONTINUED TO BE stuck in bed, Luke had to continue fending for himself. And he became irritable.

One morning, Jacob refused to eat breakfast. Luke had gotten up extra early to make bacon, eggs, sausage, and orange juice. He tried everything he could to persuade Jacob to eat.

"You're going to get sick," Luke warned. "How can you learn on an empty stomach? Do you know how many chickens and pigs and oranges gave up their lives so you could enjoy this meal? Do you know how much this cost?"

"Two dollars?" Jacob said in all seriousness.

Luke didn't want Jacob sitting in class with hunger pains and a growling stomach. He didn't want to be judged by Jacob's teacher for not providing him with a decent breakfast. No good father would send his son to school hungry. He wondered if Jacob had discovered where Luke had hidden the Halloween candy stash from the previous year and was siphoning off Snickers and Butterfingers in the middle of the night.

After dropping off Esther at the high school, then Brian at the junior high, Luke had Benjamin and Jacob all alone in the back seat on the way to the elementary school.

"I can't believe you didn't eat anything this morning, Jacob," Luke scolded. "You're going to regret it."

Perturbed, Luke turned on the sports radio station.

"Dad," Benjamin said quietly from the back seat, "do you know why Jacob didn't eat today?"

"Why?" Luke said, turning down the radio. "I'd like to hear this."

"He's fasting for Mom, and the baby, so that Heavenly Father will take care of them."

Luke looked at his young sons in the rearview mirror and felt like an amalgamation of Darth Vader and Lord Voldemort. For Luke, fatherhood was a crash course, with an emphasis on crash.

He pulled over to the side of the road because he couldn't see anything.

"Dad, why are you crying?" Jacob asked.

"I'm just proud of you," Luke said. "You are way more mature and spiritual than I am. You're like your Mom, thank goodness. I'm sorry for getting upset with you. Hope you can forgive me."

"Yeah, I'll forgive you," Jacob said. "I've had lots of practice."

Luke loved the kids' unvarnished honesty and childlike faith.

He unfastened his seat belt, reached behind him and gave Jacob and Benjamin a hug.

"I love you guys," he said.

"It's going to be okay, Dad," Benjamin said. "Heavenly Father is helping us. Just like He helped Nephi build a boat and like He helped Moses part the Red Sea."

All Luke could think of was a Bible verse — *and a little child shall lead them.* Then he got misty-eyed again as he watched the boys get out of the car and walk into the school.

Later that morning, while Luke was at the church gym, shooting layups, Hayley called him.

"It's time to go to the hospital," she said in somewhat frantic tones.

"I'll be right there," Luke said, tearing out of the gym.

That afternoon, the Mannings welcomed a healthy, seven-pound baby girl into their family. They named her Sarah.

Luke again marveled at Hayley's enormous capacity to love, endure pain, and make sacrifices on behalf of others.

When Luke held little Sarah for the first time, he could see her mother in her.

"You're a lucky girl," he whispered in her tiny ear.

As it turned out, Sarah was a quiet, calm infant that smiled often and rarely cried or screamed — unlike her twin sisters. Hayley said Heavenly Father had sent them the perfect baby to offset the craziness of twins.

After a while, Luke figured it out in his head. He realized by the time Sarah would be graduating from high school he would be almost eligible for Social Security, if it were still around by then. If *he* were still around by then.

When Luke gave Sarah a name and a blessing in sacrament meeting a few weeks later, she lay serenely in Luke's arms, sucking on a pacifier, looking wide-eyed at the gathering of men huddling around her with bowed heads and closed eyes.

Luke remembered when he blessed Ashley and Lindsay (fortunately not at the same time), they both arched their backs and screamed like Sam Kinison, nearly drowning out the words of Luke's blessing, even though it was broadcast with a microphone.

Hayley's dad, Grit, had a habit of aggressively bouncing infants up and down during baby blessings, apparently under the impression that newborns enjoy Tilt-a-Whirls. Amid the circle of arms under the baby, Grit would start the undulating process. Luke figured the babies would get seasick. When the twins fussed, Grit's solution was to bounce them higher and higher. Luke feared they were going to be flung into the tenth row of pews and vomit all over everyone.

Anyway, just like that, Luke and Hayley had seven kids under the age of 15, and Luke joked that he was running a Boys and Girls Club.

But Luke tried his best to make things happy and fun at home, though he didn't always succeed.

When it came to throwing birthday parties, Luke became an expert, at least in his own mind. As a kid, he didn't really have any memorable birthdays, at least no *happy* birthday memories. He recalled that when he turned seven, he wanted a new bike.

His dad returned home after disappearing for several days, which happened frequently. Luke thought his dad had remembered his birthday.

Instead, his dad stomped angrily into Luke's room, stole some money out of his piggy bank, probably so he could buy more alcohol.

"Damon, it's your son's birthday," Luke's mom, Sheila, told him.

His dad looked down at him and uttered some expletives before adding, "Birthdays don't mean nothin'. The sooner you realize that, the better off you'll be. As it is, you won't amount to much anyway."

Then he left, slamming the door behind him.

CHAPTER 7

IN MANY PLACES IN THE WORLD, a weekend meant having Saturday and Sunday free. In Mormonville, Luke learned long ago, Saturdays were extremely busy because Latter-day Saints had to cram all their weekend activities into one day.

Compressing 48 hours into 24 hours was no easy task.

Sundays were supposed to be a day of rest. But as elders quorum president, Luke found that Sundays were just as exhausting as the other six days, if not more so. Luke would spend ten hours or more in his suit, going to meetings, conducting personal priesthood interviews, and making visits.

While Hayley felt much better not being pregnant anymore, her headaches increased in intensity. Since high school, she had suffered from migraines, but nothing like this. Migraines spurred her to get into nursing, to help alleviate others' pain. She could empathize.

In the days after Sarah was born, Hayley spent long days back on self-mandated bed rest. In the middle of the afternoon, she had the blinds closed and she placed something over her eyes because even a sliver of light would make her head pound as if burly lumberjacks were alternating swings at her cranium with a pickaxe.

With Hayley out of commission for much of the day, Luke continued to shoulder much of the load around the house. He was grateful that Esther was willing and able to help all she could. Luke relied on her heavily.

Hayley spent the next two weeks in bed except for when Luke took her to doctors' appointments. Doctors had no answers. Luke attributed the cause of the headaches to being married to him, not to mention being the mother of seven children, but he kept his diagnosis to himself. Luke took Hayley to a specialist, then to the emergency room, where doctors took a CT scan.

Luke was more scared than Hayley about possible outcomes and he asked the doctors a litany of questions, as a journalist is wont to do. His worst fear was that Hayley would be taken from him and the kids.

"Mr. Manning," the doctors would say, "we should know more after the CT scan. We're doing everything we can for her."

While the doctors couldn't find anything wrong, Hayley's pain was real. They ruled out a tumor, which was good news. The doctors prescribed her medication that helped reduce the frequency and severity of the migraines.

Hayley asked Luke for a blessing. He called Ben to assist him. Before Ben arrived, Luke suggested to Hayley that President Kimball administer the blessing.

"Luke, you hold the same priesthood he does," she said. "I'd like you to give me the blessing. Besides, ultimately the blessing comes from the Savior and in it's Him that I place all my faith."

Those words both instilled an overwhelming sense of confidence in Luke, and took a lot of pressure off him.

Luke helped Hayley into the living room and she sat down on a chair. The children gathered around as Luke and Ben placed their hands on Hayley's head. Luke blessed Hayley with the ability to continue to be a wonderful wife and mother. He felt prompted to say that, as a family, they should cherish every moment they spent together. He was inspired to say that those headaches would never completely go away. But as long as she trusted in the Heavenly Father and His plan and His will, and as long as she trusted in the Lord's infinite power and intimate love, she and her family would be would be blessed.

Early the next morning, the doorbell rang. Hayley shook Luke and told him to answer the door.

"I bet it's your dad," Luke grumbled as he turned over in bed. "He's the only person in the world that would ring someone's doorbell before the sun rises."

Sure enough, Luke was right. Grit Woodard stood on the Mannings' porch, dressed in overalls and a wide-brim hat, holding a Golden Retriever puppy as a gift. While Grit didn't approve this with Luke or Hayley, Hayley was instantly smitten with the yellow ball of fur with a tail wagging madly. Luke was stunned, and not in a good way.

Hayley grew up around animals — milking cows, feeding pigs, gathering eggs from the hens, and taking care of a variety of pets. She taught her kids how to plant gardens full of tomatoes, carrots, and radishes. And she always felt the kids needed some sort of pet. Of course, Luke strongly resisted not only because of his allergies, but also because of the added expenses and added responsibilities an animal brings.

For years, people had asked Luke, "Have you thought about getting a dog?"

To which Luke would always reply, "No, we have kids."

Hayley was delighted with her dad's surprise and the children were even more so.

"This dog will teach the kids responsibility," she said to Luke.

"I'm predicting right now that I'll be the one taking care of it," Luke said, sneezing.

"Maybe this dog will teach you some responsibility then," Hayley joked.

For family home evening that week, Luke held a vote. The kids decided to name the dog "Buzz" because his head looked like a barber had styled it into a flat top. Buzz's head was so flat, Luke imagined crushing a ball with his nine-iron off it.

So in between doing loads of laundry, sweeping the kitchen floor, and picking up the carpool, Luke fed Buzz and cleaned up his messes. And at night, Buzz would serenade him with a constant whine from his cardboard box in the garage. It was like having another newborn.

Even when Buzz was quiet, Luke could hear that canine whimpering in his mind, a sound that he couldn't get rid of, as much as he tried. Buzz shed all over the house. Sometimes Luke would find dog hair as he folded laundry or put away the dishes. Plus, Buzz gave Luke hives and itchy, watery eyes, and cold-like symptoms. Luke was popping allergy medication three times a day.

Fortunately for Luke, Grit would come over on a regular basis to help potty train the dog and teach it how to sit and stay. The kids, especially the boys, enjoyed teaching Buzz new tricks.

During those times when things were relatively calm, and the kids were being entertained, Luke withdrew to the solace of his office and opened his laptop. His office was a Buzz-free zone.

"Time to get some work done," he would say to himself, exhaling.

He had just done so one day when Ashley and Lindsay walked in, having awakened from their afternoon naps sporting Donald Trump-in-a-windstorm hair. He ushered them into the kitchen for some fruit snacks and returned to his office, only to hear the boys chasing each other throughout the house with baseball bats, with Buzz in tow.

Luke knew the Lord was trying to teach him patience but he didn't think he had time for such lessons.

In his weakened state, Luke yelled at the kids, then ordered Esther to cease and desist playing the violin.

"Esther!" he shouted. "There's enough noise in this house as it is! Mom doesn't feel well! She needs it to be quiet!"

Luke realized his yelling was louder than everything else that had been going on.

Esther stopped playing and the rest of the kids stood frozen in place and stared at him. They stared at him the same way he stared at his dad when his dad got mad. He saw fear in their eyes.

The twins began to cry. Luke wanted to press the rewind button on his life to about 10 minutes earlier.

Luke apologized to the kids and to Hayley. Later, Hayley told Luke, "I know Esther plays loudly but please don't tell her to stop. I love it."

"Even when you have a migraine?"

"Yes. It actually helps my head when she plays. It calms my nerves and my head. It's soothing."

That night as he tried to sleep, Luke doubted that he could ever become the kind of father Hayley and the kids needed him to be. Then he thought about his old friends from New York, going to chic restaurants, attending Broadway plays, and sitting in the luxury seats at ball games. By contrast, Luke felt like he was stranded on a barren island inhabited by wild kids. Sometimes, he silently wished he were somewhere else. Then he'd feel guilty for such thoughts.

Of course he loved his family. But was this what he signed up for when he joined the Church and got married? Was this some sort of elaborate bait-and-switch? Why wasn't family life as blissful as described in the pages of *Ensign* magazines and general conference talks?

Whenever the kids were giving Luke and Hayley trouble and all heck seemed to be breaking loose, Hayley would calmly say, "Luke, how else is the Lord going to teach us to love them like He loves them? One way or another, these kids will teach us to become true disciples of Jesus Christ."

"Or inmates in an insane asylum," Luke would reply.

When the boys put another hole in the downstairs wall, Hayley would take a deep breath and say, "It's OK. We're raising kids, not trying to make an issue of *Better Homes and Gardens*."

CHAPTER 8

THE ALARM SOUNDED AT 5:30 a.m. It was a high-pitched, shrill noise he always dreaded, especially at that hour.

Sunday had come again. And so had a winter storm.

It was two weeks before Christmas, and it was time to get up and get ready for Ward Council. Luke was tempted to push snooze on the alarm clock but he remembered on the news the night before the TV weatherman predicted a heavy dumping of snow. He walked to the front room window and peered through the blinds. In the pre-dawn twilight, he saw snow blanketing everything he saw. So he shoveled a couple of inches off the driveway. All the while, the snow kept falling faster and faster. He could barely keep up. By the time he finished the driveway, it needed to be shoveled all over again.

After shaving, showering and putting on his suit, Luke fixed breakfast for the twins, who had awakened early, as usual, and kissed Hayley goodbye.

"See you at church," he said.

Luke hated leaving Hayley alone to get the kids ready by herself. But he was encouraged that her chronic headache spells seemed to be subsiding.

Still, those early-morning meetings got him out of doing a lot of tasks at home on Sunday mornings, including curling the twins' hair. Esther had started helping out with that duty, which made everybody happier.

The meetings went relatively well, except Luke had to nonchalantly jab himself in the back of the leg with his pen a couple of times to stay awake.

And it was always a little discouraging to hear the run-down in Ward Council about all the troubles ward members were experiencing.

Sister Haynes had goiters. Brother Stephens lost his job. The Taylors were on the verge of declaring bankruptcy. There was plenty of service to render.

The Lord indeed was hastening His work, and Luke had a bad case of whiplash.

Luke tried to lighten the mood in the meeting by sharing a joke that his son, Benjamin, had told him.

"Knock, knock."

"Who's there?" Bishop Tompkins said, reluctantly.

"Lettuce."

"Lettuce who?"

"Let Us All Press On," Luke said. "You know, like the hymn."

Groans, some courtesy giggles and polite smiles, all around.

The Ward Council reviewed the monthly statistics and the bishop pointed out a concerning trend. The elders quorum home teaching percentages had dipped below 80 percent for the third straight month. This from a ward that had a tradition of 95-100 percent home teaching every month.

"Not that it's about the numbers, but the numbers reveal something about the dedication of our ward members," the bishop said to Luke. "Do you know how we can get those numbers up and make sure every family is visited?"

"How about incentivizing home teaching," Luke said. "Bishop, if we get 100 percent home teaching next month, will you shave your head?"

"No, President Manning," the bishop said. "I'm not comfortable with giving incentives for home teaching."

"I would suggest you should probably do home teaching interviews with all of the elders," said Brother Vinson, the high priests group leader.

"Does that work?" Luke asked.

"Well, we've had 100 percent home teaching in the high priests for 15 straight months, so I would say yes," Brother Vinson replied.

Bishop Tompkins provided all the auxiliary leaders with a copy of the projected budgets for the following year to review.

Luke saw the figures for all the auxiliaries. The elders quorum and the high priests were at the bottom with $75 apiece. The Relief Society, Young Men's and Young Women's each had thousands of dollars in their respective coffers. It was like looking at a Monopoly board, with the elders and high priests taking up residency on Mediterranean and Baltic Avenues while the others were occupying Park Place and Boardwalk.

"I know I'm kind of new here, and I'm not trying to rock the boat," Luke said, "but there's not much we can do with $75. Maybe buy every member of the quorum a plastic comb and fingernail clippers? I would really like to organize some get-togethers and parties to improve the unity of our quorum. Bishop, can we do fund-raisers like the Young Men do?"

The bishop looked askance at Luke though his bifocals, then thumbed through the Church Handbook.

"What did you have in mind?" Bishop Tompkins asked, meaning: *How much longer until I'm released?*

"Maybe we could sell a Chippendales-like calendar featuring various men in the ward," Luke joked. "Brother Vinson, I was thinking you would be a perfect fit for January."

"I'm flattered, Luke, but I'm very self-conscious about my pacemaker," Brother Vinson said. "I'm not taking my shirt off for anyone but my cardiologist."

The Relief Society and Young Women's presidents sat aghast at the mental image.

"President Manning, the answer is no to fund-raisers for the elders quorum," the bishop said, closing the Church Handbook. "I'm sorry."

Then inspiration, or something, struck again.

"Well," Luke said, "would you be OK if we used that $75 to go bowling as a quorum?"

"Sure," the bishop said, "as long as you incorporate the gospel and fellowshipping in some way into the activity."

The bishop hurriedly moved on to the next item on the agenda before Luke could make another suggestion or ask another question.

"The stake's goal for the next year is to have every member focus on family history and take names to the temple," Bishop Tompkins said. "We need to bring family history, the spirit of Elijah, into our lessons, all the way to the Primary. We'd like the Young Men and Young Women to do indexing and go on trips to the temple on youth nights for baptisms for the dead. We'd like the elders, high priests, and the women of the Relief Society to research their family history and prepare thousands of names for temple work. Our stake president, President Kimball, promised our stake that we'll be blessed greatly if we do this."

Luke made a note of it in his planner but he planned to delegate this item to one of his counselors. Family history wasn't something that he was interested in. In fact, he avoided it like the swine flu, even though he knew it was something he should be doing. Hayley had told him this hundreds of times. Being a convert, Luke figured he probably had bunches of people dangling from his family tree like overripe fruit. On the other hand, from what he knew about his ancestors — like his degenerate dad — they were probably whiling their way in spirit prison anyway and wouldn't be upwardly mobile.

When Ward Council ended, Luke raced to the chapel to see if he could help Hayley and the kids into sacrament meeting. He found them straggling to their seats. The twins were lifting up each other's dresses while Jacob and Benjamin were shoving each other and hitting each other MMA-style with their scripture cases.

Esther was holding Sarah and Hayley was holding her Primary opening exercise bag. Hayley looked beautiful, as usual, but she also looked like she had just climbed Mount Kilimanjaro.

"How it is out there? Is it still snowing?" Luke asked her, noticing her hands were red.

"Yeah," she said, snowflakes melting on her forehead. "It's still coming down."

The storm continued throughout sacrament meeting and gospel doctrine. Some blamed the accumulating snowfall on Brother Hightower because he had profusely thanked Heavenly Father for "the abundant moisture that we so need" in his opening prayer.

Right after priesthood opening exercises started, while the priesthood brethren were singing "The Time Is Far Spent," President Kimball burst into the culture hall and made his way to the bishop.

"Uh oh, someone's in trouble," Brother Vinson said, nudging Luke.

"Yeah," Luke said, "it's probably me."

Everyone noticed the bishop and stake president whispering to each other. It was all highly unusual, and most stopped singing altogether, although that might have also been because they didn't know the words to the hymn.

After the prayer, the bishop turned the time over to President Kimball.

"Brethren, in case you haven't looked outside in awhile, we're being hit with the Storm of the Century," President Kimball said. "I have consulted with the rest of the stake presidency and we feel it's expedient that we cancel the rest of the block of meetings."

The deacons, teachers and priests cheered out loud and gave each other high-fives.

"It's dangerous out there already with all of the snow and it's going to get worse. What I am asking of you brethren is, instead of going to your priesthood meetings, put your priesthood in action today. Please help the widows and elderly to their cars so they can get home safely. Please help shovel driveways. There are bound to be cars slipping and sliding all over the roads, and some are sure to get stuck. Please spend the next couple of hours seeing what can be done to help your neighbors."

Then he looked at Luke. "President Manning, I'll put you in charge of that in your ward. If you wouldn't mind reporting to me a little later in the day, I'd appreciate it."

Luke looked at Ben like he was the President of the United States, calling on the National Guard in a federal emergency. He caught himself before he said, "Yes, Mr. President."

"Yes, President Kimball," he said.

Just then, the power went out in the building. The cultural hall went pitch black. People pulled out their smartphones for light and everyone started moving out of the hall while trying not to incite a panic.

In somewhat orderly fashion, Ben dodged his way through the crowd and reached the hallway, where he explained in a calm but authoritative voice to everyone that church was canceled and he directed them out of the building. Families negotiated their way through the darkened hallways. Everyone seemed rather jovial. Nobody seemed to be too broken up by the change of plans, including Brother Taylor, who didn't remember until sacrament meeting that he had been assigned the elders quorum lesson that day. Saved by the snowfall.

But it was anything but a relaxing afternoon for the elders

quorum. Luke brushed off the snow and scraped the ice off 80-year-old Sister Perkins' car, and turned on the engine and heated it up for her before escorting her to the parking lot.

Sister Perkins gripped Luke's arm so hard, he'd have a bruise by that night. She was a hefty woman and she didn't walk very well due to double-hip replacement surgery the previous summer.

She almost fell a few times on the ice on her way to the car but Luke somehow kept her upright. He did rip his suit pants when they got caught on a fender. Luke placed Sister Perkins in the passenger's side of her car, drove her home, and helped her into her house.

"Thank you, Brother Manning," she said. "You're such a gentleman."

After making sure his family returned home safely, Luke changed into Levi's, a sweatshirt, snow boots, thick gloves, a wool snow hat, and heavy coat. Then he walked out the door and braved the elements with his oldest son, Brian, a deacon dressed in a Gore-Tex snowsuit.

"We may be a while," Luke warned Hayley as they left.

By then, the neighborhood power outage was over but the Ward Snow Patrol's work had just begun.

Luke and Brian spent the next three hours shoveling driveways and sidewalks and pushing cars out of snowdrifts. It wasn't something Luke ever expected to be doing on a Sunday, but he liked it. Not just because he got out of a meeting, but also because he figured it was what the Savior would be doing on a snowy day like that.

Every once in a while, Luke would look out into the winter wonderland and see his fellow quorum members working together, serving, smiling, and contracting frostbite. It was a better lesson on unity than they could have had sitting in the church merely talking about it.

Luke also enjoyed spending quality time with his son.

Many ward members expressed their gratitude for the help, including the only non-members — the Morris family — in their ward boundaries.

They were the family that seemed to deliberately mow their lawn on Sunday mornings in the summer just as everyone headed to church, seemingly to send a message — a public act of defiance.

The Morris family brought Luke a cup filled with a warm beverage.

"It's hot chocolate, not coffee, by the way," Mr. Morris assured him.

When Luke got home, all he wanted to do was take a hot shower, change into his favorite sweats, and go to sleep. But Hayley and Esther were doing the dishes and there were kids to take care of and play with.

Luke read scriptures with the kids, gave the twins "airplane rides" by lying on his back and propping them up in the air one at a time on his feet while holding their arms. They laughed and asked for more. Luke felt a sharp pain in his back. Then he got all of the kids ready for bed, and led family prayer.

Before going to bed himself, Luke threw on his snow boots and removed a dusting of snow that had accumulated in his driveway.

A morning that began with shoveling snow ended the same way. Though achy and sore, Luke slept well that night.

CHAPTER 9

BROTHER GREG HARDING, A MEMBER of the elders quorum, was always positive and joyful. He pretty much embodied every characteristic listed in the Scout Law.

Those were his distinguishing traits and that's why everyone liked being around him. If Brother Harding's smile had an odometer, Luke decided, it would have already exceeded the 400,000-mile threshold. He could charm a meter maid. He, his wife and three young children had moved into the ward about two years earlier and he served faithfully as a ward greeter.

"If anyone could be foreordained for a calling," Luke once told Hayley, "that would be it."

Brother Harding was kind and friendly without being annoying. He was genuinely happy to see people walk through the chapel doors and cheerily greeted each one. He would stand on one side of the chapel and call each person by name. If he didn't know the person, he would introduce himself and welcome them to the Helaman 6th Ward. If they were joining the ward, he'd even track down their Church membership numbers and give them to the ward clerk before the meeting was over.

Having served in the Texas McAllen Mission, Brother Harding liked to say he was tri-lingual — English, Spanish, and Tex-Mex. He particularly enjoyed fellowshipping the Latino members of the Church, and sharing the gospel with non-member Latinos he met.

Brother Harding actually volunteered for more home teaching assignments. Three weren't enough for him. If Latter-day Saints gambled, Brother Harding would have been the odds-on favorite to be the next bishop.

Instead, Brother Harding was called to be the ward mission leader. The bishop planned to release him as a ward greeter but Brother Harding convinced the bishop to let him keep that calling because he figured he would be greeting everyone anyway as the ward mission leader.

In elders quorum meetings, Brother Harding always said the right things to encourage and inspire his fellow elders. He had a talent for edifying and uplifting those around him.

As ward mission leader, Brother Harding, a software engineer, would walk throughout the ward boundaries a couple of nights a week, visiting the less-active, coordinating meals for the full-time missionaries, and serving others anonymously. He'd stop and help someone by pulling their weeds or just chatting with them.

Luke noticed this and thought Brother Harding should be the elders quorum president instead of him. Brother Harding had a way of making everyone he came in contract with feeling better about themselves. Nobody, including Brother Harding's wife, was aware of him saying a negative word about anyone or anything.

So people were curious how long that positive outlook on life would last when Brother Harding was diagnosed with stage-two lung cancer.

It didn't make any sense at all. Brother Harding never smoked, never even thought about smoking. He was rarely around second-hand smoke. Yet lung cancer had invaded his body and was ravaging it. And he had no clue.

Before the diagnosis, during a ward basketball game, Luke and Brother Harding both dove for a loose ball at the same time. Luke landed hard on Brother Harding's chest.

Brother Harding came up with the ball and, despite Luke's body perched on top of him, he threw a perfect pass down court to Brother Richins for a layup.

Luke picked Brother Harding up off the floor and asked him if he was OK.

"I'll be fine," Brother Harding said. He was either smiling or grimacing — Luke couldn't tell.

Brother Harding played the rest of the game, scored 10 more points, and didn't complain. He acted normal.

That night, his wife insisted he go to the hospital because she figured he had broken ribs.

At the emergency room, hospital personnel took some X-rays. The Hardings waited a long time for the results. They finally took the Hardings into a doctor's office in a different part of the hospital.

That's where they received the devastating news.

"Mr. Harding, you have a couple of broken ribs," the doctor said, "but the X-ray revealed something else much more serious. You've got lung cancer."

Sister Harding gasped.

"Can I finish the basketball season?" Brother Harding asked, trying to diffuse the tension.

"Mr. Harding," the doctor warned, "you don't have much time to live. Unfortunately, your condition has advanced to the point that there's not much we can do. I'm sorry."

"But I feel fine," Brother Harding said, "except for my ribs."

"There aren't any signs of lung cancer for people like you who are otherwise healthy," the doctor said. "But you're lucky you came in for this X-ray. Now you know what you're facing. You can make preparations."

"How much longer do I have?"

"Three to six months," the doctor said.

When Luke found out about this stunning diagnosis, he dropped by the Hardings for a visit.

Brother Harding was helping his nine-year-old son, Tanner, with his homework.

Luke didn't know what to say. He just knew it wasn't fair.

"I'm sorry for that collision the other day," he stammered.

"No reason to be sorry," Brother Harding replied as he led Luke into another room so they could talk privately. "I am glad you broke my ribs. It was a blessing in disguise. Now I know what I'm dealing with. The good news is, I've already met my insurance deductible for this year."

"I'm just so, so sorry," Luke said. "I just want to help if I can."

"I think we're fine," Brother Harding said. "My wife is taking it the hardest. We haven't told the kids yet. How do you explain to your young kids that their dad is leaving for the rest of their lives?"

Brother Harding's eyes filled with tears and so did Luke's.

"Just pray for my wife and children," Brother Harding said.

CHAPTER 10

BESIDES ESCAPING TO THE GYM to shoot baskets and run around to get exercise in the mornings, a healthier diet led Luke to shed close to 12 pounds over a six-month period.

Or maybe, he thought, it was due to the stress of his new calling. Either way, he felt much better overall and much better about his appearance.

Brother Harding's illness gave Luke even more motivation to get healthy. He contemplated his own fragile mortality — that life can change quickly, without warning. Luke couldn't understand why someone as righteous and Christ-like as Brother Harding, an all-around good guy, could be afflicted in this way.

Luke was grateful that Hayley's health seemed to be improving. He could only imagine what Sister Harding was going through.

While Luke loaded the dishwasher one morning, Hayley walked into the kitchen and thanked him.

"I'm getting too good at this," Luke said. "I'm afraid if I don't find a real job soon, I'm going to end up getting groceries at the Bishop's Storehouse. I don't think I could handle that. I don't want us to get to that point."

"What are you saying, Luke?"

"Well, with freelance opportunities not panning out, I think I need to apply for a real job."

"Doing what?"

"I was thinking about doing what I do best — writing for a newspaper. I won a bunch of awards when I worked in New York, you know."

"Yeah, I remember," Hayley said. "It's hard to forget when they are strewn all over your office. But last I checked, newspapers are laying off people, not hiring."

"Yes, it's a dying industry," Luke said. "Newspapers are going the way of MySpace, it's true. But newspapers are one of the pillars of our society. The venerable Fourth Estate. Maybe there's a news outlet out there looking for someone like me. Our country and the free press will always need good reporters."

"I agree that something needs to be done. I'm really worried about our financial situation. Soccer signups are coming up. My medical bills are starting to come due. And we're almost out of diapers again …"

"Remember how we decided when we got married to raise our family here in Helaman?" Luke said.

"Yeah."

"What if my new job requires me to move away? Like out of state?"

"Then if that's what we have to do, that's what we'll do," Hayley said. "I've mentioned that possibility to my dad before and he wasn't happy at all about the idea of his daughter and grandkids moving away. We'd have to break it gently to him."

"That would be *your* job," Luke said. "Tell me when you do. I'll make sure to be out of the state at that time."

Against his better judgment, Luke continued grousing about all the chores he had been doing around the house.

"It's time for me to do some real work," he said, putting away the vacuum.

"What do you mean by *real* work?" Hayley asked.

"I mean something that pays money. A paying job."

"Why don't you write a blog? Those are pretty popular. You'd be good at it. I'm sure there are ways you could monetize it."

Luke laughed. "Like a daddy blog? Puh-leeze. I would never do that. Those are so corny. I've got to find something lucrative, something substantive. In the meantime, I feel like I might go nuts here at home. I feel like wasting my life sometimes. If this is the way the

Lord wants us to live, after the manner of happiness, then why is this so miserable?"

Oooooooops.

Luke immediately realized that he had just stuck an entire Nike Outlet store in his mouth.

"This is what it means to be a husband and father," Hayley said. "It's your responsibility. No, being a parent is not easy. It's hard, backbreaking work. But it's the most important work in the world. I'm sorry that you're so miserable with me and the kids."

"I didn't mean to say miserable..."

"No, but you always say you might go nuts here at home and you just said you are wasting your life. I know you're not happy. You feel trapped. Don't let me and the kids stand in the way of your happiness."

Then Hayley walked out and closed the door behind her.

Just like that, by opening his mouth and letting words tumble out, Luke made everything worse. He was good at that. That night, he tried apologizing, but it wouldn't be that simple. He just continued trying to help out with the work at home with his mouth sewn shut. Luke had never seen Hayley so mad and frustrated.

While on the receiving end of the silent treatment, Luke decided to e-mail his résumé, and samples of his work, to editors that he knew, and some he didn't know, all over the country.

Days later, Luke's heart fluttered when he saw an e-mail from *The New York Times*. Yes, *that New York Times*, the bastion of liberal newspapers. Luke had sent a résumé to one of its editors that he knew, inquiring about freelance opportunities.

But *The Times* was offering much more than that. The newspaper editor asked about his interest in moving back to New York City and working full-time. *The Times* wanted to fly him out to the Big Apple for a series of interviews and to discuss the details, such as salary, and the type of stories he would write.

For the first time in years, Luke was excited about a job-related opportunity, although he wondered how he could reconcile working for one of the most liberal newspapers in the country when his views had taken a slightly conservative U (as in Utah)-turn over the years.

Then again, how could he turn down a chance to write for the prestigious *New York Times*?

With trepidation, Luke approached Hayley that night, after the kids were in bed, to talk to her about the e-mail invitation to interview with the *New York Times*.

"If that's something you feel you should do, then go for it," Hayley said. "Luke, you know I love you. But I feel like I'm suffocating you. You like your freedom and you feel like that's been taken from you. But the reality is, we are the parents of seven children that we love more than anything. We're responsible for loving them and caring for them. There's no sense in having a bad attitude about it."

"I'm sorry about my attitude," Luke said. "I'm sorry for saying I was wasting my life. You know I didn't mean it."

"I appreciate what you do for me, and for the kids, but something has to change."

Luke gave a lot of thought to what kind of change it should be.

Unable to sleep, he arose at four in the morning. He quietly tiptoed into the bathroom, shut the door and turned on the light. His marriage seemed to be flat lining. He was struggling with his church calling, feeling like there was always more to be done, feeling like his best efforts were never good enough.

His goals of being a Pulitzer Prize-winning journalist or a best-selling author not only seemed elusive, they seemed to have passed him by. He figured he was destined to be a mere footnote, at best, in the history of American journalism. He felt his writing abilities were atrophying.

Here he had this possibility of joining *The New York Times*, yet he knew his wife wouldn't be happy about relocating to the East Coast. Perhaps his family would be better off if he were living in New York. By himself.

So he accepted the offer to fly to New York, meet with *The New York Times* editors, and explore his options.

Within a couple of days, the arrangements were made. He received e-mail confirmation of his upcoming flight to New York City.

One night, Brian begged Luke to take him to the temple to do baptisms for the dead. Luke tried to come up with excuses why he couldn't go but Brian was persistent.

When the temple workers asked if they had family names to do work for, Luke sheepishly reported that he didn't.

"It's fine if you don't have family names prepared this time," the temple worker said. Then he added with a smile and a wink, "If you invest a little bit of effort in doing some research on behalf of those who haven't received their ordinances, it makes this experience so much better!"

The guilt he felt from the sweet old man's comments struck him like a Mohammed Ali right cross.

CHAPTER 11

HAYLEY WASN'T A BIG FAN of social media, though she did like logging onto Pinterest from time to time to search for sharing time ideas and for economical, healthy recipes. Luke didn't have much interest in social media, other than occasionally checking his Twitter account for sports and news updates.

When they'd get on their joint Facebook account, Luke and Hayley would shake their heads at what they considered to be frivolous items people would post.

"So many selfie-absorbed people out there," Luke said. "So many lonely people looking for attention, fishing for validation. You look at this stuff and after a while, it gets depressing. You only see one side of people — their best side. And you start to feel like your life is not as fun or glamorous as theirs, and that something is wrong with you and your life. It comes off sometimes like people are bragging and boasting about how great their lives are."

"Remember when Brother Barker posted that long, sappy love letter to his wife on their 30th anniversary on Facebook? That was so awkward," Hayley said. "Why couldn't he have just written that to her personally in a card? Some things shouldn't be shared in a public forum like this."

"It's cool that people have a platform to speak their minds or share ideas," Luke said, "but unfortunately, some people's brains are in neutral when they're posting stuff. Not to mention the blatant disregard for good grammar."

"People judge the quality of their lives, and their number of friends, by Facebook," Hayley said. "They equate their self-worth to their Twitter and Instagram followers or Facebook friends. If some people don't get a bunch of 'likes' on their posts, they feel like a failure, as if their happiness depends on such things. And then there are people tearing down others in their posts like they're bullies on a school playground."

One day, a member of the ward posted a photo on the ward Facebook page of the stake center, with the sidewalks covered in snow. Luke, as elders quorum president, was responsible for the church being shoveled. The post pointed out that someone, or some quorum, was being "slothful."

The Mannings didn't appreciate that attempt at public shaming, whether or not it was at their expense. Little did that woman who posted the photo know, but Luke had spent most of his day removing the snow from the driveways of various widows in the ward. The church sidewalks were shoveled later in the day, before meetings took place, but that post remained up much longer.

Brother Bosworth always seemed to cause controversy on social media, either deliberately or unwittingly. Like the time he strapped a Go-Pro to his head during the Primary Program, then posted video of his kids singing.

One Sunday afternoon, Hayley was scrolling through the Helaman 6th Ward Facebook page searching for an update on the missionaries serving from the ward when she spotted trouble.

Earlier, the Clarkson family, who lived just a few houses down from the Mannings, posted a photo of themselves frolicking at the beach in southern California for spring break.

Brother Clarkson, a Sunday school teacher, was shown with his wife, who was a counselor in the Relief Society presidency, with their three daughters — a Beehive, a Mia Maid and a Laurel — who were wearing swimsuits that some in the ward deemed to be somewhat immodest.

The caption with the photo: "Greetings from Zuma Beach in Malibu! Great way to spend the day! I love my family! #Maliburules #familiesareforever #waterisactuallywarm #funandsun

In most places, that would have been considered an innocuous post. But not in Helaman. Ward members reacted on both sides of what became a heated ward Facebook controversy. It seemed to polarize the entire ward.

The post had 38 "likes" on Facebook with comments like, "What a gorgeous family. Have fun!" Or "That is my favorite beach in California!"

Meanwhile, one ward member commented, "I don't think playing at the beach is considered keeping the Sabbath Day holy. Why post this?"

That comment got five "likes."

Back-and-forth it went until late Sunday night. Numerous ward members weighed in and several were downright snarky.

One mother said, "This is so disappointing. I teach my young daughters that we don't go swimming on Sunday and to wear modest suits."

Other replies: "Let's get down from our Rameumptoms and stop being so judgmental. What better way to get closer to God than to be in nature with picturesque views and the Pacific Ocean! #mykindofchurchmeeting"

The Mannings stayed out of it.

"This is why I'm going on a one-year fast from Facebook," Hayley told Luke. "This post is tearing our ward apart. If you 'like' it, you are seen as condoning Sabbath-breaking and wearing immodest clothing. If you don't 'like' it, you are seen as a Pharisee and a hypocrite. You can't win. Everybody loses."

A couple of days later, Sister Clarkson logged onto Facebook again and was mortified by the controversy she had inadvertently caused.

Sister Clarkson tried to clear up everything.

"I'm very sorry for posting the photos the other day on Facebook," she wrote. "I had terrible timing. I never should have posted those on a Sunday. The photos were actually taken on Saturday. On Sunday we attended church in Malibu and didn't go to the beach. As for my daughters' attire, we believe it falls in line with what is outlined in *For The Strength of Youth*. I apologize for the problems I caused."

After that, some ward members got back on Facebook and apologized for making assumptions and for comments they made about the Clarkson's' beach vacation.

But the damage had been done.

Bishop Tompkins, who everyone assumed was nearing the end of his tenure as bishop, addressed the issue during a Fifth Sunday meeting with the adult members. He had to meet with several members privately in an attempt to repair strained relationships and hurt feelings. Bitterness over the controversy continued for a while and made things a little uncomfortable at times at church.

Bishop Tompkins counseled ward members that instead of fretting about how many Facebook friends they have, they should remember that Christ wants to be our "friend," and we should "follow" Him. Instead of being so eager to post a "like" on someone's post, he said, we should be "like" Him.

Luke thought that was pretty clever, and effective.

Then the bishop concluded by quoting Jacob 6:12: "O be wise; what can I say more?"

Luke felt blessed that he didn't have to deal with the problem in elders quorum but the Relief Society President did. She referred the tougher cases to Bishop Tompkins, who was looking more and more haggard all the time. His hair looked to be thinning, and graying, by the day.

"I hope these bad feelings don't linger for years," Hayley said.

"All I know is," Luke said, "I feel bad for the next bishop of the ward."

Luke hoped Bishop Tompkins would be put out of his misery soon. That's one of the many things he really liked about the Church. A bishop could preside over a ward of hundreds of people for six years, then a week later, after being released, he would sit in the congregation like a regular member of the ward with no authority, or responsibility, whatsoever among the same group of people. From time to time, Luke fantasized about what it would be like to be released as elders quorum president, with its time commitments serving as the equivalent of a part-time job.

If he were to land a full-time job in New York, one of the unintended consequences would be a release from his calling.

And he would have been just fine with that.

71

CHAPTER 12

AS LUKE MOPPED THE kitchen floor at home, he listened, and sang along, to Frank Sinatra's hit, "New York, New York."

The day that he was to leave for New York City, and his job interview with *The New York Times*, had arrived. He would be heading to the airport late that night for a red-eye flight.

New York City was on Luke's brain, and he focused his attention on landing that job at *The New York Times*.

It had been several years since Luke had been in New York, and he was giddy at the prospect of returning to The City That Never Sleeps. He packed his suitcase and Hayley encouraged him to throw in a stack of Pass-along cards and a few copies of the Book of Mormon to give away.

Hayley had a doctor's appointment that day, and then she needed to take Esther to a school function. Luke promised he would pick up Benjamin from soccer practice, and fix dinner.

In terms of culinary skills, Luke was more 10-year-old child than Julia Child, though he had improved significantly since he became a father. He could manage pretty well if it involved something frozen and a microwave.

Luke went to Kimball's Market and bought dinner for that night as well as a large food supply to last while he was in New York. Ben Kimball joked that his store would someday re-name aisle 13 —

the frozen food aisle — in honor of Luke. With a shopping cart brimming with food, Luke approached a checkout stand and noticed a sign that read, "Lane Closed." He had seen that sign many times before, but on this occasion, he thought of his dad, and his middle name — Damon Lane Manning.

Why? Luke wondered. Was it because he was returning to New York? In his mind's eye, the phrase "Lane Closed" conjured up an image of his dad not just in a New York prison — where he had spent many years of his life — but also in spirit prison.

The thought left quickly as the cashier in another lane started to ring up his purchases.

Luke returned home and put away all of the groceries. Then he got so caught up in preparing for his trip — thinking of questions he might be asked during the interview, reading everything he could in *The New York Times* — that he completely forgot about picking up Benjamin and fixing dinner.

When Luke heard the garage door going up, he finally took his eyes off his computer. He looked out the window. It was almost dark.

"Where's Benjamin?" Hayley asked Luke when she walked into the house.

"Uh-oh," Luke said.

"Don't tell me you forgot to pick him up."

"I'll go right now."

Luke raced to his car, his pulse pounding. He arrived at the park a couple of miles away to find Benjamin sitting on a park bench, alone, and shivering in the dusk.

"I'm so sorry," Luke said to Benjamin. "I was busy and forgot to come get you. Are you OK?"

"I'll be fine, dad," Benjamin said, his breath filling the air. "No permanent damage done. I knew you'd come eventually."

"What have you been doing the past 90 minutes?"

"After practice, my coach asked if I needed a ride. I said, 'No, my Dad's coming.' Then I kept practicing by myself until it started getting dark."

Luke felt like nominating himself for World's Worst Dad.

When Benjamin walked through the door, Hayley hugged him.

"You're ears are frozen," she said. "It will be a miracle if you don't get an ear infection."

"I could have ammonia," Benjamin said.

"You mean pneumonia," Hayley said.

Just like that, Luke found himself back in the doghouse. Buzz seemed to be smiling at him, gloating at Luke's latest demotion.

"Luke, I can't believe you forgot him," Hayley said. "That's really irresponsible."

"You strand one kid at soccer practice for a couple of hours and you're labeled for life," Luke sighed.

"I really hope Benjamin doesn't get sick," Hayley said, "just as you're leaving."

Even after re-dedicating his efforts on making his family happy, he had blown it again. In a matter of a few short hours, he had undermined all of his work.

Before putting the younger kids to bed, Luke placed his suitcase in the entryway, and called the family together.

"Dad's going on vacation," Hayley said.

"Dad, you're not supposed to go on vacation by yourself," Benjamin said.

"This is no vacation, trust me," Luke said as the twin girls grabbed each of his legs and squealed. "I'm going for a job interview. I'll be back in a week."

Luke let the kids know there was a slight possibility that they could be moving.

"Where?" Esther asked.

"New York City," Luke said.

"Is that the place where you said there are rats as big as pigs?" Jacob asked.

Luke laughed. "Did I say that?"

"Yes," everyone responded in unison.

"Look, I need to go to New York for some interviews, then we'll see what happens."

"Dad, we can't move," Esther said. "That's not fair. I don't want to move to New York. I don't want to start over at a new high school. Are you deliberately trying to ruin my life?"

"Esther, nothing's been decided yet," Luke said. "Don't start telling anyone that we're moving. It's not a done deal. It's only a possibility."

"But do you want us to move?" Brian asked.

"Not necessarily," Luke said. "Let me go through the interview process first and then we'll talk about it."

Luke was conflicted. He knew he would miss his family, but he thought about how great it would be to catch a Mets game. Visit Grand Central Station. Walk across the Brooklyn Bridge. Eat at nice restaurants.

Then he thought about Hayley being left alone to fend for herself with all of the kids, eating macaroni and cheese and chicken nuggets, watching Barney videos, and chasing that darn dog around.

Maybe I am going on vacation, Luke thought.

Hayley went to bed before Luke left. He quietly knelt beside her.

"I'm leaving now," he said.

Hayley's head didn't move on her pillow. "I hope you find what you're looking for," she mumbled.

"What's that supposed to mean?"

"I hope you're going somewhere that makes you happy."

"I'm happy here. The whole reason I'm going to New York is to find a real job so I can provide for our family. I'm tired of working so hard for nothing."

Luke had done it again — he said the wrong thing at the wrong time.

"Well, the work I do here isn't for nothing, you know."

"I know," Luke said. "You know what I mean. I need a job. This is the best prospect I've got."

"And it's 2,000 miles from home."

"I thought you were fine with me going."

"You just seem pretty happy about this and the possibility of uprooting our family."

Luke didn't know how to respond to that without digging a deeper hole for himself.

Dejected, he stood up from Hayley's bedside and trudged out to the car with his luggage in hand.

Maybe, he thought, it was time to make a new life for himself where he came from, in New York City — a place he once felt very comfortable.

As he drove to the airport, Luke was consumed by dark thoughts about how his past seemed to be lurking and luring him back to a place he once knew. It was a place he had left behind, but at times, he felt like Lot's wife, fighting the temptation to look back. As he approached the Salt Lake City Airport, and the Great Salt Lake, he was afraid he might be turned into a pillar of salt.

Maybe, he thought, he was genetically predisposed to the ways of the world. Maybe his fate was sealed — he would eventually turn out like his father, dragging his family to the depths of a black, freezing ocean like the Titanic.

Maybe, he thought, his wife and children would be better off without him.

CHAPTER 13

JUST BEFORE MIDNIGHT, Luke boarded the red-eye out of Salt Lake City bound for John F. Kennedy Airport in New York City.

The New York Times sprung for a first-class ticket, which he appreciated. It was like flying in a Barcalounger. The flight attendants brought him a basket of snacks to choose from, drinks in glasses — instead of plastic cups they gave the coach passengers — and hot towels.

Somewhere over the Midwest, Luke leaned his chair back and stretched out his legs. Most passengers were sleeping but Luke couldn't.

He was excited about going home to New York yet anxious about the interview and dismayed about the latest blow-up with Hayley. A number of scenarios played out in his mind. Perhaps he could take the job and stay in New York and live out of his office. That way, his family could remain in Utah. He could provide for his family, and visit monthly.

Or maybe he could move his family to New York City and take Hayley away from her parents, and extended family, and run the risk of alienating her and the kids. Luke knew for sure that Hayley, and Esther, didn't want to live in New York. What if he got the job but lost his wife and children?

If his family did move to New York, the Mannings would have to sell their home in Helaman. Housing would be expensive in New York, and such a move would require new schools, a new ward and quite possibly a 45-minute commute to and from church on Sundays — not to mention a new lifestyle for his family.

And if he weren't offered the job, how would he support his family? He had no backup plan. There was no ideal solution, no matter what happened.

Finally, Luke drifted off to sleep. He awoke when the pilot announced the final descent into JFK. Luke looked out his window and gazed on the place he used to call home. The sun was coming up, splashing bright gold below, revealing the vast expanse of the famous New York City skyline. Having lived in Utah for so long, he noticed the lack of mountains, and he also noticed that the city was built on nothing thicker than pizza crust and was surrounded by water.

How can people live here? Luke caught himself thinking.

Once he retrieved his luggage, he haggled for a few minutes with a couple of cabbies — just for old time's sake — then boarded the crowded subway and headed to Manhattan on a brisk, windy morning. Luke's lungs burned. He squeezed inside the train.

"Lord, thank you for bringing us safety here," a middle-aged African-American woman, decked out in a red outfit and red-brimmed hat, exclaimed with a Jamaican accent from her subway seat. Her weathered hands clung to a pole. "And, Lord, please close that subway door. It's cold outside."

"Amen, sister," Luke said.

On cue, the door closed. Luke grabbed a pole while trying to balance himself, and hold on to his luggage.

The woman looked up and smiled.

"You know, Jesus can do anything that He wants to," she said.

"Absolutely," Luke said. "I agree with you. Right now, I'd like to ask Him to stop the wind from blowing. It's freezing here."

"Oh, He can do that, honey," the woman said, her eyes twinkling. "All you have to do is ask Him. If He wants it done, it will be done."

"Amen," Luke said.

Then the woman began rattling off New Testament scriptures from memory.

"I've heard that somewhere before," Luke joked.

"It's from the Bible."

"It's a bestseller for a reason."

"Where are you from, honey?"

"Utah," Luke said. "I'm originally from New York but now I live in Utah."

"Utah?" the woman asked.

"It's out West."

"Never been there. What's it like?"

"It's dry."

"You mean like a desert? Or dry, like no alcohol?"

"Both."

The woman laughed.

"What's your name, honey?"

"Luke."

"Luke? I like that name. Just like one of the apostles."

"Yes, ma'am. And what's your name?"

"Angel. My mama named me that because she said I am like an angel. I try to live up to that."

"You do, indeed."

"Are you a religious man, Luke?"

Luke looked around him inside the crowded train. "Yes, I am."

By this time, bystanders were listening in, whether they wanted to or not.

"You believe in the Bible?" Angel asked.

"Yes, I do."

"Did you know the Good Book says that if you have just a mustard seed of faith, you can move mountains? In his name, you can do anything. But it's not for you. It's not for your own glory, but for His."

"I believe that, too."

"Are you a born-again Christian?"

"Sort of. I'm a born-again Christian Mormon. I'm a member of The Church of Jesus Christ of Latter-day Saints."

"*Mormon?*"

Luke suddenly felt the penetrating stares of everyone on that subway car.

"Have you seen that *Book of Mormon* musical on Broadway?" a man next to him asked. "It's pretty entertaining."

"No, I haven't seen it," Luke said. "But if you think the musical is good, you should read the book. It's God's other bestseller."

"You're a Mormon, *and* you believe in Jesus Christ?" Angel asked.

"Yes," Luke said, realizing he was about to teach an impromptu first discussion to about 20 people within earshot. "Some people claim we're not Christians. But in the Book of Mormon, in Moroni, Chapter 7, there's an eloquent treatise about what it means to be a Christian — written by a prophet named Mormon. You should read it."

Luke removed a copy of the Book of Mormon from his backpack and handed it to Angel, marking Moroni 7 with a Pass-along card.

"Thank you, honey," Angel said. "What else do Mormons believe?"

At one time, Luke had memorized the Articles of Faith with Esther and Brian. But his mind drew a blank, so he improvised.

"We believe that we are all children of a loving Heavenly Father. We believe that His son, Jesus Christ, was sent to Earth to atone for our sins, our mistakes, our weaknesses, our sufferings," Luke said, feeling like a missionary. "We believe that through obedience to the commandments, we can not only return to live with Them again, but that we can also be like Them."

"Amen!" Angel shouted like a Baptist preacher, and pumped her pink-gloved fist.

"Thank you," Luke said, realizing he had just borne his testimony on a crowded subway. "Thank you very much. I'll be here all week."

"Have you been saved by grace?" Angel asked.

"Yes," Luke said. "As members of The Church of Jesus Christ, we also believe in being transformed by grace through the Atonement of Jesus Christ."

"Amen," Angel said.

"Jesus Christ is my Savior. He doesn't just save me once, like a one-time event. He's saved me many times, both physically and spiritually, and he saves me constantly, sometimes from myself."

"Amen," Angel said.

As the subway moved closer to The City, making its usual stops, Luke shared more passages with Angel from the Book of Mormon. She shared more of her favorite New Testament verses. It was a congenial conversation devoid of contention. They felt like they were learning, and gaining a new perspective, from each other.

"Forty-second Street, Times Square," the subway conductor announced as the train screeched to a halt.

"That's my stop," Luke said. "I've got to go. But it was very nice meeting you, Angel."

"You, too, Luke," Angel said. "May God bless you."

"Thank you. Same to you."

It wasn't the way Luke imagined his first hour back in New York City would go.

He stepped off the subway then made his way to the stairs. At the top, he emerged into the blinding sunlight and a bone-chilling wind.

Luke jaywalked three times with dozens of other pedestrians and, right away, he felt like a New Yorker again.

He had a couple of hours to kill before his meeting with the *New York Times* editors so he decided to check into his hotel, the 49-story Marriott Marquis Times Square, a five-star accommodation located on Times Square at Broadway and 45th Street.

Luke wandered over to the elevators, some of the most famous in the world. The Marriott Marquis features high-tech cylindrical, glass elevators that ascend 45 stories through the atrium lobby, rising to "The View," the city's only rooftop revolving restaurant and lounge.

Just trying to get on the elevator took some work. In the lobby, he pushed the floor number and waited to be told, via an electronic voice, which car to get into. He noticed a man wearing an all-camouflage ensemble waiting for the same car.

Luke did a double take. "Oh, sorry," he joked. "Didn't see you there."

The camouflaged man wasn't amused.

Once inside the car, the elevator rose at about 1,000-feet-per-second to the eighth floor where the front desk is located. Luke made the mistake of looking out the glass windows on the way up, which gave him a case of vertigo and acrophobia. He decided during the rest of his stay, while he was on the elevator, he'd just stare at the floor.

Luke schlepped his luggage to the front desk and the man stationed there looked at him a little dismissively.

"How may I help you, sir?"

"Hi, I'm here to check in, please," Luke said as the phone at the front desk rang.

"Excuse me, I need to get this," the man said.

Luke then waited for a few moments while the man engaged in a curt conversation with someone. Then he abruptly hung up.

"Do you have reservations?"

"About staying here? No, I'm pretty sure I like this hotel. I've seen the reviews."

"I mean do you have a reservation here, sir?"

"Yes."

"Your name?"

"Luke Manning," he said, handing the man his driver's license. "And you're Nicholai?"

After being addressed by his name, Nicholai was momentarily flustered.

"How do you know my name?"

"It's on your nametag."

"Oh, yes," Nicholai said, cracking a slight smile.

"How's your day been?" Luke asked.

Nicholai wasn't used to this line of questioning from a guest.

"Now that you bring it up, not good," Nicholai said. "My alarm didn't go off this morning and I was late for work. Then a customer got angry with me. It's been one of those days."

"I hope it gets better for you," Luke said.

"Me too," Nicholai said, looking at Luke's driver's license. "You're from Utah?"

"Yes, sir. Originally from New York."

"Utah? That's where my childhood hero — Kresimir Cosic — played basketball in America."

"Yeah, he was a BYU star," Luke said. "And a member of The Church of Jesus Christ of Latter-day Saints."

"Kresimir Cosic is a legend in my homeland and around Europe, too. It was very sad when he died. I was just a kid but I remember it well. I've always associated him with Utah. Because of that, I'm a big fan of the Utah Jazz and that famous singing group."

"You either mean The Mormon Tabernacle Choir or Donny & Marie."

"Yes, the Mormon Tabernacle Choir. I used to watch them sing on TV on Sunday mornings when I first arrived in this country from Croatia. So I have a question for you, Mr. Manning from Utah. If Utah is famous for that choir, why is the basketball team there named the 'Jazz?' I've never heard that choir sing jazz."

"Oh, they sing jazz from time to time," Luke said. "I once went to a concert and they sang 'When the Saints Go Marching In.' You can't get any more jazzy than that. As for the name of the basketball team, it moved from New Orleans to Utah in the late 1970s. They decided to keep the 'Jazz' nickname. The 'Utah Mormon Tabernacle Choirs' was a little too long. Wouldn't fit on the jerseys."

"Well, I've always been a fan of the Utah Jazz, because of Kresimir Cosic. Back when they played the Chicago Bulls in the NBA Finals, I loved John Stockton and Karl Malone. I loved the way they played the game. I wanted the Jazz to win even though Toni Kukoc, who is also a national hero in my home country, played for the Bulls. That's how much I love Kresimir Cosic — and Stockton and Malone. I wanted the Jazz to beat Michael Jordan and the Bulls so much. Too bad it didn't happen. I like you, Mr. Manning. It's an honor to meet someone from Utah."

"You can call me Luke."

"Tell you what I'm going to do for you, Luke. I'm going to upgrade you to a bigger, better room, one of our suites, at no extra charge. How does that sound?"

"Thanks," Luke said. "That's nice of you."

"No problem. You're the best thing that's happened to me all day."

"Your day's been that bad?"

"You just seem like a really good dude. I can't explain it, but I get a really good vibe from you. I know, that sounds weird. I just met you, but you're different from most people I deal with. It's as if I would trust you with my life and I barely know you."

"You've probably just caught me on a good day."

Nicholai laughed and handed Luke a key card. "It's Room 2211. Eleven was Cosic's number at BYU."

"I see what you did there," Luke said. "You know, BYU retired that No. 11."

"Yeah, I know," Nicolai said. "Now that you're checked in, do you have any baggage?"

"Yeah," Luke said, "but most of it's emotional."

"You're pretty funny," Nicholai said, laughing. "Are you a standup comedian or something?"

"Not hardly. My own kids don't laugh at my jokes."

"Well, I hope you enjoy your stay."

"Thanks, Nicholai."

When he got to his room, Luke immediately felt guilt-ridden. Nicholai had upgraded him to a Deluxe King Suite that featured a view of Times Square, two televisions, a separate living room area and a work desk with an ergonomic chair.

My whole family could fit in this room, he thought.

Luke placed his bags on the bed and removed various framed photos of his family and placed them on the desk.

Before taking a shower and changing into some clean clothes, Luke grabbed the ice bucket in his room and sauntered down the hallway to the ice machine and filled it with ice.

While his room was plush and the king bed was comfortable, Luke knew he wouldn't be able to rest, so he decided to walk around New York City.

As he strode through Times Square, which was teeming with gawking tourists and its typical assortment of eccentrics, Luke reveled in the city's ubiquitous diversity. In just over two blocks, he counted six different languages spoken — English, German, Spanish, Japanese, Italian and, of course, New York-ese.

Luke stopped to buy a "hot dawg" — one of his epicurean pursuits when he lived in New York City — and then he kept walking through the seamier side of The Big Apple. Subconsciously, he started to sing the Bruce Springsteen song, "It's Hard To Be A Saint in the City."

No, Luke wasn't in Utah anymore.

Back in his heyday, Luke had hung out at New York City clubs like McFadden's, eating, drinking and being merry, as if life had no consequences. Back then, he wanted to live it up before he died.

But after living a large chunk of his life in Utah, nothing really seemed to matter to Luke without his wife and children. He regretted how he left home with bad feelings between himself and Hayley.

In a city of 8.5 million residents, people came from all backgrounds and cultures. Luke was sure every nationality, religion, and belief system imaginable was represented. There were Catholics, Evangelists, Hindus, Buddhists, and atheists. They all belonged to Heavenly Father's universal family, and yet so few knew about His plan or the Savior's Atonement.

What if he had never gone to Utah? It's a thought that had penetrated his mind thousands of times over the years. Luke probably never would have found the gospel. Or met Hayley.

But didn't it seem like life was so much simpler without the gospel? Ignorance really was bliss. Life without the Church meant being able to sleep in on Sundays; keeping 10 percent more of his money; not feeling guilty all of the time; not having to worry about home teaching percentages.

In this return to New York City, Luke's memories about his lifestyle when he lived here haunted him. He thought about all of the sins and mistakes he had committed in his life, even the ones he hoped he had been forgiven of, then he started doing the math. The numbers were staggering. Luke couldn't remember all of the times he violated the commandments and he knew it was incalculable. He multiplied an estimated number by every person he saw, all of the people in Times Square, and then all of the 8.5 million people of the Greater New York Metropolitan Area. Then he imagined the Savior paying the ultimate price for all of those sins.

And what about the rest of the country? The rest of the world? What about those who have died? And all of those who would be born in the future?

Luke's head started to hurt. So did his heart.

Then he thought about the agony and angst he saw etched in the faces of certain individuals he saw around him. If only they knew about the Savior and His ability to succor them.

To his mind came a favorite quote by Elder Jeffrey R. Holland of the Quorum of the Twelve Apostles: "However late you think you are, however many chances you think you have missed, however many mistakes you feel you have made or talents you think you don't have, or however far from home and family and God you feel you have traveled, I testify that you have not traveled beyond the reach of divine love. It is not possible for you to sink lower than the infinite light of Christ's Atonement shines."

Those words buoyed him and comforted him when contemplating how often he fell short while striving to live a gospel that beckons perfection. It was comforting to him knowing that perfection was not man-made; it could only be found in, and created by, Jesus Christ.

A part of him wanted to ask for a few minutes to share the good news of the gospel, like he had on the subway, over one of the Jumbotrons in Times Square. Or take a megaphone and proclaim it to people, David Letterman-style — or Samuel the Lamanite-style — from the top of the Empire State Building.

As the wind chapped Luke's lips, he walked into Modell's

Sporting Goods, just to escape the crowds and the elements.

"You wanna buy some elliptical equipment?" the proprietor asked him.

"Are you suggesting I need elliptical equipment?" Luke asked.

"Hey, buddy, we could all use some. Know what I mean?"

"A little too pricey for me," Luke said as he left. "I'll exercise the old-fashion way by walking."

Luke's feet carried him to Columbus Circle and an entrance to Central Park.

By this time, the wind had calmed down, so Luke sat down on a Central Park bench and soaked in the spring sun as joggers and bicycle riders passed by. He looked at his watch. Hayley and the kids were probably eating breakfast, Luke thought.

A strange feeling overcame him. Luke loved feeling like a New Yorker again. But at the same time, he wasn't one of them. He only used to be. He lived in Utah with his wife and seven children. He wasn't living the dream as a journalist eating pricey lunches, wearing Armani suits, interviewing celebrities and power brokers, taking luxurious vacations and collecting a six-figure salary. He remembered when his face used to grace the buses in New York City — advertisements imploring people to read his newspaper stories.

Now he was just a non-descript face in the crowd.

As a Latter-day Saint, Luke knew he was a minority in New York. He knew his beliefs were starkly different from almost everyone he could see. He wasn't a real New Yorker anymore. Yet he didn't feel completely like a member of the Church, either. Saddled with an inferiority complex, something he never had when he was a resident of New York, Luke felt almost like a man without a country, a man without a true identity. What was his identity? But he came up with something — he was a child of God, a member of the Church of Jesus Christ, a husband, and a father.

Wandering through Central Park, he recognized his former self in the people he passed. The language peppered with profanity. The hardened looks. The skepticism of everything and anything.

Luke was shocked by how much he had changed over the years. Had living in Utah made him stronger? Or softer?

Just as he had testified to a subway full of people earlier, all New Yorkers were God's children. They were all loved. The Savior had purchased them and their salvation, just as He had his. Luke knew he was fortunate enough to have learned the gospel and to have been baptized.

Despite the uncertain circumstances in his life at the moment, he felt an enveloping peace — a trust that everything would work out for him and his family according to the Lord's timetable. It was as if the Spirit were whispering the words, "Have faith. Don't doubt. Just believe. Have you forgotten all the times He's already helped you? Why don't you trust Him now?"

Two spiritual experiences in New York City, all in the same morning. Who would have predicted that?

Luke looked at his watch again and realized he needed to return to the Marriott Marquis and get ready for his interview. He tried to muster the confidence he once had as a young, brash investigative reporter. In his former life, Luke felt perfectly comfortable staking out, and stalking, people for the sake of a good story.

The last time he had done any staking out and stalking involved his daughter Esther and a stake dance.

CHAPTER 14

IT HAD BEEN A LONG TIME since Luke had gone through the job interview process. He put on his suit, the same one he conducted business in as an elders quorum president.

Luke picked up his cell phone a few times to call Hayley, but he couldn't do it. All he could think about was how mad she was with him when he left. He didn't know what to say.

Once, Ben Kimball gave a talk on marriage in the adult session of stake conference. Something he said stuck with Luke.

In the best marriages, a husband and wife see themselves as teammates, helpmeets, and best friends, not as competitors or adversaries. They fight for the same goals, not with each other. Every day, we should be thinking, 'What can I do serve my spouse, make my spouse's life better?' If we consistently act on that, I promise you, the result will be a happy marriage."

Just by being in New York City, Luke felt a little like he was not being a very good helpmeet. But how was he supposed to support his family?

Walking out of the Marriott Marquis, he walked the couple of blocks to the New York Times Building on 242 West 41st Street.

Tom McDonough, the managing editor, greeted Luke. Tom praised Luke for his previous work for the *New York Daily*

News. He said he enjoyed Luke's book about being held captive in Africa.

Things were going well, Luke thought. Even better than expected.

"When I received your résumé, I was surprised," Tom said. "I had wondered what became of you. It was as if you disappeared or had joined the Federal Witness Protection program. What have you been doing in a place like Utah all of these years?"

"I've been doing some freelancing," Luke said.

"I really like your style. We'd like you to write a couple of investigative pieces a month plus biweekly blogs with incisive analysis about the big stories of the week," Tom said, thumbing through a stack of Luke's clips from his days with the *Daily News.* "We've got an office for you and we'd like you to be part of our daily editorial meetings. We'll pay for you and your family to relocate here."

"It sounds like a great opportunity," Luke said. "Of course, I'll have to discuss it with my wife."

"Of course," Tom said, stroking his white, close-cropped beard. "You are a gifted reporter. My one concern is you've lived far away from New York for a long time. Can you produce stories like you did for the *Daily News?*"

"I believe I can," Luke said, "and I will."

Tom took Luke on a tour of the *Times* building and met several employees. Luke remembered how much he loved the rush of adrenalin of the newsroom and he looked forward to being part of that again.

That evening, Tom invited Luke to a dinner meeting with a few other members of the newspaper's staff at an upscale restaurant located near Rockefeller Center.

Luke and Tom were ushered to a table near the back of the restaurant, and they were joined by Bruce Remington and Mandy Adams, a pair of *Times'* desk editors. Luke had known Bruce and Mandy for a long time. He respected their skills as journalists, and he enjoyed their company.

Then Luke saw a familiar face approaching the table, and he suddenly lost his appetite.

"Luke, you remember Peter Bartholomew, one of our senior reporters," Tom said.

Luke had spent years trying to forget about him.

"Yeah," Luke said, extending his hand. "Peter, how are you?"

"Never better," Peter said, projecting all the warmth and charm of a tapeworm.

The two awkwardly shook hands.

Peter and Luke had been rivals, even enemies, years earlier. Peter still had that smug look that made Luke want to remove Peter's larynx with a broomstick.

"I had heard that for many years," Peter said sardonically, "you've been living in a catatonic state — Utah."

Everyone around the table laughed. Luke forced a smile.

"I went to Utah once," Peter continued. "Moab and Park City are the only normal places. Everywhere else, all I saw were mountains and a bunch of deranged people. Everyone seemed to be smiling. It was like being trapped in 'Mr. Rogers' Neighborhood.' Creeped me out."

The waiter asked the group what they wanted to drink.

"Bourbon," Peter said.

"Scotch, on the rocks," Bruce said.

"Dom Perignon," Mandy said.

"Vodka," Tom said.

The waiter turned to Luke. Finally, Luke looked up from his menu.

"Water, bottled — on the rocks," he said theatrically.

Everyone at the table laughed again.

The waiter waited a moment to make sure he was serious.

"Did you say *water*, sir?" the waiter said, realizing he wasn't going to make much tip money off this guy.

"Yes. But not tap water, please. I've read in *The Times* what's in the New York City water system. How about Dasani?"

The Times crew smiled. The waiter nodded and scribbled on his notepad. "Okay, I'll bring your drinks right out for you."

"No alcohol for you, Luke?" Mandy asked. "I remember when you used to drink everybody under the table. Are you someone's designated driver tonight?"

"Just myself. I don't drink," Luke said. "I'm a member of The Church of Jesus Christ of Latter-day Saints."

"You mean you're a Mormon," Bruce said.

"Yes," Luke said, "I'm a Mormon."

As soon as he said that, he realized it sounded like he was participating in the Church's national "I'm a Mormon" media campaign.

I'm the father of seven, the wife of one, a journalist, I'm trying to land a job with a liberal newspaper in New York City. And I'm a Mormon!

Everyone at the table, meanwhile, went silent. And just like that, the tone of the dinner meeting changed.

"Mormons don't even drink coffee, right?" Bruce asked.

"I can confirm that, yes," Luke said.

"I really should keep my drinking to Mormon levels," Mandy said. "I've known a few Mormons. How can they be so perky — without coffee?"

"We eat a lot of ice cream and a lot of chocolate," Luke explained.

"Luke, what's happened to you?" Bruce asked. "You used to be one of my favorite drinking buddies. It's like you've been brainwashed or something. Did you have to do Alcoholics Anonymous? No wine? No beer?"

"That's right."

"And no women, besides the person you're married to?" Bruce said. "I couldn't live like that. I'd rather be dead."

"I hear you have three-hour church meetings on Sundays," Mandy said. "That alone would kill me."

"And they force you to cough up a big chunk of money," Peter said. "The Mormons are rich thanks to the contributions of their dumb-as-sheep minions."

It bothered Luke that people felt members of the Church were fair game to poke fun at and to use as a punch line and a punching bag. Even in this age of political correctness, any joke aimed at the Mormons was acceptable, whereas the same joke made at the expense of any other religious group or race would result in a public outcry or a revolt or a lawsuit or a resignation or a boycott.

But Luke realized that he used to make similar mean-spirited, misinformed jabs at the expense of the members of the Church back in his younger days. In fact, he had become an expert at it. Wrote a whole book about it, though it was never published. As he looked around the table at those sitting with him, he realized he needed to be forgiving. He, like them, once had been one of those pointing, laughing, and mocking with scorn from the upper floors of the Great and Spacious Building.

"Legally, I know I'm not supposed to ask you about your religion, so this isn't part of the interview process," Peter said. "But are you a bona fide Mormon or is it just an act? You can't actually believe the outlandish stuff Mormons believe. I can't imagine a grown man, particularly a decent journalist, could swallow such frivolous fairy tales. It's hard to take anyone seriously, like, say, Mitt Romney, who believes in that garbage."

Luke was actually grateful that someone asked him that so he could explain exactly what he believed and what he stood for.

"Yes, I really am a Mormon," Luke said. "I am a member of The Church of Jesus Christ of Latter-day Saints. Some might even say a devout member of my Church. I would take that as the highest compliment."

"I'm appalled by the arrogance of the Mormons, calling themselves 'Saints,'" Peter said. "What hubris. How self-righteous."

"A Saint is simply a believer in Christ," Luke said, "also known as a sinner who keeps on trying."

Before he could continue disabusing Peter of that notion, Peter kept talking.

"Luke, you have some talent, but I have serious concerns about you working at *The Times*. I'm afraid your views will color the way you cover stories. How are you going to separate your personal beliefs from your reporting?"

"When has that ever stopped you, Peter?" Luke responded.

"Are you going to have your church leaders in Salt Lake City edit and approve your stories before you submit them?" Peter seethed. "I mean, do you really believe that nonsense about angels, that Joe Smith character, the stories he fabricated, the fraudulent book he wrote? It's one of the biggest scams ever perpetuated on the world. I would go so far as to say you can't be a Mormon and a serious journalist. You can't purport to report the truth when in your personal life you believe in the fiction foisted upon us by the Mormon Church."

"First of all, Peter, I'm a professional. I report what I see and hear. I report the truth," Luke said. "And you need to get your facts straight. Joseph Smith didn't write the book. It was written by prophets that lived in the Americas centuries ago. He translated the book from gold plates. Like it or not, the Book of Mormon is true."

Luke couldn't believe it — he was bearing his testimony, again, this time to a pack of liberal journalists clad in fine-twined linen as they imbibed their alcoholic drinks.

"You believe it's true even though there's no shred of proof that an ancient civilization lived in upstate New York more than two thousand years ago?" Peter asked.

"Wow, I'm being grilled like the food back in the kitchen," Luke joked. "Look, Peter, the proof is in the book itself. Don't judge it until you've sincerely read it."

"Luke, I didn't realize how much Mormonism was part of your life," Tom said. "Looks like you've changed quite a bit since you were living in New York."

Luke wanted to tell Tom that he should have checked his sources before he invited him to New York for an interview. It felt like an ambush, but he thought that maybe he should have been more transparent about his beliefs from the beginning. Luke was determined not to develop a persecution complex about the experience.

"I respect your beliefs," Tom said, "but do you think you can check your Mormonism at the door every day?"

In that moment, Luke started to think about Mitt Romney and his two unsuccessful presidential runs. He had harbored some misgivings about Romney running for President of the United States. His high-profile candidacy put the members of the Church, and their beliefs, under the microscope. Everywhere Luke turned, he was reading scornful pieces and spiteful comments from politicians, pundits, columnists and talking heads about the Church, and most of it was extrapolating half-truths, claiming outright falsehoods, and making wild accusations.

Though Luke considered himself an independent voter, not a Republican, he did like Mitt Romney — so much so that Romney might have been the first Republican he ever voted for in his life. Mitt was a guy Luke would have wanted to sit down with and enjoy a root beer. Luke never bought into that media characterization of Romney being some ultra-rich, out-of-touch white guy. He knew Romney had been a stake president, someone who dealt with welfare situations and many other real-world issues that people at large didn't realize.

As much as Luke liked Mitt Romney, and the way he represented the Church, he wasn't sure he would have liked seeing that kind of vitriol directed at the Church, and its members, for four years while Romney resided in the White House.

Luke didn't agree with all of Romney's political views but he admired him for the way he didn't shy away from his faith amid criticism and tough questions.

Sitting in that upscale New York restaurant, Luke wondered how Mitt would handle some of the questions he was fielding. Having lived in Utah for so long, Luke wasn't used to being confronted with this line of questioning.

"All I can say is, being a member of The Church of Jesus Christ is who I am, and I can't check it in at the door," Luke said. "It is deep inside me. All I know is that my faith makes me happy and I'm a better man than I would be without it. I am also a reporter. To me, being a reporter means shedding light on dark places and telling the truth to our readers. If anything, my beliefs help me do that."

"That's debatable, but I'm just glad we didn't have a Mormon president," Peter said. "Not that Romney ever had a real shot."

Luke couldn't resist the bait.

"I don't know if this country will ever elect a Mormon president," he said, "but you know, if the government would follow the Church's example, a lot of society's ills could be alleviated."

"Can't wait to hear this," Peter said. "Please explain your delusions."

"Some of our problems as a country include a complicated tax code," Luke said. "Well, God gave man the law of tithing in the Bible. Everyone pays 10 percent — rich and poor. You make 10 million dollars, you pay one million. You make 100 dollars, you pay ten. It's fair for everyone."

"What about those who are unemployed, or unable to work, or those who don't have jobs and don't pay taxes?" Mandy asked. "How do we help them?"

"In the Church, we fast once a month for 24 hours. We go without food or water. The money we would have spent on food that day we pay to our bishops. We have what is known as a Bishop's Storehouse. Then those who are struggling financially for any number of reasons can obtain what they need. The Church helps those who receive assistance to learn how to provide for themselves. Imagine if everyone engaged in that practice of fasting and giving money to the poor. We could probably eradicate hunger and maybe even poverty."

"So you're suggesting that going on little 24-hour diets could improve our country's economic problems?" Mandy asked.

"It's not a handout, like food stamps. The bishops work with those people who receive assistance and help them put together a plan to be self-reliant and self-sufficient. Then, in many cases, they work for what they have received. It gives them a sense of giving back and it helps them avoid feeling a sense of entitlement. Like I said, the government could learn from the Church."

"Your church is one of the richest organizations in the world and you're tax exempt," Peter said. "Your proselyting efforts are nothing more than a way to keep revenue flowing in. You even expect the poorest of your church to pay. Like other churches, your church leaders prey upon the weak to build ornate buildings and accumulate wealth. Plus, you can't defend the crazy history of your church. How can we have a member of this cult work for our paper?"

Tom decided to change the subject.

"How many kids do you have?" he asked.

"Seven, last I checked."

"Seven!?" Mandy exclaimed, almost spitting up on her Dom Perignon.

"Are you trying to overpopulate the world?" Peter snickered.

"Nope. Just my house," Luke said. "Hey, would you like to see my kids?"

Luke dug his smartphone out of his pants pocket and looked up his family pictures. He started swiping through photos of Brian and Benjamin playing baseball. A video of Esther playing at her violin recital. Hayley holding Sarah on the day she was blessed. Photos of the twins' most recent birthday party. The Fathers and Sons outing. The Pinewood Derby. Jacob getting stitches in the emergency room. Christmas morning.

"Your kids are so cute," Mandy said. "And your wife, she is beautiful."

"Yes, she is," Luke said. "Thank you."

"*She* had seven kids?" Tom asked.

"Yep. And four C-sections."

"Has she done any modeling?" Tom asked.

"Just when she helped me and my sons build some miniature airplanes."

"What does your wife do?" Mandy asked.

"She's a full-time, stay-at-home mom."

"She doesn't work?" Mandy said.

"Oh, she works. Way harder than many people with a paying job. And it's full-time in every sense. It's 24-7 with no days off, no vacation days."

"Well, seven kids would keep you busy," Mandy said. "She's a brave woman."

"Yes, especially considering that she's married to me. She's also a registered nurse, but she hasn't worked in that field since we started having kids."

"But what does she do for fulfillment?" Mandy asked. "She must get tired of being cooped up with a bunch of kids all day."

"Yeah, she sacrifices a lot for the kids and for me," Luke said.

"Is she from Utah?" Tom asked.

"Yes."

"I'm surprised," Bruce said. "I thought all Mormon women were, you know, frumpy and unattractive. I thought they wore bonnets and 'Little House on the Prairie' dresses.'"

"You shouldn't be surprised by the beauty of Mormon women. That's how they grow them out there in Utah," Luke said. "Prettiest women I've ever seen, per capita."

"Is that why you believe in polygamy, too?" Peter said.

Suddenly Tom, Bruce and Mandy put their heads down and stared at their menus.

"I'm married to a great woman," Luke said. "One woman. I caught my limit. We believe in abstinence before marriage and fidelity within marriage. A lot of societal issues could be resolved — fatherlessness and abortion, to name a few examples — by living the law of chastity."

"Yeah, but you Mormons practice polygamy, right?" Peter said. "That's just wrong no matter how you look at it."

"The Church stopped practicing polygamy over a hundred years ago, Peter. You know that. Show some intellectual integrity," Luke said. "I'm not going to sit here and defend polygamy, something the Church abandoned a long time ago. But it's funny how a lot of people feel it's perfectly fine to be with women that you're *not* married to. And those same people say it's not okay to be with women that you *are* married to, in the case of polygamy as it was practiced in a different era. Isn't that a little hypocritical?"

"Hypocritical?" Peter shot back. "How about you Mormons fighting so hard against same-sex marriage, against 'redefining' marriage, yet you Mormons tried to redefine marriage in the form of polygamy?"

"Peter, c'mon," Bruce said, "why don't you stop with your witch hunt. Enough is enough."

"I just like to expose religion for what it is, a blight on human intelligence," Peter said. "To me, it makes no sense that you send missionaries all over the world, aggravating people like door-to-door salesmen, trying to bring them into your religion but you deny them access to your secretive temples. And you live with your heads in the sand. I'd bet you don't believe in climate change."

"Yes, I do," Luke said. "Did you notice how windy and cold it was early this morning? Then by noon, I was sweating like an ice cube in Death Valley."

Then Luke's phone started buzzing.

"Please excuse me," Luke said as he stood from the table. "I've got to take this."

Luke was relieved to be able to escape for a moment. He was beginning to feel a little like Abinadi, and he was noticing the heat coming from the kitchen. He was even happier when he saw it was a call from home.

When Luke returned, Peter started piling on again.

"Were you telling your seven kids a bedtime story about angels?" he said, laughing.

Luke didn't even bother to sit down.

"It actually was one of my kids," he said. "He's working on an English paper and asked for my help. Look, I want to thank you for dinner, or, at least, the bottled water. It was great catching up with all of you. But I think we can see that this isn't going to work out. As much as I would love to work for *The Times,* I don't think I'm a good fit. The more I think about it, Peter's right. A Mormon like me working at *The Times* makes as much sense as a cow working at a hamburger stand. I belong back in Utah, with my family."

And with that, Luke smiled, shook everyone's hand, wished them well, placed $20 on the table, and left.

Luke walked out into the cool Manhattan night and never looked back.

As he made his way to the Marriott Marquis, Luke wondered

why the Lord would allow him to go all the way to New York for an interview if it were going to end up like this.

His flight wasn't scheduled to leave for another week. He had planned, if all had gone well, to accept the job, then scout out a place for his family to live, and introduce himself to his new bishop. That would no longer be necessary.

After arriving at his hotel, he called the airline and tried to change his flight to the next day, but it would have cost him $1,200 in penalties and fees. Though he missed his family, he decided to remain there rather than book an earlier flight and pay all that money. Luke realized he would have to find a place to stay for the rest of his time in New York.

As he thought about it, there was some unfinished business in New York he knew he needed to take care of.

A part of him was disappointed that the *New York Times* job didn't work out. It was exactly what he wanted to do. It would have paid him handsomely, and provided his family with stability and security, at least financially.

But he knew he had done the right thing.

Suddenly, as he was pacing in his hotel room, he received a text from Hayley.

"Luke, I'm so sorry I got upset with you," she wrote. "It's been bothering me all day. Please forgive me. I know you're trying hard to support us and I appreciate your efforts. I am praying for you. I am grateful for all you do for the kids and me. Be careful. Love you forever."

Those words made Luke's heart soar. Overcome with relief, Luke called her.

"Hayley, I just got your text. Thank you. I haven't been able to handle this tension between us," he said. "I am so sorry for all the dumb things I say and do."

"I'm sorry, too."

"I've been a real jerk. I want you to know that you and the kids mean everything to me."

When Luke told Hayley about his disastrous job interview, he sensed that she was thrilled that her husband wouldn't be working for *The Times* — she didn't know how she was going to explain that to her family anyway — but it didn't alleviate her fears about their financial future. Luke needed a job, and quickly. He didn't want to have to sell their house in order to survive.

Luke assured Hayley that things would be fine but he didn't know what the Lord had in mind for him. He didn't want to be picky, but it had to be something that felt right for him, and for his family.

"Well," Hayley said, "if you're going to be in New York a while longer, maybe you could do some family history research while you're there."

"That's a good idea," Luke said. "I will. How's everything at home?"

"Things are going well," Hayley said. "How's your hotel?"

Luke downplayed how nice it was. He didn't mention the French-milled soap in the bathroom or the 50-inch, high-definition TV in front of the king-sized bed or the nightly turndown service with a mint left on top of one of the eight goose-feather pillows.

"It's OK, I guess," Luke said. "You know, a typical hotel room. Nothing to text home about."

CHAPTER 15

LUKE AWOKE EARLY the next morning to a phone call from Nicholai at the front desk.

"Hey, somebody from the *New York Times* just called to inform us they are canceling the rest of your reservation. Just wanted to make sure you knew that you need to check out today. Are you in some sort of trouble?"

"No, I knew that would happen," Luke said. "I'm going to be here in New York several more days. Can I reserve another room?"

"Sure. We've got rooms starting at $339 per night."

"Um, that's too expensive for me."

"I tell you what. With my employee discount, I can get you a room for $150 a night."

"I'll take it. Thanks, Nicholai."

Luke bought an Egg McMuffin and then walked around Central Park to clear his mind. When he got tired, he sat down on a park bench, desperately seeking inspiration.

His thoughts turned to his elders quorum, and the stake challenge to do family history. Then he thought about Hayley's challenge to do family history. Brian had been begging him to do temple work, too.

Weeks before, Hayley had stumbled across the name of a

woman on the Internet, on an ancestry website. She seemed to have done a lot of genealogy research. Her name was Maureen Manning, and it appeared that she might be related to his dad. All Hayley knew was that she lived somewhere in New York City.

Of course, Luke knew next to nothing about his ancestry. In fact, he intentionally avoided family history, despite the Church's emphasis on it. He didn't really care before he became elders quorum president, but President Kimball and the other stake leaders were encouraging all members of the stake to research their family history, and perform vicarious work.

Once he returned to the hotel, Luke reached into his backpack and pulled out a manila file folder titled "Family History." It held just one piece of otherwise blank paper with the name *Maureen Manning* scrawled on the top line.

Luke had been told many years earlier that his family line included an Ezekiel Manning, his great-great-great-grandfather, who apparently joined the Church, or at least that's what someone had claimed. Luke was skeptical. There were a lot of people named "Manning" in the United States. He was certain that it was an apocryphal story that some well-meaning member of the Church had told him. Maybe it was some sort of clerical error. Regardless, as a journalist, he felt it was his duty to investigate. He wanted to know more about Ezekiel, and he felt strongly that he needed to start doing temple work for his relatives. Luke was curious and intrigued.

And he happened to be in New York City.

After spending a few minutes on the Church's family history website and doing some detective work, he found what he thought to be an address for a Maureen Manning. Maybe she could help him. It was worth a shot.

So Luke took the No. 2 train, the Seventh Avenue Express, to Brooklyn, in search of his roots.

It had been many years since Ben Kimball's daughter, Brooklyn, had died. She was just a young girl when she was involved in a car accident that claimed her life not long after Luke had arrived in Utah. She had made such an impression on him that from that point on, whenever he heard the name "Brooklyn," he thought of her, not the borough in New York.

When he got off the train, Luke realized that he disembarked too soon. But he didn't mind walking. Luke reached Greenwich Street and found a three-story Brownstone townhouse. He walked up the six stairs, knocked confidently on the door. He could hear classical music playing inside.

Luke waited a full three minutes before knocking again.

A woman in her 60s, wearing a peace medallion and an oversized sweater, opened the door abruptly. She looked like an eclectic spinster, which is how Luke had imagined her.

"Whatever it is, I'm not interested," she said in a thick Brooklyn accent.

Luke's first impression was that she was a Manning.

"Hi, my name is Luke Manning," he said, extending his hand, "and I think we might be related."

The woman declined to shake his hand. "I'm not falling for one of your scams. Get off my stoop!"

"Beethoven," Luke said as she started to close the door. "You're listening to Beethoven. Beethoven's 9th, I believe. My daughter plays the violin. She taught me everything I know about dead composers."

"Like I said, whatever you're selling, I'm not interested," the woman said as she started to shut the door.

"Are you Maureen Manning?"

"I'm calling the police."

"Maureen, I know you don't know me from Adam Sandler, but I just would like to talk to you for a few minutes. I'm trying to find out more about my family history, and I think you might have some answers."

Slam!

The door nearly amputated a few of his fingers. Luke figured that getting some genealogical information from his lady was going to be akin to Nephi trying to get the brass plates from Laban.

"Why is everything always so hard?" Luke asked himself, exhaling in frustration.

He knocked again.

The door swung open. Maureen was holding a pink can of Mace.

"Get away from my door or I'll shoot," she said.

Luke raised his hands in the air and scrambled down the stairs.

The woman slammed the door again.

OK, Luke thought, *time to get creative.*

He said a little prayer in his heart, then walked down the street, and sat down on the curb and tried to think up a way to get this woman to talk to him.

Within 10 minutes, he noticed her leaving. She wore a bright pink hat, a matching pink jacket, pink scarf, and black boots. She shuffled down the street, and when she disappeared from view, Luke ran back to her townhouse and peered through the window. Inside, he saw a baby grand piano, some black-and-white pictures of austere people from the 1800s and early 1900s next to a John Travolta Saturday Night Fever poster from the 1970s. Luke jiggled on the door handle but it was locked. He planned to confront her again when she returned.

While crouched behind a parked car, Luke saw her in the distance, carrying a large bag in her arms.

As he approached her, a man came out of nowhere and snatched her purse off her shoulder, knocking her down.

Maureen yelled at him from the pavement. "Get back here, you creep!"

The man, wearing baggy jeans and a greasy Levi jacket with a maroon cobra stitched on the back, started running down the street. Luke sprinted toward the man and tackled him like he was playing in the Super Bowl. The man hit the ground with a thud.

"What are you doin' man?" the robber groaned.

"Just doin' my good turn daily," Luke said.

"I'm just tryin' to make a livin'."

"Well, thanks for your help."

"Help?"

"Yeah, you're an answer to a prayer. No wonder they call this place 'Crooklyn.'"

Luke grabbed the purse. The man complained that his ribs and knee hurt and couldn't stand up. Soon, the police arrived and made an arrest.

When Luke caught up with Maureen, he gave back her purse, and she thanked him begrudgingly.

"Who are you, one of those street thug vigilantes?"

Luke laughed. "I wish."

"You're not a Guardian Angel?"

"No, I am not an unarmed citizen crime patroller. I'm just trying to help out a long-lost relative."

Maureen shook her head. "What makes you think that we're related?"

"Just a hunch," Luke said.

Maureen's sack of groceries broke, spilling parsley, potatoes, onions, celery, and bread onto the sidewalk. Before she knew it, Luke was on his hands and knees, gathering up the contents in his arms.

"Let me carry this for you," he offered.

"I can do it."

"Please, allow me."

"I don't trust you."

"What do you mean? Didn't I give you a reason to trust me?"

"What do you want?"

"I just want to talk, that's all. I'm doing some research about my family. Please, I need your help. You may be the only one who can."

Maureen silently led him into her apartment.

"OK," she said, looking at the grandfather clock. "I'll give you fifteen minutes. That's when *Jeopardy!* starts."

"I love that show," Luke said. "We must be related."

"You're a real wiseacre," Maureen said as she put away her groceries.

Luke offered to help but she ordered him to sit down. He took a seat on colorful fabric couch that looked to be straight out of the '70s — like one from his childhood, like one he had once seen at Deseret Industries back in Utah. A colorful afghan, made of crocheted wool, was draped across the back of the couch. A nightstand next to the couch featured a lava lamp and rotary phone.

The drafty house smelled musty and moldy, with a slight hint of formaldehyde wafting in from the electric fan on the ceiling.

Luke considered making a sarcastic comment about the couch, lava lamp, and phone, but he needed Maureen's help. Plus, he was running out of time.

Then his heart sank. On a dresser sat baseball cards of Billy Martin, Thurman Munson, Reggie Jackson, Derek Jeter, and Joe Torre, in pinstripes.

Tragically, Luke thought, Maureen was a Yankees fan.

"Would you like some tea?" Maureen asked.

"No, thanks."

"Coffee?"

"No, thanks."

"You must be thirsty after chasing down that thief," Maureen said.

"A glass of water would be just fine," Luke said.

Maureen returned with some bottled water. "OK," she said, "You're down to ten minutes."

"All I really know is that Damon Lane Manning is my father. According to my research, you and I are related somehow to Wayne Manning, who is my grandfather."

"What did you say your name was?"

"Luke. Luke Manning."

"Do you have a birth certificate?"

"Excuse me?"

"A birth certificate."

"No," Luke said, "but I do have a valid Utah driver's license."

Maureen's eyes grew as big as silver dollars. "Did you say *Utah?*" "Yeah, why?"

"You live in Utah *now?*"

"Yeah."

A slack-jawed Maureen started coughing, and quickly popped a cherry lozenge in her mouth.

"Can I see your license?" she asked.

"Do you have a background in law enforcement by chance?" Luke asked as he pulled out his wallet.

Maureen studied the driver's license up and down.

"I know who you are," Maureen said. "Didn't you write for the *Daily News* years ago?"

"Guilty as charged."

"So you're a reporter?"

"Yeah, I've dabbled in reporting."

"I thought you looked a little familiar. You look older, you're clean-shaven, and you've put on some weight."

"Thanks for noticing."

"I used to read your stuff all the time when you wrote for the *Daily News.* I always figured we were related. Your articles sounded just like my dad."

"Your dad?"

Maureen paused. "Wayne Manning is my father. Damon, your dad, is my brother."

A shiver went down Luke's spine.

"I'm no genealogist, but I believe that would make you my aunt," he said.

Luke reached over to give her a hug, which she hesitantly accepted. "Sorry, I've never had an aunt before," he said. "I never knew I had an aunt."

Maureen was expressionless as she sipped on her cup of tea.

"If you thought I might be related to you when I was with the *Daily News*, why didn't you ever reach out to me?" Luke asked, wondering to himself why she smelled of bug spray.

"Well, I wasn't completely sure, and I was scared to find out. Enough people think I'm a crazy lady. Knowing the way you write, I figured you would have a field day with me and make me a laughingstock in the New York papers. Besides, I didn't want to disrupt your life. I knew a little about your dad's marriage and had heard you had been through some bad experiences and I didn't want to dredge them up, I guess. Plus, you didn't seem to be the kind of guy that would be interested in talking to a woman like me. Your father and I were estranged for many years before his death. Maybe I felt guilty."

"I was pretty arrogant back then," Luke said. "In fairness, I probably wouldn't have responded to you anyway."

"I can see some of my dad in you," she said as she turned and pointed to Wayne Manning's photo above the couch.

"So this is Grandpa, huh?"

Luke stood up and examined the black-and-white picture — in some ways it was like looking in a mirror. He looked at the many other photographs hanging on the walls.

"Why are you so interested after all of these years?" Maureen asked. "What do you want from me?"

"Aunt Maureen, my intentions are pure. All I want is to get to know you and our family. It's important to me. I don't want any money, if that's what you're worried about."

"Good thing, 'cause I don't have any money to give. And all of my 1970s memorabilia is earmarked for 'Save the Whales' when I die. It's in my last will and testament. And please don't call me 'Aunt.'"

"OK, fair enough," Luke said. "Could you please tell me about yourself?"

"Well, there may be some things you don't want to hear."

Those fifteen minutes turned into three hours.

Maureen told Luke about how she grew up in Syracuse, and

after graduating from high school, she left to enroll at New York University. She eventually graduated in library science and worked at the Brooklyn Public Library for 40 years. She never married.

"I'm what you would call an eclectic spinster," Maureen said with a laugh.

"Now I wouldn't say that," Luke said.

"Some might say that I'm caught in a 1970s time warp, judging by much of my décor, and I guess I am. In my mind, I'm still 25 years old. And yet I'm kind of obsessed with my ancestors. I feel a deep connection to them. I probably should have lived in the 1870s."

Maureen explained that her father, Wayne, Luke's grandfather, served in World War II as a fighter pilot. He had been shot down over the south Pacific, was captured by the Japanese, and held in a prison camp. The enemy had imprisoned Wayne for months and he was tortured and beaten. After the war, when he returned home, he battled alcoholism, and, as a result, was frequently distant and unfriendly and prone to unprovoked outbreaks of rage.

"I'm sure he had post traumatic stress disorder from his time spent in Japan," Maureen said, her eyes turning red. "He was at times aloof and at times angry. That's the environment that your dad and I grew up in. My dad was regarded as a war hero and a part of me always saw him that way. I feel that my dad was a good man but the war took a terrible toll on his life. He survived the war but dealing with the aftermath almost destroyed him. He had a difficult time relating to us, his children, and to anyone else. He never talked about his experiences at war. He kept it bottled up inside him, so he'd turn to a bottle of alcohol to cope. When he wasn't haunted by his demons, he could be warm, loving, and humorous. But we rarely saw that side of him. Dad would lash out at mom and us kids. Then there would be times when he would withdraw completely and avoid us for weeks at a time. It was hard on us. Eventually, dad drank himself to death."

"What about my dad?"

"Damon and I were close when we were young. He was handsome, had a great sense of humor, and he was quite charming. He had so much potential. But I think he was starving for dad's approval. He never received it. So he became a troublemaker by the time he was a teenager. He was on his own, on the streets, and basically lived unsupervised. He followed dad's example by drinking heavily, starting at a young age. Well, you know what they say. If parents can't discipline a child, society will. I think that's what happened to your dad. He was disenfranchised from my parents when he was 16. I think that's when he met your mom. I left home to attend NYU, and I lost all contact with him. I was angry with him because I knew he was wasting his life. The only time I went back to Syracuse was for the funerals of my parents. Damon didn't have the decency to show up."

Luke knew from public records searches that his dad had died in a car accident while he was out on parole. But he was dead to Luke long before that.

"The last time I saw my dad, I was 11 years old, and he waved goodbye with his fist across my jaw," Luke said stoically.

"Something that you should know," Maureen said, leaning forward. "Our family has a history of mental health issues, like depression. Dad had it. My sister had it. I think your dad had it, too. He had a lot of issues during his life. The older I get, the more I realize that between your dad's genetic makeup and his environment, he didn't have much of a chance. I'm not trying to excuse his behavior or his choices, but the odds were stacked against him from the beginning."

To Luke, Damon Manning had always been an unequivocal failure, and a despicable human being.

But Maureen was providing details and insights that Luke never knew. Luke started to see him in a different light.

"My parents died in the early 1980s. Then Damon died, then my sister, Cybil, died of brain cancer about 10 years ago. You actually have two aunts," Maureen said. "She didn't have any kids, either. That makes you my only living relative."

"Not exactly," Luke said.

"What do you mean?"

"I've got a wife and seven kids — four girls and three boys — at home in Utah."

"Seven kids? Are you goofing me?"

"No. Would I goof you?"

"Well, at least you're keeping the Manning name alive."

Luke removed his smartphone from his pocket and showed her pictures of his family. She was stunned to see the faces of nieces and nephews she never knew she had.

"Beautiful family," she said. "I feel bad I've ignored you all of these years. I've spent all of my time on dead relatives, not living ones. When you stopped writing for the *Daily News*, I guess I kind of forgot about you."

"Don't feel bad," Luke said. "I'm just glad I found you."

Luke looked at the genealogical charts and photographs that filled the walls of Maureen's home. It was like a shrine to the Manning family.

"Thomas Manning, your great-grandfather, was a respected newspaper reporter and editor in Buffalo for 35 years," Maureen said. "He won numerous awards during his career."

"I had no idea," Luke said in amazement. "I thought I stumbled into journalism by accident. It looks like ink does run in the Mannings' blood."

"Would you like to see more?"

"I would love to."

"OK, then, I'll need your help."

Maureen took Luke into a back room, where there were a bunch of large, dust-covered boxes.

"My grandpa was quite a pack rat. He liked to collect baseball cards, ticket stubs, string, teapots, and books. He passed it on to my dad. I inherited all of it when dad died."

"And you've kept all of it?"

"I guess I inherited his tendency to hoard things, too. About 40 years ago, I started a new hobby, genealogy," Maureen said. "I read Alex Haley's book, *Roots*, and I was hooked. It's been a passion ever since."

"How far back have you traced our family line?"

"Back to the 1400s," she said proudly. "But I've run into a dead end with some lines."

Luke felt like he had just discovered a gold mine — his family history mother lode. But he tried to subdue his enthusiasm as to not frighten her. Back in Utah, everyone seemed to have an aunt that was fanatical about family history. Suddenly, he had one of his own.

"I've always felt this mystical desire to research my ancestors, and keep all of this stuff," Maureen said. "But I've been concerned about what would happen to it when I die. I thought about donating it to the local library. But maybe now I've found someone to bequeath it to."

Luke was flattered by that sentiment but he wondered what Hayley's reaction might be to storing the Manning junk collection in their home in Helaman.

Together, Maureen and Luke dug through boxes, looking at photos, collections, documents and letters. It got late, so Maureen invited Luke to stay with her rather than go back to Manhattan.

Luke made himself at home on the '70s couch, though it wasn't exactly comfortable. He Skyped Hayley and the kids from his computer.

Esther was working on her science project, and the boys were watching a basketball game. The twins, who were supposed to be in bed, were playing with, and secretly eating, Play-Doh.

"I'm staying with a relative, a long-lost aunt," Luke whispered to Hayley. "I'll explain it all when I get home."

"A relative?" Hayley said. "You found that woman, Maureen? Wow! I can't wait to hear about it. Is it safe to stay with her?"

"I hope so. But she is armed with Mace, so I'll be on my best behavior."

Luke had a hard time drifting off to sleep — he was discovering new information about himself and his family, which was exhilarating. Besides, the broken couch springs were jabbing him in the ribs, and all the faces hanging on the wall seemed to be scrutinizing him. It was like spending the night at a cemetery.

The next morning, Luke awoke early and continued combing through boxes. Maureen fixed him breakfast — scrambled eggs, bacon, orange juice, and wheat toast. Maureen didn't offer him coffee this time.

"We've talked all about me and your dad, and your grandfather and great-grandfather," she said. "You haven't told me much about yourself. I have to admit I didn't sleep very well last night, knowing that you spent so many years in foster care. I should have stepped in to help but I didn't think it was my place. I regret that now."

"It's all right," Luke said. "No need to feel guilty. I turned out somewhat normal."

"What happened to you after high school?"

"I graduated from Syracuse University, got a job with the *Daily News,* and ended up in Utah."

Maureen started to say something about that but she decided to hold back.

"No offense," she said, "but I can't imagine anyone willingly living in Utah."

Luke laughed. "I used to think that, too."

"You're a Mormon, aren't you?" Maureen asked.

"Yes, I am. I'm a member of The Church of Jesus Christ of Latter-day Saints. What was it that gave it away?"

Maureen's eyes narrowed.

"It was all adding up. No coffee. Lots of kids. Living in Utah. I would have bet, dollars to doughnuts, that you were a Mormon. And I was right. I know about how you Mormons love genealogy. I've read that you baptize dead corpses. Is that why you're here?"

"Actually, we don't baptize corpses. We do baptisms by proxy, and only with permission from living family members."

"Years ago, I actually toyed with the idea of going to Salt Lake City to visit the genealogical library there. But I'm too old to go now."

"No, you're not," Luke said. "You should come to Utah. In fact, I insist that you go to Utah. You can stay with my family and me. Let me repay the kindness you've shown me. I'll take you to the genealogical library myself."

Maureen continued removing items from one of the boxes until she came across a thick, black book.

"Your great-great-great grandfather was also a writer," she said.

"Who's that?"

"Ezekiel Manning."

Luke recognized that name right away.

"See this journal? Ezekiel was a prolific writer and he filled several journals throughout his life," Maureen said. "These journals will probably be of interest to you. I think you'll find that you share more in common with him than just a love of writing."

Luke practically drooled. He excitedly took the leather-bound journal from Maureen's wrinkled hands, and brushed dust off it like he had found a priceless treasure.

Luke held the tattered book in his trembling fingers. He leafed through its pages and discovered a yellowed, 12-page attachment that had been folded and placed at the front of the journal. He unfolded the document, and started reading.

My name is Ezekiel James Manning. I am writing my abridged life history in the hope that my descendants, and anyone who may care, will know something about me, who I was, the experiences that shaped me, and what I believed.

I was born in the year of our Lord 1829 near Staffordshire, England. I was the oldest of two children, which consisted of myself and my sister, Sarah. My father, Elias Manning, was a gunsmith. He was an honorable, respected man. He was known for his honesty and integrity. My mother, Elizabeth, was a noble woman. They were courageous, kind, and God-fearing.

When I was aged 12, my father met two missionaries from The Church of Jesus Christ of Latter-day Saints, all the way from the United States of America. One of them was named Elder Parley P. Pratt. My father said their manner of preaching was different from any other minister he had heard. He believed them to be messengers from God. My father and mother were both raised Protestants, but they always enjoyed listening to the various pastors and evangelists that would pass by our farm.

My father saw something in those Mormon missionaries, and he viewed them as emissaries of the Savior. He eagerly accepted the invitation to listen to their message and read the Book of Mormon.

My mother was skeptical of the book and wondered why my father showed so much interest in it when they already had the Bible. Early one morning, as my father told it, he read several chapters, then went out to be alone in an open field on our farm and did as the missionaries told him to do. He asked God if the Book of Mormon were true. He told us he received his answer through a soft but powerful feeling that pierced every nerve of his body. It was a confirmation he could never deny. At that moment, he knew that book was true and he knew that he must join himself with the Mormons.

I remember him spending hours and hours reading and studying that book. I would ask him about it, and he would tell me, "I believe this book is God speaking to us and this Church is the restoration of the Lord's everlasting gospel."

When he shared that conviction with my mother, she said that he was rushing into his decision. But he calmed my mother and told her it was God's will that he be baptized. There was no reason to delay. My mother, who loved my father deeply, then started reading the Book of Mormon with my sister and me.

We all attended my father's baptism in a nearby river, the River Penk. Elder Pratt performed the baptism and we all witnessed it. My mother said she felt something profound that day as she watched my father being submerged in the water. Not long after that, my mother, my sister, and I decided to be baptized. Like my father, I received my own witness of the truthfulness of the Book of Mormon. On our baptism day, mother was violently ill. She could barely walk. But Elder Pratt promised her if she would exercise faith in the Lord Jesus Christ, she would be healed. Mother told us when she came out of the water, she was not only healed, but that she felt like a girl aged 15. Her arthritis went away.

My father decided it would be best that we leave our home and congregate with the Saints in America. My mother did not want to leave her family in England. So they decided on a compromise. My mother agreed to go to America but made my father promise that if either one of them were to die in America that the surviving spouse would take us children back to England to be with our extended family.

Leaving England was difficult. Our friends and family wept. Some warned us that we were making a terrible mistake. But when my father made his mind up about a thing, neither heaven nor hell could change it.

I was excited to board a ship for the first time. Going to America, in my young mind, seemed like a grand adventure. I suppose I was too naïve to realize the dangers and hardships we would confront. All we took with us on the ship was a few possessions, including a gun (for protection), a copy of the Book of Mormon, and our testimonies of the restored gospel of Jesus Christ.

We sold almost all that we had in order to book passage on a ship and we secured berths in the steerage.

Several times I became sick during the journey and I would empty the contents of my stomach — mostly soup, rice and sour biscuits — off the side of the ship. Sometimes the waves lashed at our ship with a fury, and I wondered if the vessel would be destroyed and that we would drown in the depths of the Atlantic Ocean. During those times, when I was scared, my father and mother would calm my nerves. They would read us passages from the Book of Mormon about Nephi traveling with his family in a ship across the ocean. My father promised that if we were obedient, we would be blessed.

Finally, after 45 days on the tempestuous waters, we arrived in America. Boston to be specific. It wasn't at all what I had expected. I had imagined America as a place gilded in gold, a place where everyone was wealthy and happy. But we saw many other poor immigrants like ourselves, struggling to find their place in this strange land.

There were times when I noticed my mother softly crying, when she didn't think my sister or I could hear her, telling my father how she missed home and her family. My father held her in his arms and listened to her. Then he would remind her that this is where the Lord wanted them to be. This was the Promised Land. He knew that we would be blessed for our sacrifices.

Our ultimate destination, we believed, was Zion, where the Saints dwelt, in Nauvoo, Illinois, more than 1,000 miles away from Boston. In order to travel to Nauvoo, we needed to earn money. My father found employment at the docks, where he worked 12-hour days loading and unloading cargo from various ships that arrived at the port. My father would return home very tired to our small, cold abode that we shared with other families. It was a difficult time for my parents, who had enjoyed a reasonably comfortable lifestyle in England. But my parents never lost hope or faith. My father would smile when he returned home from work. He made us feel loved. My mother worked as a seamstress and she made dresses and quilts to earn money. I worked also, selling newspapers, and shining shoes.

After months of hard labor, my father told us one night that we had enough money to make the journey to the gathering place of the Saints, in Nauvoo. To us, it sounded like heaven. A man we met in Boston, Eldrick Stimple, had lived in Nauvoo for a time and told us all about it. The Prophet Joseph Smith lived there and owned a store. He told us about a magnificent temple — a House of God — that was going to be built there. I looked forward to being in a place with so many Saints working and living together. I wanted so much to meet the Prophet of God.

We purchased a horse and a wagon. We loaded food and a few possessions onto the wagon and made the journey to Nauvoo. After weeks of deprivation, we finally arrived in Nauvoo, the City of Joseph.

It was a bustling town built on the banks of the Mississippi River. We constructed a log cabin that leaked whenever it rained or snowed. Later, we built a modest brick home and I fully expected to live the rest of my life there. One winter, my mother fell ill with chills and fever. My father and sister and I did everything we could to make life more comfortable for her. Illness was common in Nauvoo. We saw many children die while we lived there.

The people were so friendly and happy. We enjoyed meeting so many from places all around Europe who had left their homeland, like us, for a common purpose — to build the Kingdom of God.

When we first arrived in Nauvoo, my father began helping on the construction of the temple. After a few days, he determined that I was old enough to help. It was arduous work. But we felt joy in our service and every little bit of progress was a triumph for us all.

My mother, due to her work as a seamstress, on occasion visited the home of the Prophet. When my father and I were working at the temple, my mother would take my sister to his house. The Prophet treated them like family. When I first saw him, I thought, "That is how a Prophet of God should look." Then I had this undeniable sensation in my bones that told me, "This is a Prophet of God."

I remember the first time I shook hands with Brother Joseph, when I accompanied my mother to the Smith home. He was a tall, strapping man with a powerful grip, an easy smile and a friendly demeanor. I would describe Brother Joseph as a noble man. He intimidated me at first but he quickly put me at ease.

"May the Lord bless you for your help on the temple, Ezekiel," Brother Joseph told me. That he knew my name was thrilling. Those may have been the sweetest words I've ever heard.

I also remember Brother Joseph playing games with us children. He had as much energy as we did. I admired him and felt something special when I was around him.

That's why I cried uncontrollably when I heard the news that Joseph, and his brother, Hyrum, had been killed in a jail in Carthage, Illinois. I couldn't understand why anyone would want to hurt them. Many of us were scared, wondering what the fate of our young church, and our beautiful city, would be.

What made matters worse — angry, marauding mobs that hated Joseph and the Mormons, threatened by our presence, would come frequently to Nauvoo. My father was called upon many times to protect the temple. Despite all of our hard work to build the temple, there were those that wanted to see it destroyed.

My father carried his gun with him on those occasions. He said he would never fire the gun at anyone, unless he had to, but he hoped it would be enough to protect himself, his family, and the temple. My father kept his gun buried under a floorboard in our home. Only my father, mother, and I knew where it was. The mobs would ride into town and burn down homes and shops. They would destroy or steal property, tar and feather certain men, and try to intimidate us. In this effort, they succeeded. But they couldn't destroy our faith.

I remember the mob marching toward the temple carrying torches and whips. They hollered and yelled and cursed at the Mormons. Their intention was to burn down the temple that night. When they approached my father, they told him to step aside. My father told them to be on their way and leave them in peace. When they threatened him, my father removed his gun.

"Leave us now," my father told them. "We don't want any trouble, but this is the House of the Lord. You don't want to tangle with Him, or my gun."

The men rode away but promised to return. Unfortunately, they kept their promise.

At nights, we kept our lights off so the mobs would not bother us. One evening, four men on horseback came to our home and ordered us to leave. My father stepped outside — against the wishes of my mother — and pleaded with the mob to let us be. My mother gathered my sister and me close to her and we quietly prayed for our safety.

My father told the mob about how his wife was very tired and sick. By the grace of God, the mob moved on.

But we knew it was time to follow Brother Brigham Young and depart Nauvoo. We packed up our belongings and started our journey to Zion, out West, the new gathering place of the Saints. When the Saints left Nauvoo, the mob took away all of the firearms from the Mormons, or so they believed. We arrived at the banks of the Mississippi, ready to cross by boat, when I overheard my mother tell my father that they had forgotten the gun at our home. Without my parents noticing, I turned around and ran home to retrieve the weapon. I knew we would probably need it during our journey, either for protection or as a way to hunt for food.

My mother and father were distraught when they discovered I was missing. In retrospect, I feel bad for making them worry, but I only wanted to help. The boat was preparing to cross the Mississippi River and my parents were frantic. I entered our home, lifted up the floorboard where the gun was hidden. I placed the gun in my trousers and hid it from view with my coat.

My heart was racing as I traversed through Nauvoo's burning houses as men on horseback fired guns, cursed and laughed. I prayed that they would not see me and do me harm. The Lord answered that prayer, because they paid me no mind and I was spared.

I finally reached the boat just before it departed. Upon being reunited with my family, my father scolded me. When he found out what I had done, he hugged me, thanked me, but he also told me never to do anything like that again.

I had a difficult time understanding why the Lord would have us leave that place, Nauvoo, behind. I still do. Many of us had worked so hard to make what had been worthless swampland into a glorious, thriving community. Why, I wondered, wouldn't the Lord protect Brother Joseph? Why wouldn't he preserve us from the mobs? And what about the temple? So many had sacrificed too much to build the temple, only to leave it behind.

The temple was eventually burned down. How could God allow that to happen? I did not know, but I hoped and prayed that He would compensate the Saints for that loss somehow. Under the direction of Brigham Young, our family traveled with the other Saints to where we would prepare for a journey to what is now known as Utah.

We had heard stories about visions both Brother Joseph and Brother Brigham had about a place, in the Rocky Mountains, where the Saints would be able to gather, live, and be protected by God from all of our enemies. We all longed to be there. My father read us a passage of scripture from the Book of Isaiah in the Bible: "And it shall come to pass in the last days, that the mountain of the Lord's house shall be established in the top of the mountains, and shall be exalted above the hill; and all nations shall flow unto it."

During our movement westward, my mother's health deteriorated. We arrived at a place on the prairie called Winter Quarters. We were destitute and we lived in a hovel built on the side of a hill. We had a dirt floor and the wind constantly blew. There were times when it seemed like it always rained, turning our hovel into a miserable mud pit. Our wretched conditions did not help my mother. She was powerless to leave her bed. One morning, I awoke to hear my father kneeling at my mother's bedside, sobbing and praying. I knew she had died and I felt a part of me die with her. We buried her in the cemetery, with many others who had lost their lives in that place. Wracked with grief over the death of his beloved Elizabeth, my father decided to abide by mother's wishes.

As much as my heartbroken father wanted to be with the Saints in Utah, he knew he needed to go back to England, for my mother's sake. He had made a promise. But he told us he was determined, once there, to teach the gospel to his wife's family. It would be our mission. He would tell stories about building the Nauvoo Temple and testify about the Prophet Joseph. He would baptize our family members and together we would all return to the United States and to Zion. We would live there forever free from strife and persecution. That was his dream and my sister and I shared that dream.

Though we never talked about it, it pained us to go back East. Why did we travel all that way, and suffer so much, only to return?

We settled in the city of Syracuse, New York, because there was work there. My father worked in the salt mines and lumberyards to earn money for passage to England. I worked in horse stables and my sister worked as a seamstress, a trade she learned from our mother.

After just two months in Syracuse, my father died suddenly while working at the lumberyard. They said his heart gave out on him. That left me and my sister to fend for ourselves. At first, we planned to go back to England, but we were robbed of all our money and we had to start over. We became very discouraged. We remained in Syracuse for much longer than we had expected. I didn't know any members of the Church in Syracuse. In fact, many of those who knew about the Church I found to be hostile toward it.

One time, when someone denigrated my beliefs, I stood up to defend them. Before I knew it, a group of men pummeled me senseless. My sister found me in the street, bleeding from the head. She nursed me back to health and warned me to keep my mouth shut or I would be killed. I admit I was tempted to use my father's gun to teach those men a lesson. But I had a dream wherein my father appeared to me and told me not to use the gun. He urged me to spend all my energy making preparations to go to Utah with the Saints. I had not made a promise to my mother about returning to England, so I determined to go to Zion.

I eventually met, fell in love with, and married Mary Keaton. She was a good woman but she did not share my convictions about the Church. She belonged to another denomination. She was fine with me practicing my religion but when I would tell her about my dream of going to Zion, she decided she would not go and that I would have to go alone. But I believed that over time, I could convince her otherwise.

By this time, my sister had decided not to go back to Utah. She said following the Mormons had caused too much suffering and that she could do it no longer. She eventually married, too, and she moved with her husband to New York City.

Disillusioned, my dear sister became estranged from the Church.

My wife and I had two sons, Edward and Jonathan. I taught them about the Book of Mormon and Joseph Smith. I told them stories about living in Nauvoo and how I wanted to go to Zion someday. When they reached the age of eight, I asked my wife if I could baptize them. She insisted that they wait until they were older to make up their own minds about what, if any, church to join.

The years went on and while my desire to go to Zion never waned, I did become discouraged. My wife died after a lengthy illness and it affected my sons greatly. When I tried to tell them about God's glorious plan of happiness, they told me they did not believe in that. They asked me, "Why would God take away our mother?" They attended college and married. In college, Edward and Joseph studied history, biology, and philosophy, and they told me God did not exist, that the Book of Mormon was false, and that I was a fool for believing such things. They were antagonistic toward the Church, publishing articles about the "lies of Mormondom." As I told them many times, I respectfully disagreed. I will never deny what I know to be true. Though my sons broke my heart, I never stopped loving them.

I am an old man now. I have witnessed the birth of a new century. I have faced bouts with cancer. Though I am in my 70th year, I still hope to go to Utah and be with the Saints and see the beautiful temple in Salt Lake City, which I have read, was recently completed. One day I was reading in the publication, *Scientific American*, that the temple was "a monument to Mormon perseverance."

When I read those words, I realized how much I wished that my life could have been a monument to Mormon perseverance.

But, regrettably, in this aim, I have utterly failed.

I fear I have displeased my father. He is probably frowning at me, disappointed that I have not gone to Salt Lake City with the Saints. I regret to say that my family's association with the Mormon Church will end with me when I die.

However, I take some solace in my patriarchal blessing that I received from the hands of Hyrum Smith, the Prophet's brother. The blessing promised me that my posterity would embrace the gospel and become strong, faithful members and leaders in the Church.

I am hopeful that my descendants will eventually embrace the gospel, go to Utah and worship in the temple there and live among the Saints. As of this writing, I don't know how this promise will be fulfilled. But I have faith in God and I know that with Him, all things are possible.

— Ezekiel Manning

CHAPTER 16

BY THE TIME LUKE HAD finished reading Ezekiel's life story, he was brushing tears from his eyes and he noticed the hairs on his arms were standing at attention.

To him, it was like reading a gripping novel, knowing that it wasn't fiction. It was part of his family history. It was part of *him*.

For hours, Luke thumbed through the pages of Ezekiel's journal and read excerpts. Ezekiel suddenly became much more than just a name on a fan chart.

For the first time, Luke carefully studied his. He realized it could be called a "fan chart" not just because of its shape, but also because it looks like a vast arena of names, revealing a person's ancestor-fans in heaven, cheering them on.

Luke never could have imagined what some of *his* ancestors had given up for the Church, and he couldn't wait to share these stories with Hayley and the kids. To Luke the journal was like sacred writings: The Book of Ezekiel.

Maureen noticed that Luke had finished reading Ezekiel's abridged personal history.

"Ezekiel died in Syracuse in 1906," Maureen said as she walked into the room carrying bowls of homemade vegetable soup on trays for lunch. "He is buried right next to his father at a cemetery in Syracuse.

I've known for a long time about his desire to go to Utah. Now you can see why, when you told me you lived in Utah, it freaked me out a little bit. He wanted so badly to go to Utah and never did. Now you live there. It's a little like *The Twilight Zone*."

Luke wondered what might have happened had Elizabeth Manning not died in Winter Quarters. What might have happened if the Mannings had arrived in the Salt Lake Valley? Maybe Luke would have been a born-and-raised Mormon like his wife, like Ben Kimball, like so many others he knew in Utah.

Elizabeth's death prevented the Mannings from going to Utah; what took Luke there was an opportunity to write a scathing exposé of the Mormons. *Yes, God moves in mysterious ways*, he thought.

Luke wondered what Ezekiel Manning's reaction must have been in the spirit world when he learned that his great-great-great grandson would be going to Utah.

"It's almost spooky that you ended up in Utah, not knowing all the background, isn't it?" Maureen said.

"Spooky is one word for it," Luke said, thinking that the more operative word might be "destiny."

"I can tell this journal means a lot to you," Maureen said. "I want you to have it."

"I can't take this," Luke said. "It belongs to you."

"It belongs to our family. You should have it. I think Ezekiel would want you to have it. I'm an old woman. I need to start getting rid of this stuff anyway. He was a Mormon and you're a Mormon. Besides, I've got plenty of his other journals and writings. He was a prolific writer. He wrote a lot of poetry and personal essays. I'll let you read those, too."

Luke realized that he was the fulfillment of Ezekiel's dreams and that he was fulfilling prophecy. He had always wondered if going to Utah in the first place was happenstance or luck.

Apparently, it was all part of a plan. If there were any doubts before, there weren't any doubts anymore.

Luke envisioned ol' Ezekiel Manning, looking down on him, smiling, when Luke got baptized. At that moment, Luke realized that he had ancestors who died for the Church. The least he could do was live for it. He wanted to uphold the family honor and heritage that he never knew existed.

For the first time, Luke saw his ancestors in a new way, and suddenly he revered a man named Ezekiel Manning. For years he had heard pioneer stories from members of the Church. Now, he had his own. Luke wondered if Ezekiel had taught his dad, Damon, the gospel and now his dad was waiting to receive his ordinances. Maybe there were many other relatives waiting, too.

I can't believe I've squandered so much time without helping them, Luke thought. He was surprised that Ezekiel didn't appear to him at some point and slap him upside the head.

Feeling a sense of eternal urgency, Luke decided he had better get to work.

He and Maureen exchanged contact information.

"I appreciate your kindness and generosity," Luke said. "You'll never know how much meeting you has meant to me. You've helped me connect so many dots the past 24 hours. Thank you."

"I have to admit, I'm glad you tracked me down. Sorry I was so stubborn at first. I've enjoyed getting to know you. I think I would like to meet your family someday."

"We can make that happen," Luke said. "You know, I really like you. Even if you are a Yankees fan. We need to get you out to Utah."

"Oh, I don't know," Maureen said, "that would be like breaking the devil's dishes."

They said their goodbyes, and Luke promised to keep in touch.

Having connected with Maureen and her treasure trove of family history, Luke felt an overwhelming gratitude for the life-changing events that led him to meet Maureen and obtain Ezekiel's journal. He knew that the Lord was guiding him. And he suddenly felt the eyes of his ancestors watching over him.

Wanting to express that gratitude in some way, Luke prayed in his heart that he would be an instrument in the Lord's hands to bless someone's life. Preparing ancestors' names for temple work would take some time but he knew he could do something *now*.

What could be a better place to positively impact someone's life than on a subway? Luke knew there were all kinds of people he could meet on the New York City subway system — the spiritually starved, the discouraged, the troubled, the haunted.

When Luke boarded the train to Manhattan, a man sitting behind him was talking to himself in a loud voice, and apparently was afflicted with Tourette's syndrome.

A young couple a few rows ahead of him were arguing over a

cell phone bill. Luke decided it might be best to keep to himself.

He was scrolling through his texts and e-mail messages — he received a notice about another stake meeting coming up — when at a particular stop, a bunch of people boarded the train. Luke stood up and gave up his seat to an elderly woman.

Satisfied that he had done a good deed, Luke slung his backpack, containing Ezekiel's journal, over his shoulder and held on to a pole.

Then Luke noticed a commotion coming from the back of the train. People began screaming. Luke craned his neck to try to figure out what was going on.

"He's got a gun!" someone shouted.

A 20-something Hispanic man was brandishing a pistol and making his way toward Luke. The man wore a flat-brim Mets cap and a trench coat. He had a tattoo on his neck and an angry glint in his red eyes. Everyone tried backing away from him, and some started shrieking.

For Luke, it brought flashbacks of the time he was taken captive in Africa. He shifted into survival mode.

"Give me your money, or people on this train are gonna die!" the man barked.

Emboldened by his poignant and stirring experience reading Ezekiel's journal, Luke felt obligated to get involved. He felt he would be protected by his ancestors somehow.

The man with the gun appeared to be under the influence of alcohol or drugs.

"You really don't want to do this," Luke said to the gun-toting man, who strode toward him.

"Do you have a death wish, buddy?" someone whispered to Luke. "He's got a gun."

"If you don't shut up, you gonna die today!" the man yelled at Luke. Then the man fired a shot, shattering a subway window. Passengers screamed.

"Everybody put their money and credit cards in my hat right now and put your phones on the ground!" he yelled as he removed his Mets cap.

Passengers frantically dropped their phones and placed whatever they had — cash or coins or credit cards or anything of value — into the hat.

"Hey, I'm a Mets' fans, too," Luke said to the robber.

"I said shut up!" the man slurred, pointing a gun at Luke's chest.

A college student sitting a few rows away from Luke dropped his phone then he stealthily pulled out another one and started live-Tweeting the incident on Twitter with the hashtag #crazymanontrain.

The student's thousands of followers read his tweets and those tweets were re-tweeted thousands of times.

Soon, concerned people on Twitter were waiting to learn details of the event and how it was unfolding. In a manner of minutes, #crazymanontrain began trending in New York City.

Luke usually only carried a credit card. But on this trip, he happened to have some cash. He was looking through his wallet when he spotted a Pass-along card that he brought with him. It had a picture of the Savior appearing to the Nephites.

"I'm not going to let you rob me," Luke said to the robber. "Instead, I'm going to give you this money because you must really need it. So, I'm giving you this money as a gift, in hopes that the Lord blesses you."

Luke placed a $20 bill, and the Pass-along card, in the hat when it came to him.

Puzzled, the robber lowered his gun.

"What the &$% is this?" the man said as he picked up the card. He stared at it and became transfixed by it.

"It's a picture of Christ when he visited the Americas after his resurrection," Luke explained. "And there's more where this came from. With one phone call, you can get a free copy of the Book of Mormon."

"Where are you from?" the robber asked.

"Utah," Luke said. "I could tell you more. I'm a Mormon, a member of The Church of Jesus Christ of Latter-day Saints."

By this time the subway stopped and people ran off the train as fast as they could, leaving their phones behind.

Noticing the train had stopped and the people escaping, the man became flustered. Meanwhile, tweets continued proliferating with a flurry of 140-character missives.

People running out of train now to safety, the college student wrote. *Mormon guy just saved us all by distracting #crazymanontrain with a picture of Jesus.*

On Twitter, dozens of people responded to the tweets:

Is everyone okay?

Any shots fired?

Which train is this happening on?

Did the Mormon brainwash the guy?

Wait, the Mormons believe in Jesus?

Is the guy talking about the Book of Mormon part of the cast of the musical?

Which guy is the #crazymanontrain, the robber or the Mormon?

Meanwhile, the robber was asking questions, too.

"Jesus came to America?" he asked Luke. "Where? Staten Island?"

"We don't know exactly where," Luke said. "Scholars believe it may have been Central America."

"Puerto Rico? I'm from Puerto Rico."

"Could have been. What's your name?"

"Emilio."

"Well, Emilio, the Book of Mormon talks all about the appearance of Jesus in America."

"My mama made me go to the Catholic church every Sunday when I was a kid. She died last week. Right after I lost my job. Then my girlfriend left me."

Sounds like the lyrics to a Hispanic country song, Luke thought.

"Mama always taught me to believe in Jesus," the robber continued. "She told me Jesus came to Puerto Rico. Then you give me this picture. It's like this is a sign from her."

"Your mama sounds like a great lady," Luke said. "I'm sorry she's gone. But you'll be able to see her again."

"I don't want to see her right now, not like this. My mama would kill me. My mama must have sent you to me."

Just then, the police showed up, a contingent of New York's Finest, with guns drawn.

"Hands up!" yelled a couple of officers.

Both Luke and Emilio threw their hands into the air.

"Drop the gun. Now!"

Emilio dropped the gun.

"Drop everything!"

Emilio dropped the Pass-along card.

"Get on the ground! Now!"

Both Luke and Emilio did as they were told.

Officers flew onto the train, frisked both men and handcuffed Emilio. The cops ordered the subway station to be cleared.

The student that was live-tweeting the episode explained to police that Luke was the one who defused the situation.

This Mormon dude's a hero, the student wrote on Twitter. He posted a grainy, out-of-focus photo of Luke before leaving the station. By that evening, it would get 17,456 likes and 10,894 re-tweets.

Officers eventually started questioning Luke and they read Emilio his Miranda rights.

Once the suspect was in custody, and removed from the train station, passengers wanted to get back on the train to retrieve their phones and other possessions. The Pass-along card was confiscated by police and taken into evidence along with the gun.

Some passengers wanted to thank Luke and take selfies with him. But the police had cordoned off the area with yellow tape. It was just as well. Luke didn't want to be an instant subway celebrity. After he answered questions from investigators, he managed to escape before the media could swarm him.

The police would only confirm that the anonymous subway hero was a Mormon but wouldn't offer a name or any other information to the media.

The front page of the *New York Post* the next morning proclaimed, "Thou Shalt Not Steal!" with a full-page photo of the Pass-along card featuring the Savior among the Nephites. The subhead read, "Mysterious Stormin' Mormon saves the day on Subway."

The story was filled with eyewitness accounts, including those from the live-Tweeting student, of what had happened. It made Luke sound like Indiana Jones and Mahatma Gandhi rolled into one. It earned him an automatic spot in New York subway lore.

All of the missionaries serving in the New York City missions benefited from the positive publicity.

For days, reporters searched in vain for the mythical subway Mormon. Peter Bartholomew of the *New York Times* was one of them, suspecting that Luke Manning might be the Stormin' Mormon in question. Peter acquired Luke's cell phone number from his editor, and he called numerous times and left messages.

The last thing Luke wanted to do was give Peter Bartholomew an exclusive interview. When Luke returned to the Marriott Marquis after the subway incident, Nicholai approached him.

"Luke," he said, "I left a message in your room. Did you not get it?"

"No, I haven't been here. I was visiting family."

"Someone from *The Times* called again today, looking for you. I told them you hadn't checked out yet. Are you in some sort of trouble?"

"I could be," Luke said.

"Are you a fugitive or something?"

"No. Well, not from the law. I have a feeling a guy from *The Times* will be here any minute and I don't want anything to do with him. Could you do me a favor? Check me out of the hotel, then check me back in for another couple of nights."

"Okay, I'll do it."

"Thanks for your help, Nicholai."

Soon thereafter, the relentless Peter Bartholomew entered the Marriott Marquis lobby from Times Square. Peter took the elevator to the eighth floor. Nicholai asked if he needed assistance.

"I'm looking for Luke Manning," Peter said. "It's very important that I find him."

"I'm sorry sir," Nicholai said. "Mr. Manning just checked out."

"Are you certain?"

"Yes. He was just here but he left."

"Do you have any idea where he was going?"

"He didn't say where. Maybe LaGuardia?"

With that, Peter bolted out of the hotel, and flagged down a cab to take him to the airport.

Nicholai called Luke's cell phone, and reported what had happened.

"Good work, Nicholai," Luke said. "I appreciate it. I'm sending a letter to your manager today to recommend you for Marriott employee of the month."

"No problem, my friend," Nicholai said. "I hope someday you explain all of this to me."

CHAPTER 17

ONCE HE GOT SETTLED BACK in his hotel room, Luke figured he had better call Hayley. Where to start? What should her tell her?

Luke gave her a brief overview of the previous 24 hours and told her not to worry. He filled her in on the momentous meeting with Aunt Maureen, Ezekiel's journal, and his harrowing experience on the subway, which he tried to downplay.

That was the good news.

The bad news was, he was no closer to landing a job than the day he arrived in New York. As great as it was to find his roots, that wouldn't help him when it came to supporting his family and easing their financial distress. Luke told Hayley that he was paying $150-a-night at the Marriott Marquis. Another expense she hadn't been counting on.

Maybe Maureen will take me in again for a few nights, Luke thought. *Isn't that what family is for?*

Luke was starving but he was too exhausted to go back on the streets to get something to eat. When he found out room service charged $18 for a club sandwich, he left and walked several blocks to Gray's Papaya, and ordered the hot dog with the signature red onion sauce for old time's sake.

After eating, Luke returned to his room, turned on the TV, and saw the reports about the robber on the train in New York City and how a Mormon managed to subdue the suspect and defuse a potentially explosive situation with a card that had a picture of Jesus on it. It was one of the day's top stories in New York.

Luke shook his head. He wanted to report the news, not make the news. He turned off the TV, and lay on the king-sized bed. Bored, he reached over to the nightstand and opened the top drawer. Inside was a Holy Bible, placed by the Gideons, and a copy of the Book of Mormon, placed by the Mormons. Seeing that familiar blue-covered book was comforting to Luke at the end of a hectic, emotional day. He knew that because Marriott hotels are owned by the Mormon Marriotts, copies of the Book of Mormon are placed in all of the rooms.

This copy looked like it had never been touched before. He brushed off a layer of dust, cracked it open, and turned to a random page.

His eyes were quickly fixated on a particular scripture in Mosiah, and a sermon given by King Benjamin in that famous session of general conference in about 124 B.C.

"For the sake of retaining a remission of your sins ... ye should impart of your substance to the poor, every man according to that which he hath, such as feeding the hungry, clothing the naked, visiting the sick and administering to their relief, both spiritually and temporally, according to their wants."

As Luke pondered those words, he rose off the bed, knelt down and began to pour out his soul in prayer. He expressed gratitude for meeting Maureen, for reading Ezekiel's journal, and learning about his ancestors. He promised to do vicarious work for the Mannings that had passed on. He asked for strength and courage to live up to Ezekiel Manning's expectations of him. He promised to turn his life over to the Lord and serve Him like never before at home, and in his calling.

Then he remained quiet to listen for promptings, to find out what to do next. As he did, he kept seeing his father's face, which wasn't too surprising after seeing all of the pictures of him at Maureen's place. His dad, as a young man, bore a strong resemblance to his son Brian.

Luke didn't see his dad as an incorrigible human being anymore, but rather almost like a helpless child. If anything, Luke wanted to help him.

Sleep proved to be elusive that night. In the darkness, he tossed and turned, and kept reflecting on the events of the previous 24 hours. Thoughts bombarded him about his ancestors and his place in the gospel. He was reminded of all the times he had fallen short of the Lord's standards and expectations. But at the same time, he was granted a view of his grand potential. It was as if the Spirit — or maybe Ezekiel Manning — was working on him. It reminded him of Ebenezer Scrooge being visited by the Ghosts of Christmases Past, Present and Future, with his whole life playing out in front of him.

Motivation behind real, Christ-centered change can't be to get what you want, but to bless the lives of others, he swore Ezekiel was telling him as part of some sort of spiritual pep-talk. *Paradoxically, the person that benefits most from service is the one who serves. Like when you got baptized, get fully immersed in the Church and the gospel. What's the point if you're not fully committed? 'A double-minded man is unstable in all his ways.' Devote and dedicate your life to the Lord today and every day! Instead of asking, What do I want for myself? it's better to ask, What does God want from me and for me?*

Luke was startled by the clarity and directness of the words. He promptly wrote them down as if he were taking dictation.

One of his favorite pastimes since becoming elders quorum president was listening to sessions of general conference on his smartphone. One of his favorite all-time speakers was Elder Neal A. Maxwell. He thought Elder Maxwell's talks were always good to the last drop.

Before going to bed, he clicked on the Gospel Library app on his phone and dialed up an archived session of general conference.

He let the conference session play while he listened as he fell asleep.

That night, he experienced some poignant — bordering on psychedelic — dreams, with the words of general authorities and living prophets providing the soundtrack.

When Luke awoke, as soon as the closing prayer of the Sunday afternoon session was offered, he woke up; it was 8:15 a.m.

Luke wasn't one to remember his nightly dreams or pay much attention to them. But on this morning, he vividly recalled some indelible images — Luke was playing basketball at the Conference Center in Salt Lake City, during general conference, with his sons, Brian, Benjamin, and Jacob.

Instead of 21,000 seats filling the Conference Center, there was a single basketball hoop sitting in the middle, with a podium and the red seats behind it.

As they played, a kid, wearing all-white clothing, showed up, looking scared and lost. Luke recognized him as his father, in his youth. Damon begged Luke as his sons to play with them and, of course, they were happy to oblige.

They shot baskets together, and rebounded for each other, in a non-competitive way as speakers expounded on a variety of gospel topics. The Tabernacle Choir belted out hymns that reverberated off the upper deck of the Conference Center.

Every once in a while, the ball would bounce over the podium, over the stand, into the flowers behind the speakers, and bang into the iconic organ pipes. The speakers and Tabernacle Choir members seemed unfazed by the interruptions.

Damon wasn't very good at basketball, Luke noted, but he seemed to be enjoying himself, and Damon thanked them profusely for letting him play.

That's all Luke could remember.

But what did the dream mean, if anything? Was someone trying to tell him something? Was it the conference talks? Or was it just the hot dog with the signature red onion sauce from the night before?

Of course, Luke knew he needed to help his father. Ezekiel was going to haunt him until Damon Manning's temple work was done. There was nothing he could do at that moment for his dad, but he could help others.

One thing Luke had learned was that whenever he felt bad about himself, he knew he could feel better by serving others. He got an idea. It was time for some empirical, rather than theoretical, gospel-living.

Instead of showering and shaving that morning, he let himself go. He didn't touch his disheveled hair, and he wore dirty clothes. He didn't even brush his teeth.

Luke took the elevator to the first floor and walked out of the Marriott Marquis, and into the unforgiving New York City streets.

In an attempt at participatory journalism, Luke found a piece of discarded cardboard, wrote, "Love one another, even as I have loved you. — John 13:34" on it, then sat down on a random street corner.

Most people walked past him without making eye contact.

Some looked down, and then ignored him. He wasn't asking for money, but a few gave him some, including a kind woman who said she liked his sign. She gave him a $5 bill and told him things would get better.

Luke thanked her but she was the only one who showed concern. Loneliness and a sense of discouragement shrouded him for hours. He felt invisible.

A few people yelled at him to "get up and get a job." Some pointed and laughed. Children gaped. Mostly, though, people went out of their way to avoid him. Luke realized he would have done the same. It felt like he was being kicked over and over again in the backside by the Rockettes, not far from Radio City Music Hall.

Even Peter Bartholomew, who presumably was still searching for Luke, walked right past him without noticing. If nothing else, it was a brilliant disguise.

At that moment, in downtown Manhattan, Luke vowed to make an effort to acknowledge those he would pass on a street and try to help them in some way, even with just a smile and a "hello."

When his experiment ended, Luke saw a man asking for assistance on the sidewalk. Luke stopped, offered some words of encouragement, then took him to a nearby deli and bought him a Pastrami sandwich with the money he had just collected. The man opened up and told him his sad story about how he had lost everything in his life and how everything seemed hopeless. Before they parted ways, Luke gave him a copy of the Book of Mormon.

Luke couldn't help but think about Brother Harding's passion for missionary work, and how it was rubbing off on him. Then he sent a quick text to Brother Harding to find out how he was doing.

And he thought about the impact Ezekiel Manning's story was having on him.

While Luke was returning to his room — a hotel security guard stopped him, and made him show him his key card to prove he was a guest there — he packed his belongings. It was almost checkout time so he didn't have time to shave or shower or brush his teeth.

Before checking out, Luke opened the nightstand drawer and pulled out a copy of the Book of Mormon again. He took a piece of paper, Marriott stationery, and wrote his testimony.

To whomever reads this:

My name is Luke Manning and I would strongly encourage you to read this book. It has changed my life. It was written by ancient prophets on the American continent, and it teaches us about the true nature of God and His dealings with us, His children. I promise you that if you read this book with a sincere heart, then ask Him if it is true, he will reveal to you that it is. That's what I did. Now I know that it is true. If I can do it, anyone can. I want to share this with you because I know of the blessings this book can bring into our lives. I know this is another Testament of Jesus Christ, like the Bible. If you have any questions, please feel free to contact me.

At the bottom of the paper, Luke left his e-mail address and phone number. He tucked the paper inside the cover of the book with a part of it sticking out at the top, hoping someone might read it someday.

Luke figured it was yet another simple way to share the gospel in New York City.

As he walked to the front desk to check out, Luke saw Nicholai standing there.

"Luke," Nicholai said, looking at Luke's unkempt appearance, "Is everything okay? Who did this to you?"

"Nobody," Luke said, laughing. "I've been busy."

"It's like I tell people," Nicholai said, "a few days in New York can break even the best of them."

"Really, Nicholai, I'm good. Trust me. I just wanted to stop by and thank you for making my stay here so great. Thanks for the room upgrade. And for the discounted rate. And for getting rid of that *New York Times* reporter."

Luke handed him a Pass-along card with his home address on it. Luke wanted to give him a copy of the Book of Mormon, but he didn't want to Nicholai to think he had stolen a copy from his room and was re-gifting it.

"Hey," Nicholai said, "this looks like the same picture from that subway robbery yesterday."

Nicholai paused, then looked at Luke again. "Hey, you're the Stormin' Mormon guy, the subway vigilante, aren't you?"

"I can neither confirm or deny," Luke said, winking. "If you're ever in Utah, look me up. We can go to a Jazz game and attend the Mormon Tabernacle Choir's 'Music and the Spoken Word.'"

Nicholai grinned, then looked again at the card. "You got it. Godspeed, brother."

CHAPTER 18

UPON LEARNING OF LUKE'S PLIGHT, Maureen invited him to stay at her place. So Luke returned to Brooklyn. He decided he had his fill of subway rides so he took an expensive cab ride to her house.

It wasn't until he was sitting in Maureen's kitchen that he realized, much to his horror, that his wallet was missing. He remembered having taken it out to pay the cab driver, but he didn't remember putting it back in his pocket. Luke traced his steps from the street into Maureen's house, but could see nothing. He could have dropped it, he thought, and somebody had probably already charged $2,000 on his credit card.

While Luke was on the phone set to report his card missing and cancel it, there was a knock on Maureen's door. It was Hakim, the cabbie.

"Mr. Manning, you left your wallet in my cab," Hakim said in broken English. "I want to give it back to you."

Luke thanked him and offered him $20 for his trouble.

"No, I will not accept that," Hakim said. "Allah forbids it. In my religion, we do not accept payment for kindness."

"Same with my religion," Luke said.

As the cabbie drove down the street, Maureen told him how lucky he was to get his wallet back. It served as another reminder to Luke that Latter-day Saints don't own a monopoly on goodness.

Then Maureen insisted that he take a shower since he smelled like he had been treading water in the East River.

All that night, Maureen regaled Luke with more stories about the Manning family tree. Before she went to bed, Maureen confided to Luke.

"I'm not a religious woman by any stretch. I'm certainly not a praying woman. I've never really believed in God or anything," she said. "But about six months ago, I was looking at Ezekiel's picture over there and I asked God to let me know if there's life after death. If it's possible, I want to meet all of these relatives that I've studied for so many years, and be reunited with family members, like your dad. I guess I was asking for a sign and nothing happened — until you showed up. I can't believe I'm saying this but if there's a God, I think He sent you to me. I think maybe you have the answers to my questions."

Luke shared with Maureen a *Reader's Digest* version of the plan of salvation, and explained why Mormons do baptisms for the dead. He convinced Maureen to let him do temple work for their deceased relatives.

"I still think it's strange," she said, "but I don't see any harm coming from it, I suppose. But if our ancestors start haunting me, I'm revoking permission."

"If you want to know the answer to all of your questions, read the Book of Mormon," Luke said, "and God will show you the answers."

"It's hard to believe all that you're telling me, though the way you explain it, it makes a lot of sense. If nothing else, I admire you for your convictions, like I do Ezekiel. I wish I believed in something as strongly as you do. If what you believe is true, I can see why doing these rituals for our ancestors is so important."

Luke spent his final few days in New York holed up in Maureen's townhouse, poring over journals, photos and documents, collecting as much information as he could, as if he were working on an in-depth, investigative news story. With Maureen's help, he filled out his pedigree chart, and somehow it made him feel whole. He showed Maureen the resources available on LDS.org. She didn't necessarily get along with computers, but she was fascinated.

Sitting on a shelf in Maureen's kitchen was a New York firefighter's helmet. Luke asked her about it.

"It belonged to my uncle, your grandfather's brother. Jerry Manning worked for FDNY for 26 years," Maureen said proudly and reverently. "He died in the line of duty, God rest his soul."

Maureen then shared in great detail stories about Jerry rescuing numerous people from raging infernos during his career. Luke took copious notes. Jerry died in 1972 when he re-entered a building that had burst into flames while trying to save a child.

"He was a true hero," Maureen said. "I remember when your dad was a kid, Jerry would take him to the fire station. He would let him go down the fireman's pole, let him help wash the fire engine and let him turn on the sirens. When he was growing up, your dad would tell everyone that he wanted to become a firefighter."

At night, when Luke used his laptop to Skype Hayley and the kids, he wanted to introduce Maureen to them. But she politely declined.

When Sunday rolled around, Luke looked up a local Latter-day Saint meetinghouse in Brooklyn. He could almost feel Ezekiel nudging him to invite Maureen to go with him. Against his better judgment, he asked Maureen to accompany him to church.

Maureen almost choked on her marble rye.

"I haven't been to church since I was a little girl," she said. "If I were to step foot into a church, it would probably crumble to pieces."

"Nonsense," Luke said. "You might like it. I'd love for you to come with me."

"You go on ahead," Maureen said. "I'm glad to have you to stay with me but asking me to go to church is asking too much. I've never been a churchgoing woman, and I'm not about to start now."

"OK, but you're missing out," Luke said as he tied his tie and slipped on his church shoes. And he went alone.

As Luke walked down the streets of Brooklyn, he felt as if Ezekiel were walking beside him, urging him not to give up on Maureen. He caught himself carrying on a conversation with an invisible person — which wasn't uncommon in New York City. It was as if Luke had reverted to his childhood, and had conjured up an imaginary friend named Ezekiel.

Luke arrived at a box-like building that featured a familiar sign that designated it as belonging to The Church of Jesus Christ of Latter-day Saints. The majority of the ward, he learned, was comprised of transplanted members from the West. But it also featured a diverse cross-section of native New Yorkers.

People in this Brooklyn ward weren't concerned about their attire or appearance, like many churchgoers were back in Utah. Some wore their Sunday best, but instead of a white shirt and tie, it was a Legion of Honor uniform.

Luke observed that the hymns, the messages, and the spirit were pretty much the same as back home in Utah. The gospel, Luke reminded himself, is indeed universal.

During sacrament meeting, an African-American woman sang a soulful rendition of "I Know That My Redeemer Lives." While it was a version that he probably never would have heard in Utah, Luke felt the spirit strongly.

After sacrament meeting, Luke met a fellow elders quorum president, Hal Randle, whose father was one of the first African-Americans to receive the priesthood after the landmark 1978 revelation.

And Hal happened to be a New York City firefighter.

Hal informed Luke that the building the Latter-day Saints met in used to be a longshoreman's hall.

"A tough crowd used to meet in this place," Hal said. Then, he laughed, "There are rumors that there are some people still buried in the concrete. They're pretty reverent, though."

Luke also learned, to his surprise, that there was a stake in Brooklyn that featured Spanish-speaking and Chinese-speaking wards.

"What brings you here?" Hal asked Luke.

"I'm here visiting my aunt, Maureen," he said, giving Hal her address. "She's not a member of the Church but I'm trying to plant some seeds."

"And you'd like me to water those seeds?"

"Yes, please. But I'll warn you, if it's anything like my experience with her, just trying to get past her front door, it might require plenty of fertilizer, too."

Hal laughed. "What's Maureen like?"

"She loves genealogy and baseball," Luke said.

"That's great. So do I."

"Well, then, you've got the perfect icebreaker. Stop by some time and tell her you know me and mention genealogy and she just might invite you in. And be sure to let her know you're a firefighter.

She's got a soft spot in her heart for firefighters."

Luke knew that Maureen would be upset if she knew that he had been endeavoring to sic the local elders quorum president on her. But by the time she found out, Luke would be back in Utah anyway.

"How was church?" Maureen asked when Luke returned.

"I met a lot of good, friendly people," he said.

Luke and Maureen ate together and regaled each other with stories from their lives. They laughed and cried together.

The day that Luke was scheduled to fly home, they said their goodbyes with hugs and they promised to keep in touch.

"Somehow," Luke said, "I'm going to convince you to visit us in Utah."

"I haven't left Brooklyn in decades," Maureen said. "Long ago, I decided I would never take an airplane again. I have this paralyzing fear of flying. But for you and your family, I just might make an exception."

Before leaving Brooklyn, Luke decided to walk across the Brooklyn Bridge and enjoy the panoramic view of the city, and the Statue of Liberty, while dodging bicyclists. As he was moving briskly across the bridge, Hayley called to tell him about more bills that had come in the mail. Their financial situation was getting more dire by the day.

"Are you walking across the Brooklyn Bridge by yourself?" Hayley asked.

"No, of course not," Luke replied. "I'm here with a bunch of Chinese tourists, and I fit right in. They keep asking me to take pictures of them with their cameras. I've already passed out about a dozen Pass-along cards and a few copies of the Book of Mormon. Just wait until the China Beijing Mission opens up for missionary work. They'll be lining up to get baptized."

After crossing the bridge into Chinatown on the Manhattan side, Luke took Uber to JFK Airport in Queens. He gave a copy to the Book of Mormon to his driver, a man from Ghana.

I think I've given out a Book of Mormon to someone from every continent except Antarctica, Luke thought.

On the flight home, Luke reflected on his whirlwind week in New York City, where he learned a lot about himself and his family. The revelation from Maureen about the Mannings' history of mental illness made him aware of something to watch out for in himself —

and his children.

Luke was consumed by four distinct impressions, which he wrote down in his notebook.

First, he decided he was going to buy a replica John Stockton Jazz jersey, sans the postage-stamp shorts, for Nicholai.

Second, he knew he needed to visit his friend, and fellow elder, Brother Harding. Texts from the bishop indicated that Brother Harding's days were numbered. As his quorum leader, Luke felt a responsibility to do whatever he could for him and his family. What exactly, he didn't know. But he trusted that the Lord would guide him.

Third, he knew he needed to do whatever he could to perform temple work for his father as well as all of his previously unknown ancestors.

Finally, Luke felt strongly that he needed to take his whole family to New York City that summer. He wanted his kids to visit that place, have a cultural experience, see how other people live, and appreciate what they have. Maybe a trip from Utah to New York and back to Utah could vindicate and validate Ezekiel Manning's legacy.

Besides, he wanted his kids to meet Aunt Maureen.

Luke wasn't sure how Hayley would feel about this, especially given their dreadful financial situation.

He knew they didn't have enough money to fly his family to New York. By driving, he thought, his family could visit church historical sites and United States historical sites all over the country along the way. Luke figured it would be the perfect way to teach the kids about their ancestors and introduce them to the world outside of Utah County.

The biggest obstacle would be convincing Hayley that they should take this kind of vacation. Not only would it be expensive, it wouldn't be easy traveling with young kids.

Luke couldn't let go of this idea. He was so excited about the prospect of a journey across America that on the flight home he started mapping out all of the sites they could visit. He tried to figure out all of the expenditures, from gas to hotels to food. Luke knew it might cost a small fortune. He might have to sell the house.

Luke did his homework so he would be well prepared for the cross-examination he'd surely get from Hayley when he proposed the idea of a cross-country trek.

So Luke hatched a plan to create just the right environment in which to propose it.

The kids were thrilled when Luke walked through the front door that night. Hayley let the older kids stay up past their bedtime. Luke spent a while sharing with them some of his adventures in New York City. He told them about some of the people he met, including Aunt Maureen, and he showed them photos he took. He was laying the groundwork for a potential trip to New York, so he emphasized all the good parts.

"Dad, are we moving to New York?" Esther asked.

"No," Luke said. "We're not moving to New York."

Esther gave Luke a big hug.

"That stinks," Brian said. "I really wanted to go to New York."

After the kids went to bed, Luke told Hayley, "Well, as it turns out, I didn't go to New York for a job interview after all. That's not the reason the Lord wanted me to go to New York. So much happened there that I want to tell you about. But before I do, I have an important question to ask you."

"OK, what is it?" Hayley said.

"Will you go out with me Friday night?"

CHAPTER 19

IT HAD BEEN A LONG, LONG time since Luke and Hayley had gone on what could be considered an official date. Maybe during the first term of the George W. Bush Administration.

Folding laundry, cleaning bathrooms, and tandem feeding babies their formula at Oh-Dark-Thirty didn't count, Luke decided, as scintillating as those moments together could be.

Ben Kimball had strongly advised Luke to make time for date night every week, even though Luke insisted they had no time. Or money.

When they were first married, and even after Esther was born, they'd go out regularly. But after Brian was born, date night was one of the first casualties.

So Luke knew he needed to be creative if he were going to resurrect this tradition, especially knowing he would be broaching the sensitive subject of taking an ambitious trip.

This couldn't just be a typical dinner and a movie. Luke had to dig deep into his bag of romantic tricks to make it a memorable night. And he needed to hit a home run.

The element of surprise was crucial, although Hayley had some sort of sixth sense about surprises.

Even before working out the details of the date, the first item of business was figuring out what to do with the kids on a Friday night. Normally, Luke would trust Esther with them but she already had plans with her friends.

Luke didn't want to bother Hayley's parents, because they came over to the house a lot, but Luke knew that Hayley would feel comfortable knowing the kids were with her mom. So he called her.

"Hey, this is your favorite son-in-law," Luke said, which is usually what he said to his mother-in-law, though he felt certain that he wasn't. He got along well with her but sometimes he wondered if she was just humoring him.

"Luke, welcome home from New York," Sister Woodard said. "It's good to hear from you. Can I help you with something?"

"Can you keep a secret?" Luke asked, knowing how to get her attention.

"Of course," she said.

Luke then laid out his plan for the date night and explained that her help was vital if it were going to pull it off.

Hayley's mom was not only on board, she seemed thrilled.

"I love this idea," she said. "You know how hard it is to surprise Hayley."

Yeah, Luke was aware.

So after tedious planning, Luke told Hayley they would be leaving Friday at 6 p.m. It took a few minutes for Luke to convince her that he was being serious.

"What's the occasion?" Hayley asked, "What are going to tell me? Did you really get the *New York Times* job, and you're trying to break it to me gently?"

"I assure you I didn't get that job."

"Why are we doing this?"

"It's Friday night. We're going to go out like normal married couples do. Like we used to do."

"What about the younger kids? Esther and Brian aren't available to watch them."

"I know. I got a sitter. A great one. Trust me."

"What should I wear?"

"Something comfortable."

"We're going bowling, aren't we?"

"I'm not saying. Just trust me."

143

"OK. I just hope this doesn't cost much money."

Luke spent the week helping clean the house and doing laundry so Hayley could feel relaxed. Hayley tried all week to figure out what Luke was up to and her mom feigned ignorance.

Friday afternoon, after taking a shower, Hayley put on her makeup, curled her hair, and got dressed. She wore her favorite blouse and skirt.

When Luke saw her, his blood pressure spiked.

"You look beautiful," he said. "How are you feeling?"

"I've got a slight headache," she said. "I hope it doesn't get worse."

So did Luke.

At the appointed time, Sister Woodard knocked on the door.

"Mom, what are you doing here?" Hayley asked.

"I'm here to watch the kids."

"Why are you smiling like that?" Hayley asked.

"Oh, no reason," her mom said. "I'm just so happy you two are doing something together, alone."

Luke wanted it to be a perfect night and he had butterflies, as if it were their first date.

Of course, just before they walked out the door, Sarah spit up in her playpen, and Jacob spilled a plate of spaghetti all over the kitchen tile.

"Don't worry, I'll clean it up," Hayley's mom said. "You two go on and have a great time."

Luke escorted Hayley out the door. Luke led them past the driveway and toward her mom's house.

"We're not taking the car?" Hayley asked, puzzled. "Are we walking somewhere?"

"Sort of," Luke said. Then he placed a blindfold over her eyes. "I'll try not to mess up your hair."

"Luke, what are you doing? This is really weird."

"Not weird," Luke said. "Romantic."

"We'll see."

The night air was crisp and Luke pulled out Hayley's jean jacket, which he had strategically placed in the yard.

"You might need this," he said, slipping the jacket over her shoulders.

Soon they arrived at the Woodard's barn, which smelled like, well, a barn, in all of its bucolic splendor. Luke had downed plenty of allergy medicine earlier in the day to compensate.

"What's going on?" Hayley asked.

Luke opened the barn door and removed the blindfold.

"This place is highly recommended on Yelp," he joked.

Hayley's eyes beheld a steel fire pit containing an inviting fire; a table adorned with a tablecloth, dishes, silverware; and candles flickering, strategically placed around the barn.

"Scented candles?" Hayley said.

"Yep," Luke said, smiling with pride. "It's called Summer Sunrise. I must have smelled 300 scents before I found the right one. I may have done permanent damage to my olfactory senses."

"Well, you did a good job," Hayley said. "I don't know whether to be impressed or shocked."

"We're just getting started," Luke said.

He turned on the speaker connected to an iPod, which played country music, Hayley's favorite. Luke had consulted Esther on which songs Hayley might find romantic since, personally, country music ranked just above dysentery on his list of things he disliked.

"Shall we dance?" Luke asked.

Hayley nodded her head and smiled. "I can't believe this," she said, desperately trying to figure out what prompted this odd behavior.

Luke took her hand. Even after all of these years, her touch still sent shockwaves throughout his body. Her sweet-smelling perfume wafted over him and sent him to another stratosphere.

Luke locked eyes with Hayley's as they swayed to the music.

"You hate country music," Hayley said.

"Hate's a strong word. I harbor an aversion to country music. But this is tolerable."

Hayley laughed.

After a few minutes, she pulled Luke close and they embraced.

"Thank you for doing this," Hayley said. "I know you went to a lot of trouble. But I'm still trying to figure out why you are doing this. Do you have something bad to tell me?"

"No, of course not," Luke said.

"Are you trying to butter me up?"

"No. Speaking of butter, are you hungry?"

"I am hungry, actually."

"Great."

Luke ushered Hayley to her seat at the wood table, one that Grit built with his bare hands years ago. Luke presented a chilled salad sitting on ice next to a bale of hay. Then he pulled out a crock-pot filled with roast beef, potatoes, and carrots.

"Dinner is served," he said as he poured two glasses of fresh strawberry lemonade, Hayley's favorite beverage.

"Hope you don't mind that your mom helped me make all of this," Luke said.

"What do you mean by 'helped'?"

"By that I mean, she made all of it."

"I knew my mom was involved somehow. My mom's cooking is better than any restaurant. I like how economical this place is and how quiet and intimate it is."

"Yeah, and the occasional mooing coming from the corral is so romantic, right?"

"Is this what life was like before we had kids?" Hayley asked as they ate.

"Let's not talk about the kids for now," Luke said. "We always talk about the kids. Right now, it's just you and me."

"Why did you pick this place when you're allergic to hay and livestock?"

"I picked it for nostalgic, sentimental reasons. This is where you kissed me for the second time."

"I kissed *you*? I don't think so. I think you kissed *me*."

"Well, that's how I remember it."

After dinner, Luke cleared the table and moved his chair next to Hayley's. He took a giant photo album out of his backpack.

"What are you doing with that?" Hayley asked.

"I thought we could reminisce a little bit."

They flipped through the pages of photos of them dating, notes they wrote to each other when Luke was held captive in Africa, which were always signed the same way, "Love You Forever."

They examined pages and pages of wedding photos, including many of them standing in front of the Salt Lake Temple.

Hayley and Luke soon found themselves holding hands, laughing. They both felt 20 years younger in that barn, which transformed into a Fountain of Youth of sorts.

Luke was reminded of how deeply he loved his wife, stronger than the day they married. He could remember kneeling across from her at the alter at the temple, unable to comprehend that she actually picked him.

The love he felt in that moment certainly wasn't some sort of fleeting puppy dog infatuation, but it was built on a strong foundation tested by time, adversity, graying hair, wrinkles, and stretch marks.

As Luke gazed into her brilliant eyes, and stroked her silky hair, he thought about all she had done for him over the years, all that she had taught him, all the sacrifices she had gone through for him. He didn't feel worthy of such a blessing but he was grateful for it.

When they finished looking at all of the pictures and re-reading old letters, Luke placed his hand on Hayley's flushed cheek.

"This is a perfect night," she said. "Thank you. Thank you for being an excellent husband."

"You think I'm excellent?"

"Well, I do tonight," she said with a smile, then hugged him tight.

"I'm only sorry I didn't do this sooner," Luke said. "I can't promise you that our future dates will be like this one, but I can promise you that I'll make a better effort for us to spend time together like this more often. Every Friday night, we need to do something together, no matter what. We can go out to dinner, hike 'Y Mountain.' Heck, I'll even go country dancing with you. I want to show more appreciation to you for all you do for the kids and me. Love you forever."

Hayley was misty-eyed.

"I love you, too. Thanks for all you do for me."

"How about we re-enact our first and second kiss?" Luke suggested.

He moved his lips to hers. After a deep kiss, Luke pulled her close and breathed in her intoxicating scent.

"Is there anything else you need to tell me?" Hayley asked.

"Yes. I almost forgot. While I was on the plane coming home from New York, I had the strongest impression. I really think we need to take a vacation this summer. A real vacation. Not just an afternoon at the waterpark."

Some of the Mannings' friends in the ward would travel to exotic places around the world for work, then take their families to Hawaii or Florida on vacation. Meanwhile, the Mannings were always stuck at home. The last family vacation they had been on consisted of driving to St. George for the weekend.

"Luke, we really don't have enough money to do anything extravagant."

"Yeah, I know."

"So what do you have in mind?"

"I just want us to get out of the daily routine, the rut, that we're in. I want us, as a family, to see new things and gain a new perspective, like I was able to do in New York. I think a change of scenery would do everyone some good. The kids have never been east of Vernal. I would love for them to go where you served your mission in Rochester. Plus, I just learned a lot about my ancestors in New York. I think it would be great to take our kids on a journey to the East Coast and help them learn about their history and heritage. And to meet a relative, my Aunt Maureen."

Hayley looked uneasily around the barn. "Luke, you know we don't have the money to fly to the East Coast."

"I know. I was planning on driving."

"Luke, you know we don't have the money to drive to the East Coast. Would you really want to drive all the way across the country? You get ornery just driving past the Point of the Mountain."

"I know. But I really feel this is what we need to do."

"You're joking, right?"

"No, I'm serious. What if we could do it cheaply?"

"How cheaply? Do you know the price of gas? You do remember that we're in some financial trouble."

"I remember."

"Is this just an elaborate scheme to get away from, and get rid of, the dog?"

"No," Luke said, laughing, "but we'll have to ask your dad to watch Buzz during the five weeks that we're gone."

"Five weeks? We can't be gone that long. What about your calling? Would the bishop be OK with that?"

"I've already talked to him about it and he said he's fine with it. It's going to take five weeks to drive to the East Coast and back."

Hayley placed her index fingers on her temples and pressed.

"Another headache?" Luke asked.

"No, I just don't know about this. Can you imagine us being crammed in our car for a month? I don't know that we'd survive."

"I'm glad you brought that up. This trip will teach our kids real-world survival skills," Luke said. "Think of all the Church history sites we could visit. You didn't go to the East Coast until your mission. Didn't you tell me you lost a lot of your innocence on your mission because of all the things you saw and dealt with? Why don't we help our kids get a little taste of that now, in a controlled setting? Think of it as a little inoculation before they face the big, cruel world. Why don't you think about it and we'll talk about it again tomorrow."

"OK," Hayley said. "I will. I knew you had some sort of ulterior motive with this date."

"No, this date was about renewing a tradition that we need to uphold on Friday nights — Date Night."

Luke kissed Hayley again.

"That was a lot like the first time we kissed in this barn," Hayley said.

"Yeah, but let's set the record straight," Luke said. "You kissed me first."

CHAPTER 20

THE NEXT MORNING, AFTER the kids were settled, Hayley was sitting on the bed, deep in thought, while Luke was shaving.

She said she was ready to talk about The Proposed Trip.

Luke prepared for the worst.

Hayley opened up the checkbook and produced a stack of bank statements. Then she exhaled.

"Our savings are almost depleted," she began. "We've already spent our Child Tax Credit for the year. I've thought about it and I've prayed about this last night and this morning. We can't afford to take a trip like this."

Luke was about to respond with a gentle, rehearsed rebuttal when Hayley quickly added, "But I've also realized that we can't afford *not* to take a trip like this."

Luke wasn't sure he heard her correctly. "Can you repeat that?"

"You made some good points last night," she said.

"Can I have that in writing?"

"You're right. I see that our kids need this kind of experience. It would be a lot of money, but this would be an investment in them. I would like it to be a trip where the kids see how others live. It's easy to get along with those who share our beliefs. Our kids need to learn to interact with, and love, those who are different from us. It's hard to teach them some of those lessons in Utah. It would be great to give the kids an appreciation for church history, our nation's history, and our ancestors. Especially your ancestors, now that you've found out about them. I want our kids to be confident about being a member of the Church. I want them to be bold when it comes to sharing the gospel. I want them to know who they are and what they stand for."

"You're reading my mind," Luke said.

"The only obstacle is — and it's a big obstacle — I don't want to go deeper into debt in order to take this trip. We've got to figure out how we can save money and do this as economically as possible."

"Or I could just set up a Go Fund Me account," Luke joked.

"I want this trip to be an unforgettable experience. We can take the kids to Winter Quarters, Nauvoo, and Kirtland. My old mission stomping grounds in Palmyra and the rest of upstate New York. We need to go to Washington, D.C. We can visit a bunch of temples along the way. I'm really worried about spending so much money at a time when we have so little. But I feel good about this and I'm going to exercise faith. If this is the Lord's will for us, He'll provide the way."

"I agree completely," Luke said. "I've done a lot of research on this. We can make the arrangements and do it as economically as possible. I talked to Brother Toolson and he said we could borrow his RV. It's big enough for all of us. We can stay at Walmart parking lots for free along the way. We can load up with cheap food before we leave. We'll just need to pay for gas."

"Have you ever driven an RV?"

"No. But how hard could it be? I've been driving a Suburban for five years."

"If we're going to do this," Hayley said, "I say we plan opportunities to do service and share the gospel. So often it feels like our family is expending a lot of energy, keeping busy, but I wonder what we are accomplishing. So often what's most important is sacrificed at the altar of what's most convenient. I know the only way to change chaos into peace is to live the gospel every day. This trip can't be about us. It's got to be about serving others, teaching our kids to look outside themselves."

"You're preaching to the choir, Hayley," Luke said. "Let's take a leap of faith on the wheels of an RV."

For the next couple of weeks, after the kids would go to bed, Luke and Hayley would stay up late into the night planning the journey. They bought a giant map of the United States and they hung it up in the kitchen, marking places of interest and destinations with a Sharpie. They painstakingly plotted their course, figuring out where they would stay each night by finding a Walmart parking lot in the nearest town where they could sleep.

It was hard to tell who was more excited about the trek, Luke or Hayley. When they told the kids about their upcoming journey during a family home evening, the kids were a little confused, especially the younger ones.

"It's not going to be just a trip," Hayley said, "it's going to be an adventure."

But the kids liked the general concept of living in a motor home, a bus-like vehicle that had a bathroom, and a refrigerator. Plus, Luke told them the RV had a DVD player and a flat-screen TV. Luke and Hayley planned to gather up as many DVDs they could find to entertain the kids for the many hours they would be on the road on a trip that would take 30-plus days and cover thousands of miles.

Hayley bought each of the kids their own bags for clothing. The older kids would be allowed to bring some books and an electronic device and the younger kids would be allowed to bring a couple of toys. Esther planned to pack her violin so she could continue practicing while they were gone. Brian, Benjamin and Jacob were relieved there wasn't room in the RV for a piano.

The kids only had a few weeks until school was out for the summer and they were counting down the days.

One afternoon, Brother Toolson agreed to meet Luke at the church parking lot for a few tips about driving an RV. It was a 31-foot, 1989 Winnebago Chieftain, Class A motor home with 91,000 miles on it.

"Relatively brand new for how old it is," Brother Toolson said. "We've taken really good care of it over the years."

"I believe you," Luke said. "You're not trying to sell this to me, are you?"

"No," Brother Toolson said. "It's our pleasure to let you borrow it. It's for a great cause."

Brother Toolson gave Luke a ten-minute tour inside the RV. It featured, among other things, a dinette, swivel rockers, captain chairs for the driver and the front passenger, a generator, sink, stove, oven, microwave, refrigerator and freezer, queen-sized bed, overhanging cabinets, a bathroom with toilet, shower, and vanity sink. Brother

Toolson had put in the flat-screen TV himself a few years earlier.

"This is like a condominium on wheels," Luke said. "And it's so clean."

Brother Toolson reviewed all of the features of the RV, and taught Luke had to drain the septic tank.

"I'd do that every couple of days," Brother Toolson warned.

"Disgusting," Luke said. "But I guess that's the price you pay for having a bathroom in your vehicle. Any advice for driving this monster?"

"It's easy to drive," Brother Toolson said. "Even you can do it, Luke. Just takes some practice."

Brother Toolson advised Luke to leave plenty of room between the RV and other cars, and to remember to leave a large turning radius.

"And make sure when you go under a bridge there's enough room to get under it. Check your mirrors frequently. Know where other vehicles are at all times. And you need to regularly check the tire pressure."

"We'll do."

"We've really enjoyed this RV. We've taken it to Yellowstone, Disneyland, Zion's, and the Grand Canyon. We've never had a problem. You'll love how smooth it drives on the freeway. Let's practice here in the parking lot."

Luke jumped into the driver's seat, high above the ground, put the key into the ignition and turned over the engine.

"This is like *driving* a Walmart," Luke said.

Brother Toolson had Luke practice parking, turning, and other maneuvers. He then took him for a test drive on the freeway, which was a frightening experience for both Luke and Brother Toolson. Driving a vehicle that is 8 ½ feet wide in a highway lane that is only 10 feet wide would take some getting used to.

Luke pulled into his driveway in the RV, drawing squeals of excitement from the kids, who immediately ran inside and started exploring.

"This is very safe to travel in," Brother Toolson assured Hayley.

"Thanks so much for letting us borrow this," she said.

Luke and Hayley called the kids in for family home evening. They unfurled the large, colorful map of the United States on the living room floor and gathered the kids around it.

Luke explained they were going on a journey to see Church

history and United States history sites that he pointed out on the map.

Then Hayley read a scripture found in Matthew: "Ye are the light of the world. A city that is set on a hill cannot be hid. Neither do men light a candle, and put it under a bushel, but on a candlestick: and it giveth light unto all that are in the house. Let your light so shine before men, that they may see your good works, and glorify your Father which is in heaven."

Hayley asked the kids the meaning of the scripture.

"That dad shouldn't be so obsessed with making sure all the lights in the house are turned off all the time?" Brian said.

"It means we need to share the gospel," Esther said.

"That's right, Esther," Hayley said. "We have been given the gospel, and we need to share it. Not only with our words, but also by our actions. We can make a difference in the world in small and simple ways. I hope that on this trip we can do just that. When we do, maybe people who we meet, or who see us, will be inspired to learn more about Heavenly Father and Jesus Christ. Even if we can positively impact just one person, it will have been worth it. During our trip, I know that if we pray for missionary experiences, they will come. Every day we're going to pray for the Lord to help us be good examples for Him and guide us to someone we can help. When people see us, I hope through our actions and our countenances, they can feel the Savior's love. This isn't a trip where we see what we can *get*, but what we can *give*."

"Isn't it going to be boring driving so much?" Brian asked.

"Well, a lot of that depends on our attitude," Hayley said. "I hope we have the same attitude that our Pioneer ancestors had. They didn't complain. They sang 'All is Well!' even when all wasn't well. They dealt with sickness, hunger, pain and even death. But they focused on their destination — the Salt Lake Valley. Not only did they take care of each other, but they also had compassion on those who would follow them. Did you know they would leave supplies and plant crops for those who would come later on the trail? They weren't thinking only about themselves. That's why they were happy despite all the hardship they faced. I hope we can try to have that same attitude."

Then Hayley told Esther that they would not be using their smartphones on this trip to text (except in emergencies or if it had to do with their callings). They could take pictures with their phones but they were executing a ban on social media.

"But mom," Esther said. "How am I going to talk to my friends while we're gone?"

"Esther, we want to focus on our family and talking to each other rather than texting, OK?"

"OK," Esther sighed.

A few weeks after deciding to take the journey, everything came together. Luke unexpectedly received some checks in the mail for several freelance articles he had submitted months earlier and were accepted for publication. He had forgotten all about the article on the origin of the peculiar names of cities and towns in Utah. In another one, he wrote about the first names, with peculiar spellings, that parents in Utah give their children.

The total of those checks, Luke and Hayley realized, was almost exactly the amount they had budgeted for their journey, including gas, food, and entertainment.

"This is a miracle, an answer to prayer," Hayley said. "I guess this is another sign that we need to go."

Hayley stressed again with Luke she thought it would be best if they didn't post pictures or blogs on any form of social media during their journey.

"I don't want this trip to be a spectacle," she said. "I want us to have private family time without broadcasting it to the world. We've seen from sad experience what happens when people post pictures of their trips on the Internet. I want us to serve others anonymously with no fanfare or attention. Will you promise me you won't put any of what we do on the Internet?"

The journalist in Luke wanted to chronicle this epic journey for public consumption, but he respected Hayley's wishes.

"I promise," he said, somewhat reluctantly.

As excited as Luke was to take this trip with his family, he also knew he couldn't leave without supporting Brother Harding.

While in New York, Luke texted Brother Harding regularly, but he gleaned no helpful information from him. Everything was blue skies and sunshine. When Luke returned from Utah, the bishop informed him that Brother Harding was beginning to cough violently and having trouble breathing. He was weak and barely able to get around. He was coughing up mucus and blood.

Luke dropped by on a daily basis.

"Can I ask you something?" Luke asked.

"Anything," Brother Harding said.

"You have boundless hope. Where does that come from? I come over here to provide you with some comfort and you end up comforting me. How do you do that?"

Brother Harding didn't hesitate.

"I'll admit, at first, I was angry and confused about this trial. It took a lot of prayer and humility to submit to the Lord's will. I am dying, but, in a way, I am truly living like I never have before. The reality that my body is mortal and my spirit is immortal is truly sinking in for me. It's like I'm stripping life down to its simplest form. One of the greatest blessings of this trial is that the Lord has blessed me with an eternal perspective. My eyes see everything through that prism. All that really matters is my faith and my family."

"Please let me know what I can do for you," Luke said.

"Will you offer the opening prayer at my funeral?" Brother Harding said.

That request, and the matter-of-fact way he requested it, caught Luke by surprise.

"I'd be honored," he stammered.

"I'm in the middle of planning the program. I'd like Esther to play *Come Thou Fount of Every Blessing* on her violin."

"She would be happy to," Luke said.

"Remember what Yogi Berra said, 'You gotta go to your friends' funerals or they won't come to yours,'" Brother Harding quipped.

Luke smiled faintly at the gallows humor.

"Can I ask you something else?" Brother Harding asked.

"Of course."

"As my elders quorum president, could you give me a blessing?"

"Absolutely."

At first, Luke felt a lot of pressure being in this situation. But he was grateful for the opportunity. He called one of his counselors, Brother Owens, to help him. After Brother Owens took care of the anointing, Luke placed his hands on Brother Harding's head. The spirit filled the room and the words flowed. Luke blessed Brother Harding with peace in knowing that he had lived a good life and soon would be reunited with his Heavenly Father and Savior.

"Thank you, Luke," Brother Harding said, tears in his eyes.

Sister Harding, meanwhile, was almost seven months pregnant.

She was crying. They gave her a blessing, too.

Brother Owens blessed Sister Harding that the pregnancy would go well and that she would be able to meet the challenges she would be confronted with in the coming days, months and years with faith.

Brother Harding had been confined, for the most part, to home with palliative care, with the goal of providing him relief from the symptoms and improve the quality of life for him and his family in his final days.

Luke stopped by every day at a time when he figured Brother Harding would not be sleeping or resting. Luke noticed he was getting weaker and frailer by the day. But his spirit was indomitable.

"Could you do me a favor, Luke?" Brother Harding said. "Could you go visit the Martin family tonight? They've been less active these last few months. Could you see what you can do for them? If you're lucky, Sister Martin will make you some of her famous enchiladas."

As usual, Brother Harding was the one imparting encouragement.

"You're doing a great job as elders quorum president," he said. "I've heard nothing but good things about the lessons and activities. And you have an awesome family. I'm really impressed with your daughter, Esther. She really plays the violin well. And your boys are so well behaved. You're doing things the right way. I hope my kids grow up to be like yours."

"Oh, well, um, thanks …"

"And I heard about your big trip coming up. I wish I could have taken my family trip like that. You'll have a great time."

After a while, Brother Harding could barely speak due to low oxygen levels.

"Remember how you asked me how you could help?" Brother Harding whispered.

"Yeah."

"Could you play catch with my son, Tanner, when I'm not here anymore?" he said, his voice cracking.

"Of course I will," Luke said.

"And will you play basketball with him? When I became a dad, that was one of the things I looked forward to most — playing catch and playing basketball with him. I'm going to miss that."

Luke gently placed his hand on Brother Harding's shoulder.

As Luke was leaving, Sister Harding gave him a hug.

"Thanks for your visits," she said. "It means a lot to Greg."

Luke patted six-year-old Tanner Harding on the head.

The next day, Luke walked over the Hardings' house to find Brother Harding pulling weeds in the front yard alone. He had his oxygen tank and was sitting down in the middle of a weed patch.

"Greg, what in the world are you doing?" Luke asked. "Your wife would be mad if she knew you were out here."

"That's why I'm here. I know how my wife hates the weeds. She can't pull them, being pregnant. So I thought I'd get rid of them."

"You shouldn't be out here," Luke said. "You go inside and lie down. I'll relieve you."

"Okay. I am a little tired. Thanks, Luke."

Luke had been pulling weeds for about 30 minutes when Brother Garcia arrived and started helping. Then a few more elders in the quorum showed up. Sister Harding returned from her doctor's appointment and was pleasantly surprised to several men from the ward working in the yard.

Then a few other members of the ward stopped what they were doing and joined the impromptu weed-pulling party.

When Brother and Sister Harding looked out their window that evening and saw all those who had come to help, they were overwhelmed with gratitude. They felt the love from their ward family.

Within eight hours of that visit, Luke received a phone call from the bishop, informing him that Brother Harding had passed away.

As requested, Luke offered the opening prayer at the funeral and Esther played her violin. And as part of the emotional services, President Ben Kimball offered the concluding remarks.

"Brother Harding hasn't been released from his calling as ward mission leader," he said. "He's just received a transfer. He's still doing missionary work — on the other side of the veil."

CHAPTER 21

THE MANNINGS METICULOUSLY planned their trip — 20-plus states in 32 days. They mapped out in advance where they would park their RV each night and what sites they would see, though they didn't want their trip to be too structured for fear they might miss out on some spontaneous, unscripted experiences.

Hayley said she wanted the family to be led by the Spirit as they traveled.

She and Luke knew it would be a long month and that the kids would get tired of all the travel. But they hoped it would be a once-in-a-lifetime, spiritual pilgrimage.

"Can we take Buzz on our trip?" Brian asked.

"Not a chance," Luke said.

Friends and family recommended to Luke and Hayley that if they were going to embark on this kind of summer vacation that they should leave the three youngest kids at home. Hayley was grateful for the offer but adamant that they go as a family — the entire family.

Some thought Luke and Hayley had lost their minds.

"If I were in your shoes, with seven kids," a ward member told them, "a drive to Logan would be long enough."

Plenty of well-meaning people questioned the wisdom of such a trek. It would be a lot of driving, a lot of long days and even longer nights, and it would cost a lot of money. Some people in Hayley's family gave it three days before Luke would become unhinged and come home.

"I think Luke will make it to the Utah-Wyoming border, then turn that RV around," Hayley's brother said.

To most people, the idea of sleeping in an RV in Walmart parking lots didn't sound like a vacation but purgatory.

Nevertheless, Luke and Hayley were committed to this road trip. They hoped the older kids could remember and appreciate this experience. They hoped the twins could be entertained and contained. And they hoped that baby Sarah would continue to be as even-keeled as an infant could be — she possessed the perfect temperament for a series of long drives.

Bishop Tompkins was a little worried about losing his elders quorum president for an extended period of time, but he also realized this would be good for the Manning family.

"You have great counselors that can cover for you while you're gone," he said.

The Mannings stocked up on as much cheap food — mostly boxes of macaroni and cheese, Cup-o-Noodles and Top Ramen — as they could fit in the RV and packed a few days' worth of clothes (they would regularly do laundry on the road) and a box of copies of the Book of Mormon and piles of Pass-along cards.

Hayley purchased a six-month supply of hand sanitizer that she would use frequently — like anytime the family re-entered the RV.

Esther's purse and Brian's wallet were bulging with cash earned from babysitting and lawn mowing so they could buy souvenirs along the way. Brian, Benjamin and Jacob each brought basketballs as a way to entertain themselves, though Luke warned them not to dribble in the motor home.

Hayley reminded Esther about the moratorium on texting, and looking at, and posting on, social media. After being impacted by a lesson given by her seminary teacher, Esther decided it might be a good thing to go a month without her phone because she was worried about becoming addicted to it. So, for the trip, Esther would put her smartphone in airplane mode.

Before departing, Luke gave final instructions to his counselors and told them he would be checking his messages if they needed to communicate with him. Hayley's mom and dad agreed to take care of and the family garden while they were gone.

Luke and Hayley provided each of the older kids with a binder that included a map of the route they would be following so they could see exactly where they were going and the itinerary of each day's activities. Luke figured it would cut down on the kids asking, "Where are we going now?" and "Are we there yet?"

Hayley prepared several pages of historical background information on many of the places they planned on visiting. Each binder also included numerous sheets of lined paper. Luke and Hayley encouraged the older kids to write in these "journals" every night so they could record their experiences.

The first day of the trip, the Mannings awoke at 5:30 a.m. to get an early start. Hayley had already been up since 2:30, finishing up the packing.

Every morning of the trip started the same way — with a reading of a few verses of the Book of Mormon, followed by a prayer for protection and safety, and for missionary opportunities. Every morning they would ask Heavenly Father to guide them to someone they could serve; that they might be an instrument in God's hands to help someone in need.

"Each exodus has its genesis," Luke announced as he recorded the number showing on the odometer so he could keep track of their mileage. Then he started the engine. "And this is it for us. On your mark, get set, let's embark our trip of biblical proportions."

Hayley and the bleary-eyed kids settled into their seats, and Luke revved up the RV and pulled out of the driveway. The plan was to drive to Cheyenne, Wyoming, on the first day, since the Mannings figured there wasn't much to see or do between Helaman and Cheyenne. Their first and only planned stop of the day would be the Mormon Handcart Historic Site at Martin's Cove.

Hayley turned on the GPS on Luke's phone to ensure he wouldn't get lost. It featured a woman's voice guiding them.

"Hey dad," Benjamin said, "do you know the name of the woman talking on your GPS?"

"Um, I don't know. Siri?"

"No, her name is Leah. Leah Ona. Get it? Liahona?"

Luke and Hayley laughed.

"I don't get it," Jacob said.

"The Liahona is what the Lord gave Lehi and his family to guide them through the wilderness and to the Promised Land," Esther said. "And dad's GPS, hopefully, will guide us the right way so we don't get lost in the wilderness."

Luke tired of Leah Ona's voice somewhere near Bountiful, but he was glad to have that technology at his disposal.

Before leaving, Luke had vowed to himself that he wouldn't raise his voice once on this trip. He was going to be a happy dad for the next month. But he broke that vow in Evanston, Wyoming. He yelled at a semi-driver that cut him off, and then he yelled again at Jacob for spilling trail mix all over the floor of the RV.

Both times, Luke apologized, and then encouraged the kids to enjoy the view out the windows. There wasn't much to see.

"This has to be one of the loneliest, longest, ugliest, most desolate stretches of road in the world," Luke said as he drove east across I-80.

"This is what I imagine the wilderness that Nephi's family traveled through looking like," Esther said.

"Well, some of our pioneer ancestors actually traveled on this same road, though it wasn't paved back then," Hayley said. "Can you imagine the pioneers trudging through here with handcarts on dirt and rocks and sage brush? They didn't have a luxurious, air-conditioned motor home with a flat-screen TV and refrigerator like we have. And as bad as it might seem now, in the middle of June, can you imagine this road in the dead of winter, with six-foot snow drifts, minus-30-degree temperatures and the wind howling and whipping at 60 miles per hour? Now that's what I call a trial of faith. It's no coincidence that the pioneers had to go through this land. I think it was their final test before entering the Salt Lake Valley."

Hayley tried entertaining the kids with pioneer stories and pointing out unusual rock formations, including Devil's Gate in central Wyoming.

"Devil's Gate?" Benjamin asked. "I thought you said this trip was supposed to be a spiritual thing."

"Members of the Martin Handcart Company found shelter near Devil's Gate," Hayley explained. "It's now called Martin's Cove. The Willie and Martin Handcart companies left late in the summer and camped here during harsh winter storms. Many of them died. Survivors were found and rescued by search parties sent from Utah." The Mannings spent an hour or so at the Mormon Handcart Historic Site and Martin's Cove. They pushed handcarts and learned more about the pioneers but the kids got bored quickly. That didn't bode well. It was only Day One. The trip was only hours old.

"Can we go now?" Jacob said.

"I'm hungry," Benjamin said.

Luke and Hayley silently prayed that their entire trip wouldn't be like this.

"This isn't a good omen," Luke whispered to Hayley.

After Martin's Cove, Hayley finally resorted to allowing the kids to watch movies or letting them play on their hand-held gaming devices. Technology was a lifesaver for the kids, not to mention Luke and Hayley's sanity.

Luke and Hayley limited the time devoted to electronic devices and organized games to encourage family interaction. Hayley led games involving naming the books in the Bible and the Book of Mormon and naming prophets, ancient and modern. Luke led games that had to do with going through the alphabet and naming a college or pro team that started with each letter. Luke also quizzed the kids on state capitals and state nicknames.

Awards, in the form of extra snacks, were doled out to the winners.

The twins mostly entertained themselves by playing with each other's hair, giggling incessantly, and watching animated movies. Baby Sarah just seemed happy to be there. She ate when she needed to eat, and she slept when she needed to sleep.

Every few hours, Luke would stop somewhere safe and the kids would jump out of the RV and run around. When they were sufficiently worn out, and fed, they would pile back in. Sometimes, the boys didn't want to get back in.

They pulled into Cheyenne, and drove to the gold-domed state capital building. They ate on the capitol grounds before parking at the local Walmart.

The novelty of riding in a motor home wore off quickly.

At night, the RV got broiling hot and most of the kids slept next to each other on the seats or on the floor. Luke dreamed he was roasting in a barbecue oven. Hayley slept lightly because she was scared to death that one of the kids would wake up in the middle of the night, walk out of the RV, and end up in the Walmart toy aisle. Or someplace worse.

One good thing about sleeping in a Walmart parking lot — if the Mannings needed something, they didn't have to go far. One night, Jacob woke up with a bad cough. Luke walked into the open-24-hours-a-day store at 3:30 a.m., and bought cough suppressant. Problem solved.

Every time the Mannings crossed a state line, Luke and Hayley made a big deal about it to the kids with a drum roll and a list of facts about that state. Generally speaking, the kids weren't all that impressed.

Day Two featured a drive from Cheyenne to Mount Rushmore National Memorial in South Dakota. Once the Mannings entered the Black Hills National Forest, the driving became more distressing for Luke, as the narrow road to Mount Rushmore was winding and full of switchbacks. A couple of kids announced that they felt like throwing up. Luke wondered if the RV was too big for the road and he constantly worried he was going to clip other cars.

When they arrived at Mount Rushmore, they made their way to the viewing deck, and they witnessed the grandeur of the regal rock formation standing in the middle of the prairie that immortalized renowned figures from history. Carved into the mountain above were the larger-than-life sculptures of George Washington, Thomas Jefferson, Theodore Roosevelt, and Abraham Lincoln.

Having never been there before, Luke was taken aback by the enormity of it. The detail and work that had gone into creating this monument was staggering. There were the four of the greatest presidents the country had produced, seemingly surveying the nation they helped build.

"I wonder what they think about what America has become," Hayley said to Luke.

Benjamin and Jacob wondered aloud what they would find inside the noses of those presidents. Ashley and Lindsay were frightened by the sight of the giant visages and refused to look at them.

"They were great presidents," Luke said to the kids. "George Washington was the father of our country and our first president; Thomas Jefferson wrote the Declaration of Independence and expanded our country's size thanks to the Louisiana Purchase. Teddy Roosevelt oversaw the building of the Panama Canal; and Abraham

Lincoln freed the slaves and saved the Union. They are men to admire in their own way."

"But you've always told us 'not to get a big head,'" Brian said.

Luke laughed.

Hayley read to the kids from a brochure about how Mount Rushmore was sculpted by Gutzon Borglum, the son of a Danish immigrant. He started the project in 1927 and it took him 14 years to complete. It was finished in 1941, not long before the Japanese attack on Pearl Harbor. She read that the Mount Rushmore granite is so durable that it erodes at a rate of one inch every 10,000 years. She read about how workers were lowered over the face of Mount Rushmore on sling chairs, and that jackhammers and dynamite were used to do much of the carving.

Jacob, who loved rocks, let out a bored sigh. The kids got so restless they decided to leave. They needed to get to Omaha, Nebraska, that night.

As they left the Black Hills and turned toward Rapid City, Luke asked the kids who should be on the Mormon Mount Rushmore.

"That's easy," Esther said. "Joseph Smith, Brigham Young, Nephi, and David Archuleta."

"What about Captain Moroni? Jimmer Fredette? LaVell Edwards? Ty Detmer? Steve Young?" Brian suggested.

Due to road construction, Leah Ona commanded Luke to get off I-90 and take a two-lane road that dipped into Nebraska. The Mannings were amazed at the landscape of the Cornhusker State, which was flatter than cheap root beer.

"Dad," Jacob asked, "where are the mountains?"

"Mountains are illegal in Nebraska," Luke joked.

"You can see forever in every direction," Esther said. "Without mountains, how do you know where you are? I'd get lost if I lived here."

Later that night, in the darkness, on a lonely stretch of road about an hour outside of Omaha, Luke heard a loud popping sound, then the vehicle began to sway and rumble, and he felt like he was losing his grip on the steering wheel. Then came a rhythmic, and frightening, thumping noise. Blown tire.

Luke somewhat calmly applied the brake, wrestled the monstrous RV down to a slower speed toward the shoulder, leaving a choking cloud of gravel in its wake.

All the while, Hayley was wide-eyed, yelling, "Luke! Be careful! Luke! Luke! Luuuuuuuuuuuuuke!"

The kids were screaming, some with joy, some with fear.

"This is better than a roller-coaster!" Brian exclaimed.

"Don't crash!" Esther shouted.

Ashley and Lindsay were crying. Sarah slept through the whole episode.

By the time the RV came to a rest on the side of the road, Luke exhaled. He tried unsuccessfully to turn on the hazard lights.

"I know Brother Toolson showed me where the hazards are on this beast," Luke said. "But you can never remember when you need to."

Frustrated, Luke placed his head on the steering wheel. "I just checked all the tires at that last gas station," he said, then leaped out the door to check on the damage.

The back tire on the driver's side was shredded, and smelled, like a plate of burnt hash browns. Luke felt blessed that he was able to avoid an accident.

He reminded himself what Brother Toolson had told him about fixing a flat tire on an RV. He remembered that Jacob had lost the flashlight somewhere during a rest stop in Wyoming. A flashlight would have come in handy.

But his most pressing concern at the moment was the constant whirring of semi-trucks passing by at 80 miles per hour. Every time one did, it nearly knocked Luke over and caused the RV to shake. Then, suddenly, the winds kicked up and sheets of rain started pounding the ground, and him.

Dripping wet and shivering, Luke returned to the driver's seat and shut the door.

"We could be in a bit of trouble," said Luke, looking like a dog that had just jumped into a river. "We have no cell phone service. We have no light. There's a storm unleashing its fury on us and there are 18-wheelers flying by like it's the Indianapolis 500."

As usual, Hayley knew exactly what to do.

"We need to say a prayer," she said, trying to keep a stiff upper lip.

By this time, the kids, realizing the exigency of the situation, were silent and submissive. The bowed their heads and closed their eyes. Trucks continued whizzing by at breakneck speed, just feet from their RV, which seemed to be rocking as it was being pelted with a torrential downpour.

"Why don't you say it," Luke said to Hayley.

"Heavenly Father," she began, "we are so grateful to be taking this trip together as a family, but right now, we need thy help. We are stuck and we can't do this on our own. We pray the storm can be calmed and that we can receive the help we need. In the name of Jesus Christ, Amen."

Luke took a deep breath. "I'm going back out there to figure out how to fix this tire," he said. "This is quite an adventure, isn't it?"

"Be careful," Hayley said.

"Can I help, dad?" Brian asked.

"Absolutely not," Hayley replied. "Dad will handle it. We've prayed. We need to exercise faith and Heavenly Father will help us."

The rain subsided, and as soon as Luke made his way to the back of the RV, he was blinded by a pair of headlights cutting through the night. Soon, he was bathed in light. It was so bright, Luke half-expected an angel to appear.

Turned out, it was an angel of sorts — as a muscle-bound, corn-fed man in a pickup truck stepped out of the cab.

"Need some help?" he asked.

"Yessir," Luke answered. "We just had a blowout, and I've got my whole family in the RV. I've never changed an RV tire in my life."

The man had a cartoonish chin that jutted prominently from his jowls and looked as hard as a coconut. He wore a cowboy hat, work boots, and a grimy Nebraska Cornhuskers football T-shirt. He spit out some tobacco juice, and chuckled.

"Well, you're in luck," the man said. "I'm a mechanic in the town about 10 miles up the road. I'm Buck Wooten."

"Nice to meet you. I'm Luke Manning. We'd really appreciate your help."

Buck went back to his truck and grabbed an armful of tools. He turned on a headlamp.

As he started jacking up the RV, Luke asked, "How did you see us out here?"

Buck answered without looking up from his work. "Now you mention it, I really don't know," he said. "Something told me to pull over. I didn't know why until I saw you."

"Well," Luke said, "we're glad you did."

Luke helped Buck loosen the lug nuts and remove the spare tire.

"Utah, huh?" Buck asked, having noticed the license plate.

"Yep," Luke said. "Ever been there?"

"Nope," Buck said, sending a stream of tobacco juice onto the road.

Buck had the spare tire on the RV in record time.

"This should get you by for about 50-75 miles, so I'd get a new tire as soon as possible, in Omaha."

"Thank you so much," Luke said. "I owe you."

"No, don't worry about it," Buck said. "All in a day's work."

"I've got something for you."

"You don't need to pay me."

"It's not money," Luke said. Then he opened the door and asked Hayley to hand him a copy of the Book of Mormon.

"I'd like to give you this for helping us," Luke said. "It's the most valuable thing we could give you. It's a book about Jesus Christ and His teachings."

"I couldn't take it," Buck said.

"Do you like to read?"

"Not really."

"Well, will you please take it and give it to someone who does like to read?"

"OK," Buck said, stretching out his greasy, black hand. "Maybe I'll put this in the waiting room at my shop."

Luke shook Buck's hand and thanked him.

When Luke got back into the driver's seat, Hayley said, "He seems like a very nice man. He was an answer to prayer."

"Heavenly Father sent him to us, didn't he?" Jacob asked.

"Yes," Hayley said.

"He's a really good guy," Luke said. "He said something told him to pull over. That's one of the fastest answers to prayer I've ever seen."

"Well, the kids and I were just having a discussion about what happened," Hayley said. "And since you talked to the man yourself, maybe you could clear something up."

"What's that?"

"Esther said that man was one of the Three Nephites. Brian and Benjamin say he's not."

"I don't know," Luke said. "He could have been."

"What did he say when you gave him a Book of Mormon?" Esther asked.

"He didn't really want any part of it," Luke said, "but he could have been just pretending that he didn't so he wouldn't blow his cover."

Luke didn't mention anything about Buck chewing tobacco.

"He wasn't one of the Three Nephites," Brian said. "What would one of them being doing in the middle of Nebraska at night?"

The Mannings drove another 60 miles until they arrived at a Walmart in Omaha and parked for the night. As they fell asleep, Hayley whispered to Luke.

"It's funny that we set out on this trip with the idea that we were going to offer service to others," she said, "and before we can, we're the ones who are recipients of service."

CHAPTER 22

AS SOON AS THE MANNINGS woke up the next morning, Luke bought two new tires and he had a mechanic check out the others.

After pointing out once again how their prayer the night before had been answered in dramatic fashion, Hayley and Luke encouraged the kids to look for opportunities to serve, even in small ways. They continued to pray for missionary experiences.

But there was plenty of complaining. While the twins always wanted out of their car seats, one problem or another beset the other kids.

"Mom, Esther's music is too loud."

"Mom, Brian and Benjamin are acting like Laman and Lemuel again."

"Mom, why are you taking away my free agency?"

"Mom, Jacob's breath smells like Uncle DaVerl's feet."

Hayley *and* Luke were now getting regular headaches.

In Omaha, the Mannings went to Boys Town, established by Father Edward Flanagan, a Roman-Catholic priest, in 1917 as an orphanage that for decades has been dedicated to the treatment, care and education of at-risk kids.

On the way, Luke played for them the famous song, "He Ain't Heavy, He's My Brother."

Luke shared the backstory of the song and lyrics, saying he had read that there was a Scottish girl in the 1800s that was carrying her brother, almost her same size, on her back. When someone told her how difficult that task was she reportedly replied, "He's not heavy, he's my brother."

Luke hoped that story would make a lasting impact on the kids when they saw the famous bronze statue of a boy carrying his younger brother on his back at Boys Town.

Hayley took photos of Brian carrying Jacob on his back, next to like the statue.

"He *is* too heavy," Brian said.

Jacob wanted down so he started flailing his arms and legs and he fell off, landing hard on the ground — possibly sustaining a minor concussion, bruising his shoulder, scraping his arm, and ripping his favorite shirt. They wrestled on the ground for a moment until Luke broke it up. It wasn't the type of brotherly love Luke and Hayley were trying to instill in their sons.

The Mannings took a quick tour and heard stories of orphans overcoming adversity to become happy, well-adjusted adults. Luke could relate, having spent much of his teenage years in foster homes, though at the moment, he questioned how happy and well adjusted he really was.

As they left Boys Town, Luke noticed Esther place a $10 bill from her hard-earned baby-sitting money in a glass case for donations.

For lunch, Luke and Hayley decided to splurge by stopping at a Dairy Queen, spending $55. After eating, the boys said they were still hungry.

Luke needed to take a longer break from driving. Taking advantage of having an oven in the RV, Hayley and Esther decided to bake six-dozen chocolate chip cookies. The first dozen would be for their family. The rest would be for strangers, they decided.

There in downtown Omaha, near Ameritrade Park, Hayley positioned the kids on a street corner by the stadium entrance during a matinee College World Series game. Esther and Brian held plates of cookies with the twins standing next to them.

"Free cookies," the twins announced.

"Are these Mrs. Fields cookies?" one woman asked.

"No," Brian said. "I don't know a Mrs. Fields. These are Mrs. Manning's cookies."

Benjamin and Jacob handed out Pass-along cards with less success.

Some people were bemused that these kids were giving out free cookies. Some accepted a cookie, smiled and thanked the Mannings. Some looked at the family strangely.

"Are these poisoned?" a man wearing a Louisiana State baseball T-shirt asked. "Are you an Alabama fan?"

"No," Esther said, hurt by the accusation. "I've never even been to Alabama. These are my mom's chocolate chip cookies."

"Why are you doing this?" a woman asked Esther.

"We just want to brighten your day," she said.

The cookies were gone in about 15 minutes. While the cookies were a hit, the kids watched a few people who had accepted Pass-along cards throw them away in a garbage can.

Brian and Benjamin got bored so they took out their basketballs and started doing their dribbling routines, which drew attention from passersby as well.

"Wrong sport," said a guy in an Oregon State replica jersey. "This is baseball, not basketball."

"We forgot our baseball gloves," Brian said.

It was such a strange sight — a family handing out cookies and dribbling basketballs, that a man started filming them on his camera phone without the Mannings realizing it.

By that night, his footage was up on Facebook, titled, "Family hands out cookies, dribbles basketballs at the College World Series."

Luke wanted to stay and catch a game but Hayley reminded him they had a schedule to keep.

Later that afternoon, it was on to The Mormon Trail Center at Historic Winter Quarters and the Winter Quarters Temple in Florence, Nebraska. During the winter of 1846-47, Winter Quarters served as an encampment of about 2,500 pioneers as they waited out the brutal winter of that year before making their way to the Salt Lake Valley, Hayley explained to the kids.

About 500 cabins were built at the settlement that housed many Saints that had been driven from their homes in Illinois and Missouri that were looking for refuge. Due to an outbreak of illness and other conditions, about 400 died in Winter Quarters, about half of whom were two years and younger.

"Winter Quarters has a special feeling to it," Hayley said.

The cemetery next to the temple was a sobering reminder of what the early Saints endured before their arrival in Utah, especially when Luke shared with his family the story about his great-great-great-great grandmother, Elizabeth Manning, who had died in Winter Quarters.

"Elizabeth Manning had a son named Ezekiel and a daughter named Sarah, like our Sarah," Luke said.

After searching the cemetery, the Mannings found Elizabeth's name included on a mural listing those who had lost their lives there.

"This is your great-great-great-great-great grandmother," Luke said, snapping pictures with his camera phone. Luke couldn't help but think about what Ezekiel must have gone through. He traveled to a foreign country, endured privations, and lost his mother.

"This place is kind of like *Poltergeist*," Benjamin said.

"What do you mean?" Hayley asked.

"You know, like the movie. I saw it at my friend's house a while ago. It's about people building houses on top of a graveyard. Isn't this temple built on top of a graveyard? But it's not scary here. It's pretty peaceful."

The Mannings posed for pictures on the temple grounds and Luke imagined a young Ezekiel Manning standing on that same spot.

As they left Winter Quarters, Luke noticed he was driving on a street called "Mormon Bridge Road," which prominently featured a Baptist Church.

"I wonder how the Baptists feel about their mailing address?" Luke said to Hayley.

The Mannings made the five-hour drive to their next destination — they found a Walmart parking lot in Keokuk, Iowa — where they planned to stay for a few days to see all of the sites in nearby Nauvoo, a place that Luke playfully nicknamed Mormonville East.

"Nauvoo is a weird name," Benjamin said.

"Nauvoo is a Hebrew word that means 'beautiful place,'" Hayley said, pointing to the Nauvoo Temple on the hill. Luke told the kids about how Elias and Ezekiel Manning were among those who had helped build the original Nauvoo Temple before it was destroyed.

The highlight for Luke was taking Esther and Brian inside the Nauvoo Temple to do baptisms for the dead. It was the first place that baptisms for the dead had been done in this dispensation, Luke explained to them.

Before the trip, Luke, with family's help, had researched and prepared about 20 names for proxy baptisms, including his father; his grandfather; his great-great grandfather, Edward (who had published anti-Mormon literature back in his day); Jerry, the New York City firefighter; and Ezekiel's wife, Mary.

One of the temple workers explained the significance of the font, which sits on the back of twelve oxen, representing the Twelve Tribes of Israel — a replica of the "molten sea" in the Temple of Solomon, as described in the Book of Jeremiah in the Old Testament.

Standing in the baptismal font, baptizing Esther and Brian on behalf of his ancestors, Luke felt the same quiet elation as when he baptized his own children.

When his dad's name, Damon Lane Manning, came up, it almost took his breath away. In his mind's eye, he saw his father, dressed in white. Luke gripped Brian's wrist a little tighter and his voice quavered as he uttered the baptismal prayer.

At that moment, Luke felt all the resentment he had been harboring toward his father wash away in that font. He didn't know if his father would accept the sacred ordinance that unlocked the door of salvation, but for Luke the ordinance was a restorative event that brought peace to his heart. Tears rolled down his cheeks.

Luke knew this experience wouldn't have been possible without Maureen's help. Thanks to her, these weren't just obscure names printed on index cards. He felt like he knew about their lives.

Each time Luke raised his arm and baptized Esther and Brian in behalf of an ancestor, Luke felt a powerful witness that he was doing something with eternal consequences. It was a much different feeling than doing temple work for strangers. It was as if his relatives, like his dad, were standing there, watching the ordinances performed. He could feel their presence.

As Luke walked into the dressing room when they were finished, he imagined all of his ancestors lined up, nodding in approval. He imagined Ezekiel winking, saying in true Manning fashion, "Hey, Luke, it's about time you got around to this. What took you so long?"

While leaving the temple, Luke felt nothing but good feelings toward his father.

It was a feeling he didn't know how to process, but he liked it.

He felt unburdened from a load he had been carrying since childhood.

Later, the family congregated near a bronze statue located immediately west of the temple called "Calm As A Summer's Morning" that depicts Joseph Smith and his brother, Hyrum, on horseback before they rode from Nauvoo to Carthage.

Later, Luke told the kids more about his ancestors who had lived in Nauvoo. He read them a poignant excerpt from Ezekiel's journal. It didn't make quite the impact Luke was hoping for.

"Any questions?" he said.

"What's for lunch?" Brian asked.

Over the course of a few days, the Mannings enjoyed visiting the Nauvoo Visitors Center, the Joseph Smith homestead, and the Red Brick Store. They liked learning how to make candles and rope at the Family History Center. They pushed handcarts for a mile as a family through a muddy trail and through herds of angry cattle. They walked the "Trail of Hope," where families, like Luke's ancestors, loaded their wagons and waited their turn to cross the mighty Mississippi River when they forced to leave Nauvoo.

The Mannings couldn't get enough of the Mississippi River. They spent nearly an hour simply admiring its vastness. Brian, Benjamin and Jacob had a contest seeing how far they could throw a rock into the river.

"I think I read a story about how Joseph Smith threw a silver dollar across the Mississippi River," Benjamin said.

"You're thinking of the story about George Washington throwing a silver dollar across the Potomac," Luke said. "Unfortunately, neither story is true."

Luke did tell them the true story about Ezekiel Manning running back to their home to grab his father's gun before crossing the Mississippi. The kids enjoyed that one.

Meanwhile, everywhere the Mannings went, everyone made a fuss about all of the kids, especially Ashley and Lindsay.

"They're adorable," strangers would say.

"We not adorable," Lindsay would say. "We twins!"

On the down side, amid the muggy conditions of Nauvoo, Brian and Jacob got allergies — red, swollen eyes; constant sneezing; itchy hives — from touching horses and oxen. Luke suffered a little from the allergies as well, but he knew not to touch the livestock. Hayley put Brian and Jacob on a dosage of allergy medicine that made them act like zombies. Meanwhile, one night Benjamin and the twins started throwing up, creating a wretched smell in the RV. Fortunately, the vomiting party lasted only one night.

The Mannings visited the sites owned by the Community of Christ, the church formerly known as the Reorganized LDS Church, which, Luke and Hayley told the kids, branched off The Church of Jesus Christ of Latter-day Saints in Nauvoo. They explained that many of Joseph Smith's family members decided to remain in Nauvoo rather than go West to Utah with the rest of the Saints and they established a new church.

"Let's just say they weren't big fans of Brigham Young," Luke said.

So Luke smiled sheepishly when he realized that inside the Community of Christ visitors' center, Benjamin and Jacob were wearing BYU T-shirts.

The Mannings took the short drive from Nauvoo to Carthage to tour Carthage Jail. It was an especially memorable experience for the kids when they learned more about the history of what happened at that place to the Prophet.

"This is where Joseph and his brother, Hyrum, were martyred," Hayley said.

"Mom, I think it's pronounced 'murdered,'" Benjamin said.

"Well, you're going to learn a new word today," Hayley said. "A martyr is someone who is killed because of their beliefs. That's what happened here to Joseph Smith."

Luke felt like he was walking on holy ground as he visited Carthage Jail. Besides, he could relate to being unjustly imprisoned, from his experience in Africa, but he couldn't imagine enduring what Joseph went through, dying for a celestial cause.

Before the Mannings left Carthage Jail, Esther asked the missionaries serving there if she could play her violin on the grounds outside the jail. She had been practicing a couple of hymns that were appropriate for the occasion. They gave her permission.

Esther stood near the statue of Joseph and Hyrum together in front of Carthage Jail and started playing "A Poor Wayfaring Man of Grief" — the song that John Taylor sang to Joseph not long before the Prophet was killed.

People milling outside the grounds became very quiet as they listened to the girl's touching rendition. Grown men wept. Then Esther performed "Praise to the Man."

Everyone stood still watching her play that swelling anthem.

Two or three people with camera phones videoed the entire thing and put it on Facebook and Instagram.

When Esther finished playing, about a dozen people, including senior missionaries and non-members of the Church, embraced her and thanked her for sharing her talents with them.

"I'm not a Mormon," one man said to her, "but you really enhanced my experience here today."

"Can you stay all summer and play all day?" asked one of the senior missionaries.

The Mannings would have liked to oblige, but they had a schedule to keep.

CHAPTER 23

AFTER SPENDING A FEW memorable days in Nauvoo, the Mannings drove to the Windy City.

"Dad, why do they call Chicago 'The Windy City'?" Benjamin asked.

"All the hot air from the politicians," Luke joked. "It's also called 'The City of Broad Shoulders.'"

"Is that because of the Chicago Bears?" Brian asked.

"No, that nickname comes from a poem by Carl Sandburg," Luke said.

"Oh, yeah," Brian said. "He was the Cubs' Hall-of-Fame second baseman, right?"

"No," Luke laughed, "you're thinking of Ryne Sandberg. But close."

On the way to Chicago, the Mannings had to drive through toll roads.

"Why do they make you pay to drive on their roads?" Brian asked. "It slows everything down."

"They've got to pay for these roads somehow," Luke said. "One of my favorite things about Utah — no toll roads."

They arrived on the North Side of Chicago, where they visited another temple — featuring six spires and gray marble — and took more family photos. They found a place to park the RV and took an "L" train to Wrigley Field. They didn't have tickets to the matinee game between the Chicago Cubs and Los Angeles Dodgers, but Luke wanted his family to see "The Friendly Confines" of Wrigley and they took pictures with the famous red "Wrigley Field, Home of Chicago Cubs" sign.

Then they took the train to Grant Park. They visited the Art Institute of Chicago. They dined on slabs of famous Chicago thick-crust pizza.

People seemed to be gawking at the Mannings, counting their gaggle of kids. It would be a common occurrence on this trip, especially in big cities.

Spurred by her positive experience playing at Carthage Jail, Esther carried her violin everywhere she went. On Michigan Avenue, the Mannings passed a blind African-American man playing a harmonica for money. It wasn't going well for him. Esther noticed just a couple of coins in a cup. Luke urged her to play with the man.

"Can I play with you?" she asked.

"What do you play?"

"The violin."

"That would be fine. What should we play?"

"Do you know 'America The Beautiful'?"

"Sure do."

So the odd couple — a teenage Mormon girl from Utah with a violin named Esther and a blind, homeless man from Chicago with a harmonica named Jasper — collaborated to create a sweet rendition of a patriotic song. And folks noticed, including some who held up their camera phones and pushed play. A dozen or so stopped to listen, and filled the blind man's cup with money.

When they finished, people clapped and asked for an encore.

"Got time for another?" Jasper asked.

"Sure. What would you like to play next?"

"Do you know 'Amazing Grace?'"

"Yes, I do."

As they played, people congregated around. Luke took off his baseball cap (hoping they would ignore the Mets logo on it) on the ground next to the cup so people could donate more money.

"How long have you two been playing together?" a woman

asked during a break.

"About 15 minutes," Jasper said with a smile.

"If you ever put out an album together," the woman said, "I'd download it. That was just wonderful."

The Mannings introduced themselves to Jasper, who related to them his story of losing his vision due to glaucoma years earlier. When he lost his sight, he lost his job as a Chicago bus driver. As times got tough, his wife and daughter left him. He had been living on the streets and in homeless shelters in Chicago for five years. His only real possession was that harmonica, which he had learned to play as a child. Jasper taught himself to play hundreds of songs.

Before leaving, Esther gave Jasper a hug.

"Thank you, Esther," he said. "Now I have enough money for dinner tonight."

Upon hearing that, Esther burst into tears. She put $20 from her babysitting money into his cup.

While Esther was playing the violin, Brian and Benjamin started dribbling their basketballs and people stopped to watch, as if they were part of the entertainment.

"Yo, you boys can ball," one of the kids told them. "You wanna play with us?"

"Can we dad?" Brian asked.

"OK," Luke said, "but we can't stay long."

They went to a park and played an intense game. Luke was impressed that his sons held their own.

"Do you guys know Jabari Parker?" Brian asked, referring to the former Duke star and NBA player who is from Chicago.

"Yeah, he's our boy," one said.

"He's our boy, too," Brian said. "We belong to the same Church."

"Really?"

"Yeah, we're members of The Church of Jesus Christ of Latter-day Saints. Some call us Mormons," Brian said. "You should go to our church sometime. And watch out for me and my brother. We're going to be in the NBA someday."

"Whoa, Brian," Luke said, "let's not get ahead of ourselves. A little humility would go a long way."

"I'd become a Mormon if it helped me get to the NBA," one of the boys said.

"How about we play another game — to 20," one of the Chicago boys proposed. "If we win, you give us one of your basketballs."

"OK," Brian said. "And if we win, you have to read the Book of Mormon."

Just like that, the boys had consummated a bet. Hayley didn't approve but it was too late.

Brian drilled the game-winner, a jumper from the corner, to give the Mannings a dramatic 21-19 victory.

The Chicago kids reluctantly took the Book of Mormon. "I bet Jabari Parker will sign it for you," Brian said. Then he gave them his basketball anyway, which left the young Chicagoans speechless.

Luke, impressed with Brian's generosity, ended up buying him another basketball on the trip.

A man passing by noticed the game, filmed parts of it and uploaded it to Facebook under the title "Black and White Kids Hooping It Up in Chicago."

Somebody commented on it: *Maybe there's hope for good race relations in this city after all.*

The Mannings stayed longer in Chicago than they had planned. They had about a two-hour drive ahead of them to their next stop in South Bend, Indiana.

Some of the kids wondered why there were stopping there.

"It's a great place for our family to visit — a Catholic enclave and home of Notre Dame University," Luke explained.

The following day, the Mannings toured the Notre Dame campus to see the attractions — Notre Dame Stadium; the Golden Dome; Grotto of Our Lady of Lourdes; the statues of Knute Rockne, Ara Parseghian and Lou Holtz; Touchdown Jesus; First Down (or We're No. 1) Moses; and Fair Catch Corby.

"I know that BYU's campus has that statue of Brigham Young," Luke said, "but they should have other Mormon-themed, football-related monuments on campus like they have here at Notre Dame."

"Yeah, like 'Illegal Motion Nephi' or 'Pass Interference Alma,' or 'Touchback Moroni,'" Brian said.

"Exactly," Luke said, laughing.

The Mannings entered the Basilica of the Sacred Heart, which prompted a bunch of questions from the kids about what went on inside, like infant baptisms and the burning of incense, among other things. Luke figured it was good for the kids to learn about other religions.

Hayley emphasized the importance of being respectful of others' beliefs, just as she hoped to receive respect from others for her beliefs.

After that detour at Notre Dame, the Manning headed due east toward Kirtland, Ohio.

Luke stopped for gas at the Indiana-Ohio border. The cheapest he could find was $3.82 a gallon. With all the travel, the RV burned up absurd amounts of fuel. Every time he filled up the 55-gallon tank, he would spend over $210 and feel physically ill.

Luke drove so much that at nights when he tried to sleep, he'd find his hands automatically go to the 10-2 position.

The following day, on the way to Kirtland, Luke stopped to fill up the propane tanks and clean out the septic tank again. When he did, he always returned smelling like a pig after wallowing in a trough. Hayley would spray him with spritzes of Lysol and bathe him in hand sanitizer.

"Can we try to find another person like Jasper that we can help?" Esther asked.

Hayley looked up an address of a homeless shelter in Cleveland on her phone. Upon arriving, the Mannings were greeted by a man who ran the shelter.

"We're all filled up for tonight," he said. "I'm sorry."

"Um, no," Luke said. "We're not here for food or a room. We're here to help."

The man was confused. "Really?"

"Could we volunteer to feed people?" Luke asked. "Afterward, my daughter could provide some entertainment. She plays the violin."

Before they knew it, the Mannings were serving up chicken, rolls, and vegetables to grateful patrons. After the meal, the man in charge of the homeless shelter introduced Esther, who played her violin for 30 minutes straight. She played well-known tunes and sneaked a few Church hymns in there as well.

"What is this song?" a homeless man asked Luke. "I really like it."

"Yeah," Luke said. "It has a great beat and it's easy to dance to."

"What is it called?"

"'Come, Come Ye Saints,'" Luke replied.

"Never heard of it. Do they ever play it on the radio?"

"Probably not in Cleveland," Luke said.

When Esther finished, Brian and Benjamin started performing their basketball tricks, wowing the crowd. They were excited to show off in the city where LeBron James starred for the Cleveland Cavaliers. Cleveland was only 40 miles south of King James' hometown of Akron.

"Can we go to Akron, since we're close by?" Brian asked.

Hayley Googled Akron on her phone and discovered that the crime rate there was 76 percent higher than the national average.

"No," Hayley said, "we won't be going to Akron."

The Mannings spent the night at a Cleveland Walmart parking lot and arrived in Kirtland the next morning.

When Hayley told the kids they were headed to the Newel K. Whitney Store, Benjamin asked if they could buy food there.

"I'm sick of Cup-o-Noodles," he said. "It's like Cup-o-Sludge."

While taking a tour of Kirtland, Luke realized it was underrated as a Church history destination, obscured by the more famous Nauvoo and Palmyra stops.

Luke hadn't realized all the amazing things that had happened there — how half of the revelations found in the Doctrine and Covenants were received in Kirtland; how Joseph Smith had interacted with prophets of other dispensations there; how the School of the Prophets was held there; how the Pearl of Great Price was translated there; how the Savior was seen by Joseph at least six times there; how the Father and the Son had appeared in vision four times there; how at one time the headquarters of the Church was there; how the first temple of this dispensation was built there; how the first temple ordinances of this dispensation was done there; how Section 76 of the Doctrine and Covenants, the vision of the degrees of glory, was revealed there; how the Apostle Peter, John the Beloved, Moses, Elijah and Elias all appeared there; how the keys of sealing power were conferring there; how the hymn "The Spirit of God Like a Fire is Burning" was written and published there; and how the Saints first sang that LDS anthem at the temple dedication and concourses of angels appeared there.

It made Luke feel bad for suggesting earlier that his family visit the Rock and Roll Hall of Fame in downtown Cleveland, or the Pro

Football Hall of Fame an hour's drive south in Canton, instead of Kirtland.

At the Newel K. Whitney Store, the Mannings stood in the very spot that Joseph received the revelation about the Word of Wisdom.

At John Johnson's home in Hiram, missionaries told the story about Joseph being dragged out of his home in the dark of night and being beaten, tarred and feathered. The next day, Joseph preached a sermon and subsequently baptized three new converts.

Luke had always regarded northeast Ohio as the armpit of the United States. He had thought of the area built on the banks of Lake Erie as Lake Eerie.

"They call Cleveland 'The Mistake on the Lake,'" Luke said to Hayley. "But I won't think of it like that anymore. With all the cool Church history stuff that happened here, maybe Cleveland really is 'Believeland' after all."

The Mannings visited the historic Kirtland Temple, which is owned by the Community of Christ. While walking around the temple grounds, Brian tried to hand out Pass-along cards.

"You're Mormons?" a man asked.

"We're members of The Church of Jesus Christ of Latter-day Saints," Brian said.

"We're not interested."

As fun as it was to see new things and learn about Church history, Brian was a little discouraged.

"Every day we pray for missionary opportunities, but nothing ever happens," Brian said.

"What do you mean?" Hayley asked. "Every stop we've made we've had missionary experiences."

"Yeah, but I want an experience where someone gets baptized."

"That would be awesome," Hayley said. "Those things take time. We just need to be patient and keep exercising faith. I think we're having a bigger impact than you think. We're planting seeds. We're not necessarily harvesting."

"Who knows?" Luke said as he guided the RV east onto I-90, "maybe one of you will end up serving a mission in one of these places we've visited."

"Kirtland was a testing time for the early members of the Church," Hayley told the kids. "Had the Saints not gathered in Kirtland, the Church might have been destroyed in New York.

Remember all the incredible things that happened here."

"We're kind of going backward through Church history," Esther observed. "Nauvoo came after Kirtland and Kirtland came after Palmyra."

"You're right," Hayley said. "Hopefully by the time we get home it will all make sense. And you'll know your history in chronological order. Esther, you'll be studying the Doctrine and Covenants this year for seminary. You will have been to many of the places that are mentioned in the D&C."

At Niagara Falls, the kids marveled at the majesty of the famous waterfall and the millions of gallons of water cascading into Lake Ontario below. The Manning decided to forgo a voyage on the "Maid of the Mist" due to the cost.

Hayley kept the twins in the double stroller and Luke had Sarah on his back. Hayley held on to Brian, Benjamin and Jacob, making sure they didn't fall through the railings that protected them from the raging waters below.

The Mannings marched on through upstate New York, visiting Rochester, the headquarters of Hayley's mission. But the place she couldn't wait to take her family was Palmyra, the cradle of the restoration. This was one of the destinations that Luke and Hayley were looking forward to most. Hayley had spent a significant part of her mission in Palmyra.

"I only wish we could be here for the Hill Cumorah Pageant. It's the Church's flagship pageant and we used to get a lot of referrals from it," Hayley said. "But we'll miss it by a month."

"What is a pageant?" Brian asked.

"It's like a giant outdoor roadshow on the Hill Cumorah," Hayley said.

"What's a roadshow?" Brian asked again.

"Um, it's something the Church used to do," Hayley said. "Roadshows were like school plays, but with Church themes."

"The Church was really weird back then," Brian said.

In town, the Mannings went to Grandin Books, where the first copies of the Book of Mormon were published. At Hill Cumorah, the boys sprinted to the top to see the monument honoring Angel Moroni. Then they stopped to walk around, and take photos of, the Palmyra Temple.

Luke and Hayley couldn't wait for their kids to experience the

Sacred Grove and reflect on the First Vision of the Prophet Joseph Smith.

"We are about to go to one of the most special and sacred places on Earth," Hayley explained as Luke drove toward the Grove. "What happened here was one of the most important events in the history of the world. You know the story. Joseph Smith, who was between Esther's and Brian's age at the time, wanted to know which church to join. He decided to ask God, believing he would get an answer. That answer came in a way he never thought it would. Heavenly Father and Jesus Christ appeared to him and told him not to join any of the churches. Through Joseph, the Lord restored His Church in the latter days. I know the First Vision happened here. One of the greatest experiences of my life was to spend time here during my mission and tell the story of the First Vision, and bear my testimony of it to many visitors. As we would say, 'This is where it all began, where the heavens opened, and the world changed forever.'"

It was a bright, sunny afternoon. Once they arrived at the Sacred Grove, the Mannings stepped out of the RV and walked into the visitors' center and learned about how the Smith family lived and about Joseph when he was a boy.

Then they entered the Sacred Grove as a family.

"This is so beautiful, it doesn't seem real," Esther whispered, standing on the pristine, manicured trail.

"It's just like it was when I served my mission," Hayley said. "It's like standing in a painting."

"Why is it so quiet?" Jacob asked.

"It's a very special place," Hayley whispered.

"Where exactly did the First Vision happen?" Benjamin asked.

"We don't know exactly where," Hayley said. "If we did, everyone would crowd around that place and probably detract from the sacredness of it. I just like walking through the grove to feel the Spirit and contemplate what happened here and what it means to me."

"Can I go exploring?" Jacob said.

"No," Luke said. "This is not a place to go exploring."

"What are we supposed to see here?" Benjamin asked. "There's just a bunch of trees."

"It's not what we *see* here," Hayley answered, "it's what we *feel* here."

As they strolled through the Grove, the kids, even the twins, stayed mostly silent.

Luke remembered the other time he had been at the Sacred Grove, many years earlier, after he had gone to Utah and before he was baptized. He remembered the powerful feeling he had then and the memories came rushing back.

"Can we camp here?" Jacob asked. "This would be a perfect spot for camping."

Luke was surprised that he didn't have to remind the boys to be reverent, even though they had been cooped up in an RV for more than a week.

"There are some trees here — we don't know which ones — that were probably here when Joseph had his vision," Hayley whispered. "This may be very similar to what it may have looked like way back in 1820, nearly 200 years ago."

"I wonder what the Church will do to celebrate the bicentennial of the First Vision," Luke said.

"I doubt we'll see fireworks over Palmyra," Hayley said.

The Mannings were surprised to find there were no other visitors in the Grove at that time. They had the place to themselves. At one point, Luke offered a family prayer, thanking Heavenly Father for the opportunity to be there on that day.

When the Mannings left the grove, Esther, with permission of the missionaries, took out her violin, stood next to the Visitors' Center, and played "Joseph Smith's First Prayer."

During the hymn, the Mannings noticed a middle-aged man and his wife walking toward them. The burly man with a large belt buckle started filming Esther playing the violin.

"That was so beautiful," his wife said. "Hope y'all don't mind we got that on video."

"Thanks," Esther said. "And, no, I don't mind."

"I'm so sorry to disturb you," the woman said, "but we came through here a couple of hours or so ago. I believe I lost my wedding ring somewhere in there. Did you happen to see it?"

"No," Hayley said, "but we can help you look for it."

So the Mannings spread out and walked down the pathways of the Sacred Grove searching for a ring.

"That ring set me back a fortune," the husband whispered to Luke, "so I'd really like to find it."

The Mannings learned that the couple, Jim and Paula Briggs,

was from Austin, Texas, and had been spending time at Niagara Falls. Someone told them to check out the Sacred Grove, though they had no idea what it was.

"It's so pretty here," Paula told Hayley. "There's a different feeling here. It's something I've never felt before."

Hayley told Paula an abbreviated version of the First Vision, how The Church of Jesus Christ of Latter-day Saints came about, and then explained the doctrine of eternal families. She presented her with a copy of the Book of Mormon. It was just like she was back on her mission.

"Have you seen the temple here in Palmyra?" Hayley asked.

"I think so," Paula said, her eyes glistening. "Is it that building with the gold angel on top?"

"Yes, that's it."

"Yes, we drove by it."

"Temples are where families can be sealed for eternity."

"That's a beautiful thing," Paula said. "Jim and I have been married 25 years. I've often wondered what becomes of marriages when we die. I'd hate to think our marriage would end. When I get home, could I go to one of your temples and learn more?"

"Well, you have to be a member of the Church to go inside the temples," Hayley said, "but you're always welcome to go to one of our meetinghouses. Just look for the sign that says, 'The Church of Jesus Christ of Latter-day Saints, Visitors Welcome.'"

"We have churches all over the United States," Luke said, "like IHOPs."

"Would anyone mind if we showed up on a random Sunday?" Paula asked.

"To the contrary, people there, especially the missionaries, would be thrilled to see you," Luke said.

"They would be more than happy to answer your questions and share more with you," Hayley said.

Suddenly, Jacob burst out with a yell.

"Jacob!" Luke said, "please be quiet."

"I found the ring!" Jacob said.

The Briggs moved quickly toward Jacob, who held an eight-carat diamond in his palm.

"That's it!" Paula said, trying to keep her voice down.

"How did you find it?" Jim asked Jacob.

"I just started walking around, looking at the ground. Then I saw something shiny by these leaves."

"Thank you," Paula said, placing the ring on her finger. "When we came through here, my hands started to swell up. I thought I put my ring in my pocket but I must have dropped it. Thank you!"

"Young man," Jim said to Jacob, "I'm going to give you a little reward for finding our ring."

"You don't need to," Luke said.

"I insist," Jim said.

"We can't take anything from you," Luke explained. "We're just glad we could help."

"That was so nice of all of you to help us look for my ring," Paula said. "What's y'all's names?"

"We're the Mannings," Luke said. "This is my wife Hayley and these are our children — Esther, Brian, Benjamin, Jacob, Ashley, Lindsay and Sarah."

"Are you guys related to the Mannings of the NFL — Archie, Peyton and Eli?" Jim asked.

"No," Luke said. "We're the Mannings of Mormonville. We're from Utah and we're driving across the United States in an RV."

"The Mannings of Mormonville," Jim said with a laugh. "That has a nice ring to it, no pun intended."

The couple smiled, said goodbye. The Briggs left, walking hand-in-hand.

The kids begged to stay at the Sacred Grove. They didn't want to leave so they tarried a little longer. A man wearing a New York Mets cap, and using a wooden cane, walked past, drawing Luke's attention.

"Like your hat," Luke said quietly to him.

"Thank you," the man replied. "Big Mets fan?"

"Yes, sir. All my life."

"Where are you from?"

"Utah."

"Ah, Mormons."

"Yes," Luke said.

"Well, my name is Ed. I'm from Buffalo. I've come here every summer for years. This is one of my favorite places in the world. Let me tell you folks, there's no doubt in my mind that Joseph Smith saw God in this spot, and that it happened the way he said it did. How else to explain the serenity you feel here? There is no other explanation."

"How long have you been a member of the Church?" Luke asked.

"Oh, I'm not a member of your Church," Ed replied, chuckling. "I don't belong to any church. I believe in God and I'm religious in my own way, I guess you could say. Every time I come here, the missionaries flock to me like seagulls to a piece of bread. I'm always flattered by the attention, and I appreciate what the missionaries are trying to do. It's their job. But I like to be left alone, so I can soak in the aura of this magnificent place. I know something special happened here. There's no other explanation for it."

"If you ever want to join the Church, we could teach you," Brian said.

"Thank you, young man," Ed said. "I'm sure you'll be a fine missionary someday. I'll let you know if I'm ever interested in joining your Church. Good to meet you. Hope you enjoy your time here."

The Mannings returned to the motor home. Luke unlocked the doors and the kids jumped in.

"Hey Dad," Brian said, "there's something stuck in our windshield wiper."

"What is that?" Luke asked. "It looks like an envelope. They don't give parking tickets here, do they Hayley?"

"Not that I know of."

Luke stepped out of the motor home and removed the envelope from the windshield. He got into his seat, ripped open the envelope and read the note inside.

Dear Mannings of Mormonville,

It was so fun to meet you. It's been one of the highlights of our vacation. You have such a cute family. Thanks again for finding our precious wedding ring. I know God meant for us to meet today. When we return home to Texas, we're going to go to one of your churches. While we respect that you don't want a "reward" for finding our ring, we would like to give you something as a token of our appreciation. Enclosed is $100. We're sure you'll put this to good use. Thanks again. Have a great vacation.

Jim and Paula Briggs
Austin, Texas

Luke looked at Hayley. The kids stared at the $100 bill.

"We can't very well give back this money now," Luke said.

"Is that money for me?" Jacob asked excitedly.

"Maybe we could have a pretty nice dinner or buy gas with this money," Luke said.

"We could do both at once," Brian said. "Think of all the tacos and burritos you could buy at Taco Bell with that."

"Maybe we could donate the money to someone who needs it more than us," Esther said.

"I like that idea, Esther," Hayley said. "Is everyone OK with that?"

"I guess," Jacob said.

"Hopefully, Heavenly Father will guide us to someone who needs this money more than we do," Hayley said.

"What if we're the ones who need this money?" Brian said.

"Then I guess we'll use it," Hayley said. Then she paused. "How was that for a missionary experience, Brian?"

"But nobody got baptized."

"No, not yet," Hayley said, "but we planted some more seeds."

As Luke started up the RV engine, two fully loaded tour buses filled with high school kids from Utah pulled in.

"Just in the nick of time," Luke said as he pulled away.

CHAPTER 24

FROM PALMYRA, THE MANNINGS drove the 68 miles to Syracuse, where they spent the night at a Walmart.

"This is where your Dad grew up, and where I served part of my mission," Hayley told the kids as they approached the city limits.

"Is this where you met Dad?" Jacob asked.

"No. Don't you remember?" Hayley said. "Dad had left Syracuse a long time before I got here. I have to admit that while I was serving here, I never imagined I would marry a man from Syracuse, or anywhere in Upstate New York."

While Hayley had nothing but pleasant memories of her time in Syracuse, and the New York Rochester Mission, Luke had plenty of bad memories.

It was in Syracuse where Luke was abandoned by his father, and later by his mother. It was in Syracuse that he bounced from foster home to foster home. It was in Syracuse that he felt lonely and learned at a young age that the world could be a cruel, dark place.

On the other hand, he spent his college years at Syracuse University, where he studied journalism and dated just about every cheerleader and broadcast journalism coed on campus.

Luke took his family to the cemetery in Syracuse where his great-great-great-grandfather, Ezekiel, and his grandfather, and his dad were buried. Luke had researched where the headstones were located.

The headstones were simple and faded, but he felt like he was connecting with his ancestors.

"What was Grandpa Manning like?" Esther asked Luke.

Luke didn't know quite how to answer that question.

"You mean my father? He was a free spirit and lived life his own way," he said. "He left my mom and me when I was 11. I've learned that we can't judge him. He had a rough childhood. Now that we've done work for him in the temple — remember Brian got baptized for him in Nauvoo — I'm hoping he'll accept the gospel and someday, we'll see him again."

Luke felt bad that his dad would never get to know his grandchildren in this life.

After leaving the cemetery, Luke drove past the apartment complex he had shared with his mom decades ago. It brought back both happy and painful memories of his childhood.

"I used to play baseball in this street," Luke pointed out.

Hayley thought it would be a good idea for Luke to give back to the children and family services in Syracuse. They found the Onondaga County Foster Care building at the John H. Mulroy Civic Center and asked for someone in charge.

"We have a donation," Luke explained.

Ten minutes later, a woman who introduced herself as Dawn Lippmann, entered the lobby.

"How can I help you?"

"My name is Luke Manning. I grew up here in Syracuse and I'm a product of the social services you provide. I just wanted to say thanks. As a token of our appreciation, my wife and daughter have made these quilts and we were hoping you could give them to kids that need them. I remember when I was a foster kid, I moved around quite a bit. I know that having something you can call your own is a big deal."

"Wow," the woman said, "it's not often we have anyone do anything like this. In fact, I'm pretty sure this is the first time that's happened here. These quilts are beautiful. Thank you. I will make sure they are given to needy kids."

The woman posted pictures of the Mannings, and their donated quilts, on the Onondaga County Foster Care Facebook page.

Luke took his family to the campus of his alma mater, Syracuse University. The highlight was a brief visit to the Carrier Dome, home of the Syracuse Orange football and basketball teams.

"This is the largest domed stadium of any college campus in the country," Luke said proudly. "I watched a lot of football and basketball games here."

The next day, a Sunday, the Mannings visited a Syracuse ward that Hayley had served in. The bishop saw the Mannings walk through the chapel doors.

"Looks like we're going to double the size of our Primary," he told one of his counselors.

The bishop was subsequently disappointed to learn that the Mannings were just visiting.

After sacrament meeting, one member Hayley knew from her mission, and had kept in touch with on Facebook, introduced her to a woman, Sister Pickering, who was about Hayley's same age.

"I need to tell you something," Sister Pickering told Hayley. "One dreary afternoon many years ago, I was in my apartment with my baby daughter. I was a single mom on food stamps, struggling to keep us alive. I'd look at my daughter sleeping, and I'd cry. I didn't want her to grow up in such a miserable world. Then I looked out the window and I saw two sister missionaries walking down the street. They looked so happy. So clean and well dressed. So beautiful. So confident. They had purpose in their lives. I had no idea at that time what they were doing or what they believed. I only knew that they were Mormons. I said a prayer at that moment, that if God could grant me anything, it would be that my baby daughter could grow up to be like those two young women. At the time, it seemed impossible. Well, it wasn't until months later that another set of missionaries knocked on my door. I think I shocked them because I let them in so quickly. I told them I had been waiting for them to tell me why they were so happy because I wanted that in my life. A month later, I was baptized. While I was thrilled to be a member of the Church, I always wanted to thank those two sister missionaries that I saw out my window. I wrote it all down in my journal, and I put the dates together, and Sister Wells tells me one of those sister missionaries was you."

Crying, Hayley gave Sister Pickering a hug.

"Thank you for sharing that story," Hayley said. "I just wish we would have knocked on your door that day."

"That's OK. The Lord has His own timing. I went through some things between the time I saw you to listening to the discussions that helped prepare me to accept the gospel."

"I would love to meet your daughter," Hayley said.

Sister Pickering smiled. "I wish you could. That's the best part of the story. She is serving a mission right now in the Ecuador Quito North mission. She's been out for eight months."

Sister Pickering pulled out her smartphone.

"Look, here she is," she said, showing a picture of her daughter smiling and eating a lamb — the whole lamb — with an Ecuadorian family dressed in their colorful native attire.

"Now, she's the sister missionary that's happy, clean and well dressed, beautiful and confident," Hayley said.

"Yes, she is."

"The Lord certainly answered that prayer."

"He did. I'm so grateful to you for being such a great missionary and such a great example to me without saying a word."

Hayley spent a couple of hours renewing acquaintances with some of the members of the ward. Sister Wells invited the Mannings to dinner. The Manning were grateful, and thrilled, to eat a home-cooked meal for the first time in a long time.

The next morning, the next stop on the itinerary was Cooperstown, New York, home of the Baseball Hall of Fame. Luke, Brian and Benjamin could have spent weeks there but they only stayed a couple of hours.

One of Luke's favorite players when he was a teenager was Dale Murphy, even though he didn't play for the Mets. Murphy was a mainstay of the Atlanta Braves in the 1980s, and a two-time National League Most Valuable Player. At the time, all he knew was that Murphy was the nicest guy in baseball and that he was one of the most feared hitters in the game. It wasn't until Luke was older that he realized that Murphy was a member of the Church. Luke liked him even more when he found out Murphy was a convert.

As a teenager, all Luke knew about Murphy was that he signed autographs, he was polite, he didn't drink, he didn't swear, and he didn't take steroids.

Luke long believed that Murphy, and his 398 career home runs, deserved to be in the Hall of Fame. Other than the fact Murphy was conspicuous by his absence in the Hall, Luke loved his time in Cooperstown.

Hayley and the girls were not as enthused about the experience.

The plan was to go to Susquehanna, Pennsylvania — the Priesthood Restoration Site — about two hours south of Syracuse. But when Luke came out of the Baseball Hall of Fame, he noticed a giant screw embedded in one of the tires of the RV. Replacing the tire took a while so the Mannings returned to the Baseball Hall of Fame, much to Luke's delight.

"Looks like you planned this," Hayley joked. "If you wanted to stay longer, you could have just said so. You didn't need to go to such elaborate means."

Hayley was kidding but it wasn't lost on her that had they driven very far with a tire in that condition, it could have been disastrous.

Because of the tire trouble that took until late that afternoon to repair, Luke and Hayley made the difficult decision to skip Susquehanna, and stay at a Walmart near Cooperstown.

Hayley told the kids about Susquehanna, where Joseph Smith began translating the Book of Mormon, and where John the Baptist, and Peter, James and John, restored the Aaronic and Melchizedek Priesthoods, respectively, to Joseph Smith and Oliver Cowdery.

Meanwhile, unbeknownst to the Mannings, something was happening on the Internet.

That couple from Texas, Jim and Paula Briggs, posted a video of Esther playing at the Sacred Grove with a message about how grateful they were for a family from Utah that was nice enough to help them find their lost ring.

They called it "Mannings of Mormonville and Our Little Miracle at the Sacred Grove."

Elsewhere, avid social media users had uploaded videos of the Mannings — Esther playing the violin, the boys playing basketball, and the twins just being the twins — on Facebook, Twitter, Instagram, and YouTube. The video of Esther playing with Jasper on Michigan Avenue in Chicago already had accumulated 259,342 views.

A YouTube employee, and member of the Church, who lived in the Bay Area in California, realized that all the videos featured the same family, though he didn't know the Mannings.

So, on his own, and on their behalf, and without their permission, he seized the opportunity and created a YouTube channel titled "Mannings of Mormonville" where he aggregated all of the videos. He advertised the "Mannings of Mormonville" channel on

Facebook, and, suddenly, people from all over the world were watching, and following, the Mannings' trip around the country.

The best part about it was, the Mannings didn't have a clue. They were blithely unaware of the stir they were creating.

While the Mannings were getting ready for bed in their RV at a Walmart parking lot, Luke received a text message from Ben.

"You guys are turning into quite the celebrities," he wrote.

"What do you mean?" Luke texted back.

"All of your videos. My Facebook timeline is filled with them. Everyone is watching you guys. Especially Esther. She's a superstar!"

"Facebook? What videos? Superstar?"

"You mean you don't know? Someone created a YouTube channel, and a Facebook page, called 'Mannings of Mormonville.' Tell Brian that without even realizing it, he's probably already completed his Eagle Scout Service Project."

Luke didn't know how to break this unexpected news to Hayley, who had been so adamant about not putting anything, not even photos, on Facebook about their trip. She wanted any service rendered, and experiences had, to be kept within the family.

But it was too late.

Hayley was mortified to learn of her family's high-profile presence on social media.

"I swear I had nothing to do with this," Luke said.

Mannings of Mormonville had become an overnight sensation. They had a large and loyal following.

Hayley cringed when she saw her family all over the Internet, something she desperately wanted to avoid.

"Now everyone knows we're out of town," Hayley said. She texted her dad to keep a close eye on the house while they were gone.

Hayley did feel a little better when she saw a news report that a Chicago restaurant owner had seen the video of Jasper and Esther. He offered Jasper a job playing his harmonica for patrons.

But overall, she was not happy about it.

"Are our children being exploited — especially Esther?" Hayley asked.

"No, I don't think so," Luke answered. "I'm looking at it as missionary work."

"How could people just post videos of us like that, without asking us?"

"Hayley," Luke said, "we've been asked by Church leaders to use the Internet to share our testimonies and spread the gospel. Looks like that's happening. We've been praying for missionary experiences, for opportunities to share the gospel, right?"

"Yeah, I guess you're right. We have had a lot of missionary experiences so far."

"I think the lesson to be learned here," Luke said, "is be careful what you pray for."

CHAPTER 25

BEFORE HEADING TO BOSTON, Massachusetts, the Mannings took a couple of detours, first passing through Glens Falls, New York, a quaint town located in the foothills of the Adirondack Mountains.

Hayley Googled Glens Falls and discovered its crime rate was significantly lower than Akron's, so she relented.

The reason for that stop? Brian and Benjamin requested it. Begged for it, actually. Glens Falls is the hometown of BYU legend Jimmer Fredette, whom Brian and Benjamin idolized and tried to imitate on the basketball court. They always picked number 32 when they played for their Junior Jazz teams.

Upon arriving, Hayley took photos of the boys, holding their basketballs, in front of Glens Falls High School, where Jimmer launched his hoops career.

Then the Mannings trekked northeast to Sharon, Vermont, the birthplace of Joseph Smith.

"Dad," Brian said as he looked out the window on the Vermont highway and noticed the abundance of greenery and trees everywhere, "Utah really is a desert. Now I know what you mean."

In Sharon, the Mannings dropped in on the Visitors' Center and took pictures in front of the Joseph Birthplace Memorial, a granite monument that stands 50 feet, 10 inches.

The obelisk shaft, the Mannings learned, was 38 ½ feet tall, representing one foot for each year of the Prophet's life.

Hours later, tired and sweaty, the Mannings arrived at a Walmart in Springfield, located in western Massachusetts, that night. After a decent night's sleep, they spend a large part of the day at the Basketball Hall of Fame in Springfield. They learned about how basketball was invented there with peach baskets, and they paid homage to all of the greatest basketball players and coaches of all time, including Kresimir Cosic.

"Cosic was from the former Yugoslavia who was an All-American at BYU in the early 1970s," Luke told the kids. "He was a forerunner to Jimmer Fredette at BYU, though the two played much differently. I'll show you Cosic's highlights on YouTube sometime. He was 6-foot-11, but he played like a point guard. He was graceful and he was an excellent passer. He was decades ahead of his time."

"You can be an All-American even though you're from a foreign country?" Brian asked.

"Yes," Luke said. "Even more interesting, Cosic converted to the Church while he was at BYU. He won a gold medal for Yugoslavia as a player and a silver medal for Yugoslavia as a coach. But do you know what his greatest contribution is?"

"What?" Brian asked.

"He translated the Book of Mormon and Doctrine and Covenants into Croatian," Luke said. "He was a Church leader in post-communist Croatia before he died in 1995 of cancer. He was serving as the deputy ambassador of Croatia to the United States at the time of his death."

Luke also told the kids it was no coincidence that the birthplace of the Church, Baseball, and Basketball were all in relatively close proximity to each other.

Before leaving Springfield, the Mannings ate at a Friendly's restaurant, a New England fixture that's become a popular chain on the East Coast. The kids were excited to get a break from Cup-o-Noodles and soda crackers.

Luke had noticed a sign on the entrance of the restaurant, "Kids eat for just $1.99 on Thursdays!" That prompted him to stop there.

Unfortunately for the Mannings, it was Wednesday.

"Wow!" the waitress said. "Seven kids! I love big families! I'm sorry you missed our special by one day."

Feeling badly about the Mannings' ill-timed visit, the waitress talked to her manager, who decided to give the kids free ice cream.

"They really live up to their name here," Brian said, inhaling a spoonful of chocolate sundae. "They *are* friendly at Friendly's."

When Luke saw the bill the waitress left at the table, he noticed she forgot to charge for his meal and for Hayley's. He pointed it out to her.

"This might be the first time I had a customer correct me for *under*charging them," the waitress said. "Thanks for your honesty."

"Thanks for taking good care of us," Hayley said, apologizing for the mess Ashley made when she accidentally spilled Esther's full cup of water all over the table.

Along with a semi-generous tip, Luke also left the waitress a copy of the Book of Mormon with the family's testimony written inside.

From Friendly's, the Mannings made the 90-minute drive to Boston, the city where Ezekiel Manning and his parents landed when they arrived in the United States from England. Luke had Hayley read excerpts about that to his family from Ezekiel's journal, but after a while the younger kids were groaning with boredom, saying they wanted to watch a movie instead.

The next morning, the plan was to walk Boston's famous Freedom Trail, a 2.5-mile, redlined route that guides visitors to 16 sites steeped in Revolutionary War history.

When Luke told the kids about the upcoming hike, they were less-than-thrilled.

"That's a long way to walk," Esther said.

"We can make it," Luke said. "I'll have Sarah on my back and I can push the twins in the stroller. You'll love it. It's like taking a stroll through American history."

Finding a place to park the giant RV in downtown Boston proved to be a challenge. At one point, Luke got the vehicle stuck in the middle of an intersection as the light turned red. A group of cars started honking. Pedestrians, trying to get around the RV as they crossed the street, angrily pounded the RV with their fists.

"Get out of the road," they said, but using more, um, colorful language. "Go back to Utah!"

Once Luke parked the beast, the Mannings made their way to Boston Common and started the Freedom Trail.

"Why do they call it a 'Common?'" Benjamin asked. "It's just a park isn't it?"

"'Common' just sounds much cooler," Luke said. "It's the oldest city park in the United States. It started out as a cow pasture and it was used as a camp by the British military prior to the Revolutionary War."

"I'm impressed that you know that," Hayley said.

"Just read it on Wikipedia this morning," Luke admitted.

"When we get home," Benjamin said, "I'm going to talk to the mayor about changing the name of 'Helaman Park' to 'Helaman Common.'"

As the Mannings embarked on the Freedom Trail, Hayley noticed a woman in the distance staring at her and her brood. People staring at the Mannings was nothing unusual, of course. People would frequently ask during this cross-country journey if they were part of some sort of school field trip.

But this was different.

When Hayley made eye contact with the woman, the woman would smile. She noticed the woman had two young children. She thought about striking up a conversation but she was more concerned about keeping an eye on all seven of her kids.

Even in crowded Faneuil Hall, a marketplace that has been around since 1742, the woman didn't stray too far from the Mannings.

Meanwhile, Luke enjoyed haggling with, and chatting with, street vendors that tried to sell him Revolutionary War books, T-shirts, Red Sox paraphernalia, and other memorabilia.

Because it was so hot, Luke ended up buying everyone but Sarah a "bottled watt-ah" for two dollars each. He knew it was highway robbery to charge that much for water, but it was an awfully humid summer's day and everyone was thirsty and getting dehydrated.

As the Mannings walked toward Paul Revere's house, Hayley noticed the same woman behind them.

"Don't look now," Hayley said, "but I think we're being followed."

"Who would be following us?" Luke asked. "The Mormon Mafia? Maybe Danny Ainge?"

"Danny Ainge, the former BYU player?" Brian asked.

"Yeah, you know who he is, don't you?" Luke said. "Danny Ainge is the author of the most famous basketball play in BYU history, when he beat Notre Dame in the NCAA Tournament with his coast-to-coast layup. He got BYU to the Elite Eight for the first, and only, time. He was another forerunner to Jimmer. Now he's the general manager and President of Basketball Operations for the Boston Celtics. Being a New York Knicks fan, I didn't really like him when he played with the Celtics. But I've always respected him for being the first man in recorded history bitten by a Tree."

"He was bitten by a tree?" Brian asked.

"Yeah. Wayne 'Tree' Rollins of the Atlanta Hawks bit Ainge on his finger during a playoff game in 1983."

"Well, if you see Danny Ainge, let me know," Brian said. "Maybe he'll give me a tryout with the Celtics."

"Luke, I'm serious," Hayley said, interrupting the basketball conversation. "There's a woman back there who has been watching us for the past half-hour. Everywhere we go, they go."

"Well, this is part of the route tourists like us take. It's the Freedom Trail. We're all following the same path. Aren't you being a little paranoid?"

"But it's like she is watching us. Like she wants something from us."

"Do you know her?"

"No."

"Maybe she's seen our YouTube channel," Luke joked.

The kids complained about the heat, about being tired, about their legs hurting.

Undeterred, Luke couldn't wait to show the kids the Old North Church.

"This is the oldest standing church building in Boston and it's a National Historic Landmark," he told the kids as they walked. "It's where the 'one if by land, two if by sea' signal was sent from before Paul Revere's midnight ride. Paul Revere told three patriots to hang two lanterns in the steeple. One lantern let Charleston know that the British Army was going to march there, and two let them know they would be crossing the Charles River by boat. That was just before the Battles of Lexington and Concord, before the Revolutionary War officially started."

While Luke was caught up in the excitement of it all, the kids were underwhelmed. They were trying to comprehend a form of communication that didn't involve a smartphone or a computer.

After touring the Old North Church, the Mannings decided to pose for a photo beside the giant statue of Paul Revere on his horse. The woman that Hayley believed had been following them since Boston Common approached her and volunteered to take a picture of the family.

"That's very nice of you, thanks," Hayley said.

The woman, who spoke with a heavy German accent, took a variety of photos, patiently waiting until everyone was smiling, and looking at the camera.

In other words, it took a while.

"You have a beautiful family," the woman told Hayley when she was done. "Do they all belong to you?"

"Thank you," Hayley said, "and yes, they belong to me, forever."

Hayley surprised herself by adding the word "forever," and judging by the woman's reaction, Hayley hoped she didn't interpret that as a complaint.

"Forever?" the woman asked. "What do you mean?"

"Um, it just means that we believe in families being together forever. We are members of The Church of Jesus Christ of Latter-day Saints. Where are you from?"

"We are visiting from Germany," the woman said. "I've been watching you for a while. I've noticed something that's different about your family. I don't know what it is. I feel like there's something missing from my life. I wanted to ask you about it. You have something that I don't."

Hayley immediately felt the pressure of an unexpected missionary moment. It was the perfect setup and Hayley didn't want to say the wrong thing. Hayley introduced herself and asked the woman her name.

"Katarina," she said.

Hayley dug into her bag and pulled out a copy of the Book of Mormon that had her testimony written inside. She added her e-mail address. Hayley shared a brief synopsis of the book and why the woman should read it.

"It looks like you're a mom, too," Hayley added.

"Yes," she said, smiling. "My husband doesn't believe in organized religion. I have heard of the Mormons but I don't know anything about them. I would like to know more."

"I recommend you reading this book and then looking up The Church of Jesus Christ of Latter-day Saints when you return home. We've got churches, and missionaries, there who can teach you more."

"Where are you from?" Katarina asked.

"Utah."

"I've never heard of it," Katarina said. "But I'm going to do research on it. There's something special about you and your family."

"That's very kind of you to say. But full disclosure — we have our struggles, like anyone else," Hayley said. "We had to bribe the kids with ice cream to finish the Freedom Trail."

"Yes, but I sense you know the secret about raising a happy family."

"Well, the answers you're looking for are in that book I gave you."

"Thank you," Katarina said, giving Hayley a kiss on the cheek. "I will read it."

With that, Katarina returned to her husband and children who were waiting under a tree.

As the Mannings continued along the Freedom Trail in the broiling heat, Hayley was glad for the chance to share the gospel and give out a copy of the Book of Mormon. But it wasn't until later that she thought about other things she should have said to Katarina. She regretted not writing down the woman's e-mail address and getting her physical address to send to the missionaries in Germany. She wished she had done more.

The Mannings continued on to the USS Constitution battleship, and then on to Bunker Hill. Luke and the older kids climbed all 294 steps to the pinnacle of Bunker Hill Monument, which offers a breathtaking view of Boston. Jacob counted all 294 steps.

"This is where the Battle of Bunker Hill took place," Luke said. "It was the first major battle of the Revolutionary War. This is where that famous phrase, 'don't fire until you see the whites of their eyes' came from. This battle showed that the colonists could fight effectively against the mighty British Army. Let me put it in a way that you can understand it. The Americans were huge underdogs in this war. It was kind of like our family taking on Duke or Kentucky in a basketball game. Like a No. 16 seed taking on a No. 1 seed in the NCAA Tournament. Any questions?"

"Dad," Jacob said, his faced flushed, "my legs feel like Jell-O.

How much longer is this going to take?"

"Until we're done," Luke replied.

While Luke and the older kids went to the top of Bunker Hill, Hayley remained on the Freedom Trail, searching for Katarina. There was so much she wanted to tell her. But Hayley couldn't find her.

Ashley and Lindsay were bored and started singing their favorite Primary song, "Jesus Wants Me For A Sunbeam."

When they'd get to the chorus, Lindsay would sing, "A Sun…" and Ashley would follow with, "Beam!" as loud as she could. Someone started recording it on his phone and uploaded it to his Instagram account.

The Mannings walked to Boston Harbor and Luke explained all about the Sons of Liberty and the Boston Tea Party.

"They dumped an entire shipment of tea into the harbor in defiance of the Tea Act," Luke said.

"Well, that's a good thing," Benjamin said. "They shouldn't have been drinking tea."

"That's true," Hayley said with a laugh.

By the time the Mannings made it back to the RV, they were soaked in sweat and exhausted. Luke surprised everyone with the news that they were going to attend a Boston Red Sox game that night. The Sox were playing the Baltimore Orioles at historic Fenway Park. He had purchased tickets on Stub Hub for a decent price.

Brian, Benjamin and Jacob were the most excited about going to Fenway. Luke told the family all about the Green Monster, and Pesky's Pole, and he shared stories about famous moments that had taken place there, like Carlton Fisk waving a home run fair in the 1975 World Series; the Yankees' Bucky Dent breaking the hearts of Red Sox Nation in a 1978 playoff game; and a walk-off home run by David Ortiz to begin Boston's historic comeback in the 2004 American League Championship Series against the Yankees.

"Can we get a hot dog there?" Benjamin asked.

"Sure," Luke said.

When the game ended with the Red Sox coming from behind to beat the Orioles in the ninth inning, Luke claimed a victory too, as Brian told him, "Dad, I really liked baseball before. But I love it now. It's a lot better being here than watching it on TV."

Luke grinned and nodded his head. "We sure are converting a lot of people on this trip," he said to Hayley.

On their final day in Boston, the Mannings visited the Old North Bridge and other Revolutionary War sites in Lexington and Concord. The older kids showed mild interest as Luke told them everything he knew about the Revolutionary War.

"Are the Old North Church and the Old North Bridge related?" Benjamin asked.

"Of course. They're twins," Luke joked.

For the first time, Ashley's and Lindsay's ears perked up while he offered a history lesson.

Luke sensed the kids were getting a history overload, or overdose, so he stopped lecturing after a while.

Mostly, Luke couldn't wait to take his family to New York City, his former home. The Mannings were planning to stay there for several days. But Hayley was less enthusiastic. She kept telling Luke how worried she was about taking the kids to New York City.

"Isn't it dangerous?" she asked.

"Used to be. In the 1980s and early '90s, before Mayor Rudy Giuliani, it was like total anarchy. Murders all the time. But Giuliani cleaned it up pretty well. New York is very protective of its tourism industry. We'll be fine. Trust me."

"You weren't fine when that guy tried to rob you on the subway a few months ago," Hayley whispered to him.

"Just an aberration," Luke said.

Changing the subject, Luke asked the kids, "What's your favorite part of the trip so far? This isn't a rhetorical question."

"The Sacred Grove," Esther said, "and Carthage Jail."

"Nauvoo," Brian said.

"When we ate ice cream at that restaurant," Jacob said.

"Friendly's?" Hayley asked.

"Yeah," Jacob said. "That was the best."

As the motor home sped toward the Big Apple, Luke decided to teach his kids a little more about New York City.

"New York City is divided up into five boroughs," Luke explained.

"What are boroughs?" Benjamin said.

"Let me put it in terms that you might understand," Luke said. "If Mormons had settled New York, they'd be called the five 'Stakes' — Brooklyn, Manhattan, The Bronx, Staten Island, and Queens."

"Oh," Brian said. "That makes sense."

While planning for their stay in New York City, Luke had arranged for his family to stay at a hotel to cut down on travel time. He was smart enough to know not to drive an RV — especially with Utah plates — in midtown Manhattan. He could imagine the hubcaps being stolen at a stoplight, and guys on the street corners trying to wash the windows with a squeegee. So Luke arranged to park the motor home at an RV Park located in Jersey City, New Jersey.

While approaching Jersey City, Luke pointed out the Lincoln Tunnel, which goes under the Hudson River and connects New Jersey and New York.

"I bet Abraham Lincoln was the first president named after a tunnel," Benjamin announced.

"Let me tell you something about the Lincoln Tunnel. It costs $15 to go from the New Jersey side to the New York side," Luke said. "That's one reason why we're not driving through the Lincoln Tunnel. It's free to go from the New York side to New Jersey."

"Is that why the New York Giants and New York Jets play their games at the Meadowlands in New Jersey?" Brian asked.

"Could be. But New Jersey's real claim to fame is its most popular export — Bruce Springsteen music."

"Why is New Jersey called the 'Garden State?'" Benjamin asked. "I don't see any gardens here."

Luke considered staying at the Marriott Marquis at Times Square, where he had spent a few nights on his previous visit to New York. But it was way too expensive. Luke thought about contacting Nicholai for a discount but he didn't want to take advantage of him again.

After parking the RV, the Mannings hopped on the New York City subway. It was a production, as Hayley and Luke made sure all of the kids got on safely.

"Dad, what's that smell?" Esther asked while on the subway.

"It's just hot garbage," Luke said. "Very normal. You'll get used to it."

Mostly, Hayley and the kids just sat in their seats, mouth agape, staring at the odd assortment of people on the subway. The New Yorkers mostly ignored them.

"Are we underground?" Esther asked nervously at one point.

"Duh, that's why they call it the subway," Brian said. "It's cool. It's like traveling through a Medieval dungeon."

The subway carried the Mannings to Manhattan, where they checked into a family-friendly Marriott hotel.

"Don't they have infestations of bed bugs in New York City hotels?" Hayley whispered to Luke as they made their way to the elevator.

"Not anymore, as far as we know," Luke said. "I haven't heard about trouble with that in weeks."

The kids were excited to be staying in a hotel room instead of an RV. But they soon realized that the room was small, too, and most of the kids would be sleeping on the floor. That first night, Luke called down to the front desk to ask for a rollaway bed, extra pillows, extra blankets and extra shampoo.

Once the kids got settled that night after taking baths and arranging their pillows and blankets on the floor, Luke opened the drawer next to the queen bed.

"Look, kids," Luke said. "It's a copy of the Book of Mormon."

"Who put that there?" Esther asked.

"The Marriott hotel chain is owned by a member of the Church, Bill Marriott. The Marriott Center at BYU is named after the Marriott family. Bill's dad, J. Willard Marriott, started the company. The Marriotts stock all of the hotel rooms with a copy of the Book of Mormon. Isn't that cool? How about each of us write our testimonies on pieces of paper that we could put inside this Book of Mormon for people to read?"

Then he realized that Benjamin and Jacob were already asleep.

The next morning, the kids were happy to head downstairs for the complimentary, all-you-can-eat breakfast provided every morning. They had been eating mostly granola bars for breakfast for the past couple of weeks.

"Eat enough so that you won't get hungry again until dinnertime," Luke told the kids before going down to the free breakfast.

The Mannings thanked the hotel staff for the variety of food options.

"This is almost like Thanksgiving!" Jacob gushed. "Except without the turkey."

Esther just made one request after taking a helping of breakfast potatoes.

"Do you have any fry sauce?" she asked.

"What's fry sauce?" the woman serving breakfast asked.

"It's a Utah thing," Hayley said. "We can make our own with this ketchup. Do you have any mayonnaise we can use?"

Luke couldn't wait to take the family exploring around New York. But after breakfast, the kids, who had been traveling for two straight weeks, simply wanted to go swimming. They put on their suits and splashed in the pool for hours, releasing some pent-up energy.

By the time they showered, changed, and got ready for the day, it was early afternoon.

"We're wasting time," Luke said. "There's so much to see and do here. We're going out to the streets of Manhattan."

As a primer, Luke explained to the kids that New York City is the largest city in the United States. He told them that "Houston Street" is pronounced "House-ton Street," not like the city in Texas. He also explained that people who live outside Manhattan refer to the borough of Manhattan as "The City."

"If we're going to see 'The City,' we need to get going," Hayley said. "We shouldn't be out there past dark."

"That's just Central Park," Luke said.

"Well, I had a nightmare last night that we lost one of the kids," Hayley said. "This really makes me nervous."

Baby Sarah was strapped to Luke's back in a child carrier and he pushed the twins in the double stroller.

Hayley assigned Esther to be in charge of watching Benjamin, and Brian to be in charge of watching Jacob.

"You are to stay together at *all* times," Hayley said.

"Who are you in charge of watching?" Benjamin asked.

"Everyone," Hayley said.

Hayley had suggested having everyone wear a shirt of the same color so they could keep track of each other better.

"Wouldn't that make us more of a target for crime?" Brian asked. "It's better that we blend in."

When they were planning their trip, Luke and Hayley toyed with the idea of going to a Broadway show while they were in New York. Luke suggested leaving the kids with Aunt Maureen but Hayley flatly rejected that idea.

"I'm not leaving our kids with a stranger," she said.

"But Maureen's not a stranger. She's family."

Hayley wasn't convinced. "I'd need to meet her first," she said.

By the time they left the hotel, it was mid-afternoon. Luke decided to take his family to Central Park first. On the way, the kids asked good questions and made some astute observations as they walked.

"Where are all the apples?" Benjamin said.

"Apples?" Luke asked.

"I thought there would be apples everywhere here. Isn't New York called the 'The Big Apple?'"

"Yeah, you're right. But it's just a figurative name. It means the biggest of something. It really has nothing to do with fruit, although there was a time when New York City was known as 'New Orange.' In the 1600s, the Dutch took over New York from England and named it after William III of Orange."

"Dad, speaking of orange, why do people spray paint on all these buildings?" Jacob asked.

"There are a lot of aspiring artists, aspiring actors and aspiring gang members here," Luke explained.

"That's just graffiti," Esther said.

"What's graffiti?" Jacob asked.

"It's pedestrian art," Benjamin said.

The boys drooled when they passed the colorful food trucks parked on the city streets that emitted the smells of exotic cuisine. Brian was intrigued by the Korilla BBQ truck, which featured alluring tiger stripes.

"What kind of food is that?" he asked.

"It's a cross between Korean food and Mexican food," Luke said.

"What is Korean food?" Brian asked.

"Well, they eat a lot of Kimchi."

"What's that?"

"They take cabbage and bury it in the ground for a few months. Then they eat it. Want to try some?"

"No way, that's disgusting!" Brian said. "That sounds worse than school lunch."

"Dad, why do we always hear sirens here?" Jacob asked. "And why are there so many taxis?"

"Why do so many people have tattoos?" Benjamin asked.

"Why are so many people smoking? And swearing? And why do they have earrings in their noses?" Jacob asked.

"People make choices," Hayley said, trying to shield the kids' eyes. "It may not be ones we agree with but we respect their choices. We respect all people."

At Central Park, the kids climbed on the rocks, splashed in the fountains, played on the playgrounds, walked across bridges, ran across the Great Lawn, dodging irritated sunbathers, and took a ride on the Carousel.

"It's weird having a park like this in the middle of a city," Brian said.

"Yeah," Luke said. "It's a botanical jungle smack dab in the middle of an urban jungle. When I lived in the City, I used to attend free concerts here. Hundreds of thousands of people show up. It can get pretty crazy. The acoustics are pretty good."

Noticing it was almost dinnertime, Hayley decided it was time to go. The Mannings headed to the renowned theater district. On the way, they passed Carnegie Hall.

"I want to play here someday," Esther said. "I'm going to wait until I get really good on the violin before I perform in front of really big crowds."

"When you play Carnegie Hall," Luke said, "I'll be there."

The kids noticed advertisements on the New York City cabs for *The Book of Mormon* musical. It wasn't something they had expected to see in a busy, dirty, noisy city that their grandfather, Grit, had told them should be re-named "Babylon."

In the distance, near Times Square, a huge sign at the Eugene O'Neal Theatre heralded *The Book of Mormon* musical.

"Wow, the Book of Mormon is really popular in New York," Brian said. "We've only been here a little while and we've already seen it in the hotel room, on these taxis, and now on all these signs."

"That Book of Mormon reference is actually a sign for a Broadway musical," Luke said.

"Can we see it?" Esther asked. "It says, 'The Best Musical of This Century.'"

"Well," Luke said, "from what I heard, you wouldn't like it. It's nothing like the book. We'll just stick with the book. From what I understand, the musical has nothing to do with the actual Book of Mormon, just like 'Oklahoma' has nothing to do with the actual Oklahoma Sooners football team."

"But it has a picture of a missionary jumping," Esther said. "Is it about missionaries?"

"Not exactly," Hayley said. "It's not about real missionaries. That show actually mocks our beliefs, from what I've read. People who see the show don't find out what we truly believe in, unfortunately."

"The sign also says it has won nine Tony Awards," Esther said.

"Who's Tony?" Jacob asked.

"In New York, every other guy is named Tony," Luke said.

As they got closer to the theater, the Mannings noticed a long line of people waiting to watch the show.

After they walked by, Esther grabbed Hayley's hand.

"Can we show them what we really believe?" she asked. "Please? This is a perfect place to do missionary work. We're always praying for missionary experiences, and this could be a great one."

"Well, this is certainly a captive audience," Hayley said. "But how could we do that here? You didn't bring your violin."

"I was thinking we could sing Primary songs," Esther said. "Don't you think this is what Heavenly Father would want us to do? You're always telling us to be a light to the world and stand up for our beliefs."

"You're right," Hayley said. "I say we do it."

"Even for New York, this seems a little crazy," Luke said. "At least you can tell people when we get home that you performed on Broadway."

So the Manning kids lined up on the sidewalk near the Eugene O'Neill Theatre, next to the people waiting to get inside. Hayley used the skills she had honed over many years as a Primary chorister and started leading them in "Book of Mormon Stories." They did the hand motions, too, even the twins.

The crowd of onlookers was mostly staring at their phones at first. They were a little annoyed. Then they became curious.

"What cute kids," a woman in line asked Luke. "Are they part of the show?"

"No," Luke said, "but they should be. I hear they are actual Mormons. Can you believe that? They'll be available for autographs afterward."

"I hear this musical is really good," the woman said.

Luke repeated the official statement by the Church about the musical that he had memorized on his previous trip to New York for such an occasion.

"This production may attempt to entertain audiences for an evening," he said, "but the Book of Mormon as a volume of scripture will change people's lives forever by bringing them closer to Christ."

The woman looked at Luke strangely.

Then the Manning kids started singing "I Am A Child of God."

As they did so, one of the world's largest cities seemed to fall silent, as if the sound of traffic had stopped — at least it seemed that way to Luke. As Hayley led the kids, she was proud of them. They were all singing and enunciating every word so that the people could understand them.

Goosebumps covered Luke's arm as he listened to his kids sing in his former hometown.

He noticed that the crowd was transfixed, as if it were Josh Groban or Luciano Pavarotti or the Van Trapp family performing. The people applauded enthusiastically when the Mannings finished. A few of the people waiting in line had captured the Mannings' performance on their smartphones and uploaded it on Facebook and YouTube the next morning.

Luke overheard one woman ask a man standing next to her, presumably her husband, "What exactly does that mean, 'I am a child of God?'"

Luke knew that Broadway wouldn't be able to supply an answer to that simple but profound question.

CHAPTER 26

AFTER ONLY 24 HOURS, Hayley had already experienced her fill of New York City. The following day, she reluctantly agreed to take the family to neon-lit Times Square. Luke suggested going there at night, when it was all lit up but she quashed that idea immediately.

"You're lucky we're going at all," she said.

Luke insisted that it was part of the New York City experience. She relented, as long as it wasn't at night.

So the Mannings were about to brave Times Square in broad daylight.

Hayley had served her mission in the New York Rochester Mission, but she had never been to New York City, let alone Times Square. She knew missionaries who served in the various New York City missions weren't allowed to go there. So she didn't see the point of taking her family there.

The whole idea made her nervous based on what she had heard about Times Square — mostly from her own husband.

"Some people consider Times Square the capital of the world, the center of the universe, the crossroads of humanity," Luke told his family before breakfast. "It's the busiest place in New York City, which is saying something. About 320,000 people pass through here every day, and almost every language and nationality imaginable can be discovered there. It's home to the world's biggest New Year's Eve Party, with the famous ball that drops at midnight on December 31st every year. One million watch here and billions more watch on TV."

Luke felt a little anxious, playing the part of a tourist with his family, in a city he had lived in and knew so well.

The kids surveyed the scene in front of them at Times Square, attempting to process what they were seeing and experiencing.

"This is a place where you can smell colors and taste sounds," Luke joked.

"Dad, that makes no sense," Esther said, "and neither does this place."

"Can you feel the adrenalin rush of being here?" Luke asked.

"Dad," Brian said, "I feel like I'm in a video game. Or a foreign country. Does anyone here speak English?"

The Mannings stood out at most places, but not necessarily at Times Square, where practically everything is an anomaly.

Hayley kept counting the kids, making sure they were all accounted for.

While they stood at a street corner, Luke surveyed the scene around them, including some random bystanders and construction workers milling around the street, waiting to cross.

"Kids, I'd like to introduce you to 'The Village People,'" Luke joked.

Hayley rolled her eyes.

"Who?" Brian asked.

"Never mind," Hayley said.

One of their first stops was at the Marriott Marquis.

"Hey," Luke said, "how would you like to go on a scary ride?"

"Yeah!" the older boys shouted.

"What are you talking about?" Hayley asked.

Luke led them into the Marriott Marquis atrium, and to the famous elevator and pushed floor 45.

Once inside the car, Luke said, "This is the closest we're coming to an amusement park on this trip."

As the elevator went airborne, the boys squealed with delight.

"My stomach feels like it's in my mouth!" Jacob said.

"My ears are popping!" Benjamin said.

Hayley gripped Luke's arm. The twins turned a shade of light green and threw up all over their stroller. Little Sarah simply looked terrified, and then she started crying.

While Hayley took the twins back down to a bathroom to clean up, Luke folded some paper airplanes and let the kids throw them from the top floor, 45 stories high. They watched the planes glide and flutter down several stories before colliding with the balcony on the opposite side of the hotel.

"This place is so big," Jacob said. "Can we play hide-and-seek, dad?"

"No," Luke said. "We'd never find you."

They rode back down to the eighth floor lobby, where they met Hayley.

Nicholai spotted Luke immediately.

"Mr. Manning! Luke! Welcome back!" he said, giving him a quick embrace. "How is my favorite Marriott guest?"

"Does dad know this guy?" Esther asked Hayley.

"Apparently."

"Thanks for sending me the John Stockton jersey," Nicholai said. "I love it. I'd wear it every day to work if they'd let me."

Luke introduced his family and Nicholai to each other.

"Are you staying with us?" Nicholai asked.

"No. We're staying at another Marriott property here in Manhattan."

Nicholai looked disappointed.

"Remember, you've still got an open invitation to visit us in Utah to watch a Jazz game and a Mormon Tabernacle Choir performance," Luke told him before they left the hotel.

"Someday," Nicholai said.

The Mannings stepped back into the heart of Times Square. Hayley and the kids couldn't believe what they were seeing — the streets teeming with concourses of people; a three-legged dog; a street performer juggling bright orange bowling pins; a singing cowboy wearing nothing but a guitar and underwear ("No, Esther, you're not playing with *him*," Luke said); a slovenly, crazy-eyed, middle-aged hippie carrying a sign declaring: "Repent! The End is Near!"

The kids gawked at the giant video screens above flashing and flickering a variety of images that had Hayley scrambling to try to cover the kids' — and Luke's — eyes.

"Look away," Hayley would say. "No, not that way. Never mind. Just close your eyes."

To Hayley, Times Square made the Las Vegas Strip seem like a ward Christmas party.

"Remember that sweet, peaceful feeling we had at the Sacred Grove?" Hayley said to the kids. "I want you to compare that to the feeling here."

"There's opposition in all things," Luke said.

Meanwhile, the kids were making more keen observations.

"Dad, some of these people don't dress very modest," Jacob said.

"Dad, there are a lot of creepy people here," Esther said.

"Isn't it great?" Luke replied. "Don't you just love the diversity of this place?"

"Luke, we need to leave," Hayley said.

"There are more taxis than regular cars here," Brian said. "Look out into the street. Almost every car is yellow."

"I never had a car when I lived here," Luke said. "You can see why. Parking and traffic are ridiculous. It costs at least $90 just to park your car anywhere for an hour. If you had a car in this city, you'd spend all of your time idling in traffic, getting honked at, looking for a place to park, and paying for parking. Honking is just the way New Yorkers talk to each other. When they honk at you, it's their way of saying hello. Or telling you where to go."

The Mannings stopped to watch some performers singing and dancing to Michael Jackson songs.

A woman turned to Luke and Hayley. "Are you all here to perform?" she asked.

"You missed our performance yesterday at the O'Neill Theatre," Luke said with a smile.

While Hayley talked to the woman, she occasionally reminded Luke to make sure all of the kids were accounted for. Hayley ended up giving the woman a copy of the Book of Mormon and shared a message about the importance of families.

When Hayley finished, she turned around, counted only six kids and wanted to scream.

"Luke!" she said frantically, "where's Jacob?"

Luke had been so engrossed in the rendition of "Smooth Criminal," he hadn't noticed that Jacob had disappeared. Luke's head spun around as if on a swivel, and he started to panic. All he saw was a sea of people, and his eight-year-old son was nowhere to be seen.

Hayley began to hyperventilate. This was her worst-case scenario coming to fruition.

"Luke, why weren't you watching him?" Hayley said. "Brian, you were supposed to stay together at all times. Where did Jacob go?"

"I don't know, mom," Brian said. "I'm sorry. I thought he was right here."

"Hayley, you and the kids go into that McDonald's over there and wait for me," Luke said.

"What are you going to do?" Hayley asked.

"I'm going to the Police Station here to get help."

One of Hayley's main goals for this trip was to avoid making the news for any reason, especially for something like this.

"Mom, why don't we say a prayer?" Esther said.

So Hayley hurried with the kids inside the Times Square McDonald's. This wasn't like any McDonald's that the Mannings had ever seen before.

"Wow," Benjamin said, "a McDonald's with an upstairs."

They scrambled up the stairs and found an empty table, where they offered a quiet prayer.

Brian begged his mom to help Luke find Jacob, since he felt responsible for losing Jacob. Hayley acquiesced.

"Please don't lose him, too," Hayley said to Luke.

"Benjamin, you and Esther help mom watch the kids," Luke said.

"I will," Benjamin said.

Luke and Brian hustled to The Times Square police station and filled out a missing persons report.

While Luke was trembling, the officer, Sergeant Willie McBride, acted like it was no big deal.

"Kids get lost here all the time," he said.

"Do you always find them?"

"Yeah," Sergeant McBride said, "most of the time."

That wasn't exactly comforting.

The police made a copy of a photo of Jacob from Luke's smartphone and sent it to all of the police officers in the vicinity so they could begin searching. Sergeant McBride couldn't have been nicer but he wasn't acting with any sense of urgency.

"What kind of shirt is he wearing?" Sergeant McBride asked.

"It's blue and says, 'Helaman Elementary' on it," Luke said. "He's a curious kid. Very adventurous."

"Don't worry sir," Sergeant McBride said. "He couldn't have gone too far in this short amount of time. Stay close. We've got dozens of New York's Finest on the case. If we track him down, I'll call you."

"If?"

"I mean *when*, sir."

Truth was, Luke was more worried about Hayley than about Jacob. She hadn't felt good about going to Times Square, and now this was happening. He knew he would never hear the end of this. It would be his fault that one of their kids got lost in New York City.

Luke and Brian combed the area where they last saw Jacob. Luke called Hayley and told her the police were on top of the situation. But she was inconsolable.

"I can't believe we lost him," she said. "I had a dream about this. I had a feeling we shouldn't have come here. There are people here from all over the world. He could be kidnapped. Someone could take him and leave the country. Remember that movie, 'Taken?' He could be somewhere in the Middle East by tomorrow."

Hayley started crying.

"Hayley, let's not jump to conclusions. There are New York police officers all over Times Square looking for him. I'll get the mounted police involved if we have to. You know how Jacob is. He likes to explore. We'll find him."

"I know the Lord will help us. But I just can't sit here," she said. "I've got to look for him."

"Brian and I are looking for him and so are the police. The best thing you can do is keep the kids together and stay calm. I'm scouring the streets for anyone four-feet tall. I thought I saw Danny DeVito."

"This is no time for jokes," Hayley said.

Inside the McDonald's, Benjamin entertained the twins and bought them ice cream cones. Esther changed Sarah's diaper.

"Text me every few minutes and give me an update," Hayley said.

"I will," Luke said.

Luke and Brian continued weaving in and out of people on the crowded streets. They went to a toy store, thinking Jacob might have been drawn in by the window displays. They went to a Yankees apparel shop. They entered the Disney Store. They stepped into the Bubba Gump Shrimp Company.

No sign of Jacob.

Luke passed the Marriott Marquis again.

"Maybe he went back to ride the elevators," Brian said.

They entered the hotel and went to the front desk.

"Nicholai," Luke said, "have you seen my son? The eight-year-old? He's wearing a blue shirt…"

"No, I'm sorry, Luke," Nicholai said. "I'll notify hotel security and I'll help you look."

"Are you sure?"

"I'm scheduled to go on break right now. Let's go. Have you talked to the police?"

"Yes," Luke said.

"Where did you last see him?"

"Not far from here. We were watching some performers, then he just disappeared."

"I'll go this way toward West 42nd," Nicholai said. "You go toward West 48th."

"His name is Jacob," Luke said, showing him a photo. "Text me if you find him."

As Luke and Brian walked briskly toward West 48th, passing an army of people as they went, Luke wiped the sweat off his brow. He offered one long, continual silent prayer that they would be able to find Jacob. Luke didn't want the trip marred by anything like this.

Suddenly, in his mind's eye, he saw Jacob. He stopped and turned to Brian.

"I think I know where he is."

"Where?" Brian asked.

"Just keep up with me."

They cruised past the Ed Sullivan Theater, then onto Eighth Avenue. Luke was hoping all the while that he was being inspired by something more powerful than wishful thinking.

They walked with determined steps past Broadway Theatre, past a Dunkin' Donuts, all the way to Columbus Circle and the entrance of Central Park.

"Where are we going?" Brian asked. "He's probably at the park, climbing on the rocks or playing on a playground."

"That's good thinking," Luke said. "But I'm thinking he's somewhere else. We're getting close."

They continued past Century Theatre, Fieldston School, and Saucier Jewelry. They took a left on West 66th Street, going past the ABC News Research Center and Café 47, and the American Folk Art Museum.

Then Luke looked up into the sunny sky. "There it is!" he said.

"What?" Brian asked.

"Up there. Do you notice anything familiar about that building?"

Brian stared in amazement. "The Angel Moroni? What is *he* doing *here*?"

"It's the temple," Luke said, looking down toward the entrance, where he saw, just as he did in his mind, Jacob standing by the front doors of the Manhattan New York Temple, nonchalantly playing with his yo-yo.

Luke called Hayley to put her at ease. She began crying again.

"He's in front of the temple," Luke said.

"Don't let him out of your sight. Stay there," Hayley said. "We'll catch a cab and we'll meet you there."

After waiting for what seemed like an eternity to cross the busy street, Luke scooped Jacob up in his arms, and bear-hugged him.

"Dad! Brian!" Jacob exclaimed. "I found a temple!"

"How did you get here?" Luke asked.

"I walked."

"We've been looking all over for you."

"I took out a dollar bill from my pocket and it fell on the ground," Jacob explained. "Then the wind started blowing it. I chased it. Then I couldn't see you or mom or the rest of the family. I just started walking. I guess I went the wrong way."

"Jacob, haven't we taught you to stay where you are when you're lost?"

"Yeah, but you also told me to run away from strangers. A big, scary guy with a tattoo on his face was walking behind me. So I started to run away."

"You crossed the busy streets by yourself?"

"No. I wasn't by myself. There was a bunch of other people crossing the streets, too. I just kept walking. I said a prayer in my mind and something told me to look up. Then I saw the Angel Moroni up there. I felt safe here. I knew you'd find me."

Luke called Sergeant McBride.

"Told you we'd find him," the officer said. "Maybe get a leash for that one."

"Thanks, sergeant," Luke said.

Then he called Nicholai and gave him the good news and thanked him for his help.

"Where did you find him?" Nicholai asked.

"At the Mormon Temple."

"Where's that?"

"It's the building near Columbus Circle with the gold statue of a man playing a trumpet on top."

"That's a Mormon temple? I didn't know that. I thought that building was some sort of a tribute to famous trumpet players like Louis Armstrong, Miles Davis and Herb Alpert."

"The guy's name on top of the temple is Moroni."

"Is he a jazz trumpeter?"

"No, he's an ancient prophet who lived in the Americas hundreds of years ago. He symbolizes the spreading of the gospel and the Second Coming of Jesus Christ."

"And he plays the trumpet, too?"

"Apparently."

"That Utah Jazz nickname is really starting to make more and more sense to me," Nicholai said. "I'll never watch a Jazz game, or see a Jazz score again, without thinking of you, and the Mormons."

After getting off the phone with Nicholai, Luke noticed that Jacob seemed oblivious to the panic and commotion he had caused their family.

"This is kind of like the story in the Bible," Brian said.

"What do you mean?" Luke asked.

"Remember when Jesus was a young boy and he got lost and worried his parents? They found him at the temple."

"Good thinking, Brian. Be sure to remind your mom of that story."

Soon, a cab pulled up next to the temple and Hayley and the kids squeezed out like a bunch of little people in a clown car at the circus.

The cabbie wearing a turban asked for an exorbitant amount of money, and Luke paid it without quibbling.

Reunited at the temple, Hayley kissed Jacob's cheeks and almost squeezed the life out of him. She looked up at the Angel Moroni amid the skyscrapers and bustling, raucous New York City streets and decided it was time for a teaching moment.

"Even though I nearly had a nervous breakdown, Jacob taught us an important lesson today," Hayley said. "We've learned that you can stand in holy places, even when you're in a place that's not so holy. The temple is a powerful symbol of our beliefs and what we stand for."

"Jacob, how did you know the New York City Temple would be one of our stops?" Luke asked.

"Inspired, I guess," he said.

After a pause, Hayley announced, "Now, we are going back to the hotel, where it's relatively safe. And I'm locking the door and not letting any of you out."

As the Mannings maneuvered their way back to the hotel, Hayley was constantly counting bodies again, making sure she knew exactly where each of her seven kids were at all times.

Hayley kept worrying about what the kids were hearing and seeing. "Luke, why did we bring our family here, exposing them to all of this?" she asked.

"Like you just told the kids, I'm hoping they will learn that when they're surrounded by anything evil or negative or confusing they will know where to look for peace," Luke said.

That answer satisfied Hayley for the moment. At one point at Times Square, on their way back to the hotel, the Mannings were accosted by men dressed up as Marvel superheroes. Jacob was a big fan of Spiderman, who was more than happy to pose for a picture. Of course, Spiderman wanted a tip afterward. Luke dug into his pocket and gave him a quarter.

"Cheapskate," Spiderman responded.

That night before she fell asleep, Hayley made sure the door was dead-bolted and then she stacked chairs in front of it. She wasn't taking any chances.

CHAPTER 27

BEFORE THE TRIP, LUKE HAD arranged for his family to visit Maureen in Brooklyn.

"Maureen Manning is my aunt, which would make her your great aunt, but, as I learned the hard way when I met her a couple of months ago, don't call her 'aunt,'" Luke explained to the kids.

"What should we call her?" Brian asked. "Sister Manning? Sister Maureen?"

"No," Luke said. "She probably wouldn't like that, either. Just call her Maureen."

Luke advised the kids that Maureen wasn't a member of the Church.

"She's an older woman, she lives alone, and she doesn't like being around large groups of people," he said.

"Then why does she live in New York City?" Jacob asked.

"What I mean is, when we're guests in her home, please be polite and respectful and quiet. Don't fight. Or touch anything. Her house is like a museum. Or more like a mausoleum."

The Mannings took the subway to Brooklyn, got off at their designated stop, and walked the few blocks to Maureen's place.

Maureen seemed genuinely glad to have them in her home. She greeted them warmly, gave everyone a hug, and offered the kids a plate of "coffee cake."

"Mom," Esther whispered to Hayley, "are we allowed to eat coffee cake? Or is it against the Word of Wisdom?"

"It's OK," Hayley whispered back. "There's no coffee in it. It's called that because people drink coffee with it."

"What do you tell Maureen for giving you a snack?" Luke asked.

"Thanks," the kids said in unison.

"How old are you?" Jacob asked Maureen.

"Jacob!" Hayley exclaimed. "Maureen, I'm sorry."

"Somewhere between 40 and death," Maureen replied.

Then the twins started to play with the rotary phone and the lava lamp.

"Ashley! Lindsay!" Hayley exclaimed, picking up the girls in her arms.

"It's OK," Maureen said. "It's nice to have some visitors. It gets quiet around here."

"I didn't think it was ever quiet in New York," Esther said.

"That reminds me," Maureen said. "A man showed up here one night in his firefighter's uniform. I thought there was an emergency so I opened the door and invited him in. He said he had heard that I was related to Jerry Manning and he said he wanted to know more information about him. So I've had Hal and his wife over a few times and it turns out that he's a genealogist, too. He encouraged me to go to Salt Lake City to do more research."

"That's a great idea," Hayley said.

"Hal told me he met you, Luke, when you went to church here. He's a Mormon, too," Maureen said. "I didn't even know there were any blacks who were Mormon. He and his wife took me to a Yankees game a few weeks ago."

To Luke, going to a baseball game was an ideal way of fellowshipping.

When Maureen went into the kitchen, Luke noticed the copy of the Book of Mormon he had given her sitting on the bookshelf. He picked it up and saw pages dog-eared, and passages highlighted, which both surprised and thrilled him.

After Maureen got to know each of the kids, she spent the afternoon sharing stories about the Manning family. She pointed to each picture hanging on the wall and explained who each person was.

"Dad, this is like a family reunion for your side of the family," Esther said quietly to Luke.

"Yep," Luke said. "All that's missing is the potato salad."

Maureen had noticed that Esther was carrying a violin case. Luke, Hayley and Esther perked up when Maureen casually mentioned that one of her cousins was "a talented violin player."

All this time, they had presumed that Esther's musical ability had come exclusively from Hayley's side of the family.

Esther told Maureen that she played the violin, too, and asked more about her cousin.

Maureen asked Esther to play something.

"How about 'Yesterday' by the Beatles?'" Esther suggested. "I've been practicing."

Maureen smiled. "I love the Beatles," she said.

She tapped her toes to the beat and genuinely enjoyed the performance.

"That's one of my favorites," she said. "And that was amazing."

Then Esther played "The Spirit of God Like a Fire Is Burning." Maureen became a little emotional but she didn't know why.

"That was wonderful," Maureen said when Esther finished. "You have real talent."

"Thanks," Esther said.

"Do any of you have any more questions for me?" Maureen asked.

"Why don't you have any children?" Benjamin asked.

"Benjamin!" Hayley said. "That's not an appropriate question."

"That's fine. These kids are like New Yorkers. They say it how it is. To answer your question, I never married. I wish I could have had a family. But it never worked out. I'm just glad you kids will be able to carry on the Manning name. You need to explain to me why you Mormons are so interested in genealogy."

Esther spoke up.

"It's because we believe we are all Heavenly Father's children. We are all brothers and sisters. We want to learn as much as we can about each other and try to help them. I learned in seminary about the Spirit of Elijah. Elijah was a prophet in the Old Testament. The last two verses of the Old Testament say, 'Behold, I will send you Elijah the prophet before the coming of the great and dreadful day of the Lord: And he shall turn the heart of the fathers to the children, and the heart of the children to their fathers, lest I come and smite the earth with a curse.'"

Luke and Hayley were impressed with Esther's gospel knowledge.

"What does that mean?" Maureen asked. "Sometimes I feel smited and cursed. I love reading but I haven't spent much time in the Bible."

"It means that in the Last Days, the Lord would send Elijah to Earth to plant in our hearts the desire to do family history work," Esther said. "If we don't link all of our family members together we won't be able to be together in the next life. We did baptisms in Nauvoo for some of those people you told us about."

"Maureen, you have the Spirit of Elijah like nobody I've ever seen," Hayley said.

"Now you need to get baptized," Jacob said, "so we can live together in heaven."

Luke and Hayley smiled nervously.

Maureen looked nervous, too. "It would probably be easier if you just wait until I'm dead, too," she said with a sigh.

Before leaving, Luke and Hayley presented Maureen with a framed family photo. She proudly hung it up on her Wall of Fame, alongside Ezekiel Manning.

Though it would have normally made her uptight hosting so many people in here home, especially young kids, Maureen felt comfortable with Luke's family. She no longer felt alone in the world.

"We need to get together more often," Maureen said.

"We could get together in Utah," Luke said. "We'd love to have you. We could take you to the Church's genealogical library."

Maureen's eyes began to well up with tears.

"I'm going to miss all of you," she said. "Luke, I didn't think I would get so attached to your kids. If your dad and grandfather could see them, he would be so proud."

"I'm sure your dad's proud of you, too," Luke said.

"I might consider going to Utah someday," Maureen said. "I haven't been on an airplane in decades. I have this horrible fear of flying."

They all hugged Maureen and Luke marveled as he saw this hard-boiled New Yorker melt in their embraces.

"Goodbye, Aunt Maureen," Esther said.

"Esther..." Luke said.

"It's OK," Maureen said. "Aunt Maureen. I kind of like the sound of that. It's growing on me. I think I like being an aunt."

Tears streamed down Maureen's face as she watched Luke and his family walk back to the subway.

The Mannings' New York Experience continued with a stop in Queens — specifically Flushing Meadows.

Luke suggested they take a train there at about the same time the New York Mets were playing the Cincinnati Reds.

Though the Mets were his favorite baseball team, Luke wasn't able to purchase tickets to watch a game at Citi Field. Tickets were expensive, and they had already spent a small fortune to watch a game at Fenway Park. Besides, his lifelong love affair with the Mets wasn't quite the same since he moved to Utah and the Mets moved to Citi Field. The original home of the Mets, Shea Stadium, had been demolished to make way for Citi Field and was turned into a parking lot.

"We can just walk around the stadium a bit and take some pictures," Luke said to Hayley.

When the Mannings arrived at Citi Field, it was the top of the third inning. A stranger approached Luke.

"Hey, buddy," he said, "would you like some tickets to the game?"

"No thanks," Luke said. "It's a little out of our price range."

"I'm talking about free tickets."

"Really?"

"Yeah. It's the third inning anyway. I could use some good karma. So here you go."

The man handed Luke an envelope. He opened it to find enough tickets inside for his family. By the time he looked up, the man had disappeared.

"Now that may have been one of the Three Nephites," Luke said to the kids.

Luke had his family follow him into the stadium turnstiles to watch his beloved Mets in the left field seats.

"Why do I get the feeling that you planned this all along?" Hayley joked.

Luke identified with the Mets, who were always overshadowed by the Yankees in New York.

The Mets were an upstart franchised that debuted in 1962.

To Luke, the Yankees, born in 1913, played with silver spoons lodged in their mouths — a pinstriped and spoiled franchise, and fan base, that had a bushel of World Championships and, in his estimation, had purchased most of them. He respected the tradition, history, mystique, and aura of the Yankees, from Babe Ruth to Reggie Jackson to Derek Jeter. But he loved the scrappy, gritty, blue-collar Mets.

The Yankees possessed a button-down reputation while the Mets were the lovable, unsung bad boys sporting grimy, ragged T-shirts.

Luke always felt like an underdog, so he could relate to the Mets.

He took it as a sign that the Amazin' Mets won the World Series in 1969, not long after he was born. In 1986, the Mets beat the Red Sox in the World Series in dramatic fashion. He adored Mookie Wilson, Lenny Dykstra, Roger McDowell, Ron Darling, Dwight Gooden, Darryl Strawberry, and Rick Aguilera (whom, Luke learned later, attended BYU).

One of the highlights of Luke's pre-Utah life was standing in front of a 13-inch, black-and-white TV at his college dorm, listening to the dulcet tones of Vin Scully calling the World Series. Luke would yell, "Let's Go Mets! Let's Go Mets! Let's Go Mets!"

The Mets and Reds compensated the Mannings for missing the first few innings. The two teams ended up playing 12 innings. Luke insisted they stay until the end, and had to fork out more money to buy overpriced food for his family at a Major League ballpark.

When the game ended, with the Mets winning, 6-5, it was after midnight. The twins were sleeping in Luke's lap. Hayley cradled a sleeping Sarah in her arms. They had fallen asleep sometime during the 7th inning. They got back on the subway, and returned to the hotel late that night.

Meanwhile, the legend of the Mannings of Mormonville continued morphing into a life of its own. With each passing day, the Mannings of Mormonville Facebook page and YouTube channel were racking up more views and more comments and more attention. Little did the Mannings realize a burgeoning audience on the Internet was enjoying their good deeds and good adventures.

CHAPTER 28

WHILE EATING BREAKFAST the next morning at the hotel, Luke gave the kids a brief recap about the tragic events of Sept. 11, 2001, and how he had lost several friends, and acquaintances, that day of the terrorist attacks.

"We New Yorkers have a reputation for being loud, rude, arrogant, and self-absorbed," Luke told them. "But on that day, New Yorkers were courageous and selfless. Many lost their lives trying to save the lives of others."

The Mannings arrived at Ground Zero and stopped at the massive twin Reflecting Pools featuring the nearly 3,000 names of the men, women, and children killed that day inscribed on bronze parapets on the footprint of the World Trade Center, where the Twin Towers once stood.

"I used to meet friends to eat at Windows on the World restaurant, which occupied the 107th floor of the North Tower of the World Trade Center," Luke reflected. "It was an amazing view. Some of those friends I used to eat there with, I never saw again. Lives changed forever that day. It was my generation's Pearl Harbor. I'll never forget it."

As Luke squinted into a bright sky at the majestic One World Trade Center — also known as the Freedom Tower, which stands

1,776 feet high and is the tallest skyscraper in the Western Hemisphere — Benjamin noticed a tear dripping from underneath Luke's sunglasses.

"Are you OK, dad?" he asked.

"That was a terrible day for New York and for our country. Being here brings back a lot of memories."

Luke guided his family to see a pear tree, which became known as the "Survivor Tree" because it withstood the terrorist attack on 9/11. The tree was severely damaged but it was removed and nursed back to health before being replanted in the Memorial area. New limbs had grown from damaged stumps, symbolizing resilience and rebirth.

As part of the tour of New York, Luke also took his family around to famous churches and cathedrals — from St. Paul's Chapel (which includes a pew where George Washington worshipped), to Trinity Church to Saint Patrick's Cathedral.

These ancient, ornate churches with distinctive architecture were juxtaposed by modern, state-of-the-art skyscrapers.

"It's a powerful reminder of how important religion and God were when the country was first established by the first European settlers," Luke told the kids.

"Maybe during the Millennium, those beautiful churches will be transformed into temples," Hayley said. "People, like my dad, think of New York as a godless place but there are beautiful churches here."

"Including our temple, right?" Jacob said.

"Yes, including our temple," Hayley said, giving him a squeeze.

"Look at the paintings here," Benjamin said inside one of the churches. "It looks like Michelangelo's Sixteenth Chapel."

"*Sistine* Chapel," Luke corrected.

Luke led his family to Wall Street, where they took pictures next to the Charging Bull, then to the Brooklyn Bridge. They walked across the bridge and took pictures of the Statue of Liberty in the distance. The older kids gawked at the Brooklyn Bridge's Gothic arches, and majestic filigree of cables.

From the bridge, the Mannings marveled at the Manhattan skyline.

"There are so many people here," Esther said to Hayley. "So many people that don't have the gospel."

"That's why we're trying to help others," Hayley said. "That's why missionary work is so important. The responsibility of missionaries is to participate in the Gathering of Israel."

"What's that?" Benjamin said.

"We're all part of Heavenly Father's family, right? Well, everyone belongs to a particular tribe of Israel," Hayley said. "Those tribes are scattered throughout the world. It's our responsibility, as members of the Church, to gather them by teaching them the gospel and baptizing them into the Church, so they can rejoin Heavenly Father's family."

After crossing the Brooklyn Bridge, Luke bought hot dogs for everybody from a street vendor.

If nothing else, Luke succeeded in his goal to wear out the kids so they would sleep well that night.

As for the money the Mannings had been given from the couple from Texas at the Sacred Grove, Esther suggested they give it to a soup kitchen and homeless shelter in New York City. Luke and Hayley agreed.

Luke found a homeless shelter in Manhattan, and he called to make arrangements to volunteer that evening. When the Mannings showed up, a long line of people, clearly down on their luck, was formed outside.

The Mannings decided to pick someone, or a family, they could present with $100.

"Is this place always so busy?" Luke asked Reggie Baines, the head of the homeless shelter.

"Unfortunately, yes."

The Mannings helped serve hundreds of people that night. Among the memorable people they met was the Murray family. The father, DeVon, had served in the war in Afghanistan, where he lost one of his legs to a roadside bomb. DeVon was unemployed and struggling to support his wife, Janet, and their four children, who ranged in age from age 11 to 3.

DeVon wanted to be an engineer. He had undergone numerous surgeries related to his war injuries. He was also waiting to receive government assistance in order to go to school.

"I just want my children to have a home," DeVon explained. "It seems like we're in this deep, dark hole. But we have faith in God that He will pull us out somehow. If it weren't for places like this, and for kind folks like you, I don't know what we'd do. You give us hope."

While the homeless ate, Esther played her violin.

"Our patrons usually don't get entertainment with their meal," Reggie said.

Esther played a few hymns and some patriotic selections. When she finished, she received a standing ovation.

Before leaving the shelter, the Mannings discreetly presented DeVon and Janet Murray with $146.43. Besides the $100 they received from the couple from Texas, Esther gave some of her babysitting money, and the boys donated some of their money from mowing lawns. Jacob contributed a widow's mite six dollars, all the money he had left.

They also gave the Murrays a copy of the Book of Mormon with their testimonies written inside.

"This is a very generous thing," DeVon said. "You folks are real Christians."

"Thank you," Luke said.

"We'll never forget you," Janet said.

After they returned to the hotel, Jacob had an important question.

"Why do I feel so good inside?" he asked.

That was the kind of question Luke and Hayley loved to hear from their children.

Esther had so much fun playing her violin at the shelter she asked if she could play somewhere else.

"I'd like to perform at other places around New York City to raise money for families like the Murrays tomorrow," she said.

"No problem," Luke said.

"Are you sure we don't need some sort of permit to do that?" Hayley asked. "I don't want our daughter arrested in New York."

"Street performers don't need a permit unless they use a loudspeaker or are next to a park," Luke said.

"Can I perform inside the subway?" Esther asked.

"Actually, I did a story on this once when I lived here," Luke said. "The Metropolitan Transportation Authority holds annual auditions in the Grand Center Terminal to consider new performers for the subways. Performers are chosen based on their ability and the way they reflect the diversity of New York City. So you can't perform inside the subway station. But there's nothing wrong with you playing *outside* a subway station."

So, the next day, Luke found a spot for Esther to play near the subway station on 42nd Street.

"Dad, try not to embarrass me too much," Esther said.

"Ladies and gentlemen, all the way from Helaman, Utah," Luke announced, "Classic violinist Esther Manning!"

Luke opened the violin case while Esther, her face having turned a shade of red, played a medley of songs amid bemused people rushing around on the streets. Esther's efforts yielded $26 and change.

"Where next?" Esther said.

Luke suggested Rockefeller Center.

"There are a lot of people there," he said. "I can't believe this. My daughter's a street performer!"

"Luke, please don't that term, 'street performer,'" Hayley said. "I don't like it."

"I'm no marketing genius," Luke said, "but I think we'll raise more donations if we tell people what we're doing."

So Hayley and Esther created a homemade sign that said, "Raising money for the homeless. Every donation helps. Thanks!"

Luke explained to the kids who John D. Rockefeller was, and the history of the Rockefeller Center. He told them about the Christmas tree lighting ceremony that occurred every year and how, in the winter, skaters fill the ice skating rink. He pointed out One Rockefeller Center, the Nintendo World Store, and the *Today Show* studios.

Esther removed her violin and started scratching out beautiful melodies, from Church hymns to classical numbers to pop music.

Soon, she had attracted a fairly large crowd. People were dancing, swaying, clapping and toe-tapping. Some put coins and bills in her violin case.

"Luke," Hayley said, "I'm afraid we're exploiting our daughter."

"No, we're not," Luke replied. "She loves this. Look at her. But she's going to need an agent. I just figured out what my new job could be."

Hayley glared at her husband.

When Esther finished, the crowd applauded, and some dropped cash into her case. One woman recognized the family, snapped a photo on her smartphone, then Tweeted it out with the hash tag #ManningsofMormonville.

"I kept telling you those violin lessons would pay off," Luke told Hayley, who playfully elbowed him in the ribs.

Then Brian and Benjamin, not to be outdone, pulled out their basketballs and started performing their routine. By this time, the boys had decided to dribble in sync to Esther's violin. They knew the Harlem Globetrotters' theme was "Sweet Georgia Brown." But Esther didn't know that song. So they chose instead "Sweet Hour of Prayer." The slow music didn't exactly match the boys' fast-paced bouncing of basketballs, but people seemed to enjoy it.

A spiffy woman dressed in a business suit approached Esther when she finished a song.

"That was awesome!" the woman said. "You are wonderful!"

"Thanks," Esther said.

"My name is Marjorie Krasnik. I'm a producer at the *Today Show*."

"I'm Esther Manning."

"Aren't you the one who has been putting on little concerts all over the country during your family vacation?"

"How did you know about that?"

"A lot of people know about that. Haven't you seen the thousands of 'likes' and views you've gotten on Facebook and YouTube? I think what you are doing is great. I've been following you and your family, the *Mannings of Mormonville*. I've been following your exploits around the country. Have you ever watched the *Today Show*?"

"Not really," Esther said. "We're usually doing family scripture study during that time, then I've got to go to school."

Marjorie's brow furrowed, then she smiled. "I loved it when you played with that blind man in Chicago. It made me cry. Where else have you performed before your trip?"

"At Helaman 6th Ward sacrament meetings and the ward Christmas party."

Luke, Hayley and the rest of the kids made their way to Esther, wondering what this woman was saying to her.

They introduced themselves to Marjorie, who introduced herself.

"What an amazing family," Marjorie said. "Esther, I couldn't help but notice the sign you made. What made you want to donate to homeless shelters?"

"We met a really nice family at a homeless shelter here yesterday. We wanted to do something to help them, and other families

236

that aren't as fortunate as we are."

"So you're all the way from Utah?"

"Yes. We drove in a motor home and we've stopped at Church history sites, and U.S. historical sites, along the way. My dad is from New York originally."

"How long are you in New York City?" Marjorie asked.

"'Til tomorrow afternoon," Luke said.

"That's great! How would you feel about Esther playing her violin on the *Today Show* tomorrow morning?"

"Are you serious?" Hayley asked.

"Yes, I'm serious."

"What do you think, Esther?" Hayley asked.

"I'd love to, if it's OK with you and dad."

"It's fine with me," Luke said.

"Could we meet Nick Larimer?" Hayley asked. She was a big fan of the *Today Show* host.

"That can be arranged, absolutely!" Marjorie said, and then she looked at Luke.

"Wait a minute. Luke Manning? You wrote that book about being kidnapped in Africa, right? Didn't we have you on the show years ago?"

"That's right. You have a great memory."

"This will be wonderful!" Marjorie exclaimed. "And we may have time for your basketball-dribbling sons, too. For being on our show tomorrow morning, we at the *Today Show* promise to donate $5,000 to a homeless shelter on behalf of your family. What do you think about that?"

"I love it," Esther said. "Thanks!"

Hayley temporary lifted the moratorium on phone use and allowed Esther to text all of her friends the exciting news. Word spread throughout Helaman that she would be appearing on the *Today Show* the next morning.

Luke couldn't resist reminding Hayley of the promise he made before the trip, not to share any of their experiences on social media.

"Ironic how all this has happened after I promised you not to post any pictures on Facebook, Twitter or Instagram, huh?" Luke said. "And it seems now you're excited about being on the *Today Show*. And meeting Nick Larimer."

"Well," she replied, "I did say I didn't want anything on social media. But I never said anything about the *Today Show*."

CHAPTER 29

MARJORIE GAVE THE MANNINGS detailed instructions on their TV appearance, which involved waking up at 5:30 a.m., Eastern Time — 3:30 a.m., Mountain Time.

Esther was excited and terrified about her national television debut. She could barely sleep.

Luke let her stay in the bed with Hayley that night while he slept on the pullout couch with Jacob and Benjamin. Luke was up most of the night as Jacob kept inadvertently kicking him in the head.

When the Mannings woke up, Hayley fretted about what she, and the kids, would wear. She started combing the boys' hair, and curling the girls' hair.

The plan was for Esther to perform a song, and that would be that, Luke and Hayley figured. But when they arrived at the *Today Show* studios — a black SUV limousine with leather seats picked them up at the hotel — Marjorie informed them that she wanted all of them to be on camera for a brief interview before Esther's performance. Hayley started fussing with the kids' hair again.

Marjorie escorted the Mannings to the Green Room. The boys were impressed with the spread of complimentary food. They surrounded it like ravenous wolves.

"Go ahead and eat something," Marjorie said. "Just leave something for Jerry Seinfeld. He's going to be on later."

The kids began eating bagels and fruit. Esther couldn't eat. She felt sick to her stomach. Luke and Hayley couldn't eat, either.

"Luke, you know the drill," Marjorie said. "You've been on TV before. Nick will ask you and Esther a few simple questions about why you're here in New York. The rest of you just look at the camera and smile. Then during the commercial break, we'll go outside, and when we come back, we'll have Esther play."

This was much more than the Mannings had bargained for — they didn't realize that being a light unto the world would include being in the bright spotlight of a national television appearance.

A woman started putting makeup on each member of the family. The twins enjoyed the experience but the boys resisted.

Esther was shaking as she warmed up on her violin.

The Mannings' appearance was preceded by a segment about how to exfoliate the skin with a mixture of avocados, egg whites, and baking soda.

"I've got to try that when we get home," Luke said to Hayley, trying to break the tension.

Then the Mannings were escorted to the set, Studio 1A.

Nick Larimer, the urbane host of the *Today Show*, couldn't have been nicer or more charming during the commercial breaks.

"Just relax and have fun," advised Nick, who was tanned and had teeth so white they seemed to emit LED light. "Be yourselves."

Hayley was so nervous, she could barely speak. Esther was saying a silent prayer.

Pretty much everyone back in Helaman, as well as a lot of other places, would be watching that morning.

The director counted down the seconds until they were live again. Nick smiled, looked into the camera, and smoothly delivered his scripted lines off a teleprompter.

"We have some very special guests this morning. We're joined by a family all the way from Utah that has spurred an Internet sensation. They have a YouTube channel called *Mannings of Mormonville*."

Video clips of their adventures, taken from social media sites, flashed on the screen. The Mannings were watching many of these videos of themselves for the first time.

"During their cross-country trip across America, the Manning family has been serving up good deeds and inspirational music," Nick intoned.

The camera then panned to the family. The twins were staring at the lights, and making faces. Jacob had his right index finger planted in his left ear. Hayley cradled Sarah in her arms. Esther, Brian and Benjamin stared glassy-eyed at the camera.

"Luke and Hayley Manning have seven children," Nick continued, "including their oldest daughter, Esther, who is something of a prodigy on the violin. One of our producers found her yesterday performing at Rockefeller Center. Manning family, welcome to the *Today Show*."

"Thanks for having us, Nick," Luke said.

"First, I've got to ask, how did you train your kids to be so well-behaved?"

"Tranquilizers," Luke joked. "No, just kidding. They're good kids. It's like someone once said, we try to teach them correct principles, and let them govern themselves."

Hayley didn't appreciate Luke implying that they had drugged their kids, but she was impressed that he would paraphrase the Prophet Joseph Smith on national TV. People in Helaman enjoyed that line, too, when they heard it.

"Whatever you and your wife are doing, it's working," Nick said. "Luke, as the proud dad of this big family, tell us about your trip and what brought all of you to New York. You're Mormons, right?"

"Nick, we're members of The Church of Jesus Christ of Latter-day Saints. Some know us as Mormons. A few weeks ago we left our home in Utah in a motor home and, against the sound advice of some friends and relatives, we traveled across the country to see Church history and U.S. history sites."

"We've been seeing you and your family on Twitter and Facebook and Instagram and YouTube quite a bit the past few weeks," Nick said. "Tell us what's motivated you to help others."

"Well, it was supposed to be random and anonymous, but due to technology, it hasn't been very anonymous. Well-meaning people have been posting some of the stuff we've been doing. We just found that out recently. We weren't looking for any attention."

"You mean you didn't realize your acts of service, and your daughter's performances, were being captured on video and uploaded to social media sites by total strangers?"

"That's right," Luke said. "But we're really just a normal family."

"Did you say a normal family, or a Mormon family?" Nick said, laughing.

"We just wanted to make a little difference in the lives of those we come in contact with. We believe that when we serve others, we are really serving God."

Luke was on a roll. First he quoted Joseph Smith, then King Benjamin. All in the same segment.

"But what made you decide to do this? Most families don't do this sort of thing. They want to have fun and relax on vacation."

"We just decided that we wanted to serve others while we were traveling because we know that's the best way to be happy," Luke said. "We try to follow the example of Jesus Christ. And we've had some wonderful experiences, like helping at homeless shelters. Also, our family has been on the receiving end of service, like the kind man who helped us when we had a tire blowout in Nebraska."

"Let's look at the YouTube clip of your daughter, Esther, playing with a homeless man in Chicago. You've donated money to homeless shelters. How did that come about?"

"Esther decided to raise money by playing the violin. She saw a need, and found a way she could help. It was all her idea."

"Esther," Nick said, "how long have you been playing the violin?"

"Since I was four."

"We've done some research on the great Mormon violinists, like Lindsey Stirling and Jenny Oaks Baker. Maybe you're the next great one," Nick said. "What made you want to give money to homeless shelters?"

"We met a great family here in New York," Esther said. "We found out they were homeless and we wanted to help them, and others. The dad is a veteran and lost his leg in Afghanistan. It feels good to help. My whole family, my brothers and sisters, have helped, too."

"We encourage your viewers around the country to donate to homeless shelters, to the Red Cross, or to VA hospitals in their own cities," Luke said. "We encourage your viewers to help neighbors and strangers, too. We're all children of God. We all need help from time to time."

"That's such a wonderful cause," Nick said. "We here at the *Today Show* are going to donate $5,000 to a local homeless shelter. Do you have a website where people can find out more about your family and your cause?"

"We don't have a website, or a cause, per se," Luke said, smiling. "That's why it's kind of ironic that we're on your show because we didn't want to draw any attention to ourselves. Like I said, we're just average, everyday people. For more information about what motivates us, I'd encourage viewers to read the Book of Mormon. And go to our Church's website, LDS.org."

"Looks like you're proving that the 'Mormon Moment' didn't end with Mitt Romney's failed presidential bids," Nick said.

Luke wanted to say something about the Millennium but he remembered to be humble. "We'll take our moments when we can," he said.

"Manning family, thank you for your time this morning," Nick said. "When we come back from these messages, we'll hear from Esther Manning and her violin."

During the commercial break, the Mannings adjourned to Rockefeller Center Plaza, where a large crowd was congregated, holding corny signs, waving and screaming for the cameras, generally acting like lunatics, in hopes of getting on TV.

Esther was still scared about performing on television, but Hayley calmed her down, telling her to relax and pretend she was playing in sacrament meeting. When the *Today Show* came back from commercials, a hush fell upon the crowd as Esther calmly played a stirring rendition of "Amazing Grace."

The crowd cheered when she finished.

After the Mannings' appearance on the *Today Show*, at least when it aired later that morning in Helaman, that segment went viral. Luke's cell phone was on the verge of exploding. He received a steady stream of text messages and e-mails. Luke couldn't keep up with all of them.

Most of the messages were from ward members and friends in the stake, including Ben Kimball. They all said the same thing — that they had watched the show, and were so proud of Esther and the whole family.

But one e-mail's subject line stood out from the rest: "Reality Show."

At first, Luke thought it was some sort of joke. He knew of some practical jokers in the ward, and in Hayley's family, that were capable of this. The e-mail was purportedly from a man named Sal Randolph of RTVN, the Reality TV Network, based in New York City. He wrote that he had seen the *Today Show* that morning, and an idea for a new reality show hit him over the head while he ate his bran muffin and café latte.

Randolph proposed that the Mannings star in a reality show on his network. He said he would love to discuss the possibilities. He left his New York phone number.

Luke let it go for several hours as the Mannings wrapped up a couple of more stops in New York, including Madison Square Garden, the self-proclaimed "world's most famous arena," and the Empire State Building. At Grand Central Station, he decided to call the guy to see if it were legitimate.

Instead of calling the number Randolph left, Luke looked up the number of the network. When he called, he asked for Sal Randolph.

"May I ask who's calling?" a voice said.

"Luke Manning."

"I'll put you through."

Not more than five seconds later, Luke found himself talking to Sal Randolph.

"Luke, thanks for getting back to me," he said. "I am very excited to talk to you about my proposal. Are you still in New York?"

"Yes. For now."

"Any way we could get together?"

"Yes, I suppose so, but we'll have to hurry. We're scheduled to leave later this afternoon."

"Where are you now?"

"Grand Central Station."

"I can be there in 10 minutes. There's a restaurant there called 'La Fonda del Sol.' Meet me there. I'll treat your family to lunch. You have a huge family, so that should let you know that I'm serious about this."

"We'll be there," Luke said. How could he turn down an offer of free food, especially for his whole family?

Luke didn't really care for reality shows. Hayley had watched occasional episodes of "The Bachelor," "American Idol," and "Survivor" in the past.

Hayley listened to Luke explain what was going on. She thought he was kidding.

"A reality TV show?" she asked. "What would they want with us?"

"I don't know. It couldn't hurt to listen. Besides, at the very least, we'll get a free lunch out of it."

"Dad, you always say there's no such thing as a free lunch," Brian said.

"Well, in this case, I was wrong."

Randolph showed up in 15 minutes. The Mannings were already seated inside as Luke pulled a few tables together to accommodate everyone.

Part snake-oil salesman, part avuncular figure, part Sopranos cast member, the charismatic Randolph introduced himself to everyone. He was a heavy-set man with slick-back hair. He wore an Armani suit and gaudy rings on his fingers.

"Do you think this guy is in the mafia?" Hayley whispered to Luke.

"It's entirely possible," Luke whispered back.

After the formalities, and after the food was ordered, Randolph got right down to business. He had his pitch ready to go.

"Luke, Hayley, I watched your family on TV this morning and it was clear to me that you guys should be on TV all of the time," Randolph said. "You're naturals! You should have your own TV show! You're telegenic, you're talented, and you've got a fascinating story."

"We're flattered that you would say that," Hayley said, "but we're really quite boring."

"You mean you're Mormons? Yes, I know. That's part of the reason why I love this idea. Mormons have shown to be popular on reality shows, like *Big Love* and *Sister Wives*. My vision for this show is taking a wholesome family like yours, and then we'll take you all over the world. You can do just like you're doing on your family vacation — serving others, visiting homeless shelters, helping out at soup kitchens. It's inspiring. Ratings would go through the roof!"

"Those shows you mentioned, um, we're part of a different religious affiliation than those people," Hayley said. "We belong to The

Church of Jesus Christ of Latter-day Saints. They don't."

"Yes, of course. But the audience doesn't know that. They don't care."

"I wouldn't be required to marry other women, right?" Luke deadpanned.

Randolph roared with delight. "See! You guys are hilarious! It's organic, unscripted entertainment. That would be the strength of the show. Besides, Luke, your wife and daughter are really easy on the eyes."

Luke didn't know whether to thank him or punch him in the nose.

"And we'll make it well worth your family's time. We will pay you $50,000 per episode. We'll fly you in private jets all over the world. Plus, we'll have a nice place for you to live in Greenwich, just outside of New York City, when we're not filming."

Luke and Hayley just stared at each other, shocked by this offer.

The twins were finger-painting in their enchiladas.

"I'm sure you'll need some time to think about it. This would be a big commitment," Randolph continued. "I know you Mormons like to talk about your Church, and spread the faith. I get it. You've made a big splash around the country just with a brief appearance on the *Today Show* and your YouTube channel. We'll help you make a big impact all over the world. We'll send you to places like South Africa, India, Italy, Germany, New Zealand, Australia …"

"I've always wanted to go to Australia," Hayley said. Then she immediately regretted saying it. She didn't want to give this guy the wrong idea.

"Oh, it's a beautiful place," Randolph said. "You'll love it."

"Could we see kangaroos there?" Esther asked.

"Of course!" Randolph said. "And boomerangs and Koala bears and Aborigines and Hugh Jackman. Think of the good you could do on a global scale! Look at the attention you've drawn without even trying. With the backing of my network, this will be huge. We'll put you up in first-class hotels. We'll buy you a brand new motor home — it will be Shangri la on Wheels. We'll even provide you a driver. You'll do what you feel comfortable doing, spending a week at orphanages and children's hospitals. Esther can play the violin. She may get a recording contract out of this. We'll be there to capture it all. You'll be the Mormon version of the Kardashians."

That caused Hayley to shudder. She wanted to throw up.

"Who are the Kardashians?" Brian asked.

"Never mind," Hayley said.

The twins were sitting next to each other, giggling and talking to each other. People all over the restaurant were staring.

"You see what I mean? That's a great comedy act," Randolph said, pointing to the Ashley and Lindsay. "People love that stuff. It's organic humor."

"Yeah, it's a laugh-a-minute at our house," Hayley muttered under her breath.

"Those twins girls are the cutest things I've ever seen," Randolph said. "Those smiles, those eyes. They could be stars in TV commercials right now."

Hayley was horrified to hear this man talking about her young girls, objectifying them like that.

"You could all be stars," Randolph said.

"Well, I don't know about that," Luke said. "We're not *that* funny. We're no *Studio C*."

"Excuse me, but I'm not familiar with *Studio C*," Randolph said.

"It's the Mormon version of *Saturday Night Live*," Luke said. "Or elaborate Boy Scout camp skits."

"Oh," Randolph said. "Anyway, I already have a tentative title for the show. We'll call it *Mannings of Mormonville Abroad*, similar to your YouTube channel. We can build on the brand you've already created. Whaddya think? Who do you think came up with the *Duck Dynasty* idea? That worked out pretty well."

"Mr. Randolph, this is a lot to take in," Luke said. "We appreciate the offer. My wife and I will need to talk it over."

"Of course, by all means. Talk it over. Think about what this could mean for your family. Luke, wouldn't it be nice to pay for your kids' college educations?"

"And our missions?" Brian chimed in.

"This has the potential to make you and your family set for life. This is a life-changing opportunity."

That's exactly what frightened Hayley, how this would affect their lives. She couldn't see it affecting them in a good way.

Randolph paid for lunch, as promised, and the Mannings thanked him. Before he left, he pulled Luke aside.

"Call me after you've talked it over with your wife. I look

---

forward to working with you. Here's my business card. I have a real good feeling about this."

Hayley didn't have a good feeling about this. Luke thought about how this could solve his family's financial problems. Even if they did just one or two seasons of the show, he figured they could squirrel away enough money that he could retire. Maybe he could buy some beachfront property somewhere.

With this offer hanging over their heads, Luke and Hayley knew that the rest of the trip could be negatively impacted until they came up with a resolution.

Before checking out of the hotel, Luke had the older kids write their testimonies on a piece of paper and place it inside the copy of the Book of Mormon in the nightstand drawer.

"You think anyone will ever read these and get baptized?" Brian asked.

"I don't know," Hayley said, "but I really like what your wrote."

The hotel staff was happy to provide the Mannings with fruit, crackers, pretzels, soaps and shampoos as a going away gift. After watching the Mannings on the *Today Show*, they became huge fans, and posed for pictures with them. The hotel manager personally came out to bid them farewell.

"Nobody told me we had celebrities staying with us this week," she said.

As Luke asked for the hotel receipt, the hotel manager told him that someone had already paid their bill, saving them hundreds of dollars.

Luke and Hayley were shocked. "Who did that?" Luke asked.

"The person wanted to remain anonymous," the manager said. "We hope you enjoyed your stay with us."

Another unexpected blessing.

The Mannings took the train back to New Jersey to pick up their motor home. The stocked the RV with the food from the hotel, buckled up, and headed south on I-95 on the New Jersey Turnpike.

Next on the itinerary was Philadelphia.

Before going to see the Liberty Bell and Independence Hall, Luke taught his family about the Declaration of Independence and the Constitution.

Hayley read Doctrine and Covenants 101:80: "And for this purpose have I established the Constitution of this Land, by the hands of wise men whom I raised up unto this very purpose, and redeemed the land by the shedding of blood."

Hayley explained that, just as described in the Book of Mormon, this country is a land of promise, and will be protected as long as the people who live here are righteous. Hayley pointed out the many times the Lord had preserved America's freedom, from the Revolutionary War to the Civil War to World War I to World War II to the present day.

Hayley told her kids about how in 1877, the Founding Fathers, and others that the Lord had raised up, appeared to Wilford Woodruff in a vision and asked him to complete their temple ordinances. Wilford Woodruff performed vicarious temple work for eminent men in history, including George Washington, Thomas Jefferson, Benjamin Franklin, all the others that signed the Declaration of Independence, in the St. George Temple. And Lucy Bigelow Young was baptized on behalf of prominent women in history.

"Why didn't they just get baptized when they were alive?" Benjamin asked.

"Because the gospel wasn't on the Earth then," Hayley said. "That's why they appeared to Wilford Woodruff. The gospel had been on the Earth for quite a while by 1877, and they wanted their temple work done for them."

The older kids, who had never heard that story, were mesmerized.

"You mean all those guys that are on the money and that we learn about in history class, are actually members of our Church?" Brian asked.

"Well, they had their ordinances done for them," Hayley said. "They were good men, foreordained to help prepare the United States for the restoration of the gospel of Jesus Christ. The Declaration of Independence and the Revolutionary War all paved the way for the gospel to be restored through the Prophet Joseph Smith. That's what we've tried to show you during this trip, that American history and the history of the Church are connected and intertwined. One couldn't have happened without the other."

CHAPTER 30

THESE ARE THE TIMES THAT TRY MEN'S SOULS.

The Mannings read those immortal words by Thomas Paine at Independence National Park, and the Mannings lived them, too.

The kids were restive and they were tired of being confined in the claustrophobic RV, which was starting to feel like a prison.

Luke had enjoyed the nice break from driving while staying in New York City. If he had had the money, he would have gladly paid for his family to fly home.

Since the Mannings found themselves in close quarters all of the time, it was hard for Luke and Hayley could discuss the reality TV offer.

Of course, Hayley had already made up her mind. She knew that Luke had a different opinion. Neither of them wanted to turn this into a source of contention, especially while on the road. So they tabled the topic for the time being.

In Philadelphia, the Mannings toured Independence Hall and took pictures with the Liberty Bell. They went to see the "Rocky" statue, and Luke and the older kids ran up "The Rocky Steps" — while Luke played the *Rocky* theme song on his smartphone — to the Philadelphia Museum of Art.

The next day, the Mannings visited Valley Forge. One of Luke's and Hayley's favorite paintings, "The Prayer at Valley Forge," hung prominently in their living room at home. Then it was on to Gettysburg, where the Mannings spent a large chunk of the day learning about the Civil War.

Before going to Washington, D.C., they hung out in Annapolis and the U.S. Naval Academy. Once in the nation's capital, the Mannings walked the National Mall and saw the Lincoln Memorial, the Jefferson Memorial, the Vietnam Veterans Memorial, and the Washington Monument.

Every once in a while, people would recognize the Mannings and compliment Esther and the family, and snap photos of them. They were like B-list celebrities. It scared Hayley. She prized her family's anonymity and she didn't want to lose that. Of course, Hayley feared it would be hard for her family to stay grounded when they had been on national TV and all over social media.

Also while in D.C., the Mannings went to the U.S. Capitol Building, the Library of Congress, the Rotunda of the National Archives Building (to see the Constitution, the Bill of Rights and the Declaration of Independence) and the Smithsonian. They saw the well-protected White House from a distance.

At a souvenir store, Luke bought a Mitt Romney T-shirt on the bargain rack from the 2012 election for $2.75.

"I would have paid $8.75 for this," Luke told Hayley. "It belongs in the Mormon Hall of Fame."

The Mannings took the subway to the Smithsonian's National Zoo to see the giant pandas munching on bamboo and playing in the trees. Ashley and Lindsay wanted to take them home.

The Mannings also toured Arlington National Cemetery, the Marine Corps War Memorial — featuring the iconic statue of the soldiers raising the flag at Iwo Jima — and Ford's Theater, where Lincoln was assassinated.

Another stop in the nation's capital, of course, was the majestic Washington, D.C. temple, where they posed for more family photos.

"It's the tallest of all the temples in the world," Hayley told the kids. "It was the first temple built in the Eastern United States."

But the kids weren't listening. They were busy running toward the wooded area that surrounds the temple, searching for rabbits and other wildlife.

While in the D.C. area, the Manning visited George Washington's beloved Mount Vernon and Thomas Jefferson's beloved Monticello in Virginia.

Luke and Hayley could tell the kids were being worn out on history and tourist haunts. They were mixing up the Civil War and the Revolutionary War, among other things.

It was time for a break, or at least a change of scenery. So they decided to attend a Washington Nationals baseball game. Luke wanted to pay homage to a superstar Latter-day Saint baseball player, Bryce Harper. He was Luke's type of player — brash, with the shaggy hair, and a shaggy beard. He shattered the Mormon stereotype and Luke reveled in it. Luke only wished Harper played for the Mets.

Luke believed the three-run home run that Harper belted in the sixth inning was just for his family.

That night, after they got the kids back to the RV, and in bed, Luke and Hayley decided to discuss the uncomfortable subject — the reality TV show offer.

"Globe-trotting sounds like a fun adventure," Luke said. "Just think about how much the kids could learn by traveling all over the world."

"That's true, but won't our kids get that kind of experience serving missions?" Hayley said. "I don't want my family to turn into some sort of cable TV sideshow. And I certainly don't want to be known as the Mormon version of the Kardashians."

"What about for just one season?" Luke said. "With the money we make off of it, we could secure our financial future. What a legacy we could leave our children, not to mention our grandchildren. We could share the gospel with people all over the world."

"The money would be great, and it would solve a lot of problems but I can see it creating other problems. I just feel like if we did this, we'd be selling our souls. Our intention would be to share the gospel, but we don't even know the people at that network and what we'd be contractually obligated to do. What if they wanted us to do stuff that are against our values? We would have no control over how they portray the Church or us. They really don't know anything about our values. That scares me."

"You've really thought this through," Luke said.

"All I know is, we need to be united in our decision. I don't want this to become a wedge between us. No matter what we do, I don't want either of us to be resentful. We just need to do what's best of our family."

"Hayley, you're always telling the kids to be a light to the world and look for missionary opportunities. Isn't this a great way to do that on a worldwide scale?"

It was getting late. They were tired. They knew they should put this topic to rest and go to bed themselves. They were going to be sitting next to each other for the next 2,000 miles as they made their way home. They didn't want this decision to spoil the final week of their trip.

There were still some sites the Mannings wanted to see on their way back to Utah, but their main focus was on driving as far as they could every day so they could return to Helaman as soon as possible. The kids' attention spans had exceeded their limits.

Luke noted passing into the states of Maryland and West Virginia. He started listening to West Virginia's anthem, John Denver's "Take Me Home, Country Roads."

Luke started singing along.

It became apparent to Luke that whoever wrote that classic song was geographically challenged. The Blue Ridge Mountains and the Shenandoah River that the lyrics extoll aren't actually in West Virginia.

Meanwhile, as the Mannings drove through Kentucky, Hayley was fighting back an impression that, if followed, would result in a significant detour on their trip home. The night before, she had a dream that she couldn't get out of her head but she was hesitant to bring it up.

It still bothered her that she didn't do enough when sharing the gospel with Katarina, the woman from Germany that she met on the Freedom Trail in Boston.

"I really feel strongly for some reason that we need to go to Memphis," Hayley said to Luke as she passed out fruit snacks to the kids.

"Memphis? Tennessee?" Luke said, slowing down the RV and turning down the music. "Why?"

"I don't know. I feel like we need to go to Memphis. I had a dream about it last night. I kept seeing signs that said 'Welcome to Memphis.' I can't explain it."

"Um, Hayley, you do realize that Tennessee wasn't part of our plans. That's hundreds of miles out of the way. Have you been there before?"

"No. You?"

"No. Does this have anything with you being mad at me for wanting to do that reality show? Or do you just want some really good barbecue?"

"This has nothing to do with any of that. Like I said, I just feel like we need to be in Memphis. I don't know why."

"Maybe you mean Nashville, Tennessee. You know, the home of country music, and the Country Music Hall of Fame. Maybe Esther could sign a recording contract there."

"No," Hayley said, shaking her head. "That's not it."

Luke knew better than to question his wife's judgment. Besides, he was always up for an adventure. It might be fun going to Memphis. It was a place he had always wanted to visit.

"Memphis is famous for its rhythm and blues," Luke said. "We could go to B.B. King's."

The Mannings were approaching Lexington, Kentucky. Their plans had them stopping in Louisville, Kentucky, and then going on to St. Louis, Missouri. Memphis wasn't exactly on the way to St. Louis from Louisville. It would cost them a whole day in travel.

"According to Leah Ona, I mean, the GPS," Hayley said, studying her smartphone, "Memphis is 386 miles away from Louisville."

Of course, Luke didn't want to drive any farther than necessary. His preference would have been to shorten the trip rather than lengthen it. But he could tell Hayley was determined to go to Memphis no matter how crazy and irrational it seemed to him.

"OK," Luke said. "We'll go to Louisville and then we'll head to Memphis."

The Mannings arrived in Louisville late that night. In the morning, they toured the Louisville Slugger Museum & Factory, where Major League Baseball bats are made. They each received a miniature bat and the boys started sword fighting with them. Afterward, the Mannings dropped by Churchill Downs, where the world-famous Kentucky Derby has been run annually since 1875.

Then it was time to go to Memphis.

"What do we do once we get there?" Luke asked.

"I have no idea," Hayley said. "That's what makes this so interesting. I guess we'll just follow the Spirit."

Without having received his own spiritual confirmation of the need to go to Memphis, Luke gripped the steering wheel tighter and adjusted his seat, settling in for the drive that day.

At that point, the kids' whining was incessant. They were tired and ornery, and on the verge of staging a revolutionary war of their own. Luke wondered if keeping a family this young and this big inside an RV this long could be considered cruel and unusual punishment. If so, he thought, he'd be prosecuted.

One wrong look would send the twins into tantrums. Even Sarah, who was usually so good-natured, was starting to arch her back and scream from time to time. The boys were on the verge of going stir-crazy.

Luke hoped the Disney animated movie marathon on the TV would entertain the kids until they arrived in Memphis.

Hayley, meanwhile, prayed for some inspiration.

On the way to Memphis, the Mannings drove through a violent rainstorm, and Luke couldn't see because the windshield wipers weren't working. So he pulled over the first chance he could, found an auto parts store in Nashville, and replaced the wipers. While they were there, Hayley said they might as well look for the Nashville Tennessee Temple. So they did. The kids hopped out of the RV and ran around and took pictures. Then they ate at a fast food restaurant.

Hayley convinced Luke that, while they were in Nashville, to go to the Country Music Hall of Fame. After all, she had been a good sport about going to the Baseball and Basketball Halls of Fame.

Hayley enjoyed the displays and tributes to Kenny Rogers, Garth Brooks, Martina McBride, and Carrie Underwood, among many others. It wasn't Luke's favorite stop but he endured it well.

That night, Luke pulled into a Memphis Walmart. The younger kids had cried themselves asleep.

This trip was becoming an ordeal, Luke thought.

In the morning, the Mannings ate breakfast and got ready for the day. Then Luke asked the question du jour of this unexpected part of the journey. For the first time on their trip, the Mannings didn't know exactly where to go or what to do.

"So, where should we go?" Luke asked.

"Well," Hayley said, "I thought we'd start with the temple."

They arrived at the Memphis Tennessee Temple, located in Bartlett, about 14 miles outside of Memphis. The Mannings walked around the temple grounds and, naturally, took pictures. Hayley talked to everyone she saw around the temple, hoping to stumble upon the reason for their inexplicable detour.

Other than chatting with a kind, elderly couple from Arkansas, she came up empty.

Hayley suggested they go to Graceland, home of the late Elvis Presley, located on 3764 Elvis Presley Boulevard. On the way, Luke played some Elvis songs for the kids to enjoy, which, for the most part, they didn't.

"He was the 'King of Rock and Roll,'" Luke explained. "He had a bunch of No. 1 hits."

"I read somewhere that Elvis owned a copy of the Book of Mormon and took the missionary discussions," Hayley said. "I think he had a baptismal date set before he died."

"That sounds like a Mormon urban legend," Luke said. "My journalistic instincts tell me that it's not true. I don't know why members of the Church want to believe in celebrity conversions so badly. But I guess it kind of makes sense. A guy with a bunch of gold records being attracted to a book that came from gold plates."

"How did Elvis die?" Brian asked.

"A heart attack," Luke said. "He died at Graceland. He was young when he died. He was only 42."

"Forty-two isn't very young," Brian said.

"I remember hearing the reports that he had died," Luke said. "I was just a kid. Yeah, I guess I thought he was old when he died, too. But he was younger than I am now."

"Maybe that's why we were prompted to come to Memphis," Brian said. "Maybe we're supposed to do a baptism for the dead for Elvis."

"The Church frowns on doing temple work for celebrities," Luke said as he searched for a parking spot at Graceland. The place was packed.

"Graceland costs almost as much as going to Disneyland," Hayley said.

"Elvis probably makes more money now that he's dead than when he was alive," Luke said. "We can at least pay our respects by walking around the outside of Graceland and checking it out."

"So it costs $50 to visit Elvis' house but it's free to visit Heavenly Father's temple?" Brian observed.

"Well, Elvis is a king," Benjamin said.

"And there's a big line around Elvis' house, waiting to get in, but there's no line at the temple," Brian said.

The Mannings walked around the wall that surrounds Graceland. That wall has transformed into a shrine where fans from around the world write their name and date and leave messages for Elvis.

"A Single Star That Shines At Graceland Led Me Back Again This Year," said one.

"Never Forgotten. RIP, Elvis."

There were also a bunch of messages that insisted that "Elvis Lives."

"Why do so many people think he's alive?" Brian asked.

"Well he *is* alive," Esther said, "somewhere in the spirit world, right?"

"I wonder if he puts on concerts there," Luke mused.

If something's going to happen, maybe it's happening at Graceland, Hayley kept thinking, and hoping, considering the crowds. So she gathered the kids together and led them in singing, "We'll Bring the World His Truth." The kids always put an extra emphasis on the word in the song, *Helaman,* their hometown, as they sang the chorus, "We are as the army of Helaman."

But people didn't seem to be moved. The Mannings got plenty of strange looks but that was it.

"Was that one of Elvis' obscure hits?" a man asked Hayley.

"Could have been," she answered.

"Maybe we should have done an Elvis version of that song," Luke said.

"OK," Hayley said. "We need to leave now."

"Giving up so soon?" Luke asked.

"No, I think we should try Beale Street."

"As in the famous Beale Street? One of the most iconic streets in America? *That* Beale Street?"

"Yep."

Who was Luke to argue? He had always wanted to go there.

After parking the RV, Luke and his family strode onto Beale Street on a steamy afternoon. For what purpose, they didn't know. But

Luke didn't care. He enjoyed walking past the Jerry Lee Lewis' Café and Honky Tonk; Coyote Ugly Saloon; Hard Rock Café; Johnny G's Creole Kitchen; King's Palace Café; and The Pig on Beale.

Luke was seriously craving some barbecue.

Finally, Hayley stopped in front of a place called Blues City Café. Amid the busy sidewalk filled with tourists, Hayley asked the kids to sing "I Am A Child of God" while Esther accompanied them on the violin.

"Mom, we're tired of singing," Benjamin said. "We're hungry."

"And it's really hot," said Brian, who was drenched in sweat.

While they sang, Luke noticed a waitress from the restaurant emerge from the front door and glare at them. Luke thought she was going to tell them to leave because his family's singing violated some sort of city ordinance and scared away customers.

When the singing ended, the 50-something woman, wearing a canary yellow work dress, sashayed over to Hayley.

"Who sent you here?" she demanded. Tears streaked her face and her mascara was running, creating dark black lines down her defined cheekbones.

"What do you mean?" Hayley asked.

"That song. You're Mormons, aren't you?"

"Yes, ma'am," Hayley said, showing her command of southern vernacular. "Do you know any Mormons?"

"I used to be a Mormon," she said. "Look, if I bring you some food, can I talk to you?"

"Of course," Hayley said.

"OK. Don't go away, please. I'll be right back."

And the woman disappeared back into the restaurant.

"Kids," Luke said, "it looks like lunch is served."

Then he looked at Hayley and shook his head. "This food better be good. We came hundreds of miles out of the way for this. Seriously, though, how do you do this?"

Hayley shrugged her shoulders. "The Spirit led us here," she said.

The woman introduced herself as Julia Blackmore. She carried a Jenga-like tower of Styrofoam boxes full of southern food.

"I just got off my shift. I got you folks some seafood gumbo, barbecue ribs, turnip greens, tamales, and gumbo cheese fries. Everything here is real good."

"Thanks," Luke said. "How much do we owe you?"

"Nothin.' I just want some of y'all's time."

"Can everyone thank Julia for all the food?" Hayley said.

"Thanks!" the kids said.

"You're welcome," Julia said. "I'm just trying to think of a quiet place that we could talk."

"We've got a motor home a few blocks away," Luke said. "We could go there."

Luke and Hayley and each of the older kids carried a box of food.

On the way, Julia told the Mannings all about Beale Street, its history, the famous musicians and entertainers who have performed there.

"You should see this place at night," Julia said. "Ever been here before?"

"Never," Luke said.

"Where are y'all from?"

"Utah," Hayley said.

"Utah. Of course. I could have guessed."

Once inside the RV, Hayley put Esther in charge of feeding the kids and told them to be quiet so she and Luke could "talk to this nice woman."

"I'm not as nice as I may look," Julia said.

"You seem really nice to me," Hayley said. "It's no easy thing to feed a family of our size. How can we help you?"

Julia took a deep breath.

"I guess I'm about to tell you my life story but I'll skip the boring and the R-rated parts. My parents were teenagers when I was born in Texas. They put me up for adoption and a Mormon couple from Utah adopted me. When I was young, I was happy. My parents were really nice. I remember taking trips together, going to church, and I was baptized when I was eight. But the older I got, I had questions that nobody could answer. At first, after I found out that I was adopted, I didn't think about it much. The more I thought about it, and the older I got, I angrier I became. But I didn't know who to be angry at. My birth parents? My adoptive parents? God? I was convinced that if my biological parents didn't want me, I must be worthless. I've had those deep feelings for a long time. I thought God didn't want me, either. I started doubting everything. Commandments, to me, were restrictions keeping me from being myself and finding my individuality.

"When I turned 18, I left home. I was rebellious, defiant and bitter. I decided I would never again attend a Mormon Church meeting. I felt like I had been brainwashed and kept from the truth. I wanted to find my real parents and confront them. I wanted to find out what life was all about on my own. Thus began my 35-year search for 'truth.'

"At first I felt so free. I hitchhiked my way to Arizona, which is where I found out my biological parents lived. Basically, they agreed to meet with me but they still didn't want anything to do with me. That only made me angrier. I left Arizona and went to the East Coast. For the first 10 years, I did everything you can imagine, tried to experience everything life had to offer. It was filled with alcohol, drugs, abuse, and profound loneliness. Like I said, I'll spare you all the gruesome details, but after about a decade, I felt like I had no freedom whatsoever because of my terrible choices. I made my way the best I could, with no college education, working different jobs until they bored me or until I got a better job. At one point, I made a big mistake by getting married. I got divorced one year later. I collected a group of 'friends' in one city, and then I'd soon realize they weren't my friends at all. So I'd move on to another city and repeat the same pattern of self-destructive behavior. Truth was, my life felt hollow, and I felt more worthless than ever. I tried hard not to form close bonds with anyone because I never again wanted to be rejected. But that is such an empty way to live. I thought many times about just ending my life. I was so lost and so desperate, I decided to turn to God for help.

"About five years ago, I moved to Tennessee to live with my boyfriend — that didn't last long, either — but I did find plenty of churches here. So I studied them all. From the Catholics to the Jehovah's Witnesses to the Southern Baptists to the Episcopalians to the Evangelicals. I even attended a Muslim church and a Hindu church for a while. I bet I attended almost every church in the Memphis phone book. I read the Bible. I read the Koran. I studied Zen. I practiced Yoga. I read self-help books by Southern Preachers. But I never felt at peace with any of it. The one church I always avoided? The Mormons. I thought I knew everything about the Mormons. The doctrine and the stories of the Mormons were too fantastical for me. Last Sunday, I decided not to attend any church at all. I went to a park and sat on a bench and, in my heart, I poured out my soul to God. I was going to give Him one last chance to help me. I asked him what church I should join, if any. While I was saying those words, I remembered something from my childhood about Joseph Smith asking God that same question. But I quickly dismissed that thought. I asked God for some sort of sign to know what church to join. Maybe I just wanted a sign that there was a God. And then, this afternoon, as I'm finishing up my shift, I walk out the door and onto Beale Street — Home of the Blues — for the millionth time and what do I hear for the first time in decades? I hear y'all singing, 'I Am A Child of God.' It stirred something within me, from the days when I attended Primary as a little girl. It was a little like stepping into a time machine. I can't explain how I felt. It was something so familiar and comforting. It was as if God was answering my prayer, wrapping his arms around me, saying, 'I am aware of you. This is where the truth is. You had it all along.' And I don't know how much longer I would have suffered if I hadn't heard your family singing that song. When I heard it, I realized that He knows me. He loves me."

Julia broke down and couldn't speak.

"So you asked me before who sent us. Well, I can tell you now. It was the Spirit of God," Hayley said. "We're on a cross-country trip. We drove all the way here from Louisville. We had no plans to come here. But we felt like we should for some reason. As it turns out, it was for you."

Julia embraced Hayley. "Thanks for comin'," she said.

"You're right, Heavenly Father does know you," Hayley said. "He loves you enough to answer your prayer."

"Here's another thing that freaks me out," Julia continued, pulling napkins out of her pocket and dabbing her eyes. "During my breaks the past few days, I've been writing a letter to my adoptive parents, who I now realize are my *real* parents, on these napkins, apologizing to them for what I must have put them through. I decided that I would not give them these napkins unless I could hand-deliver them. Then you guys come into my life. I think they still live in Utah, in Provo, if they are still alive. Would you mind taking these napkins to them?"

"It would be an honor," Hayley said. "But I've got a better idea. Why don't you just come with us and deliver them yourself? We're on our way home."

"No, I can't do that. I have no idea how they would react to me after all of these years," Julia said. "I treated them real bad. I must have broken their hearts into a million pieces. I hope they can forgive me. But I wouldn't blame them if they didn't."

"Just come with us," Luke insisted. "Speaking as a father, I'd be willing to bet anything they'll be thrilled to see you. If they're not, I'll drive you back to Memphis myself."

"Would that be OK to go with you? I don't want to impose. Do you have room for me?"

"You're not imposing," Hayley said. "We'll make room. It would be a privilege to take you home. You're the reason we came to Memphis."

CHAPTER 31

THE MANNINGS PICKED UP Julia at her apartment the next morning — she packed herself a small bag — and they left Memphis, heading north toward St. Louis, Missouri.

On the drive, the Mannings presented Julia with a copy of the Book of Mormon and she spent time reading and asking questions about it.

"Why did an angel tell Nephi to kill Laban?" Julia asked.

"Because Heavenly Father won't allow one bad guy to ruin all of His plans," Benjamin said. "Heavenly Father gave him a bunch of chances. He gives everyone lots of chances."

"Even me?" Julia asked.

"Everyone," Esther said.

"I see a lot of Laman and Lemuel in myself," Julia said, "rebelling against my parents."

"We all do that sometimes," Esther said. "At first, I murmured a lot when my parents told us we were going on this long trip. I thought my dad was a 'visionary' man. But now I'm glad we came. It's been worth it. In fact, I've decided that I want to serve a mission when I'm old enough."

Luke nearly drove off the road.

"Esther, that's great!" Hayley said.

"I wish I would have served a mission," Julia said. "I wish I could have found a nice guy to marry. I wish I could have made something of my life. I wonder how different my life would be now."

"It's not too late," Brian said.

"It is for me," Julia said.

"Just have faith," Brian said.

Luke and Hayley liked that the kids were teaching the gospel and sharing their testimonies.

"Yeah, I noticed that when the Lord commanded Nephi and his brothers to go back to Jerusalem to convince Ishmael and his family, his daughters, to go on their journey, Laman and Lemuel didn't complain about that," Julia said. "They were all about getting married."

"You can still get married," Esther said.

"No, I just feel like I've missed out on so much," Julia said. "How can I ever be accepted by God?"

"Julia, are you familiar with the Provo Tabernacle?" Hayley asked.

"I remember it. It was built by the pioneers, right? I remember going to meetings there as a kid. Why do you ask?"

"Well, it burned down by accident. It was sad to see that inspiring building reduced to charred rubble. But guess what? The Church has transformed it into a temple and it's more beautiful than ever. That's what the Atonement of Jesus Christ can do for us. The Lord can transform our lives, if we let Him. He can rebuild us."

Julia didn't respond. She just sat quietly and stared out the window, lost in thought.

In St. Louis, the Mannings bought tickets to ascend the famous St. Louis Arch. When they arrived at the top, they enjoyed the views, with Mississippi stretched out on one side of the Arch, and the St. Louis Cardinals' Busch Stadium on the other.

The Mannings stayed the night in St. Louis and the next day, instead of taking I-70, they headed northwest to visit some Church history sites.

As fate would have it, they passed through Hannibal, Missouri, the hometown of Samuel Langhorne Clemens, aka Mark Twain, the father of American literature.

For Luke, it was serendipitous, and not something he had planned. But nobody else was interested in going there. He felt like since they were this close to Hannibal, they should pay homage to one of his favorite all-time writers — even though Mark Twain wasn't kind to the Mormons in his writings. In fact, during his first, yearlong visit to Utah, Luke tried to derive inspiration from Twain's irreverent musings about Utah and the Church.

Adventures of Huckleberry Finn was one of his favorite books. As a kid, Luke could relate to Huck's experiences, and moments when Huck learned important lessons about God and life.

As the Mannings, and Julia, walked around Hannibal, Luke looked up his favorite passage from Twain's book about Huckleberry Finn and read it to everyone:

"And I about made up my mind to pray, and see if I couldn't try to quit being the kind of a boy I was and be better. So I kneeled down. But the words wouldn't come. Why wouldn't they? It warn't no use to try and hide it from Him. Nor from ME, neither. I knowed very well why they wouldn't come. It was because my heart warn't right; it was because I warn't square; it was because I was playing double. I was letting ON to give up sin, but away inside of me I was holding on to the biggest one of all. I was trying to make my mouth SAY I would do the right thing and the clean thing … but deep down in me I knowed it was a lie, and He knowed it. You can't pray a live — I found that out."

"You can't live a lie, either," Julia said. "I found that out."

Luke explained to everyone that the name "Mark Twain" was a Mississippi River term that referred to the second mark on the line that measured depth signified by two fathoms, 12 feet, which was a safe depth for steamboats that regularly made their way down the river.

Near the river, they found a statue of Twain, gripping the wheel of a steamboat. The statue sat on top of a slab of rock that was donated by someone from Utah, a person known, as it said, as "a good Mormon."

It surprised him a little, knowing the rocky relationship between Twain and the Church.

Then Luke thought about that phrase, "a good Mormon." That sounded like a pretty good compliment to him, something he wouldn't mind engraved as an epitaph on his headstone.

It reminded him of something Ben Kimball liked to say: "If you were accused of being a Christian, or a Mormon, would there be enough evidence to convict?"

The Mannings enjoyed one last spectacular view of the mighty Mississippi River. They also took pictures of the kids next to Becky Thatcher's house, and the white picket fence that Tom Sawyer tricked his friends into whitewashing.

From there, the Mannings drove to Adam-ondi-Ahman, located near the community of Gallatin, Missouri in Daviess County.

Hayley explained to the kids, and Julia, that this was where Adam and Eve went after they were forced to leave the Garden of Eden. Before his death, Adam bestowed one last blessing upon his righteous posterity here.

"Joseph Smith taught that Adam-ondi-Ahman means 'the place or the land of God where Adam dwelt,'" Hayley explained.

When they walked to the site, they looked out into a lush, verdant valley.

"It's just a big open space," Esther said. "There's nothing here."

"Not yet. But one of the most important gatherings in the world will take place here someday," Luke said. "This is where, after Christ's Second Coming, a giant sacrament meeting will be held. Adam will be here. So will many other great, resurrected beings. The Savior will be here, and this is where He will take back the priesthood keys, and begin his millennial reign on the Earth. That's going to be a tough ticket to get."

"I bet those tickets won't be available on Stub Hub," Brian said.

"Christ's Second Coming will usher in the Millennium. That will be one thousand years of peace, with no disease or death," Hayley said. "It will be a time when the righteous who are on earth will be very busy teaching the gospel and doing temple work. When people die, they won't be buried. They'll be resurrected in 'the twinkling of an eye.'"

"I want to be alive for that," Benjamin said.

"This is such a beautiful, peaceful place," Julia said. "I just wish I would have known about places like this."

"Well, we're going to another amazing place right now," Luke said as he loaded everyone back into the RV.

That would be the Liberty Jail Church Historic Site, where the Mannings learned about Joseph Smith's five-month imprisonment in abysmal conditions. The visitors center featured a replica of the jail cell.

"See," Luke joked with the kids, "being stuck in a motor home for a month isn't as bad as you thought, huh?"

As they ate a picnic lunch, Hayley explained that what Joseph

Smith suffered Liberty Jail was instructive to all members of the Church.

"Kind of ironic — a jail named 'Liberty,' right? Some have called Liberty Jail a temple because of what Joseph learned there about how to deal with opposition and trials, and what he learned about Heavenly Father always being there for us. Sometimes the most sacred experiences we can have in life, including receiving revelation, happens when we are in miserable conditions. Then we're humble enough to be taught by the Lord. Dad went through something like that when he was in Africa."

"That's right," Luke said. "I know what it's like to be a prisoner. And I can tell you, even though I was in a horrible prison — I thought I might die — I never felt closer to Heavenly Father. I won't bore you with the story again."

"It's not boring," Brian said. "They should make a movie about it."

"That would be cool," Luke said.

While driving to Kansas City, Julia had Luke tell her the whole story of his abduction in Africa.

"You can read more about it in a book my dad wrote," Esther said.

"I would love to read it," Julia said. "But I've got to get through the Book of Mormon first. But it sounds like they should make your book into a movie."

After touring the Independence Visitors' Center and the Far West Temple site, Luke parked near the Harry S. Truman Sports Complex, which houses Arrowhead Stadium, home of the Kansas City Chiefs, and Kauffman Stadium, home of the Kansas City Royals.

The Royals were playing later that night, so the Mannings decided to give away free cookies and some of their last copies of the Book of Mormon. They set up and most Royals fans, and others they came in contact with, were very friendly. A few even took a copy of the Book of Mormon.

Two men in their 30s approached the Mannings and each grabbed a cookie.

"Would you like a free copy of the Book of Mormon?" Benjamin said.

"Wait," one of the men said, "you're Mormons?"

"Yes," the kids replied in unison.

The men threw their cookies in a garbage can, and whirled around with disdain in their eyes.

"You Mormons are bigots," one of the men said. "You may preach love, but you don't believe in love. You hurt people. You think you can win people over with your cookies when you judge and try to tell people what to do? Go away. We don't want you here. Hate is not a family value."

"We don't hate anyone," Julia said. "These kids are just trying to do something nice. Y'all stop being so rude."

The kids were shell-shocked and confused by the accusations and display of anger.

"You should seek Jesus, not His 'church,'" one woman told them with a sneer.

"The trouble with that," Julia said, "is nobody agrees on all of His teachings. We believe Jesus has His Church on Earth today. It's called The Church of Jesus Christ of Latter-day Saints."

Julia surprised herself how easily those words came out of her mouth.

The woman huffed and walked away. Then security showed up and told the Mannings they needed to leave.

"Apparently, Mormons still aren't welcome in these parts of Misery. I mean Missouri," Luke joked. "Sounds like we're being exterminated again."

The Mannings, and Julia, piled back into the motor home. Luke and Hayley had a long discussion with the kids about why some people dislike the Church. It was a foreign concept to them.

"Prophets have said in the last days, we will be persecuted like our pioneer ancestors were in Nauvoo and Missouri," Hayley said. "Our beliefs, and the world's beliefs, are growing farther and farther apart. We need to be strong and be prepared to defend our faith when necessary."

As Luke drove through pancake-flat Kansas, with nothing to see for hundreds of miles at a time, he had a lot of time to think. He felt like he had been driving through the wilderness for 40 years, like Moses.

Luke pondered the reality TV show offer. Was it the answer to all of his prayers? What else was he going to do to support his family?

Since Julia had joined the Manning traveling party, Luke had almost forgotten about Randolph's offer — until Randolph started text messaging him, asking if they had made a decision.

The Mannings stopped for gas in Lawrence, Kansas, and Luke decided to end the debate. He turned to Hayley.

"I think you're right. We can't be on a reality TV show. That's just crazy, right? What was I thinking? While you guys go to the bathroom, I'll call Randolph and tell him thanks but no thanks."

Hayley relieved, and somewhat surprised by Luke's willingness to respect her perspective without a little more resistance. She had figured that this discussion would continue for a while after they returned home.

"That's your final decision?" Hayley asked.

"Yes, I've thought a lot about it. You're right. That's not for us. I mean, I thought it was a temporary solution to our financial issues, but I feel the Lord has something else for us to do. What it is, I don't know."

Hayley smiled and placed her hand on his shoulder.

"I'm glad you came around," she said. "I knew you'd figure it out on your own."

"Yeah, I'm a little slow," Luke said.

"Look on the bright side, with all this experience driving this RV," Hayley joked, "maybe you could drive a school bus."

"I'm qualified now, that's for sure," Luke said.

Yes, he was still unemployed. Returning home meant facing that harsh reality, as well as the fact that money would probably continue to be tight for quite a while. All of the funds Luke had earmarked for the trip, from those freelance articles, had been spent. In fact, they had gone over their budget.

Hayley tracked every penny they spent on gas, but Luke didn't want to know how much that total was.

After fueling up, Luke called Randolph on his cell phone and told him their decision.

Randolph was disappointed. He offered an increased amount of money per episode, but Luke bit his lip and held firm.

"Again, we're flattered that you would consider us for a show. But after spending the past month traveling all over the country, we've decided that we belong in Helaman, Utah."

"I respect your decision," Randolph said. "What your family can offer is the kind of entertainment a lot of people in the world are starving for — humorous, unscripted, wholesome, inspirational. There are all sorts of videos on YouTube of families doing all sorts of stuff that go viral. Millions of hits. Like that 'Charlie bit my finger' on YouTube. I still laugh every time I watch that. And what your twin girls were doing in the restaurant the other day — that was cyberspace gold."

"When Jacob bit Benjamin's finger a few days ago, Benjamin put Jacob in a headlock," Luke said. "It wasn't pretty."

"If you ever change your mind, you know how to get a hold of me," Randolph said. "I hope you realize what you have, Luke. You've got an amazing family. You know, in a way, I envy you. I never married. I never had kids. I thought that would get in the way of making money. I've worked 80-hour weeks since I was in my 20s. But the older I get, I realize that when I'm retired, I just might be alone. I'll have nothing to live for. And when I die, I'll probably die alone. All of my money will go to the government. But look at you. What a legacy you're leaving on the world."

Why, Luke wondered, did it take people like Aunt Maureen, Julia, and some big-shot reality TV producer, of all people, to make him realize, or at least remind him, just how blessed he was?

When the kids were asking for the 10,000[th] time how much longer until they arrived at home, Hayley shared some good news.

"We're almost to Colorado," she said. "We're almost one state away from home."

"So we'll be home in like 30 minutes?" Jacob asked.

"Not exactly," Hayley said. "What was your favorite part of our trip?"

"The Basketball Hall of Fame," Brian said. "And Nauvoo."

"Swimming!" Jacob said.

"Carthage Jail," Esther said. "The Sacred Grove. And Rockefeller Center."

"What was the worst part?" Luke asked.

"The driving!" Brian and Benjamin shouted at the same time.

"The driving? What are you talking about?" Luke said. "You guys didn't have to drive at all."

Then Luke's cell phone rang. Hayley picked it up to see who was calling.

"Let me guess — it's Randolph again, asking us to reconsider," Luke said.

"Nope," Hayley said. "It's Ben. President Kimball."

"Ben? What does he want? Hopefully, he's not telling us our house has burned down. Or flooded."

Hayley answered the phone. "Hi, Ben. I mean, President."

"Hayley, how's the trip going?" Ben asked. "Almost home?"

"Yes, we're about to cross into Colorado. It's been a great trip but we're excited to get home."

"That's great," Ben said. "I'm guessing Luke is at the wheel. Could you put him on speaker phone for me?"

Hayley pressed the speaker phone button.

"Luke, are you sick of driving yet?" Ben said.

"Let me put it this way — next time we drive across the country, we're flying."

Ben laughed.

"Your YouTube channel is getting more and more subscribers by the day," he said. "Before you know it, you'll be surpassing 'Kid History.' We're living your trip vicariously on the Internet. Your family has done a lot of good."

"Why do I get the feeling you are about to ask me to do something?"

"OK, I'll get to the point. As I'm sure you know, we've got stake conference on Sunday morning, and I would like you to speak."

"I thought we were friends," Luke joked. "Did someone back out at the last minute?"

"How'd you guess? Brother Wilcox broke his leg last night playing stake softball."

"That's a pretty lame excuse."

"I wanted to know if you could pinch hit."

"You really know how to let a guy ease back in after a vacation. What do you want me to talk about, and for how long?"

"The topic is right up your alley — missionary work. I need you to speak for 15 minutes. Feel free to draw upon your recent experiences of your cross-country journey."

When he hung up with Ben, Luke told Hayley, "So much for sleeping in Sunday morning."

After spending the night at a Walmart parking lot in Denver, they drove to the Denver Temple and took more photos before starting their final leg home. When they passed the "Welcome to Utah" sign, the kids cheered, waking up Julia.

As much as Luke was looking forward to returning home, a sense of doom momentarily overcame him again. He thought about the mountain of unpaid bills that would be awaiting him, and the prospect of having to do back-to-school shopping at Deseret Industries.

But the Mannings needed to make one more detour. Instead of going straight to Helaman, they got off on one of the Provo exits to stop by Julia's parents' house.

I hope they're home, Luke thought.

The Hampton family lived just below "Y" Mountain. Brother Hampton was a retired BYU economics professor.

Julia wanted Hayley to go to the door and explain the situation. Julia thought it wouldn't be wise to show up on their porch unannounced. Hayley had rehearsed 100 times in her mind what she was going to say to these strangers.

"I hope I say the right thing," Hayley said.

Julia was trembling. "This is going to be harder than I thought," she said.

Hayley kept Julia's notes-on-napkins in her pocket.

When the Mannings pulled up to the rambler house with a modestly landscaped yard, Julia gasped.

"This is my house," she said. "It looks almost the same as it did 35 years ago. And look! They still have that brown Oldsmobile. I learned to drive in that car."

As Hayley walked up to the path leading to the front door, she repeated her carefully rehearsed introduction in her mind. But after knocking on the door and seeing an elderly woman answer, all Hayley could do was cry. She could only imagine how she would feel as a mother of an estranged daughter.

The woman hugged Hayley. "Are you OK, dear? Can I help you?"

"My name is Hayley Manning," she said, trying to compose herself. "We are returning home to Utah after a cross-country trip. While we were gone, we met your daughter, Julia, in Memphis, Tennessee."

The woman placed her hands over her mouth.

"Dell!" she said, calling for her husband.

Then she invited Hayley inside.

Hayley sat down and presented the Hamptons with napkins filled with writing. She related the entire story about how they had prayed for missionary experiences, how they were led to Memphis, and how they met Julia.

The Hamptons tried to decipher the words scrawled on napkins.

"We've been praying for our daughter every morning and every night for years, ever since she left," Sister Hampton said. "We have fasted for her once a month. We didn't know what became of her. Every day we've prayed that her heart would be softened, and someday we'd be reunited."

"Well, those prayers have been answered," Hayley said. "How would you like to see your daughter?"

"I'm booking a flight to Memphis right now," Brother Hampton said, pulling out his smartphone.

"You don't need to," Hayley said. "She's here, in front of your house. But she's nervous to come in."

The aging parents sprang off the couch like they had been catapulted, and they ran as fast as they could to their driveway.

Julia was standing there, sobbing next to the hydrangea bush. A glorious reunion ensued as Julia embraced her parents. Tears flowed. No words were necessary. The Hamptons' prodigal daughter had returned, ending decades of separation and heartache.

The kids watched the scene in silence and wonder from the windows of the RV.

"I guess you're never too old to go home and see your mom and dad," Jacob observed.

The Mannings said goodbye to let them be together and drove away. They felt blessed for playing a role in helping end a turbulent and painful period for a family.

"I guess I'll admit it," Luke said as he headed back toward the freeway. "Taking that little side trip to Memphis was a pretty good idea."

CHAPTER 32

WHEN THE MANNINGS PULLED into their driveway on that Friday evening, Luke noticed the RV's trip odometer read 7,998 miles. He stared to back up and continue driving down their street.

"Luke, what are you doing?" Hayley asked.

"We need to drive around the block a few times so we can break the 8,000-mile barrier."

For some reason, that's when it all sunk in for Hayley. First, they had made it safely home, which she regarded as a miracle. Another miracle? She realized she didn't suffer any major headaches during the month-long trip.

And, to Hayley's relief, the house was still standing. Her parents rushed over to welcome them home. Buzz looked like he had doubled in size since they left. Buzz was so excited, he jumped on Luke, licked the kids' faces, then reverted to puppy-like behavior by relieving himself in every room of the house.

While the Mannings were happy to be home, after all they had seen, felt, and experienced the previous month, Luke figured that everything in their lives moving forward would be as anticlimactic as the day after Christmas.

On Saturday, Hayley had everyone help out with a major house deep cleaning, including dusting, vacuuming, and cleaning the blinds. When that was done, Luke and Brian mowed and edged the lawn, which had grown almost to Brian's shins.

Luke had arranged for one of the deacons in the ward to mow while they were gone, but it appeared he had forgotten.

Then the Mannings spent hours scouring the inside and outside of the RV, the place they had called home for the previous month.

By nine o'clock that night, Luke sat down at his desk and started formulating his talk. The words came easily. He realized that he had been preparing for this talk for a while without even knowing it.

The next morning, Ben introduced Luke as the next speaker. Luke stood at the pulpit in front of a large congregation at the stake center. He thought he would be nervous, but then he remembered he had recently been on national TV. How hard could it be?

Brothers and Sisters, my family and I just returned from an 8,000-mile, month-long, cross-country trip two days ago. It was 26 states in 32 days. That's why I may look a little haggard and act a little loopy, although my wife would say that's how I am normally. I'm dealing with a serious case of RV-lag. But that journey was a life-changing experience for me and for my family. We had some amazing spiritual experiences at Winter Quarters, Nauvoo, Kirtland, Palmyra, and Fenway Park.

I'd like to share with you some things that I learned from our transcendent trip.

First, I learned that while you don't need to go to the Sacred Grove to gain a testimony of the First Vision, if you have an opportunity to go there, or any other Church history sites, please go. There's nothing quite like being there. We deepened our testimonies of the Prophet Joseph Smith, and our appreciation for the early Saints who sacrificed so much for us.

Before our trip, when we'd try to show Church history-related movies to our kids, they'd roll their eyes. Now when they watch those kinds of films, they say, "Hey, I know where that is! I've been there!" And they actually watch them — at least for the first 15 minutes.

Pretty much every day on our trip we'd see a handful of iconic places. If one of those places had been experienced independently, we would have enjoyed spending the next year talking about it and reflecting on it. But on this whirlwind, drive-by approach to Church history and American history, we saw so many historic locations each day the kids would forget what they had seen by dinnertime. We encouraged our older kids to write in their journals each night. And every night, before they would start writing they would ask, "Dad, what did we see today?"

"Oh, I don't know," I would say. "Let's see, we saw the Sacred Grove, Joseph Smith's home, the Palmyra Temple, the Grandin Press Building, the Hill Cumorah, the Peter Whitmer Farm, Niagara Falls, and the Baseball Hall of Fame. That's about it."

"Oh yeah," they'd say while yawning.

I don't think they appreciate it all now, but hopefully someday they will.

I learned that one minute I could have tears of gratitude in my eyes thinking about how the pioneers sacrificed and suffered for us; and the next minute I wanted to scream in exasperation at the sight of my boys performing mixed martial arts on each other inside Brother Toolson's vintage RV. Don't worry, brother Toolson, we patched the holes.

I learned that being together as a family in tight, claustrophobic quarters for an extended period of time is both a blessing and a burden.

I learned that for some reason, no matter what kind of vehicle you travel together in as a family, there's always some mysterious odor emanating from the back seat.

I learned that the gospel is easy to share and easy to understand. In fact, it can be summed up in the Primary song, "I Am A Child of God." I learned it is a simple but powerful hymn when it comes to inviting the Spirit, including for those not of our faith.

I learned that if we pray for, work for, and look for miracles, God will perform them according to our faith in Him, His will and His power to produce miracles. And as our faith grows, He will produce more miracles — if we pray for, work for, and look for them.

I learned that sometimes we miss out on opportunities to experience miracles because we're too busy to notice God's hand in our lives and His willingness to intervene on our behalf.

Lastly, I learned that there will be no Mormons in heaven.

Now, as for this final lesson learned — before you tar-and-feather me, or before I am struck down for heresy — please let me explain. I love the gospel, I love The Church of Jesus Christ of Latter-day Saints, I love that we are led by living prophets and apostles, and I love the members of this Church. I am so grateful to be surrounded by so many strong members and strong examples.

However, sometimes we forget that we are all children of a loving Heavenly Father. We were blessed to meet and associate with many people during our trip. "I Am a Child of God" applies to all people. No matter what we look like, no matter what we believe, no matter where we live, no matter what we do. No matter whether we believe in the Savior or not. We are children of God, and nothing will ever change that.

That's why I don't believe there will be labels in heaven — or in what we know as the Celestial Kingdom. Labels are created by man, not by God. That's why I believe you won't find Mormons in heaven, or Southern Baptists or Nephites or Catholics or Athiests or Multi-level marketers.

I believe in heaven, you'll only find righteous, obedient, humble children of our Heavenly Father — those who make and keep covenants, those who have been cleansed and transformed though the Atonement of Jesus Christ, which was wrought for all of Heavenly Father's children.

When Jesus was asked who is the greatest in the kingdom of heaven, He "called a little child unto him, and set him in the midst of them and said, Verily I say unto you, Except ye be converted and become as little children, ye shall not enter into the kingdom of heaven. Whosoever therefore shall humble himself as this little child, the same is greatest in the kingdom of heaven."

I know we always talk and sing about being children of God, but I think we'll be surprised when we go on to the next life and discover how literally we're all related. I think we'll be shocked to realize when we pass through the veil how much we share in common. We're brothers and sisters. At church, we call each other "Brother and Sister." We're linked in ways we'll never understand in mortality.

We're commanded to "love thy neighbor as thyself." When the Savior shared the parable that illustrated how we should love our neighbor, remember, the hero of the story is a "Samaritan," a type of person that Jews looked down upon and hated. But this "Good Samaritan" had compassion and rescued the stranger. The Samaritan did not avoid the bloodied and beaten man on the road. He did not pass him by. We are commanded to "go and do thou likewise" — and that's how we love our neighbor.

Again, after this life, I believe we'll be stripped of labels. We'll all just be children of God. The challenge for each of us is being able to see everyone as a child of God, especially those who are outcasts or are marginalized on the fringes of society.

I've been assigned by President Kimball to talk about missionary work and, coincidentally, we spent quite a bit of our family trip trying to do missionary work.

Some of you may know that by profession, I am a journalist. Most of the news I've reported in my career has been bad news. I love that the meaning of the word "gospel" is "good news." It *is* good news, and it is the best news. Missionary work is simply delivering the good news of the gospel to those who haven't heard it yet — or, at least don't remember accepting it in the pre-Earth life.

We met so many people on our trip that don't look, act or believe like we do. And it was a wonderful experience. God is the author of diversity. He created us all differently. He created thousands of species of flowers because together, the differences make the world a beautiful place. And he created billions of children, and our differences make the world a beautiful place. It's like a great symphony comprised of many different and diverse instruments that together create a melodious, sweet-sounding harmony that enriches our lives.

On our trip, we left the majesty of the Rocky Mountains, drove through the plains of the Midwest, and its "amber waves of grain." We saw lush vegetation, and towering skyscrapers, on the East Coast.

As my son Benjamin put it so eloquently, "How boring would it be if every place were the same? There would be no reason to go on vacation."

I think sometimes we believe that God wants us to be exactly the same — that we must think and feel the same way. But He is not a cookie-cutter creator. In order to be truly successful in missionary work, we need to avoid being provincial. The Church is not just for white people from Utah. That's the image many people conjure up when they think of the Church. But children of God come in all shapes, sizes, colors, cultural heritages, and backgrounds. The gospel is for everyone, not just those who are clean-cut and have a Costco membership. The gospel is for those who have tattoos, Mohawks, and wear skinny jeans.

On our trip, we met many good members of the Church who hold the same beliefs, but don't have the same perspective or attitudes that many of us have in Utah. This Church is bigger than just Utah. We can't be afraid to approach those who are different from us and we can't be afraid to share the gospel with them. We never know who is prepared to embrace it. Our responsibility, as members of the Church, is to participate in the gathering of Israel.

In the Old Testament, the Lord showed Daniel a vision in which the gospel shall be as the stone cut out of the mountain without hands that would roll forth and fill the whole Earth. God's children are being prepared to accept the gospel everywhere.

We who are from Utah are peculiar. We're insulated in a bubble here of sorts. I happen to be an expert in this subject because I am a convert. I'm a New York native who lives in Utah, so I'm peculiar in more ways than one. Honestly, there have been times when I've felt out of place here, despite being a member of the Church, because of my background. But what you may not realize is how much I envy those of you who have grown up in the gospel. You may not appreciate what a great blessing that is.

I originally came to Utah to write a book, only to discover another book — the Book of Mormon — that changed my life.

Within that book, in the book of Fourth Nephi, which happens to be one of my favorite books in the Book of Mormon — and not just because it is one of the shortest — it talks about how the Nephites and Lamanites are converted to the Church of Christ after Jesus' appearance in the Americas. In verse 17 it reads: "There were no robbers, nor murderers, neither were there Lamanites, nor any manner of –ites; but they were in one, the children of Christ, and heirs to the kingdom of God."

As proud as I am to hail from Utah and be a "Mormon," that title is not what's important. The most important titles are "Child of God" and "Disciple of Christ." We all have the opportunity to choose whether we want to follow His plan or not. Remember, the Savior suffered and died so everyone could be resurrected and cleansed through His atonement, even knowing that many would reject Him. That's why we shouldn't fear being rejected by others when we try to share His gospel.

Being a member of the Church is not like being a member of an exclusive, elitist country club. Like the Lord, we invite all to come in and be one with us. Our Heavenly Father's Plan is for everyone.

As members of the Church, we have been given a precious gift — the fullness of the gospel of Jesus Christ. We take it for granted; at least I know I do. Sometimes we tend to judge people we meet and think, "This person would never accept the gospel" for one reason or another.

I'm living proof that God loves all of His children, despite our weaknesses, sins, and idiosyncrasies. I will forever be grateful to those who didn't judge me when I first arrived in Utah many years ago. Our stake president, Benjamin Kimball, never gave up on me, although I gave him plenty of reasons to along the way. He was patient, loving, and kind. He was a true friend and stood by me, even when he didn't agree with my actions or decisions. President Kimball ended up baptizing me. I never would have joined the Church without the selfless love and genuine concern for me by so many people that I met here in Utah.

My beautiful wife, Hayley, has taught me so much about the gospel by the way she lives her life. We were sealed for time and all eternity in the temple. One thing she has taught me is, life is not about what we receive, but what we give. Now we have seven children, who have also blessed my life. I know that I can be with them forever.

I arrived in Utah to learn all I could about the Church, never thinking that one day I would become a member. I was the antithesis of everything the Church represents. But the closer I looked at members of the Church here, the more I realized they had challenges and problems like anyone else in the world. But I also realized that because of the gospel, they were equipped to handle those challenges and problems. I noticed that members of the Church loved and served one another.

At the risk of getting too autobiographical, I'll tell you that my dad left my mom and I when I was young. Then my mom abandoned me, so I spent a lot of my formative years living in foster homes. While living in Syracuse, New York, as a young boy, I went into a Catholic church one day and prayed that God would help me. And because God didn't immediately snatch me up and save me at that very moment, I thought for a long time that He didn't exist. I just didn't understand His plan for me. As I look back on my life and experiences, I see that He has been with me all along. He answered that prayer in His own time and in His own way. I've seen Him do that for many others as well.

Despite my many faults and weaknesses, I've come to understand that I am His son and that He loves me. And I know that He feels that way about all of His children.

I'll admit that I've felt a little like a second-class citizen in the Kingdom of God because I am a first-generation Mormon. Or at least I thought I was. Thanks to the stake goal for this year to do more family history, I recently discovered that I come from pioneer stock after all. A few of my ancestors on my dad's side of the family were actually baptized in England, arrived in this country, and made it all the way to Winter Quarters, but had to return to the East Coast. That's where my family's connection to the Church ended. But my great-great-great-grandfather Ezekiel Manning was promised in his patriarchal blessing that his ancestors would embrace the gospel. Well, it took God a while, but He got around to fulfilling that promise.

While we were in Nauvoo during our trip, my daughter, Esther, and my son, Brian, and I were able to do temple work for a number of our ancestors, including my father. It was one of the most spiritual experiences of my life.

For my part, I have resolved to be more fully committed to living the gospel and sharing it. I know the gospel is true. I know it because of how I feel when I live it. I've had too many witnesses, too many answers to prayer, to deny that. I want to put God first. I do that by doing the little things every day — praying, studying the scriptures, and serving others. That's what has brought me true happiness in my life. Those are the most important things I can do every day.

My wife and I are striving to teach our children to do the same.

I certainly don't have all the answers, but I know that when I live the gospel, I feel peace. I feel happy. It doesn't matter how many people say that there's no God or that the Book of Mormon is a work of fiction and that Joseph Smith was a fraud.

Among the mountains of evidence that Joseph Smith was a prophet, I know that he couldn't have written the Book of Mormon. When I write a book, or even an article, I use a word processor, an Internet connection, and Google. Even with all of that, and a college degree, and years of writing experience, it's pretty hard. There's no way a young, uneducated farm boy could have written that book.

Besides that, I know the Book of Mormon is true because I asked God and He revealed that knowledge to me.

And every time I read its words, the truthfulness of the book is confirmed to my heart again.

That's one of the many things I love about the gospel. We can ask Heavenly Father, the Most Powerful Being in the Universe, to find out what's true or what we need to do. If we ask sincerely, He will answer us through the power of the Holy Ghost.

There's a big difference between the culture of the Church and the doctrine of the Church. I believe that the Lord wants us to focus more on the doctrine, like missionary work. As our family prayed for missionary experiences, the Lord answered those prayers in miraculous ways. We blessed the lives of others, and they blessed us.

On my family's cross-country trip, we saw and experienced a lot of different cultures. But the only culture that matters is the culture of the restored gospel of Jesus Christ. Let's live it every day.

I'm living proof that God doesn't just answer the prayers of members of The Church of Jesus Christ of Latter-day Saints. He will answer the prayers of all of His children. We are children of God, no matter how different we look or act or believe. He loves all of us.

May we all share the gospel with everyone.

In the name of Jesus Christ, Amen.

CHAPTER 33

NO DOUBT, LUKE'S STAKE conference talk created quite a stir.

Some stake members said it was one of the best non-general conference talks they had heard in a while.

Some called it too edgy and controversial, bordering on sacrilege and blasphemy. Someone asked Luke if he were a liberal. One guy asked him if he were a socialist. Those people missed the point of Luke's talk.

For some, all they heard was that there would be no Mormons in heaven. They gasped in shock, then tuned out and didn't hear anything else Luke said. They were too busy thinking about what they would write in their carefully worded complaint letter to the First Presidency.

Meanwhile, Luke and his family tried to return to normal life after their trip.

While the Mannings' problems didn't disappear, everyone seemed to be kinder to each other and more patient with one another. Luke noticed that the kids were a little more obedient and grateful for what they had. Luke attributed that to their newfound appreciation for the gospel on their cross-country expedition, and the fact that they were no longer eating Cup-o-Noodles and saltine crackers for almost every meal. And they loved sleeping in their own beds again.

283

Every day on their trip, the Mannings had prayed that they might be instruments in God's hands to help someone in need. The reverberations of those answered prayers continued to be felt when they returned home. Occasionally, they heard from their new friends they met, as well as complete strangers.

Luke read social media comments and feedback on Facebook and the YouTube channel written by members and non-members alike, from far-flung places like New Zealand, Chile, Brazil, Ghana, England, Tonga, and Idaho.

"I didn't know they had Internet access in some of those places," Hayley said.

"Yeah. Who would have guessed they had computers in Idaho?" Luke joked.

Luke and Hayley hoped the lessons they were trying to imbue in their kids would last forever. But they weren't always sure how successful they were in that aim.

With the hundreds and hundreds of photos and the many videos the Mannings took during their trip, Luke decided to make a slideshow, set to music, to commemorate their trip in hopes that the kids would watch it and remember this experience the rest of their lives — and show it to their kids and grandkids. The soundtrack was well represented by Bruce Springsteen, Jimmy Buffett, and Tabernacle Choir songs.

Much to Hayley's dismay, rare was the photo that captured everyone smiling at the same time. In some, the twins would be smiling, but Jacob would have his eyes closed. In others, there would be an ideal picture of Jacob, but the twins looked like they were sitting on a cactus. There were photos of Brian making bunny ears behind Benjamin's head.

But Hayley realized that those photos encapsulated her family as it really was, the good and the not-so-good. They were far from being a perfect family. They just belonged together perfectly.

There was one family photo in particular that Hayley adored — in front of the Nauvoo Temple. A nice, elderly woman leaving the temple offered to take the picture, and Hayley wondered if she had been a professional photographer. Everyone was smiling and to Hayley it seemed like a shaft of light from heaven surrounded them. She enlarged the photo, bought a frame, and hung it in the living room.

Hayley printed family photos of every temple they visited on their trip, and she framed them and displayed them on an entire wall in the kitchen.

For Luke, it was back to reality. In his elders quorum presidency meeting, his counselors got him up to speed on all the new developments while he was gone. There was plenty to be done.

Luke's biggest concern was the family's continuing financial crisis.

The trip was more expensive than they thought. Gas alone was more than $3,500. They had paid about $250 for driving on the many toll roads. Luke bought new tires for Brother Toolson's motor home when they returned to Utah.

The Mannings' savings were depleted and they had no source of income on the horizon. A bunch of bills were due.

Luke bought groceries on his credit card, not knowing how he would pay it off. He hated sinking into debt, praying that he wouldn't have to declare bankruptcy at some point.

As Luke contemplated his ominous situation one night, his phone rang. It was the stake executive secretary.

"Brother Manning, President Kimball would like to meet with you and your wife tomorrow night at seven p.m.," Brother Davis said.

As much as he liked President Kimball, Luke preferred talking to Ben instead. Luke tried to think of an excuse to postpone the meeting. He couldn't think of one that fast.

"We'll be there," Luke said.

Luke and Hayley were puzzled as to why the stake president would want to meet with them.

"Maybe I'm being released because I was gone for a whole month," Luke said.

"Maybe you're being released for saying Mormons aren't going to heaven," Hayley said, laughing.

That following night, the couple sat in the foyer outside the stake president's office.

"Do you realize it's been about one year since the last time we met with the stake president?" Luke whispered to Hayley.

Once again, Luke's intestinal tract felt tighter than a trampoline spring and his stomach was turning triple salchows.

Luke and Hayley sat on red upholstered chairs, listening to Tabernacle Choir music. The choir was singing "Faith in Every Footstep." And he couldn't help but think of Ezekiel Manning, and his own family's cross-country trip. Those thoughts calmed his nerves.

Then President Kimball's door swung open. Ben's perma-smile greeted them.

"Luke, Hayley, welcome," he said. "Come in and have a seat."

"Before you say anything, President, I apologize if I said something wrong the other day at stake conference," Luke said. "The no-Mormons-in-heaven bit? Was it too strong? I was a little worried you'd pull a lever and I'd disappear under a trapdoor beneath the podium. Or I thought you'd turn off the microphone."

Ben laughed. "I really liked your talk. In fact, something happened while you were speaking. I received an answer to a prayer."

"Really?"

"Yes. The reason I wanted to meet with you tonight is to release you from your calling as elders quorum president."

Luke and Hayley didn't know how to take that news.

"Sounds like I'm being fired," Luke said.

"No, you're not being fired. You did nothing wrong. In fact, you did a great job as elders quorum president. As I release you from that calling, I hope you feel that the Lord is pleased with your efforts. You've really blessed the members of your quorum. I know this because many elders in the quorum tell me privately how you've positively influenced their lives. What did you learn from that calling?"

"I learned, once again, that serving others brings happiness," Luke said. "I learned that the mantle of holding priesthood keys is real."

"Great answer," Ben said.

"It was my talk, wasn't it?" Luke said. "That's why you're firing me, um, releasing me, right?"

"No, no, it was a great talk, really," Ben said. "I enjoyed it. I loved your honesty and directness. It was a perspective the members of our stake needed to hear."

"Well, I guess I'll have a lot more free time now," Luke said.

"I wouldn't necessarily say that," Ben said.

"But I can grow back my facial hair, right?"

"I wouldn't do that if I were you."

"Why not?"

"Bishop Tompkins is due to be released soon, and the past few months I've been praying for inspiration to know who should be the next bishop of your ward. Then, during your talk, the name of your new bishop came to me."

"Can you let us in on the secret?" Luke asked.

"Yes, I can, actually. And I think you're going to be shocked."

Luke and Hayley braced themselves.

"Luke, the Lord would like you to serve as the new bishop of the Helaman 6th Ward."

Luke took Hayley's hand and gripped hard. Tears welled up in Hayley's eyes.

"This is crazy," Luke said. "I can't do this. Me? A bishop? A lot of people may lose their testimonies if you do this, you know. Including my wife. Are you absolutely sure about this?"

"Yes, I am absolutely sure. And, yes, you can do this. Luke, I can attest that the Lord has prepared you for this calling as bishop. We were right about calling you to be elders quorum president, weren't we?"

"The jury's still out on that," Luke said. "Isn't being bishop like a six-year sentence?"

"I would plan on serving approximately five or six years, yes. You've learned lessons the past year as elders quorum president that prepared you for this new assignment."

The words Luke had uttered in that prayer that late night at the Marriott Marquis in New York City the previous spring, when he promised to turn his life over to the Lord, echoed in his head.

"Have you forgotten that I'm unemployed?" Luke said. "I don't know how I can be a bishop of hundreds of people when I can't even provide for my own family."

"I'm going to promise both of you that the windows of heaven will be opened on your behalf because of the way both of you serve," Ben said. "Wouldn't you say that you've already witnessed many blessings in the past year?"

"Yes, we have," Hayley said.

"Now you watch and see," Ben said. "You'll be able to 'count your blessings, and name them one by one.'"

"I hope you're right. Since we got married, there's only one calling I've aspired to — team-teaching Primary with my wife. But *bishop*? Are you absolutely sure about this?"

All Luke could think of was that if fulfilling the duties of an elders quorum president was the equivalent of a part-time job, fulfilling the duties of a bishop was the equivalent of a full-time job, with no monetary compensation.

"Hayley," Ben said, "can you support Luke in this calling?"

"Of course," she said, wiping her eyes with a tissue.

"I should mention that this is a family calling, and Hayley, you will be like one of Luke's counselors," Ben said. "His most important counselor. Luke, be sure to listen to Hayley. And like I've told you before, you are a husband and father first. A bishop second. Your family should be your top priority above all else. For what shall it profit a man if he shall help rescue the whole ward and lose his own family?"

"I'll try to remember that," Luke said. "I think Hayley will do much better as a bishop's wife than I will as a bishop."

"By the way, Luke, I'd like the names of your two counselors in the next few days. We'll release you from the elders quorum presidency this week, but we won't sustain and set you apart for your new calling for a few more weeks."

"Good," Luke said. "It's going to take me at least that long to get used to this idea. I'm feeling completely overwhelmed right now. I desperately need some advice."

"Just remember that when it comes to the members of your flock, the Helaman 6th Ward, you can love them, you can serve them, you can teach them, but you can't save them," Ben said. "Only One can save them — Jesus Christ. That's the piece of advice that was given to me when I was called to be a bishop. It helped. One of your strengths is that you're non-judgmental. That actually comes in handy when you're a common judge in Israel, being able to see, and treat, everyone you meet as a child of God."

Despite Ben's edifying and encouraging words, Luke and Hayley returned home that night feeling overwhelmed. They found Esther cleaning up the kitchen from dinner. The twins were drawing pictures on the wall with crayons.

Brian and Benjamin were wrestling in the living room. Jacob was in the pantry, stuffing his face with crackers. Sarah was wearing nothing but a diaper, and sprawled out on the couch.

"Dad, what's wrong?" Esther asked. "You look really pale."

"I feel really pale," Luke said. "Mom and I have something to tell all of you."

Luke was good about keeping confidences but he knew the kids weren't. So he told them that he was going to be released as elders quorum president, and left it at that.

"Was it something you said at stake conference?" Esther asked.

"No," Luke said.

"That's cool," Jacob said. "Now can you be my Primary teacher?"

Luke smiled. "You don't know how much I would love that."

Luke and Hayley were glad they had a few weeks to prepare for and come to grips with this new calling, something neither one of them dreamed would ever happen.

They could only imagine how stunned ward members, and their own kids, would be.

As Luke looked back on the past year, he realized the Lord had been preparing him for this, just like Ben said.

But he certainly didn't have the typical profile for a Latter-day Saint bishop. Especially in a town like Helaman. Plus, having spent a year as elders quorum president, he had received a small glimpse of what bishops go through. That thought made him weak in the knees.

After Luke was formally released from his calling the next Sunday, ward members felt sorry for him, believing he had been unceremoniously demoted, and they went overboard thanking him for his service to the ward.

I appreciate the nice comments, Luke thought, *but I'm not dead or anything. Save something for my funeral.*

Many presumed the stake president didn't approve of Luke's comments at stake conference, and they believed that's why he was released.

A few others said they knew Luke wasn't prepared or cut out for a calling like elders quorum president anyway.

"He was only in for one year," Brother Bosworth told other members of the quorum. "Most elders quorum presidents serve for three years. He was in way over his head. Poor guy. Plus, he was gone for a whole month during the summer. He was an absentee elders quorum president. A change had to be made."

For Luke, the highlight of the day was being invited to stand in as the Harding's baby boy, Taysom, was given a name and a blessing by his grandfather. Luke promised himself that he would play catch with the boy as soon as he was old enough to put on a baseball glove.

CHAPTER 34

DURING THE MANY HOURS he drove on the trip, Luke had plenty of time to ponder how he could be a better father and husband. One thing he and Hayley decided to improve on was spending more one-on-one time with the kids. With this new calling, they both knew that would become even more important.

Usually, the Mannings did everything together as a family, which was a good thing, but Luke and Hayley realized they needed to invest time with each individual child, including the twins. So they resolved to do one-on-one activities with each of them. The kids needed that, and so did their parents. Also, Luke began doing one-on-one interviews with each of his kids every month, drawing upon what he learned from doing personal priesthood interviews with members of the elders quorum.

Many of those informal interviews involving buying ice cream cones and talking together at a park.

Luke asked Ben for counsel about being a good father and balancing that with magnifying his new calling.

"Fortunately, we have an ultimate role model, Heavenly Father," Ben said. "Even His title is instructive. 'Heavenly' describes not only where He lives but also *how* He lives."

Luke realized that he could be more heavenly in the way that he taught, talked, interacted, and even played, with his children. That was a way he could become more like Him.

As part of their plan to grow closer as a family, Luke and Hayley resolved to go to the temple to do work for Luke's ancestors, including taking Esther and Brian as often as possible to do baptisms for the dead.

"We have enough work now to keep us busy up to, and maybe through, the Millennium," Hayley said.

In addition to their standing appointment for date night each Friday, Luke and Hayley had a standing appointment to attend the temple together every Tuesday afternoon.

Every time Luke attended the temple, he thought about Ezekiel Manning. He realized that he was continuing to build the eternal Manning family bond and its connection with the Church — after a century-long hiatus. Luke resolved that this latest iteration of the Mannings in the Church would last forever.

Luke felt a renewed responsibility to live up to the legacy he never knew he had. With that perspective, he looked at everything differently.

Meanwhile, as President Ben Kimball had promised, the Lord opened the windows of heaven.

A local Latter-day Saint publisher that belonged to the Helaman North Stake approached Luke. He had listened intently to Luke's talk and he wanted to know if he would be interested in writing two books — one about his conversion story, and one about the Mannings' cross-country trip and how he discovered his ancestors' history.

"Hayley, I know you wanted our trip to be low-key, with no attention or fanfare," Luke told Hayley after the book offers came in. "How would you feel about me writing a book about our trip?"

"I guess I'd be OK with that," Hayley said. Then she smiled. "But it looks like the social media world already scooped you on that one."

Within a couple of weeks, Luke signed a contract for the two books, which provided a modest advanced that helped pay some bills.

While Luke was cleaning out the garage with Brian and Benjamin, his cell phone rang. He didn't recognize the number but he noticed it was from the 212 (New York City) area code. Luke wondered if Sal was coming back with another reality TV offer.

Instead, it was William Capshaw, an editor at a large, conservative web site. He wanted to gauge Luke's interest in being a columnist on family-related issues. William had seen the Mannings' *Today Show* appearance and was impressed. He had Googled Luke's work, including his newspaper articles from when he lived in New York, as well as *Grace Under African Skies*.

"Would you be interested in writing a bi-weekly, faith-based humor column about being a dad?" William asked. "There are a lot of mommy blogs out there, so we're looking for male voices that can address topics that men can relate to, including the growing stay-at-home dad audience. With any luck, we'll get it syndicated."

To Hayley, it sounded like a perfect arrangement for her husband, and she couldn't help but remind Luke that she had suggested that he write a "daddy blog" a while ago, an idea he had scoffed at.

As a columnist, the hours were flexible and it allowed him the ability to continue to help out with the kids and fulfill his calling. Plus, being around the kids would provide him with all the material he would ever need for his column. While Luke figured he wouldn't get rich with this endeavor, he would earn a steady paycheck.

Meanwhile, the Hamptons called Luke and Hayley one day to express again their profound gratitude for bringing their daughter, Julia, home. They invited the Mannings to their home to eat dinner with the entire family, so everyone could meet and thank them.

"Julia told us she would like to become a member in good standing of the Church," Brother Hampton said. "She is moving back to Utah. We are so happy that you and your family followed a prompting and went above and beyond the call of duty in bringing Julia back to us."

"That was all Hayley," Luke said. "She's the one who was inspired and insisted that we go to Memphis. I thought she was a little crazy. But she knew what she was doing."

"It says in Matthew, 'And whosoever shall compel thee to go a mile, go with him twain,'" Brother Hampton said. "Your family went with my daughter about a thousand miles. And because you did, we'll be eternally grateful."

"Glad we could help," Luke said. "We just happened to be on our way home."

Someone from the Tabernacle Choir called because he had seen Esther's performance on the *Today Show*. He was wondering if Esther would be interested in playing her violin as part of an upcoming choir concert.

Then someone from the Utah Jazz contacted Luke, asking him if his two sons would be available to perform during a halftime show of an exhibition basketball game that season. Brian and Benjamin were ecstatic.

"Dad, I told those kids in Chicago we'd be in the NBA someday," Brian said. "It's happening sooner than I thought."

Naturally, Luke invited Nicholai to Utah to watch the Tabernacle Choir concert and the Jazz game. Thanks to the kids, Luke had access to VIP seats for both events.

Nicholai came to Utah and fell in love with the mountains and the people. He enjoyed the concert, and the game. And when Luke took him to the Marriott Center to see Kresimir Cosic's retired jersey, he became emotional. It was like a spiritual experience for him.

Later that year, Nicholai transferred from the New York Marriott Marquis to the Provo Marriott.

Speaking of Marriott hotels, Luke also received an e-mail with the subject line "Marriott Book of Mormon Testimony."

Dear Brother Manning,

I am a member of the Church from Arizona. A couple of months ago, I stayed in the New York Marriott Marquis. I was there on business. I am in sales and I travel a lot for my job, all around the country.

Anyway, I happened to open the drawer by the nightstand and I saw a copy of the Book of Mormon with a piece of paper sticking out of it. I read your inspiring testimony inside. After I read it, I thought, 'Why didn't I think of that?' I always stay at Marriotts but it never occurred to me to leave my testimony inside. It's so simple. Well, I've been doing that ever since, and including my e-mail address at the end. I am writing you from my room at a Marriott in Orlando, Florida. I just received an e-mail from a woman who stayed at the Santa Clara Marriott in California. She was in the same room I had been in weeks earlier. She has been going through a divorce and her father has just died unexpectedly. As she sat on the bed, crying, she opened up the drawer and found my note inside the Book of Mormon. She began to read the book and said it brought her comfort and she could feel God's love. She thanked me for taking the time to write in it. I don't know what will happen from here with her, but I thought you'd like to know about this experience. Writing my testimony in the Book of Mormon in Marriotts around the world wasn't my idea. It was yours. I never even expected a response from anyone, but I did. I don't know you, but your simple gesture of sharing your testimony inspired me.

> *Your brother in the gospel,*
> *Reed Carmichael*

Those nights spent at the New York Marriott Marquis kept paying off for Luke, and he wasn't even enrolled in the Marriott Rewards Program.

Those nights spent in Brooklyn also paid off for Luke. He thought about Aunt Maureen every day. They traded e-mails for a couple of weeks after the Mannings returned from their trip. Ultimately, Luke convinced Maureen to fly to Utah for a visit.

Knowing of her fear of flying, Luke asked Hal Randle to give her a blessing to help her get through the five-hour flight. That, and the doses of Dramamine and Melatonin, must have worked because Maureen arrived in Salt Lake City looking calm and happy to be in Utah. The Mannings greeted her at the airport as if she were a returning missionary.

During Maureen's stay, Luke took her to the Family History Library in Salt Lake City, the largest genealogical library in the world, with more than 2.4 million rolls of microfilmed records. She was in genealogical heaven.

For years, Maureen had been stumped by a gaping hole in the Manning family line because certain census records eluded her. Names were missing. She hoped to find them in Salt Lake City.

Maureen explained her dilemma to a senior sister missionary, a retired schoolteacher, at the Family History Center. The missionary also had ancestors from the same area of England, and they discovered they were distantly related. Maureen was thrilled to find missing ancestors.

For three straight days, Luke drove Maureen to Salt Lake City in the morning and picked her up in the evening. Maureen camped at the library, sifting through records.

During those 45-minute drives, Luke and Maureen would have long, deep conversations about the gospel and the doctrine of the Church. Luke shared more about his conversion. Maureen let it slip that she went to church with Hal Randle back in Brooklyn one Sunday.

"What did you think about it?" Luke asked.

"It wasn't like any church I've ever seen," she said. "It wasn't fancy at all. It was quite plain. But the people there were very nice. I've always felt a strong kinship with our ancestors. But for some reason, I've felt it stronger than ever since I've been here in Utah. This may sound strange, but I feel like they are by my side, watching me."

"I don't think it sounds strange at all," Luke said. "It makes perfect sense. It's the 'Spirit of Elijah' we told you about."

"Well, I don't know about that, but I can't stop thinking about how different Ezekiel's destiny — our entire family's destiny — might have turned out differently had he gone to Salt Lake City rather than Syracuse. I can't figure out why, but even though I've never been here before, this place feels like home. I feel more connected with our ancestors and I feel connected with your family. It's like I've always known you."

"I think you have," Luke said. "I can't tell you how grateful I am to you for sharing so much history about our family with me. I'd been disenfranchised from our family for so long, and you brought me back. I'll be forever grateful to you for letting me in your house that day."

"As I recall, I didn't have much of a choice," Maureen joked.

Maureen mentioned to Luke a few times about her other hobby and passion, buying curios and antiques. So he took her to Deseret Industries.

"This is like a giant surplus store that's owned by the Church," Luke explained.

"Des-e-ray Industries?" Maureen said, reading the sign on the building.

"It's pronounced Des-e-*ret*," Luke said, "not Des-e-*ray*."

"Oh," Maureen said. "I thought Des-e-ray sounded like the name of a risqué French dancer."

Luke took pleasure in explaining what "Deseret" had to do with honeybees, referencing the Book of Mormon, and pointing out all the things that had "Deseret" in its title in Utah.

Luke and Hayley spent one afternoon hanging photos in their living room. Maureen had given them pictures of Manning ancestors, including Ezekiel. They hung those pictures next to the photo of their family posing in front of the Nauvoo Temple.

Maureen attended church with the Mannings, and when ward members found out that she was Luke's aunt — and a non-member — they fawned all over her as if she were *their* aunt. At first, Maureen was a little spooked but soon she felt like an honored guest.

For family home evening, Luke took his family and Maureen to This Is the Place Monument and then Temple Square for a tour. By the end of the evening, she agreed to listen to the missionaries.

"OK," Maureen said. "You've worn me down."

The Mannings invited the missionaries to meet with Maureen in their home.

She asked a lot of questions, and after continuing to study the Book of Mormon, doing plenty of soul-searching, offering many prayers, and having myths about the Church debunked, she agreed to be baptized.

In front of a large gathering of members of the Helaman 6th Ward, Luke baptized Maureen the day before she returned to New York. During the baptismal service, Esther played "Families Can Be Together Forever" on the violin while the congregation sang.

"Finally," Brian told Luke and Hayley that night, "we got a baptism!"

Luke called Maureen's bishop in Brooklyn, who already knew her. "Please take good care of my Aunt Maureen," Luke said.

Within a few weeks, the bishop called Maureen as a family history consultant.

Maureen also confided in Luke that she actually was quite wealthy. She had recently changed her last will and testament, which would leave her large savings account and most of her estate to Luke's children upon her death.

"They can use the money for their college educations, their weddings, their missions, or all three," Maureen said. "You can have whatever else you might want, including the New York Yankee baseball cards. The rest, I'm donating to 'Save the Whales.'"

CHAPTER 35

HAYLEY KNEW LUKE NEEDED a break from all the stress of his impending calling. Luke was carrying the weight of the calling without being set apart yet and it was getting to him.

So Hayley arranged for her parents to watch the kids. She blindfolded Luke, and helped him into the car. She started driving without offering any clues as to where they were headed.

"Where are we going?" Luke asked.

"You like surprises, don't you?"

"Of course. And you like blindfolding me, like I did to you, right?"

"Of course."

Besides the temple, Hayley knew of at least one place where Luke could relax, feel at peace, and shut out the outside world — a baseball diamond. She took him to a minor league baseball game in Salt Lake City. She bought him two hot dogs, a drink and some peanut M&Ms.

Luke couldn't have been more surprised or pleased. It was just what he needed.

Between innings, they talked about how they would continue to go on dates every week, no matter how busy they were.

"This has been a perfect night," Luke said, placing his arm

around Hayley's shoulder. "Let's do this again."

"How about next week, we see a chick flick."

"For you," Luke said, "I'll even go see a chick flick or attend a country music concert. And I promise I won't check my phone once to catch up on baseball scores."

After the game, Luke and Hayley stayed in their seats while the crowd filed out and the grounds crew sprayed and raked the infield dirt. They stared at the diamond with the lush green grass, and the perfectly symmetrical white baselines.

"If only life could always be this calm and orderly," Luke said. "This must be the calm before the storm."

Before Luke was sustained as bishop, Ben and Stacie Kimball went out to dinner with the Mannings to commiserate about the adventure they were about to embark on.

"I remember those years being a bishop's widow, I mean, wife," Stacie joked with Hayley. "You know I'm always here if you need someone to talk to or a shoulder to cry on. Being a bishop's wife isn't an official calling, but it's an indispensable one."

The Kimballs then gave the Mannings some sage advice.

"Schedule everything," Stacie suggested. "Our daily prayers are on the calendar. What we eat for breakfast is on the calendar. If it's not planned, chances are, it's not happening. This way, we're acting, instead of being acted upon. We're controlling what we can control."

"Are spontaneous activities scheduled, too?" Luke joked.

"This is how we've done it, and it's worked for us," Ben said. "But I'm sure you'll find a system that works for your family."

Due to the nature of his new calling, Luke was forced to prioritize his time carefully. He realized he would be able to accomplish much more that way.

Monday was reserved for family home evening. Luke's executive secretary would have control of his schedule on Sundays and Wednesday nights. Tuesday afternoon was temple day. Tuesday night was Young Men's and Young Women's. That left Thursday nights to spend one-on-one time with the kids or free up Hayley to go do something fun, like shopping, scrapbooking or reading.

Friday nights belonged to their weekly date night. Esther and Brian were usually the designated babysitters. And, of course, Saturday was a special day — the day they got ready for Sunday.

Hayley became almost fanatical about scheduling. When they

came home from the baseball game, Hayley unveiled a large whiteboard calendar, on which she created an intricate color-coded, easy-to-read schedule. On the bottom she printed a verse of scripture, D&C 88:119.

"Organize yourselves; prepare every needful thing; and establish a house, even a house of prayer, a house of fasting, a house of faith, a house of learning, a house of glory, a house of order, a house of God."

Hayley possessed a drawer full of Sharpies of every color of the rainbow and more. Each family member was represented by one of those colors. For example, all of Esther's violin lessons, Young Women's meetings, and choir practices, were written in yellow. Brian's football practices and Young Men's meetings were written in blue. Luke's bishopric and stake meetings were written in purple.

"Purple?" Luke asked.

"The kids picked the colors," Hayley said.

The weekly one-on-one time with the kids also appeared on the calendar.

Hayley hung her masterpiece in the kitchen so everyone could see it.

By being more organized, Hayley noticed her life felt more simplified and less cluttered. That allowed her family to make the most of the time they had together.

"It's, um, colorful," Luke said of the family calendar. "It looks like something that should be displayed in the Louvre Museum. Or the Smithsonian."

"Or maybe the bishop's office," Hayley said.

CHAPTER 36

THE SECOND WEEK OF AUGUST, Luke was sustained.

President Kimball uttered the immortal words, "The following individuals have been called, and we'd like them to stand when their names are presented. Luke Brian Manning has been called as bishop of the Helaman 6th Ward."

There were audible gasps — just like there were as he was sustained as elders quorum president, only louder. And longer. When he was sustained as elders quorum president it was in a quorum meeting in the chapel overflow. This was in sacrament meeting.

When President Kimball asked for a sustaining vote, Luke almost winced. To his relief, about every hand in the congregation was raised. The sustaining was unanimous in favor.

It was official. Who would have thunk it? Luke Manning was the bishop of the Helaman 6th Ward.

Isn't this one of the signs of the Apocalypse? Luke asked himself as he sat on the stand with his two counselors and President Kimball.

After the meeting, a crowd of people made their way to the stand to express their support, including Sister Harding.

"I want you to know that I am so glad you are the bishop," she said, holding her baby, Taysom, in her arms. "I sustain you with all my heart. My husband would, too, if he were here."

Brother and Sister Taylor informed Luke they were thrilled.

"I had a premonition that you would be our new bishop a while ago," Sister Taylor said.

"I wish you would have warned me," Luke said.

Brother Bosworth made it a point to shake Luke's hand.

"I sustained you, but I have to admit, I haven't received my own confirmation that you're supposed to be the bishop," he said. "I need some time to let this sink in."

"That makes two of us," Luke said. "I'm right there with you."

"I'm just going by faith here," Brother Bosworth said.

"Same with me," Luke said.

After sacrament meeting, Grit ordained Luke as a high priest. Like everyone else, Hayley's dad was incredulous about Luke's new calling but he was honored to ordain his son-in-law.

Then Ben set Luke apart as a bishop. Right after that, before Luke could even think clearly, with a blitzkrieg of feelings, emotions and impressions bursting from his heart, he sat down with the rest of the bishopric as part of a meeting in the bishop's office. The executive secretary informed Luke that he already had 12 appointments lined up for that week.

The first bishop Luke had ever met, Bishop Law, who had died several years earlier, was one of the finest men he ever knew. Bishop Law played an instrumental role in Luke's conversion. He was a true Christian, in Luke's estimation. Bishop Law was the gold standard that Luke compared all other bishops. Luke didn't feel worthy to hold the same title. He imagined Bishop Law rolling over in his grave until the resurrection.

When the dust settled, Luke met alone with his predecessor, Bishop Tompkins, in the bishop's office.

Bishop Tompkins enthusiastically handed over keys to the bishop's office, the bishop's desk, and the bishop's credenza, which was filled with confidential files. Bishop Tompkins brought Luke up to speed on pressing ward issues as Luke's capillaries were pulsating and his blood pressure soared to dangerous levels.

"Well," Bishop Tompkins said, "I wish you the best. I'll be praying for you, Bishop Manning. I support and sustain you. And I've left a bottle of extra-strength Tylenol in the top drawer of the credenza. You'll have some days when you'll need it."

"Now that you're released, what are you going to do?"

"I'm going to Disneyland," Bishop Tompkins said with a smile, like he had just won the Super Bowl. "I'm going with my family. It's been a while. I need to get away."

"You deserve it," Luke said. "Your family deserves it."

"Happiest Place on Earth," Bishop Tompkins said, looking wistfully at his former office.

"Any last advice for me?"

"Remember that confidentiality is so important when someone comes to you as bishop with a broken heart and a contrite spirit. Ward members need to know they can trust you."

"As a journalist, I've always protected and safeguarded my sources and off-the-record conversations," Luke said. "Someone could water-board me and I wouldn't say a thing."

"You can't imagine all the troubles you'll deal with and all the blessings you'll receive as you serve as bishop," Bishop Tompkins said. "While I'm glad to be released, believe it or not, a part of me envies you. It really is the greatest church calling in the world."

At home, the kids were surprised about Luke's new calling, but supportive. They had certain requests.

"Dad, since you're the bishop now," Brian said, "can you change our meeting schedule, so it's only one hour?"

"Dad, since you're the bishop now," Esther said, "can you decide where we go for girls' camp? Can we go to New York?"

"Dad, since you're the bishop now," Jacob said, "can I skip my final four years of Primary?"

Luke's first night as bishop was a sleepless one. Insomnia overpowered him. At 3 a.m., he woke up, walked into the bathroom, closed the door, turned on the light, and looked in the mirror.

In the mere hours since he was set apart, he swore his gray hairs had doubled, and a few new wrinkles had formed on his face. Training meetings, appointments, interviews, and a long list of duties swirled around in his head. The surreal moment when Ben announced Luke's sustaining kept replaying in his mind as if it were on a loop.

Bishop Manning.

To him, that sounded almost like blasphemy. Luke resigned himself to the fact that his life would never be the same — again.

He would soon learn that everyone in his ward looked at him, and treated him, differently as a bishop.

If only Ezekiel Manning could see him now. And Luke was

confident that he could — and he didn't want to let him down.

Luke took comfort in, was constantly humbled and amazed by, the realization that the Lord could utilize someone as flawed as he was as an instrument in His hands to assist him in His work.

CHAPTER 37

THE FOLLOWING SUNDAY, HIS FIRST full one as a bishop, Luke arrived 30 minutes before bishopric meeting so he could be alone.

When he got to the bishop's office, he saw dozens of letters and drawings taped to the door — courtesy of the Primary — with a sign that read, "We love you, Bishop Manning!"

His favorite message was from Jeremy Bosworth from the Valiant 8 class: "I don't care what everyone says, I think you will be a great bishop!"

Luke kept Ezekiel Manning's journal on his desk, just so he could remember his family's legacy.

Later, sitting on the stand and presiding over sacrament meeting for the first time, he looked out at the congregation. Ward members seemed to be looking at him, too. Even some of the less-actives had shown up that Sunday, maybe to see if the rumors were true. Maybe to see how Luke Manning would handle this new calling — or the other way around.

He noticed most of the chapel was full 10 minutes before the start of the meeting, which hardly ever happened. The overflow seating in the cultural hall was filling up. Luke turned to his first counselor, Brother Heimuli, who had spent the previous 10 years serving in the Primary. Brother Heimuli was famous for entertaining at ward parties by playing Tongan songs on his guitar.

"Are you sure there isn't a missionary farewell or baby blessing today?" Luke asked.

"Not that I'm aware of," Brother Heimuli said. "They probably came to see you. No pressure."

More than anything, Luke knew he would desperately miss sitting next to Hayley, and holding her hand during the sacrament. He would miss balancing the twins on his lap simultaneously, and trying to keep them quiet. What he wouldn't give to be back in one of the back pews. Luke exhaled, looked down, and noticed white powder on his suit pants. He brushed it off — he figured it was probably something from the twins' hands that had gotten on him that morning when he said goodbye to them.

Surveying the congregation populated with lifelong members of the Church, Luke was filled with love for a group of people that he didn't know was possible. Having served as elders quorum president, he was already aware of trials and struggles of almost every family in attendance.

Luke saw people in a way he never had before — he saw them as God saw them. It thrilled him but it also scared him. Ben had warned him about that. "It's part of the mantle of being a bishop," he had said.

It hit him that these members of the Church were there that day to find peace and healing. It was humbling to realize they were counting on him to ensure that sacrament meeting would be a spiritual, uplifting experience every Sunday.

When it came to being a judge in Israel, Luke knew he would always err on the side of mercy. A less merciful God, Luke knew, would have given up on him a long, long time ago.

As the prelude music swelled from the organ, Luke made eye contact with Hayley, and smiled. He noticed that he was receiving unsolicited promptings about certain individuals. He felt he needed to meet with one of the priests for some reason. Brother and Sister Gibbons should consider serving a mission. Brother Hicks could be the new Sunday School President.

Nobody in the ward could remember the start of a sacrament meeting that was as quiet as it was that day. It was so quiet that Luke could hear his heart thumping.

When the clock hit the appointed time, Luke rose from his seat, the prelude music faded, and he blurted a welcome to the congregation.

Then he made an unexpected announcement.

"In honor of the new bishopric, and the new school year coming up, for this week's youth activity, we'll be going to the temple to do baptisms," Luke said. "Afterward, we'll go to Brother Heimuli's house for a luau — kalua pork, grilled pineapple, and shaved ice. Brother Heimuli will be performing his fire knife dance."

The young women and young men let out a muffled cheer.

Though he had prepped in his mind for what he would say many times in the mirror that morning, and though he had a cheat sheet in front of him, he stumbled his way through the program.

When it came time to introduce the opening hymn, he realized he had forgotten to write it down. He glanced to see the hymn numbers posted on the wall behind him. His forehead was beaded with sweat.

"We'll sing hymn No. 2," Luke said.

"'The Spirit of God…'" Brother Heimuli whispered to him.

"'The Spirit of God Like a Fire is Burning,'" Luke said. "That's an appropriate hymn for the occasion, because it sure seems hot up here."

Luke looked out to one of the pews on the side of the chapel.

"Brother Johnson," he said, "would you mind turning down the thermostat a bit?"

Yes, there was a new sheriff in town.

"Our invocation will be offered by Brother Jim Krzmarzick. Jim Krzmarzick. Jim Krzmarzick. Am I pronouncing that correctly? It is pronounced 'Jim,' right?"

Nobody in the congregation seemed to get the joke.

Hayley took a deep breath. She offered a silent prayer for her husband.

"This is a lot harder than it looks," Luke whispered to Brother Heimuli after he sat down in his seat.

During the hymn, Luke locked his eyes on Hayley's. She looked up at him and smiled lovingly, as she wrestled with the younger kids, which calmed his nerves.

When the time came for ward business, Luke bungled things with a flurry of faux pas. He mistakenly told the members that were being released to stand up, which was against protocol. They awkwardly stood up. People were whispering to each other and chuckling at his gaffe.

Then he announced that Sister Hayes had been called to be the teachers' quorum advisor, and Brother Williams had been called as activity days leader.

Luke's counselors helped him straighten it all out.

It was a little like watching a three-year-old ride a bike for the first time, without training wheels.

"You'd think after attending church for all these years I'd know how to do this," a red-faced Luke told the congregation. "Thanks for your patience."

As the bishop, Luke quickly realized, he couldn't relax for a second. He remembered that he needed to pay close attention to the sacrament prayer to ensure that the priests were saying it word for word. Luke ensured the deacons offered the sacrament to everyone in attendance.

As proud as Luke was of Brian's athletic exploits, he was even more proud to watch him pass the sacrament on Sundays — especially on this Sunday.

Luke had to listen to every word of every talk, no matter how dry. He couldn't close his eyes or allow his mind to wander. No, he didn't like being the guy presiding. And he realized that many others, more experienced, men in the congregation could do a much better job.

Luke regarded it as a tender mercy that the closing prayer was "I Am a Child of God."

The rest of the day was packed with meetings and interviews. He found himself scrambling from one end of the church to another while trying to manage the immense weight he felt on his shoulders.

When Luke returned home from church — he jokingly referred to it as his "full-time job" — that evening, he kissed Hayley and took her in his arms. He acted like he hadn't seen her in months.

"I'll never be able to do this for five or six years," Luke said.

"Yes, you will," she said. "What did you expect for your first Sunday? There's a big learning curve. It'll get easier from here. Besides, you're so cute when you're flustered."

"Thanks, Hayley, just what I needed to hear. You know, I'm looking for a speaker in sacrament meeting next week…"

"Good thing bishop's wives have immunity from giving talks," Hayley said. "It's in the Church Handbook."

"Really? I'm going to have to study that book. There's a lot to learn."

"Even Bishop Law and Bishop Kimball and Bishop Tompkins

made mistakes from time to time," Hayley said. "Just think, in a couple of years, you'll be able to conduct sacrament meeting in your sleep."

"I think that's the approach I'll take next week. It couldn't be any worse than today's performance."

"Most people don't even realize when you make a mistake," Hayley said. "And if they do, they'll forget by the time the meeting is over. Just remember to smile more on the stand. It will help people know you care. It will help you relax."

Luke appreciated his wife's counsel, and her unconditional support.

He went into the kitchen, ate dinner — the family had eaten hours earlier, so Hayley reheated his plate — then he helped his wife wash the dishes.

"You did a really good job conducting sacrament meeting, Dad," said Esther, who was playing with Sarah. "All my friends said they had never been to a sacrament meeting like that before."

"Yeah, not bad for a rookie," Brian said.

That night, as Luke fell asleep, he replayed the day in his mind. There were plenty of cringe-worthy moments that he wished he could erase. When he woke up the next morning, he was relieved that Sunday was over, and that a new day, Monday, had come.

Then came a thought that filled him with dread — only six more days until Sunday.

Luke helped Jacob find his favorite shirt, changed the laundry, cleaned up the breakfast dishes, and tied the twins' shoes. Hayley had taken Esther back-to-school shopping, and he ended up taking the younger kids to a movie.

Later that day, after Hayley and Esther came home, Luke picked up Tanner Harding. He took Tanner, Brian, Benjamin, and Jacob to the park to play baseball. Then they went to the church to play basketball.

Playing basketball at the church gym was one of the best stress-relievers he knew of, and it was a lot more fun going with people he loved rather than going alone.

"How are you doing, Tanner?" Luke asked him as they were leaving.

"I'm doing pretty good, Bishop Manning," Tanner said. "I miss my dad but I feel like he's not far away. The other day, a kid was making fun of me but I didn't care because I felt like my dad was standing there, smiling at me."

In Tanner, Luke already saw a future missionary. Like father, like son.

Aside from the steady stream of mini-calamities he had to deal with, Luke took solace in the knowledge that as long as he had the restored gospel of Jesus Christ in his life, he and his family — known in some social circles as the "Mannings of Mormonville" — could cope with anything.

Luke resolved to believe more and doubt less. He resolved to yell less, and hug more.

Despite all of the blessings he had received in recent months, life was far from a paradisiacal glory. Raising seven kids continued to be chaotic and crazy.

Hayley continued to suffer from migraine headaches from time to time, but she seemed happier than ever by focusing on spending time with her husband and children, and maintaining an eternal perspective by remembering that she was helping to shape future generations.

And thanks to her family's trip, she made many new friends that she enjoyed communicating with from disparate places all over the world.

One of them was Katarina, the mom from Germany. Katarina reached out to Hayley via e-mail, which Hayley had left in the copy of the Book of Mormon that she gave Katarina on the Freedom Trail. Hayley answered her questions and helped coordinate a meeting between Katarina and the full-time missionaries in Germany.

Hayley also kept in touch with Jim and Paula Briggs, the couple from Texas that had lost their wedding ring in the Sacred Grove. Hayley hoped to help them get baptized, then married for eternity.

She enjoyed being a cyber-missionary, responding in her spare time to people who reached out on the Mannings' YouTube channel and Facebook page.

Esther turned 16, got her driver's license, and even though she was responsible, it scared Luke to death whenever she borrowed the car. What scared him even more was when she went on her first date. It was a group date involving four other couples, but he conducted a full journalistic background check on her date before the kid picked her up.

"I'd like her home by eight-thirty," Luke told Esther's date.

"Dad!" Esther said.

"Brother Manning, I mean Bishop Manning, with all due respect, that's like two hours from now."

"OK, eleven," Luke said. "But not a minute later. Have fun, but not too much fun."

Brian, Benjamin, and Jacob signed up for flag football, and basketball, which helped keep them out of trouble, for the most part.

One of the many blessings from their cross-country trip that Luke noticed — it seemed the older kids were attending church, reading scriptures, and serving others not because everyone else around them was doing it. Not because they felt peer pressure to do so. They were deliberately making those choices because they simply wanted to.

Nothing would make Luke and Hayley happier than to catch one of them on their knees in prayer or studying the Book of Mormon.

Ashley and Lindsay were about to start Kindergarten. Sarah was scooting around the house faster than Luke could keep up with her. She watched the twins carefully and learned from them how to get into mischief, like dumping a bottle of bubble bath into the toilet and then flushing.

When it came to providing for his family, Luke was grateful for his new opportunities. Though he figured he'd never be rich, he didn't have to worry as much about money.

There was a time when he thought that success was determined by the size of his bank account, and the number of awards he had earned. But he realized that no matter what he accomplished, or didn't accomplish, his biggest success would always be his wife, his marriage, and his children.

How ironic, Luke thought, that becoming rich and famous was what motivated him to come to Utah in the first place. After living here for a while, he discovered that the lifestyle of the rich and famous wouldn't bring lasting peace or happiness. One of the many integral lessons he had learned in Utah was that happiness is measured by eternal relationships, not by earthly wealth.

Luke wanted to make sure his family knew exactly what *Mannings of Mormonville* stood for — and it wasn't the title of a reality show or a hashtag or a YouTube channel or something trending on Twitter. He knew *Mannings of Mormonville* wasn't just some catchy, alliterative title.

It described, and reminded him, what his family stood for and represented, going all the way back to his ancestors that never made it to Utah.

Luke hoped that he and his family would strive to be a monument to "Mormon perseverance." Together, this family would press forward with a perfect brightness of hope.

The path Luke had chosen, to follow Jesus Christ, wasn't always easy, but he had proven to himself he could live the restored gospel anywhere, from Temple Square to Times Square.

It didn't matter to Luke if the entire free world thought he was insane for his beliefs or his decisions. Others couldn't, or shouldn't, be expected to understand. He was secure in what he believed, what he knew, and what he felt.

If his life in Utah so far were only a prologue for what was to come, then Luke Manning knew this new chapter he was embarking on would be the most challenging of his life. It was time, once again, to exercise faith, trust in the Lord, and cling tightly to his family.

All things considered, he wouldn't want to do it any other way.

"Hey, Dad," Benjamin told Luke one Sunday evening, "I kind of like being the son of a bishop."

Luke laughed. "Why's that?"

"I like how your name is on the front of the tithing envelopes. I like how you have a key to the church, and we can play basketball there anytime we want. I like how I don't need to schedule an appointment to hang out with you, even when you're really busy. And I like how everyone at church calls you 'Bishop,' but I can still call you 'Dad.'"

Somewhere, Ezekiel Manning was smiling.

ABOUT THE AUTHOR

Jeff Call is the author of the several books, including *Mormonville; Rolling with the Tide; Return to Mormonville; The Lost Sheep;* and *100 Things BYU Fans Should Know & Do Before They Die* — all titles that can be found on Amazon.com. He is also an award-winning journalist, having worked as a sportswriter for the Deseret News in Salt Lake City, Utah, since 1997.

You can contact him via e-mail at jeff_call_2000@yahoo.com.

Call lives in northern Utah County with his wife, CherRon. They are the parents of six sons.

54141223R00192

Made in the
USA
Lexington, KY